ROGUE PREY

A LEON CAZADOR THRILLER

NIK MORTON

Rogue Prey
Paperback Edition
Copyright © 2022 Nik Morton

Rough Edges Press
An Imprint of Wolfpack Publishing
5130 S. Fort Apache Rd. 215-380
Las Vegas, NV 89148

roughedgespress.com

Paperback ISBN 978-1-68549-097-3
eBook ISBN 978-1-68549-096-6
LCCN 2022938378

ROGUE PREY

CHAPTER 1

ENDANGERED SPECIES

2018 - *April*
Argentina

SANTIAGO THE GUIDE BANGED THE JEEP'S dashboard and pointed at the tree foliage that overhung part of the track roughly twenty meters ahead. Birds chirped, seemingly unbothered by the heat of the day.

"Lazaro, stop!" Doina ordered.

Lazaro braked.

The engine ticked over noisily.

"Cut the engine," she commanded.

The driver turned the key and the engine stopped.

In the back, Doina sensed her pulse beginning to race and her breathing had increased. She turned to Nicholas on her left. "Can you see it?"

Eyes squinting, he peered and then nodded, plump lips grinning. "About three meters, I'd say."

She reckoned the boa constrictor was at least that length as it slithered along a tree bough that arched across the track.

Santiago said, "That will be the male I told you about."

Doina nudged her elbow into the side of the man in a baseball cap sitting on her right. "Okay, Quint, take your shot while you can. Fortunately, he moves slowly."

Showing a shining white set of teeth, Quint stood up in the jeep. He raised his rifle with its telescopic sight, aimed, paused a second and then fired.

This close, she found the report was deafening.

Nearby birds fell silent, while some disturbed the foliage and flew away.

The big snake twitched on the branch and then slid off, hitting the track with a loud thudding sound.

"Good shot, mister!" Santiago said.

"Okay, Lazaro. Go get it."

Lazaro switched on the engine, put the vehicle into gear, drove up to the carcass and then braked.

Quint jumped out and with an effort lifted up the dead boa in both hands, its length draped in a loop of attractive diamond-patterned scales. He smiled broadly, posing.

Doina clicked the digital camera. "For your scrapbook."

"Yeah, it'll go with my giraffe and rhino kills."

Nicholas said, "Come on, Quint. We have a female to catch!"

Quint hefted the snake into the back and clambered into the jeep.

"Not far to go, I think," Santiago assured them.

It was not usual to find a male and female close together, Doina knew. Boa constrictors were solitary creatures, only seeking the company of other snakes when mating.

Santiago had proved his worth on previous trips, and today seemed no exception. It wasn't far, as he promised. Only its tail was visible from the track.

Doina tapped Lazaro's shoulder and he stopped the jeep and cut the engine.

Santiago, Doina, Nicholas and Quint got out of the jeep and ran towards the disappearing snake.

Boldly, Santiago lurched forward and snatched hold of the tail with both hands. He hauled hard, walking backwards, and it started to slide over the undergrowth, but then he couldn't move it further. "Come on, give me a help!" he shouted, passing the snake's body through his hands, making room for others to grab it near the tail.

With some reluctance, Doina and Nicholas joined Santiago and grasped the snake's body. She'd held snakes before, but this was slightly different. She'd never tackled one this large.

Santiago gasped. "It is using its teeth, holding onto some root, perhaps."

A hissing noise erupted from it and surprisingly swiftly for its bulk it coiled around, its head darting towards Santiago.

Its jaw clamped onto Santiago's forearm as he lifted it defensively. He swore, grabbing it around the throat, and then pulled away, holding the head with its flicking tongue inches from his face. The teeth had drawn blood.

Although the female was slightly shorter than the dead snake in the back of the jeep, it was still well over two meters in length. And now it coiled around Santiago's left leg, hissing. They only hissed when they were annoyed. This one was definitely provoked and irritated.

"Quick, the sack!" Santiago called.

Lazaro came running up with a big hessian sack.

Shoving the head of the boa into the sack, Santiago strained to unravel the coils from his leg and struggled to drop the rest of the wriggling snake into the bag. Seconds later, it was entirely inside and he pulled on a draw-string. The boa went quiet and still.

Quint said, "Will you need a shot of antivenin?"

Santiago shook his head. "It is not poisonous." He waved his bitten arm in the air. "But it hurts a little bit."

Nicholas clapped Santiago on the back. "Well done!"

"It is what you pay me for, no?"

Doina eyed the sack and flushed with pleasure. Their prepared illegal export route of the dead and living boa constrictors was all arranged. Even after taking into account all the outlay, she and Nicholas would still come away with a tidy profit from Quint's fee. Plus an attractive product to sell to a discerning client.

———

2018 - June
Southern Spain

HE HAD LARGE EYES, big ears and, surprisingly, his middle finger was very long on each hand.

"He looks cute," Leon Cazador said in Spanish, lowering the photograph of the little aye-aye.

The animal's hair was black, and he had a long bushy tail. His ochre-colored eyes seemed to be expressing surprise at finding himself in a cage rather than in the rapidly diminishing rainforests of Madagascar. Perhaps the daylight conditions affected him, too, which wasn't strange really, as his kind were nocturnal. On the reverse of the photo was scrawled a hefty price in Euros.

"But," Leon added, shaking his head in mock concern, "my fiancée wants something a bit more exotic. Know what I mean?"

"A pity, Señor Santos, because we have many aye-ayes." Lazaro Perez heaved his broad shoulders as if the fate of his primates was of great concern to him.

Leon absently fingered his false greying mustache. It was secure and not at risk of coming unstuck. In times like these, he wondered what event in his childhood had influenced him to deceive so convincingly. Although there was certainly a lady close to his heart, he had no fiancée. The shadowy world he often inhabited meant he was comfortable living a lie. His chosen calling required that he adopted an alias from time to time, and as far as Perez and his business associates were concerned, Leon was Carlos Ortiz Santos, rather than his true self. What was one's true self, though?

He shook off such heavy introspective thoughts and leveled his dark brown eyes on Perez expectantly.

Perez was short, stout, with patchy stubble and a thin black mustache which he repeatedly caressed as if it was a pet in his substantial menagerie. His dark eyes glinted, wavering, checking on any newcomer who entered the roadside bar.

The bar was typical, two-thirds of its counter dominated by glassed-in heated containers of tapas—sausages and onions, Russian salad, various sorts of fish, garlic mushrooms, and tortilla. Hanging on ceiling hooks behind the bar were three hind-quarters of serrano ham, tinged yellow and brown, with plastic drainage cups attached to the dangling foot. A fourth ham resided in a special wooden stand called a *jamonera*, from which the bartender had used his flexible knife expertly to slice off wafer-thin slivers of the deep ruby colored meat to Leon's order. The floor was littered with discarded paper tissues, tooth-picks and the shells of cashew nuts.

It was a hot day, which was to be expected this time of year in the Costa Blanca. Leon was grateful for the air-conditioning. Both he and Perez wore light tan suits with open neck shirts, no doubt simulating typical businessmen to the casual observer.

Taller than average for a Spaniard, Leon had dark brown hair edged with hints of gray, and a powerful broad-shouldered build that suggested he was younger than his fifty-four years. His movements gave the impression of being nonchalant but measured, yet for those perceptive enough to observe there was the subtle hint of a coiled spring in his demeanor. His mouth was thin, his chin firm, and his complexion tanned. Lines in his face suggested a hard weathered life, but naturally did not betray the fact that he had spent many years involved in secret intelligence work. "My allegiance is split because I'm half-English and half-Spanish," he confided more than once, though not to Lazaro Perez. "Mother had a whirlwind romance with a Spanish waiter but happily it didn't end when the holiday was over. The waiter pursued her to England and they were married."

Over the years he'd been well-traveled, working with

several government forces and clandestine agencies, and had established a useful network of contacts in law enforcement, notably Captain Silvano Lopez of the Guardia Civil. And although he was now a civilian, a private investigator, Leon was conducting this latest investigation on behalf of his friend Silvano.

Condensation formed little globules on the sides of their small glasses of Mahou beer, as it was slightly less potent than San Miguel, therefore more appropriate for an afternoon tipple. The small plates had recently held tasty tapas, including his serrano, but were now empty, save for the odd breadcrumb and blobs of olive oil. A porcelain ramekin contained dregs of alioli. His tongue still savored the nutty flavor from the meat.

Brushing a few flakes of bread off the paper tablecloth, Perez delved into his inside jacket pocket and slid across another color photograph. "This, I think, will be more to your fiancée's taste, no?"

Leon studied the image of a large boa constrictor, beautifully marked with cream, brown, tan and gray camouflage ovals and diamonds.

"That's more like it!" Leon said enthusiastically. He'd played enough poker games to know that his face betrayed none of his true emotions while appearing to pander to the greed of Perez.

Such exquisite skin belonged on the reptile, not on somebody's feet, handbag or furniture. Still, he was being marginally unkind to Señor Perez whose business was finding expensive homes for exotic pets and not slaughtering endangered species for eye-catching fashion accessories.

Perez grinned, displaying perfectly shaped if rather large white teeth. "Impressive, isn't he?"

"Yes. How big is he?"

Pursing his thick lips, Perez produced three photographs from the same jacket pocket. "We have three males and one female. They range from two to five meters in length." He added with a note of pride, "The female is pregnant, which is good news for our business."

"Your suppliers are good," Leon said, flicking the photograph to discourage a dysfunctional wine-fly, dopy due to the heat, incapable of distinguishing between beer and wine. "These animals are hard to find nowadays."

"That's why the boas are considered rare."

"And the rarity value explains the prices you charge, of course."

Perez nodded, not appreciating the ironic censure. "Much of their habitat is being destroyed. We do them a service, preserving them in the hands of discriminating private individuals like your good self, Señor."

"Indeed, I can see that." Leon discarded two photos, sliding them towards Perez, and placed two in front of him, as if undecided which to choose. It didn't matter, not really. "My fiancée has always wanted to do exotic dancing. But I think the big boa might be too heavy for her."

"Yes." Perez smirked, licking his lips, perhaps picturing a scantily clad woman draped with a big snake. "You are a discerning customer, Señor Santos, and I truly want to sell to you. But I must admit that even the small one weighs fifteen kilos."

"A lot to hold and dance with, I agree," Leon mused. "But she's a strong woman."

"I envy you, Señor." A tightening under his eyes. "I like strong women."

"I am fortunate, indeed." He pretended to study the two photographs further, turning them over to check the respective cost in euros scrawled on the back. "It's difficult." He bit his lip. "Before I decide, can I see them first?" Casting the baited line.

Perez hesitated for a beat, and then he smiled. "You certainly can."

Hooked.

Leaning forward, Perez whispered, "But to show good

faith, Señor Santos, I would ask that you pay the agreed deposit. We have overheads, as you will understand."

"Yes, I understand," Leon said. "No problem."

———

WEARING A BLACK BLINDFOLD, Leon was jostled in the back as Perez drove the Toyota Land Cruiser along rough country tracks.

The vehicle's climate control was extremely efficient and dispersed the body odor of the cadaverous man in blue dungarees who sat beside him, who had been introduced simply as Vadim. With his slicked-back black hair and leaden features, Vadim might well have escaped from a Bela Lugosi film. Maybe he was a throwback from the silent era. He hadn't spoken since they met, not even when he tied on the blindfold.

And the blindfold wasn't their only nod to secrecy. Perez had asked for Leon's smartphone before they set out. "I will leave it in my office. It will be returned to you when we bring you back."

These days, most people were aware that a mobile phone was also a tracking device.

"You can't be too careful, Señor Perez. I have no problem with your procedures." He'd recently obtained this phone specifically so that it contained no history.

Finally, after what Leon later discovered was two hours, the strip of black cloth was removed by Vadim. The blindfold, thankfully, had not touched the mustache at any time so the fake had stayed firmly attached.

As he tucked the blindfold in the pocket of his dungarees, Vadim gave Leon the benefit of his penetrating stare. Unflinching, Leon peered out the dusty window. He wasn't here to make small talk. He absently patted the bulge in his jacket.

This journey made a change, he supposed.

Normally, he was comfortable combating drug-traffickers, grave robbers, conmen, even Al Qaeda infiltrators and misguided terrorists. Dodgy Spanish developers and shady expat English had faced his wrath over the years. Traders in human beings and stolen vehicles invariably met their match, while kidnappers, crooked mayors and conniving Lotharios had come within his orbit of ire. Dealing with the purveyors of endangered species was a first.

The rest of the journey, another hour's duration, took them into the mountains. Leon didn't recognize any landmarks and hadn't expected to.

This lengthy track they drove along was bordered on either side by decapitated palm trees, victims of deadly red and black weevils, the trunks now resembling headless sentinels. In recent years the infestation of weevils had decimated the country's date and canary palm plantations and he found the bleak results of their depredation sad to see.

Then they rounded a final bend and approached a large fenced-off property in a hollow between two hills. Like all the others they'd traversed, the road was dusty but well used. The big metal gate rumbled open on rollers over rails between two grand stone entrance pillars joined by an arch. Leon recalled his friend Arturo saying, "No matter how small your house, you must have an entrance arch to be proud of."

They drove through and the gate rolled shut automatically after them. Dotted along the fence were clusters of low prickly pear bushes and red, white and pink oleander. If intruders didn't get pricked to death they might get poisoned by the oleander sap.

Ahead, the single-story buildings looked prefabricated and formed a u-shape. It wasn't a fly-by-night organization.

The Land Cruiser braked at the end of the right-hand upright of the "u".

Vadim spoke!

His voice was gritty, guttural: "Time to get out, Señor."

Without replying, Leon clambered from the vehicle. His emergence from the cool cocoon into the intense heat didn't surprise him, but it was uncomfortable and he started to sweat at once.

He deliberately lost his footing, sinking to one knee on the hard compacted dirt. Nobody moved to assist him. Vadim was woefully lacking in customer care. Leon grabbed the side of the doorframe for support and heaved himself up, massaging his right foot, adjusting the shoe.

"Are you all right, Señor?" Vadim asked in a tone that conveyed he didn't care one way or the other.

"Yes, just a bit careless. I was so glad to feel firm ground underfoot again, I slipped. Being knocked around in the back for about three hours was no fun, and I'm sure I have the bruises to prove it!"

"I thought you had your seatbelt on, Señor."

Leon ignored the comment and made a show of dusting down his trousers with his hands.

Vadim murmured under his breath, "Wimp."

The play-acting was convincing, then.

Straightening up, Leon surveyed the place.

No other vehicles were in sight, so there must be a garage entrance somewhere. Probably on the right, where most of the tyre tracks led.

Vadim walked over to stand next to Leon. Then Perez joined them, using a linen handkerchief to wipe his sweaty brow.

Leon heard the raucous sound of cicadas. They seemed to be everywhere, doubtless hiding in the bushes. But he was after somewhat bigger creatures, and they were not boa constrictors.

Double doors opened at the left-hand end of the "u" and a man and a woman strode towards them. All smiles. She was dressed in tailored blue open-necked shirt and jeans, her curves filling the clothes generously, while the willowy snowy-haired man with her wore camouflage trousers and shirt. She carried a medium-sized tan leather shoulder-bag.

The woman's handshake was firm, her hand smooth and soft.

"This is Doina Marcu, our resident zoologist," explained Perez. "She ensures you get the best product your money can buy."

Doina said, "Señor Santos, I am pleased to meet you."

She smiled with thin lips, toasted brown eyes lighting up as she appraised him. Her accented Spanish was quite good, but he detected a flavor of Romanian in there. She had high cheekbones and almond-shaped eyes. An oval face was framed by curling black hair that reached her shoulders. About thirty, Leon guessed.

"Our director, Nicholas Badescu," Perez said, as Leon shook hands with the man in camouflage fatigues.

Badescu had a hooked nose and it tended to twitch as he talked. "You have brought the money?" Business-like, but his gentle tone meant the question was not overtly rude. His veal-colored lips formed a smile that reminded Leon of a grinning lizard. His cheeks were pitted from an old serious ailment, and his complexion was sallow.

"Yes, of course." Leon drew the bulky envelope from his inside jacket pocket and handed it to Badescu. "The deposit, as agreed."

"Thank you." Badescu barely gave the envelope a glance and passed it to Doina.

Her polished nails were beautifully manicured. She eagerly slid a long finger under the flap and ripped it open, counted the euro notes, the tip of her tongue sticking out between her lips. "All correct," she confirmed, and slipped the envelope into her shoulder-bag.

Sweat soaked Leon's back. This was the moment when he braced himself for swift devastating defensive action. Would they take the money, then considering life to be cheap, attempt to dispose of him, or would they be greedy enough to want more? In this case, that meant more money from a sale. Happily for his continued survival, greed always won.

Clapping a hand on Leon's shoulder and embracing

him, Badescu gave a comradely hug. He smelled of musky cologne. "Let's show you your little snake!"

Badescu had been reasonably subtle about it. With that over-friendly gesture he'd checked that Leon wasn't carrying a weapon under his lightweight jacket. Some undercover agents never carry guns, as their argument goes that the weapons are not all that reliable, snagging on clothing or misfiring, and even give a false sense of security. Others rely on quick wits and superior unarmed combat skills. Leon wasn't particular. Today, a knife was strapped to his left calf while his right held a holstered Colt. There was no way they'd know, unless they blatantly frisked him and they weren't about to do that. For the time being he was a valuable wealthy client and wasn't to be embarrassed.

Perez said, "I will be waiting in the garage to take you back, Señor." He went over to the Land Cruiser, got in and drove it to the right, the other side of the "u". An automatic door opened in the wall as he approached and he steered into its dark recesses.

The rest of them headed towards the building on the left-hand part of the "u".

Leon walked alongside Doina. She exuded the pheromones of a sexual predator, and he was almost smitten as she talked.

"Governments make laws," she said, "but they don't see the global picture. Endangered species will disappear unless more businesses like ours get in on the act."

"I agree," Leon said. "You're preaching to the converted here, Miss Marcu."

"Doina will do. Carlos, isn't it?"

"Yes. Carlos."

They entered the double doors at the end of the "u". The relief from the sun was instant as they stepped into an air-conditioned ante-room. The doors shut behind them, cutting off the strident cacophony of cicadas.

A man stood behind a small drinks bar on the right, while on the left was an unmarked door.

"Would you like a drink before we proceed?" Doina enquired.

"I'd appreciate it," Leon said. "A small cool beer, perhaps?"

She gestured at the barman who quickly busied himself and within a few seconds he slickly came from behind his counter and brought a tray with four drinks on it: a glass of white wine with ice, a glass of rich red, a tumbler of sparkling water and a glass tube of beer.

Doina was served first, with the white wine. Badescu lifted the red and Leon took the beer. Vadim had the water.

Leon raised his glass. "Cheers! Let's hope we can conclude our business today."

She sipped at her white wine and the ice chinked. "I think we have what you want, Carlos." With her free hand she clung to Badescu's arm. She smiled up at him, eyes shining. Her throat contracted slightly but not with the act of swallowing. Definite affection there.

Badescu returned her smile with a gentle curve of his lips.

"Your journey was not uncomfortable?" Badescu enquired, and then sipped his wine.

"Comfortable enough, thanks. Your business is a long way out, isn't it?"

Doina said, "We are conscious of the danger posed by extremist animal lovers, Carlos."

"Understandable. It's laudable that they fight for animal welfare, but I do appreciate that some of them go too far and can be dangerous. That reminds me, I've been wondering how I will take it home. You know, the snake?"

Her tone was condescending. "When you have selected the one you want, I will anesthetise it and place it in a suitable ventilated traveling box. It will fit with ease in the back of the Land Cruiser."

"That's good to know." While they had been chatting Leon had sensed that his body temperature was adjusting to the cooler environment.

Badescu said, "And you are able to electronically pay us to close the transaction?"

"Oh, yes, I have the authorization. I'll key it into your computer, as stipulated, when we're ready."

"Good. Good."

Abruptly, Doina gulped the last of her wine. "Time for us to go, Carlos."

Leon said, "Then let's go."

Badescu said, "Be prepared, Señor Santos, when we go into the animal section, it will be humid, even though it is enclosed."

Leon put his half-empty glass on the bar counter. "Thank you for the warning."

Doina moved to the unmarked door. "This way, please." She opened it and went along the passage for a short distance, the others following. "You'll get a good view from the top. This way."

At the end of the passage was a narrow set of metal stairs fitted to the wall, which she began to climb. Leon tried not to dwell on her tightly clad rounded buttocks as she ascended, and concentrated on climbing after her.

At the top of the stairs was a small platform which faced a swaying walkway constructed of wooden planks.

Badescu and Vadim climbed after him. Keeping the client penned in.

Doina stepped onto the walkway first and Leon followed close behind.

The walkway was suspended from a number of ropes anchored to the glass ceiling's metal-frame joists and there were rope handrails on both sides. Lianas hung from trees that brushed the ceiling and tree-boles poked up through gaps in the glass below them, all in an attempt at conveying an impression of being immersed in the jungle. All that seemed missing was the strident call of Johnny Weissmuller.

By now Leon was again sweating, due to the limited exertion in the humid confinement.

Doina said, "We have all kinds of creatures, for all kinds of clients."

"So I see." On either side visible through glass were the endangered species, the reason he was here. He passed six enclosures of aye-ayes, two of golden lion marmosets and a dozen glass cases of desert tortoises.

Not so long ago a Guardia Civil raid had uncovered several rare Mediterranean tortoises smuggled into Spain from Slovenia, each one liable to fetch up to €12,000. That was small beer compared to this lot. He wondered what was in the building on the right-hand side of the "u".

Finally, they stopped about two-thirds along the walkway, relatively close to the far end section.

Doina gently grasped Leon's arm. An electric charge seemed to flash through him: she had that effect on him.

"Carlos, I think you'll like this exhibit," she whispered.

Vadim chuckled behind him.

Leon looked below, where she was pointing.

One of the boas was feeding on a rabbit, stretching its mouth to accommodate the dead animal.

"The boa's bite is not poisonous," Doina explained with enthusiasm. "It simply crushes the breath out of its victim. Then gobbles it up."

Leon said, "It leaves me quite breathless."

"Nice joke, Señor Santos!" said Badescu in what was probably his best buttering-up-the-client manner.

Then Doina gasped. "Oh my God, she's giving birth!"

She wasn't wrong. Next to the feeding boa was the biggest snake, and she was evacuating live writhing individuals encased in membranes and almost immediately little snakes broke free and flopped wriggling onto the straw-covered floor. Each baby boa was about sixty centimeters long. Despite having encountered snakes on a number of missions, this sight managed to make Leon's skin crawl.

Doina gripped the rope handrail. "There must be at least thirty of them!"

Leon wasn't counting, but there were too many for his peace of mind.

At that moment, Vadim's head jerked up like a pointer acquiring the scent. "What was that, boss?"

Badescu said, "I'm... not... sure."

They all heard the approaching sound.

Badescu glanced worriedly at Doina, then at Leon.

Leon recognized the noise immediately. The distinctive thrum of Pratt & Whitney turbine engines.

Now visible through the glass roof: two specks in the sky.

Closing.

Soon, Vadim and the others would see the green and white livery of the Eurocopter EC-135s.

Leon had been expecting them, since the transmitter in his right shoe heel would have pinpointed his position accurately enough. He'd switched it on when he exited the Land Cruiser and pretended to slip. He had only activated the tracker once he was convinced he'd reached a destination that would prove incriminating.

"They're Guardia Civil helicopters," Leon said helpfully. "SEPRONA." He added, for emphasis, "In case you didn't know, since you're foreign, it's the Guardia Civil service dedicated to the protection of flora and fauna."

Vadim swore and lunged at him.

Leon sidestepped on the swaying walkway and grabbed Vadim's arm, twisted it and shoved it up his back and flung him the way he'd come, straight into Badescu.

Out of the corner of his eye he noticed that Doina stood hesitantly, staring, her face drained of blood. Then seconds later she seemed galvanized, swung around and dashed towards the far end of the walkway.

As the two men collided, Leon snatched his knife from its sheath and sliced at the rope handrail on his left.

The rope that helped support the walkway parted.

The walkway tilted under his feet.

As he'd been expecting it, he held onto the remaining rail with his free hand.

But he'd moved so fast the two men were caught unawares.

Vadim fumbled in vain for a handhold but slid sideways. He shrieked as he fell the short distance to the glass ceiling of the boa enclosure, landing on his back. Fine spider-web cracks spread under him. Clearly, he was reluctant to move, his eyes wide, sweat oozing on his forehead.

"Nicholas, come to me!" Doina called from the far platform.

Seeming oblivious of her plea, Badescu held onto the right-hand rail, his feet scrabbling on the slanting walkway planks. His free hand fumbled in his jacket and withdrew an automatic.

But Leon had already switched hands on the rail, drawn his Colt from its ankle holster and now fired.

The single shot hit Badescu in the shoulder and he jerked spasmodically and let go of the rail, his face suffused with rage. He dropped the pistol and toppled on top of Vadim.

Doina screamed, "No! Oh, Nicholas!"

The sound of cracking glass grew louder.

Leon hung with his left hand, his right clasping the Colt.

He glanced at the platform at the end of the walkway.

Doina was edging backwards, anxiety on her pale face, tears streaming over her cheeks. "The boas," she shouted, "if they fall on them!"

Leon wondered if she was more concerned about the boas, rather than the men. Badescu clearly meant something to her. Maybe she was torn.

At least she was unarmed so posed no threat. He couldn't justify firing at her. And, at present, hanging there, he had no way of reaching her and incapacitating her.

He said, "I reckon the snakes can take care of themselves!"

Her face still ashen, her eyes glaring, she gave him a curt

nod. She spun on her heel and went towards the handrail of another set of stairs at that end.

"Doina, help!" Badescu shouted.

Her shoulders flinched at his words. She paused, twirled round and gave Leon and Badescu one last glance and then turned her back and began to descend the stairs, quickly moving out of view.

Leon decided she could take her chances with the Guardia who'd be landing any minute now.

Two fearful faces stared up at Leon.

Vadim was exceedingly quiet.

Badescu was far from quiet. "Save me!" he pleaded.

"Sorry, I can't do that," Leon said. "You're not an endangered species."

Finally, with an alarming cracking noise, the glass ceiling broke, and the two men fell into the enclosure containing the male boa.

CHAPTER 2

BIG PROBLEM

2019 · July
Southern Spain

THE AGUSTA WESTLAND AW119 KOALA HELICOPTER carried six passengers, and one of them was Leon Cazador in disguise. The pilot, who was probably not in disguise, had thin drawn facial features and bright gray eyes and beneath his taupe cotton flying jacket Leon had glimpsed an automatic pistol in its shoulder holster, a Sig P-232, judging by its grip. The co-pilot was stout with a squint and a bushy mustache, and didn't seem so reticent about advertising his hardware: he wore a holstered Smith and Wesson Sigma automatic at his waist.

In the confined space of the cabin the 1,000hp Pratt and Whitney turboshaft engine sounded quite loud. The aircraft's livery was white, black, blue, red and gold with, on the side of the fuselage, the emblem of an archery target and the letters DB, signifying in Spanish *dar en el blanco—Hit the Target*. It sounded like an excruciating example of admen's business jargon, but Leon knew it expressed more sinister connotations.

Yet again, Leon sported a thin false mustache and traveled as Carlos, but he'd dropped Ortiz Santos since all DB clients were known by first names only. "Friendly company policy which preserves an element of privacy" was the official spiel. He wore a tropical tan suit, a pale blue open-necked shirt and leather shoes with Cuban heels. Camouflage clothing and desert boots were packed in his travel case.

Two DB administrators, introduced as Mateo and Fabio, accompanied them. Their business jackets bulged where they concealed handguns in shoulder holsters.

Mateo was short with a stocky build and bald and his bushy black eyebrows might have been making a mocking statement about his lack of scalp hair. His close-set brown eyes conveyed contempt, while a bent nose, thick lips and a square jaw completed his unprepossessing features. His ragged fingernails indicated he persistently bit them, an activity for which his big prominent teeth were well suited.

Fabio was chubby, with jet-black lanky hair and small black pebble eyes that peered out from beneath a single black eyebrow that tended to separate his wrinkled brow from the rest of his face. Under a pug nose he nurtured a thin black mustache, not dissimilar to Leon's. He chain smoked Ducados Azul cigarettes, contributing to an unpleasant fug in the compartment. The yellow *No Fumar* sticker was openly disregarded, and the graphic shock cancer images and "smoking kills" warning on the packet was obviously ignored.

Addressing them in English, Mateo had made the introductions on the apron at Alicante's Elche airport, and complimented Leon on his English.

Leon said, "I'm half-English, half-Spanish."

"Neither one nor the other," Fabio observed, which won chuckles from the three clients.

Leon didn't respond. His three fellow clients, all wealthy amateur wild game hunters, were: Rudolf, a German, and a pair of Americans, Quint and Harley. With profuse apologies, they were asked to hand over their smartphones.

"Security, you understand," Mateo said in an unapologetic tone. "They will be waiting here at our DB office desk for your return."

Behind them secured netting held down three piles of crates containing bottles of wine, canned food, and other assorted sundries plus their luggage.

Once they were airborne and their seatbelts clipped in, Mateo instructed the four clients, "Put these on. Just another commercial confidentiality precaution." He handed each of them a black linen hood. "You will be able to remove them soon enough."

Leon was the last to don his hood and before he did he surreptitiously monitored his watch and then plunged himself into darkness. He fully understood that the company needed to keep their destination under wraps. That was one reason why he was here: to confirm that dirty secret. Breathing shallowly under the cloth hood he was reminded of the two times when he'd been in this situation before, though then he'd been a prisoner. Some memories were best kept buried. He closed his mind and relaxed.

After a lapse of time Mateo shouted, "You can take off the hoods now!"

Removing his, Leon blinked to readjust his vision, and then checked his watch: they'd been flying for about a half-hour. This aircraft's speed was roughly 240kph, he recalled, which meant they'd covered a distance of approximately 130 kilometers so far. Through the cabin windows he noticed the position of the sun and estimated they'd been flying in a north-east direction.

Of his companions, only Rudolf evinced any nervousness, his right foot constantly tapping the metal deck as he smoked his *Entre 23* cigarettes, adding to the already unhealthy atmosphere. He was about thirty, Leon estimated. Rudolf was the first to start up a conversation, and spoke in English since that seemed a common language here. He talked about himself, his favorite subject. Tall and powerfully built, he was big-boned with a florid complexion typical of a man of his profession, a banker. Leon imagined Rudolf was often impatient with customers in his bank.

Rudolf's button-shaped gunmetal eyes glinted as he spoke of the two antelope he'd killed in Africa. "I so much like the thrill of the hunt and the kill." His voice boomed above the sound of the rotors and engine. As if to match his memories to the moment, he wore jungle camouflage fatigues and black leather combat boots, ready to drop into a hostile jungle environment at a moment's notice. Leon thought he had surprisingly small feet for a big man.

"This must make a change for you, then," Leon offered. "Though it could be considered very expensive."

Rudolf snorted, running a hand through his blue-gray thatch, and his lips puckered, dribbling on a tuft of hair under the bottom lip. "I have saved for this pleasure!"

"I'm sure you will get your money's worth."

"Ah, money! You would think I would not be short of money, being a respected banker. But I want to retire early, so I am putting aside some of the money of my wife." He winked at the American, Harley, who sat opposite. "My wife, she is the wealthy one." He tapped the side of his pug nose. "One day soon I intend to leave her for my secretary, Anna." He thrust out his square jaw and pulled from his breast pocket a wallet from which he took a photo of a dark-haired buxom woman in her twenties. She had sultry eyes and high cheekbones. "She I have bedded for six months already."

"Pretty woman," Leon said, passing the photo to Harley, who nodded without comment and handed it back. Quint, sitting next to Harley, didn't seem interested, staring through the window.

Rudolf chuckled. "I wish to make the break soon." He returned the photo to the wallet and then to his pocket. "I can hardly wait!"

"I can sympathize," Harley said in a fluting voice. He was probably in his late thirties. Tall, like Rudolf, but angular and lean.

"How is that?" Rudolf asked.

Screwing up his owlish denim-blue eyes, Harley said, "I'm going through a divorce. I'd dearly love to shoot my wife *and* mother-in-law!"

Rudolf said, "I must admit to liking that idea. I would inherit my wife's wealth."

"If you don't get caught," Quint observed in a throaty voice. His small oval nut-brown eyes behind wired spectacles were leveled at Rudolf. Exhibiting the disdain of a non-smoker, he wafted away Rudolf's smoke from his face. He was about forty, overweight with a bull neck and a broad chest and a beer belly. He had a blanched complexion and salt-and-pepper matted hair. "Killing people ain't the same as wild animals, I assure you. It takes nerves of steel, and guts."

Rudolf puffed on his cigarette and switched his attention to the window, his foot continually tapping.

Harley stroked his lantern jaw and turned to Quint. "I've killed a giraffe and an old lion in Africa. Their heads are mounted on my office wall back home."

"Is that so?" Quint said. "What do you do, back home?"

"I'm in politics. It's a small town, but there's a lot going on. What do you do?"

Quint's dour mouth opened in a smile, revealing pearly teeth. "I'm a dentist. From Wisconsin."

"Do I know you?" Harley ventured. "Some bad publicity, was there?"

"Silly trolls on Facebook, is all. I'm an experienced tracker, and proud of it. I've killed a giraffe, a boa constrictor and two rhinos so far. You have to be thick-skinned in this business."

"Very amusing," Leon said.

"Eh?" Quint queried.

"Rhino—thick skinned?"

"Oh, yeah. Anyway, the social media blitz was a load of nonsense because of the death of one giraffe. It's not as if there aren't plenty more to go around."

Harley gestured at Quint's clothes—a black tight-fitting

T-shirt, black trousers, and black leather combat boots. "You don't dress like an experienced tracker." He smoothly slid a hand over his own bush-jacket, open to reveal white T-shirt and white chinos. Five cigars poked out of his top pocket.

"Like you, I shun camouflage." Quint's protruding brow ridges creased. "The prey I'm after is constantly on the move, and not concerned about blending in. It simply wants to get away and live." He eyed Leon. "You're keeping quiet, Carlos. What about you?"

"Oh, I've made a kill or two."

"Which wildlife have you potted?" Rudolf asked.

Leon said, "Plenty of wild animals." Mostly men.

"Do you collect trophies?" Harley pressed.

"No. I just kill." Never for pleasure.

The sound of the aircraft emphasized the weighty pause in the conversation.

Harley cleared his throat. "You don't seem dressed for the hunt."

"We're not hunting today," Leon replied. "The appropriate clothes are in my case."

"You're a man of few words, Carlos," Quint said, studying him.

"That's me, all right." Leon closed any further exchange with him by peering through the window, as if the terrain they flew above was more interesting. He'd noted the undercurrents in their talk. There was an elephant in the cabin, it seemed, and nobody wanted to identify it, let alone shoot it. Yet all of them were here because they'd committed themselves—at considerable cost—through a link on the dark web.

Both Rudolf and Harley exuded an air of heightened anticipation while Quint maintained a smug reserve in his manner.

The others then indulged in chat that meant very little and excluded Leon. He'd clearly been dismissed as an antisocial bore, which suited him fine, for now.

On their right he spotted a small village, red-tile roofs,

white walls, a paved square, a little church, and a couple of outlying farmsteads. The place was quite isolated. A couple of roads radiated from the center. There was a roundabout, and then fields with irrigation canals. In the blink of an eye the village was gone.

They continued to fly north, passing over lush vegetation, a vast variety of trees, which quite abruptly was sliced apart in a south-west/north-east direction by a sinuous wide gorge. Vegetation sprouted infrequently from this fissure in the earth, but he had little opportunity to discern any detail.

Over to the west he spotted a rocky protuberance, like a carbuncle, emerging above the treetops, which was doubtless called a *teta* by locals, though he might be indulging in fanciful thoughts since, apart from that village he hadn't identified the presence of any other habitation.

Ahead, an escarpment materialized, strewn with undergrowth, aloes, oleander of red and white hue, and other varieties of plant life.

At the summit of the escarpment loomed a long two-story building. The terrain on all sides of the building was wildly overgrown. He peered through the window, squinted: the gorge ran some distance to the east of this solitary sign of civilization.

Presently, the helicopter circled the building. Leon glimpsed the northern slope of the escarpment, behind the structure. There were chicken pens, vegetable patches and a cluster of fruit trees. Beyond these the sloping land was littered with the detritus of modern living: plastic cartons, unattractive random refuse of all colors that was a little like a 3D rendition of Jackson Pollock, the sun glinting on foil and metal. Varieties of big black and small brown birds swooped and foraged the human tip.

Switching his attention to peer over the pilots' shoulders through the cockpit windshield, he saw they were aiming for a helicopter pad on the roof of the building, painted with the huge "H" sign.

Mateo said, "The DB hacienda, gentlemen."

Alongside the western wall of the big hacienda Leon noted the presence of a generator in a metal cage; its plastic sheathed cables led up to the roof. On the eastern side was a fire escape that ascended from the ground floor to the roof. Air-conditioning units were fitted to the external walls next to every window.

As the pilot settled the aircraft's landing skids on the pad, Leon noticed the fuelling station on the western section of the roof. Flight endurance for the chopper was about five hours, he reckoned. So to justify the need to install refueling capacity, they must use the aircraft quite a lot in this vicinity since the journey to here from Alicante airport was barely ninety minutes. As he hadn't spotted any roads leading to the hacienda, it seemed logical that the aircraft was the only transport that provided access. Near the fuel pumps was a large white TV dish and a couple of radio antennae. Perched on the north-western corner of the roof was a square stone structure with two doors.

The pilot switched off the engine. The rotors whirred and slowed. "Please sit tight until I tell you to disembark," he ordered. At least he refrained from adding "I hope you had a pleasant flight and will fly with DB Air again soon."

Mateo unclipped his seatbelt and produced a Tough-book CF-30 laptop from his shoulder-bag. "Please stay seated. As agreed, you all will now authorize your payment." He opened the laptop, tapped at the keyboard with thick fingers and then swung the laptop round, offering the screen and keyboard. "Just key in your code and the funds will be transferred from your account."

One by one, Rudolf, Quint, Harley and Leon input their authorisation codes.

While Mateo pressed a few more keys to finalize the transactions, Leon surreptitiously leaned down and activated the transmitter in the Cuban heel of his left shoe.

Mateo said, "That's it. All done." He closed the laptop and stowed it in his shoulder-bag. "You can disembark now."

Leon and the others unclipped their seatbelts.

Mateo slid the door open and exited, the shoulder-bag clasped under his arm.

Leon went next and was immediately hit by the heat and a solid wall of energy-sapping humidity. He exited and descended the small set of steps onto the Tarmac roof surface. Sweat oozed even for this minor exertion.

The others followed.

Two men emerged from the elevator door of the corner structure, hastily pulling a trolley.

"They will see to your baggage," Fabio told Leon and the rest.

The two men first began unloading the luggage onto the trolley.

"This way, gentlemen," Mateo said and made for the fire escape.

Harley said, "Hey, Mateo, what's wrong with the elevator?"

Mateo's tone was sharp, ingratiating: "It will be used by our staff to take your luggage to your rooms directly. Besides, we all cannot fit in there at once."

"Yeah, OK."

Keeping pace, Rudolf said, "When do we get to check our weapons?"

"Please be patient, sir." Mateo produced several sheets of paper from his jacket. "As agreed, each of you will be supplied with a Beretta Sniper bolt-action rifle."

Harley said, "Why do you use that old Italian junk? What's wrong with the good old American Armalite AR-50?"

Mateo said, "We obtained a job-lot from a contact in Italy."

Quint laughed. "Open borders, don't you just love 'em?"

Mateo nodded. "You will of course only use the adjustable iron sights. No telescopic sights will be permitted."

Harley swore. "Hey, that wasn't in the agreement!"

"It was," Fabio interjected, "in the small print."

As a small town politician, Harley doubtless let his minions study the small print, and he merely signed on the dotted line. Leon *had* read the small print and expected to be issued with the rifle specified. Each marksman would be supplied with a single magazine that contained five rounds, 7.62 x 51mm NATO cartridges. A level killing field.

"Your prey is valuable, good sirs," Mateo added in a placating tone. "Surely you want the pleasure of tracking it down, rather than having a hasty turkey shoot that is over too soon?"

Rudolf made a grudging sound and scowled, shielding his eyes against the sun. "I'm a little impatient to get started, that is all. You know, we all paid good money…"

Exceedingly good money, Leon mused.

"And you will get good sport in return, sir," Mateo promised. "I assure you, the adrenaline will flow. The rush you get is like nothing else experienced."

Quint bobbed his head vigorously but said nothing.

As they reached the top of the fire escape, Fabio pointed at Leon and Quint. "Unlike the other two, you both seem content, no?"

"I believe we'll get what you promised," Leon replied. "DB comes highly recommended. I was told it will be money well spent."

"It is," Quint assured him. "This is my second time."

That explained Quint's smug manner.

Fabio preened. "Thank you, sir." Then he winked at Quint. "Welcome back, sir."

"A personal recommendation is good," Mateo said and turned to Leon. "Carlos, I like your attitude. When you have made your kills, I will suggest to Señor Baeza that you stay behind for additional exotic entertainment at the hands of a comfort girl." He made a crude gesture.

Keeping the distaste out of his tone, Leon said, "That's really good of you."

Fabio descended first.

"I will go last," Mateo explained.

Keeping the clients herded together.

"Remember," Mateo said, addressing them all, "the first to return with his trophy will receive a refund of €10,000."

Leon wondered what form the trophy would take.

Whatever it was, he didn't like the sound of it, not at all.

The metal handrails were blisteringly hot. Their descent was in silence. Perhaps each client was hoping to be the first to make a kill and earn a rebate. Not that any of them seemed strapped for cash and worried too much about money.

By the time they reached the ground, Leon's shirt and jacket clung to him with sweat, and a pool gathered at the waistband of his boxer shorts.

Mateo escorted them along a path that ran beside the building's wall, and then they turned a corner and stepped onto a dusty flat length of ground. Beyond, to the south stretched sloping land covered in undergrowth and trees. From here they had a panoramic view of tree-tops in every direction, the only intrusion being that distant *teta* he'd seen on the inbound flight.

On their right was an awning-covered raised veranda that stretched the whole width of the main building. Three fifths along the veranda were steps leading to double entrance doors. Above the veranda was a second-story balcony, the top floor.

Mateo said, "In a few moments you will meet our organizers."

Good. Now I can identify them.

Between the veranda balustrades Leon could see the legs of five people seated in wicker chairs, the bodies and faces obscured by shadow. Four of them wore gray trousers, and one was in a white dress or skirt—nice legs.

Those nice legs moved and she stood abruptly. "Stop! Everybody stop, don't move!" Strident, accented.

He vaguely recognized the voice but couldn't immediately place its owner. But his body reacted, signaling for him to flee at once.

Too late.

"Mateo, hold that man!" she ordered.

Pulling out an automatic from inside his jacket, Mateo growled, "Which one?"

"The one who calls himself Carlos!"

Mateo leveled a Glock automatic at Leon.

Though outwardly calm, inwardly Leon sensed his heart rate rising, his stomach sinking.

Had there been there a leak?

Mateo pressed the gun against Leon's side. Fabio, a pace to the left, had also produced an automatic. Within two or three seconds Leon could easily disarm Mateo, and then pivot round and thrust a deadly knife-edge hand into Fabio's throat before he could get off a shot. But a measured scrutiny had already told him two other men had appeared armed with machine-pistols.

Her voice, he knew it. His memory clicked as Doina Marcu stepped out of shadow and descended the steps, her flared white skirt swaying. She wore a smart tailored white linen belted jacket with neat pockets, open to expose the cleft between her breasts.

She jabbed a finger at him. "He's a *soplón!*" Informer, grass.

"Private detective," he corrected as he heard several men exclaim in alarm, while a few swore.

She spat on the ground and the spittle sizzled and dried almost instantly. She strode towards him, hips sashaying. "He works with the Civil!"

"Only sometimes," Leon modified.

His investigations into the whereabouts of a missing person had led him to that man's computer which used a TOR network browser, giving access to the dark web, a small domain within the deep web. Reading the posts and notice-boards, his suspicions had been aroused. He'd taken them to his contact and friend, Captain Silvano Lopez of the Guardia Civil.

"Leon, you know I am averse to involving civilians."

"You've done it before, Silvano," Leon had argued. "Look, the only way to discover what is really going on is to become a client. I have adequate private funds to engineer that. You don't have access to that kind of money. It isn't as if this is the first time we've worked together to roll up a criminal organization."

"True, my friend. I am concerned for your safety that is all. Lie down with dogs and you will get up with fleas."

"In my business I have to keep company with dubious characters. You know that."

"These people, they are likely to be ruthless. If they should detect you..."

"My alias is good and well documented. It would take your people months to infiltrate them and find out where they work from. I can do it faster and easier. And it costs the taxpayers nothing."

Silvano had sighed and clasped his hand on Leon's shoulder. "Very well. I will arrange the authorisation for you to act on our behalf. As soon as you have located their operations center, you must promise to signal us—like last time."

"I promise, Silvano."

"Take care, my friend."

"No problem."

But now it was a problem. A big problem.

Doina came to a stop and faced him. "You have a nerve, coming here!"

"If I'd known you were here, Doina Marcu, I might have taken a rain check."

"My name is now Vanda Dinescu. My encounter with you necessitated a change."

He raised an eyebrow at her. "I'm pleased I put you to so much trouble... Vanda. You know, we can't go on meeting like this."

She slapped him.

His cheek stung a little, but the blow didn't draw blood.

"You are not mistaken," she answered. "This is definitely the last time!" She turned to Mateo. "He will be armed—a knife strapped to one ankle, an automatic on the other."

Mateo raised an eyebrow but even so he stooped to pull up Leon's trouser leg.

"What a memory!" Leon complimented her.

Her eyes lanced into him and she pursed her lips.

Mateo grunted in surprise and unsheathed the knife. He tackled the other leg and removed the gun.

"You were right, Señorita." Mateo pocketed the weapons.

"Of course!" Vanda moved closer, whispered, "Now, take him below and strip-search him thoroughly."

"Works with the cops, eh?" Fabio snickered.

"Not so loud, we have clients watching. Soften him up and then put him with the others."

Mateo said, "It'll be a pleasure.

"But keep him in one piece," she added. "We need to talk to him later."

As the guards pushed Leon past her, she waylaid Mateo and whispered in his ear. Mateo gave her a crisp nod.

Vanda waved airily at the remaining three clients. "Welcome, gentlemen. My apologies for this little drama. Please do not be concerned. It is a minor inconvenience and will not affect your stay. As you have observed, our security is strict."

Quint said, "I'm sure none of us are worried, are we, fellas?"

Rudolf and Harley shrugged their shoulders noncommittally.

"Good," she said. "Now, you will be shown to your rooms. Make yourselves comfortable. All amenities have been arranged. We will dine later tonight and begin the hunt tomorrow."

Harley took a step forward. "Hey, ma'am, what will happen to the Carlos guy?"

Still in earshot, Leon thought: I don't want to know.

Vanda laughed. "Oh, I think we have delightful plans for him, and you will approve."

"Gee," Harley said, "it sure don't look like he's goin' to approve."

Leon was led away.

CHAPTER 3

EXTREMELY FINITE

LEON WAS PUSHED AHEAD BY MATEO. AT A SINGLE touch of Mateo's hand, Leon could easily turn and permanently incapacitate the thug, but Mateo wasn't alone. He was accompanied by Fabio, also with drawn automatic, a Star Megastar holding fourteen rounds, and another guard who carried a machine-pistol, a Steyr with a capacity of twenty-five 9mm Parabellum cartridges. Leon conceded that he wasn't faster than a speeding bullet, and though the prospect of being "softened-up" did not appeal in the slightest, he clung on to Vanda's words: "Keep him in one piece." He accepted that he would have to endure pain in this process, but he would live and come out of it whole. He mentally braced himself for the ordeal ahead.

They climbed the veranda steps and entered welcome cooling shade, then passed through double doors into a wide entrance hall. All the walls were painted white, the floor tiles were mottled tan. A ceiling fan rotated silently, circulating air that was not cool enough to dry sweat-soaked clothes. There were two anonymous doors on his left.

Crossing the floor, they walked into a short passage with two doors on the left labeled: *escalera* and *ascensor*—stairs and elevator.

The elevator was functional, as he'd expected. The cubicle's floor was stained, but he didn't want to know the source of the blemishes. At least it smelled all right, with a hint of pine, some hidden sanitizing dispenser probably having to work overtime behind a grill.

The operating panel showed four buttons with their options for basement, ground floor, top floor and roof. Plus a red emergency stop. His fingers itched to test that one.

According to the manufacturer's sign on the wall, the elevator's load capacity was six, yet it was cramped, since all four of them were broad-shouldered. At such close quarters he could incapacitate two of them, possibly all three; but the drawn weapons posed a serious health risk. Anyway, he was here for a reason. He needed to know more, he needed to learn who was behind this insane unsavory business. Must quell his defensive instinct which was natural, he knew, since his body really didn't want to get hurt. He consciously lowered his pulse rate and relaxed. Go with the flow.

Mateo pressed the button for the basement.

It wouldn't be the first basement where he'd been held prisoner. But he'd been younger then.

When he was twenty-one, rather than wait for conscription, which didn't cease until 2001, he decided to jump rather than be pushed and enlisted in the Army, graduating as an Artillery Lieutenant. About a year later, he joined the Spanish Foreign Legion's Special Operations Company and was trained in the United States at Fort Bragg, where he acquired considerable knowledge about covert activities and weapons. It was during training that he was first introduced to interrogation techniques in a basement, both as captive and captor. In those days, the failure rate in training was high.

Some months afterwards, he was talent spotted and recruited into the national intelligence agency. Unlike most Western democracies, Spain runs a single intelligence organization to combat both domestic and foreign threats. Then he was transferred to the Spanish Embassy in Washington, D.C.

where he rubbed shoulders with several contacts in the intelligence community who proved useful in later years.

Towards the close of the Soviet occupation of Afghanistan he embarked on a number of secret missions with CIA operatives to that blighted land. A basement interrogation in neighboring Iran had been touch-and-go, and he'd barely managed to escape in one piece. By the time the Soviet withdrawal was a reality, Leon was assigned to the Spanish Embassy in Tokyo, where he liaised with both intelligence and police organizations and made friends with Hiroki, a member of the Yakuza. Then secret work followed in the Gulf and Yugoslavia, and also in China where he befriended Meizhen, a member of the organization Free All Chinese from Oppression.

In 1987 he was attached to a clandestine section of MI6 to assist British operatives in Colombia, infiltrating a drug cartel hideout and freeing two agents from a torture chamber —yet another basement.

A year after witnessing the atrocity of the Twin Towers while stationed with the United Nations, he returned to civilian life and established a private investigation firm. The work sometimes entailed liaising with the Guardia Civil or the national police, and that was why he was here in this elevator.

The descent was smooth and quick.

A *ping* sounded and the elevator stopped. The doors slid open, and he stepped into another short passage. Ceiling lights offered illumination. There was a wall at the end on the left, so he turned right.

They reached a corner. In front of them was another short passage with two labeled doors on the right. The nearest door sign indicated "Store Room". He couldn't read the far one.

"Turn left," Mateo told him.

Comforting. At least he wasn't destined for storage.

They walked along a lengthy passage with doors on the

left and right. Unhelpfully none of them carried identifying labels.

When they reached the end of the passage Fabio fumbled with a set of keys and unlocked the door on their right. It was made of solid wood with a small square cut into it at head-height, an observation window into a cell.

Fabio moved aside.

Mateo prodded the gun barrel in Leon's back. "Open the door."

Leon pushed the door open.

The basement room was quite large, about three meters square, with no windows. A single light hung from the ceiling. No furniture. There was a cubicle at the far left-hand corner. The place was stuffy, lacking in air. Oppressive.

End of the road—for now.

He strode inside and instinctively tensed his muscles, waiting for a blow to the back of his head, perhaps, as traditionally in any softening up process the first blow was intended to disorient the subject.

Nothing—yet. Wait. Go with the flow.

Nerves jangled.

Keep calm.

Oh, easy for you to say, he told himself.

The door slammed shut behind him. Fully in control, he didn't react to the sound.

He took a couple of paces forward and turned slowly, feigning nonchalance he didn't feel.

Mateo faced him, with Fabio slightly behind and to his right side. To the left stood the guard with his machine-pistol.

Not taking any chances.

He wondered what Vanda had whispered to Mateo as they left the group of hunters.

Careful not to obscure the view of either Fabio or the gunman, Mateo moved to stand closer, mere inches from Leon.

The man's close proximity was so tempting. Leon quelled his instincts.

Mateo's free hand smoothed the lapels of Leon's jacket. "Nice suit."

"Thank you. I can recommend my tailor. Langa of Madrid."

Scowling, Mateo took a step back. "Take it off!"

Leon didn't move. "It isn't your size."

Not entirely unexpectedly, Mateo lunged, his fist catching Leon on the chin.

Leon could have used his wrist to deflect the blow, but saw little point in that, but he'd moved a fraction of an instant before the punch landed so that he rode it, the contact merely a glancing pain. But he pretended to stagger and rubbed his chin. "All right," he said, in a placating tone. "I get the message."

First, he slipped off his shoes. Surely the transmitter would have pin-pointed the hacienda by now? Then he removed his suit. He stood in his stocking feet, his shirt and black boxer shorts, the carefully folded trousers over a forearm, the jacket in his other hand. "Satisfied?"

The next punch pounded into his stomach and, despite being braced, he doubled up with the force of it.

He stumbled backwards and dropped his jacket and trousers on the dusty floor as he massaged his midriff. This time the pain was bad. Mateo brought to bear a lot of excessive weight behind his punch.

Wheezing, Leon straightened. "That is annoying. I'll have to get the suit dry-cleaned now."

"Fabio," Mateo said, gesturing at the suit.

Keeping well clear of Leon, Fabio snatched the suit jacket and delved in the pockets. He took out a wallet, which he threw to Mateo.

Catching it one-handed, Mateo said, "We'll study it later. Carry on."

Fabio then produced a switchblade and started to slit the jacket's lining.

Leon decided not to comment on the ruination of the jacket.

Then Fabio cut away the pockets of the trousers, leaving them in shreds, strips of material.

Well, Vanda had told them to perform a strip search.

Leon's heart missed a beat as Fabio stooped and grabbed the right shoe.

This is not going well, Leon thought.

How thorough was Fabio going to be?

Thorough enough, it seemed. Fabio used the blade to whittle at the heel of the shoe, plucking it off, and then discarded it.

This is it.

Fabio picked up the left shoe and attacked that heel.

Moment of truth.

Fabio looked up, grinning. "I've got it!"

Keeping his gun leveled on Leon, Mateo said, "Let me see."

Fabio upturned the shoe and tapped it against the heel of his hand. The transmitter, like a slightly large pill, dropped into his palm.

Mateo said, "Just as she guessed."

Clever Vanda.

Fabio eyed Mateo expectantly.

Waving a hand dismissively, Mateo said, "Do it."

Lips curling with pleasure, Fabio dropped the transmitter to the floor and stamped on it, shattering it into tiny pieces.

Not good, Leon thought.

Mustn't give them any satisfaction by showing despair or annoyance.

Fabio said, "Any other tricks up his sleeve?"

"Let's see, shall we?" Thick lips curling back in a snarl, Mateo snapped, "Now, damn you, take off your shirt!"

Leon rolled his eyes to the ceiling. "Oh, you should've said. I thought you just wanted the suit."

"The shirt!"

"All right, keep *your* shirt on."

For that quip he experienced another punch, again to the gut.

He'd expected it and, despite the pain, had tensed his sore muscles, which softened the impact slightly.

Slowly, he unbuttoned his shirt and peeled it off his sweat-soaked body. Disdainfully, he flung it on top of the tatters of material that had once resembled an expensive suit.

"That's better," Mateo said. "Now you're dressed more like the others."

More like the others? Standing only in his boxer shorts and socks, Leon decided not to make any further flippant comments. He wasn't sure his stomach could take much more at present.

"You've been in the wars, I see." Mateo indicated the scars on Leon's torso and arms.

Knife and bullet wounds.

But you should see the other guys—in the cemetery.

Mateo said, "Lost your tongue, eh?"

Leon recalled a Spanish proverb: Don't mention the noose in the house of the hanged man. By now, his bruised stomach was advising him not to say the wrong thing anymore. He compromised and shrugged.

Mateo said, "No matter. We aren't here to chat."

Then the so-called "softening-up" process began as advertised, interspersed with tediously repetitive but unanswered questions:

What is your name?
Who sent you?
Why are you here?

———

HARLEY WAS MODERATELY IMPRESSED with the accommodation. It was a large room with a double bed, bedstand on each side, a closet, and a green-tiled en suite bathroom with shower, basin, toilet and bidet. White stucco walls, clean and tidy. Not four star, but adequate. On the writing table was a laptop.

Mateo activated the laptop and explained, "You may choose a companion from the selection we have here." He gestured at the screen and clicked on the mouse ball. Pictures of ten scantily-clad women appeared, each with a numbered box. "Click on the number of your choosing."

Harley scanned the images, licking his lips as he did so. He experienced no guilt, since his marriage was ashes in his mouth. All he and his wife were doing now was squabbling over their relationship's corpse. He clicked on #8, a brunette with come-hither hooded eyes, long lashes and full scarlet lips. Her body was alluring. A response box appeared: available and allocated to you. He supposed the availability depended upon the other clients and their alacrity with the keys, as there was always the chance that two clients could pick the same number.

"You've chosen well. Eight is very popular," Mateo said. "I'll leave you to unpack."

As Mateo closed the door after him, Harley wondered about his choice. "Very popular." He wasn't too sure about that aspect. He'd never frequented a brothel or ever paid for sex. *Hey, I'm not paying today*, he told himself. Then, he counter-argued, *yes you are*—it's all part of the package and their promised "unique experience."

A short while later, he was still in the throes of unpacking his traveling bag and hanging his clothes in the closet, when there was a gentle tap on the door.

He called, "Yes, who is it?"

A deep female voice: "You ordered my presence."

Mouth dry, Harley threw his last shirt on the bed and went to open the door.

A woman with long brunette hair stood in the passage. She wore a sheer green silk dress. Her shoulders were bare, and the material fitted like a second skin, suggesting she wasn't wearing anything else.

"I am number eight," she said in greeting.

Despite her allure, his attention was momentarily distracted by movement in the passage behind her. Fleetingly, he noticed that standing at the door on the other side of the passage was a dark-skinned woman with black frizzy hair that fell to her shoulders. She wore a white dress and was barefoot. That door opened and Rudolf stood there. The banker's face was quite stern. The woman introduced herself as "number six" and then Rudolf quickly hustled her inside.

Harley presumed Quint was being indulged in a similar manner.

"Come in," he told the brunette.

She did as he bid and shut the door after her.

He said, "I didn't...didn't expect you to arrive so soon. I...I was going to have a shower before you—"

She ran her tongue over her thick lips, and when moistened they glinted. "We shower together." Deftly, she reached behind her and unzipped the dress, letting it fall to the tiled floor. Nude, she stepped out of the tumbled material. The picture on the laptop didn't do her justice.

"I would like that very much," he said breathlessly.

Jeezus, I've paid enough for this little jaunt. Might as well enjoy all the hospitality that's on offer.

He clasped number eight's hand and quickly led her towards the bathroom.

————

NUMBER six's dusky brown eyes were fearful, Rudolf thought. Possibly because at some point she'd suffered a broken nose. She wore a short white linen shift dress with a low-cut V-neck which complemented her exotic caramel complexion.

"Do you have a name?" he asked in German.

She said, "I—I am sorry, I speak only English, Spanish and Italian."

Typical! English, it gets everywhere! "Of course," he growled in English, "I should have known."

She said, "I'm pleased to meet you."

"No you're not." Impulsively, he launched himself at her, both hands pressing against her shoulders, forcing her bodily against the door. Hands trembling, he grabbed the opening of her dress and ripped it away, and then his mouth closed on hers, before she could scream out. His teeth bit into her lip and he tasted her blood.

She attempted to push him off her, and in response he let go and balled a fist and hit her on the temple. He took a pace back, letting her fall sideways.

As she slumped to the floor, her back against the door, she glared up at him, the back of her hand wiping blood from her mouth.

He said, "I will teach you a new language. The language of pain!"

He had to work out his frustration. Before the damnable #MeToo campaign he'd enjoyed being able to force himself on a certain number of female bank clients, those requiring business loans or financial advice at the time of bereavement. A natural predator, he could tell which ones were weak enough, susceptible enough. And they quickly understood only too well that their compliance meant he would approve the financial arrangement they sought.

But now in this current climate he was fearful, lest one of them drew strength from the vociferous militant feminists and exposed him to head office or even the media. That notoriety would not only cost him his job, and possibly his pension, but would also have worked against any divorce settlement. So since the publicized #MeToo furor, he had curtailed his overtures and satiated himself in the red light district, which proved more expensive and less satisfying. Afterwards, he always suffered regret.

As for Anna, he consoled himself with the thought that, providing he found an outlet for his base desires, she need never know this violent side of him.

LYING IN BED, Vanda watched the six monitor screens suspended from the ceiling. They showed the six client rooms. Three of them were empty. Francisco lay beside her, snoring. Not wanting to wake him, she had muted the sound.

There was no need to listen. Actions spoke louder.

Quint was business-like with the woman he'd selected.

Harley had taken his brunette into the bathroom. Number eight was thorough with the soapy lather.

Vanda liked the look of Harley. He was tall, angular and lean. A fine specimen. Maybe she'd catch them cavorting on the bed shortly.

But for now she was more interested in the German, Rudolf. He was a nasty piece of work. She stroked her throat, feeling the warmth of her flushed face as Rudolf beat and abused number six. Perhaps it was just as well that Francisco wasn't awake to see it.

What a sheer delight to view! So satisfying!

The cameras had been installed at her instigation, and Francisco was understandably enthusiastic. The antics of the clients were recorded, so she and Francisco could watch them at leisure and sometimes the viewing experience enhanced their own pleasure. But there was another reason for the recordings. Not all clients embraced the experience they'd paid for; a tiny minority were incapable of coping and were even traumatized. These individuals were ripe for blackmail, using the video film to ensure their silence and to encourage a monthly loyalty payment.

She wondered how the man calling himself Carlos was being entertained, and hoped Mateo and Fabio weren't getting too carried away.

Careful not to wake Francisco, she swung her legs out of bed and threw on a robe.

Time to check on them.

———

MATEO OPENED the door of Rudolf's room. Behind him stood an armed guard.

Naked and trembling, number six cowered in a corner, her nose and mouth blood-smeared. A fresh bruise on her forehead was prominent. The remnants of her white dress were strewn on the floor.

Rudolf was nude, sprawled face-down on the bed, asleep.

Mateo hissed, "Six. Number six."

Her head jerked up, fear in her eyes as she saw him.

He liked seeing that dread. "Put these on," he whispered and threw a small bundle of black lace lingerie and a pair of black shoes at her.

She grabbed them, covered herself with the flimsy garments. Hesitantly, she stood.

"Do it." To encourage her, he made a noisy chomping motion with his prominent teeth. That sent her shaking.

Trembling, she donned the underwear while he watched.

Then he grabbed her arm, pulled her towards the door. "You need to come with us now."

———

A POUNDING noise filled Leon's head: the builders with their pneumatic drill were quite familiar, even if it was quite a while since they last took up residence. It wasn't the first time he'd been knocked out. The bad part was recovering consciousness. It was worse than any hangover. "So far, you don't appear to have suffered deleterious brain damage," one doctor had told him. "But if you keep going on like this, it's only a matter of time. You really should change your career." Right now, he was inclined to agree.

Tentatively, he opened his eyes.

Light rushed in and tended to exaggerate the pain.

So he closed his eyes and took stock.

It felt as though his entire body ached, but the hurt was

nothing like the excruciating agony of a broken limb or cracked ribs.

He remembered. This had to be a good sign, suggesting no short-term memory loss.

Accompanied by two armed guards, Mateo and Fabio had taken him into a stuffy basement room.

He'd removed his shoes and stripped to his boxer shorts, and then Mateo had started on him. So they wouldn't strain themselves too much, they took turns to beat him up. They asked questions which he didn't answer. At the time he found himself thinking they proved themselves experts at inflicting pain without leaving too many marks. It was quite a while since he'd been so badly treated. He hadn't resisted or fought against them, since the gunman always kept his machine-pistol trained on him while the others went to work. The gunman watched impassively, seemingly bored.

Definitely too old for this sort of thing, he thought.

His tongue moved experimentally around his mouth. One tooth wiggled, slightly loose, and he could taste blood on his lips. His left cheek was tender, probably bruised. A herd of elephants had trodden on his stomach, or so it seemed. He couldn't taste or smell vomit, thankfully, but he was nauseous. His tongue slid over his slightly swollen lips and he noted that his false mustache was missing. He couldn't remember when or how that was removed.

Time to see where I am.

Again, he opened his eyes, just a little, mere slits at first.

The light wasn't that severe this time. A single bare bulb dangled on its cord from a blistered ceiling.

He lay on the floor of a windowless room. Similar to the place where they'd beaten him, but not the same venue. Still in the basement, then.

His wrists were shackled, with a length of chain between them. He could stand, if he had a mind to. For now, he settled on moving into a sitting position, back against the wall. *Don't do anything too rash.*

Somebody had taken off his watch, considering it a perk,

no doubt. He was still wearing his boxer shorts—and, surprisingly, his socks and shoes. Height of fashion, but it'll never catch on in the high street.

On seeing the shoes, his hopes rose and then sank immediately as he noticed that the heels had been cut away. He swore under his breath, and that hurt. Damn! He remembered. Fabio had found the transmitter in the heel. He estimated it had been sending its signal for maybe ten or fifteen minutes, up to the point where he'd been forced to strip. All time had lost meaning when they started hitting him. Would that be a long enough period for Silvano's crew to pinpoint his location? If the Guardia Civil made an incursion soon, would they obtain sufficient evidence? Probably. He was doubtful, though.

Despite being sore all over, he hadn't sustained any serious physical impairment.

They'd obeyed Vanda's injunction to keep me in one piece.

Be thankful for small mercies.

The technique no longer came easy, but finally he managed to steady his pulse and heart-rate.

"This is not in the plan," he berated himself aloud.

As soon as he'd regained consciousness smells, sounds and furtive movements had made him aware that he was not alone, but until now he'd ignored all extraneous stimuli, too intent on assessing his own physical and mental state.

Now, raising his head, he studied the others. He counted nine, five men and four women, all shackled and chained and, like him, in various forms of undress. Mateo's words echoed from his memory: "You're dressed more like the others."

"Welcome back to the living," intoned a breathy accented voice in English on his left. She stood next to him, leaning against the wall. "Though I fear it won't be for long." She gestured with her left hand, graphically slicing across her throat. He noticed the small finger on her left hand had been amputated.

Her graphic gesture was clear; he knew what she meant.

She was lithe, with taut muscle beneath her caramel complexioned skin. Incongruously, she wore a black lace camisole, jutting cones of full breasts pressing against it; it hung high, showing her flat stomach and navel. Her matching briefs didn't conceal much of her broad hips. Flat-soled black pumps were her only other item of apparel. Her frizzy black hair reached her bare round shoulders. She had a high forehead which sported a recent bruise, a wide mouth, its lower lip with a fresh cut, and a firm chin and sharp cheekbones.

She said, "I'm Daraja. From Lagos."

Nigeria's mega-city and one of the fastest growing in Africa. No longer the capital; that's been Abuja since the early 1990s. His memory seemed to be working fine. "I'm Leon."

She was probably Igbo, but he allowed she might be Yoruba or one of the many other ethnic minorities. She had a slightly crooked broad nose, and bright sparkling dusky brown eyes with long lashes.

He said, "It looks like you've taken a beating recently as well."

"I worked—slaved, more like—for Señor Baeza, who is the main man in this place." She scowled. "At least I used to until you showed up. Then I was brought here."

Why did his presence lead to this woman's imprisonment?

Before he could put the question he heard keys jangle and the lock clicked.

The heavy wooden door swung open and an armed guard walked in, followed by Vanda Dinescu, her face grim. She wore a silk dressing-gown with pockets, cinched at the waist, her cleavage evident. Her feet were in silver-and-gold mules. Was she ready for a bath? He thought she probably desired one after standing in here for any length of time. She sniffed and raised a handkerchief to her nose, and her heady strong scent wafted towards Leon. While lying here he must have become accustomed to the smell of the basement: it was rank with body odor and faeces: in one corner was a toilet cubicle, the only concession to privacy. Lack of ventilation meant it was stuffy, too.

"Sorry, I can't get up for you," he said. "I'm a mite sore. I usually stand when a lady enters the room."

"She's no lady," snarled Daraja.

Vanda lanced a feral look at the Nigerian. "Enjoy the German, did you?"

Daraja's cut lip twisted and her eyes became slits imbued with deep hatred.

Vanda sniggered and then turned back to Leon. "You're fortunate I checked on you." She indicated his bruised midriff. "Those two were getting carried away."

"Before I blacked out, I noticed. They were most enthusiastic. Obviously enjoy their work."

She said, "But they didn't get any information out of you. You're stubborn." She lifted from her robe's pocket a national ID card and wafted it in front of her flared nostrils. "Mateo extracted this from your wallet which was found in your jacket."

"You'd better tell him he won't get a finder's fee."

She grimaced. "It is probably a fake. But while the name Carlos Ortiz Santos may be an alias, perhaps the date of birth is accurate, no? February sixteen, 1963."

"Sorry I didn't invite you to my last party."

"Your silly quips, they hide your insecurity, your fear, I know."

"I hope you don't charge by the hour. Your psycho-analysis is sadly very wrong."

"You would say that, wouldn't you?" And then, appraising him, she came closer, and touched his bare torso, running a hand over a couple of ancient scars. No electricity between them now, he noted. "Mateo told me you'd been in the wars." The tip of her tongue wetted her lips. "For a man of your age, you have kept yourself fit. A lesser man, taking such a beating..." She lifted a shoulder fatalistically.

"I'll live."

"Not for much longer, though."

"We all must die sometime. Even you."

She curled her lip in distaste. "Nicholas was crushed to death by the boa before the Civil could get to him!"

"I'm sure you've found a replacement for him."

She slapped his face.

His lips stung and his bruised cheek tingled.

He said nothing.

"This time, don't expect your friends in the Civil to come flying in," she said. "Mateo found the transmitter in your shoe and destroyed it."

"That's not all," he snapped. He winced, for his lip hurt when he spoke harshly like that. "Somebody stole my watch. I'd like it back."

She snickered. "You don't really want to register the passing of time, Carlos Santos or whatever your name is. In your case it is extremely finite."

"The watch was a gift from a female admirer."

"Too bad. You should take better care of your *things*." She eyed his boxer shorts. "They're not exactly Calvin Klein, are they?"

"No. Hennes and Mauritz." He openly studied her cleavage. Black lace peeked on either side of the cleft. "What about your lingerie?"

Her tongue darted, licked her lips. "Wouldn't you like to know?"

"Are you flirting, Vanda?"

Her forehead wrinkled and her cheeks reddened and then she switched her gaze to Daraja. "You brought this on yourself."

Daraja hunched her shoulders dismissively. "He preferred me to you."

Vanda took a pace forward and slapped Daraja. "Slut!"

She really likes slapping people, Leon thought.

Daraja stood stock still, unflinching, while her chest swelled against the lacy fabric with suppressed emotion. Her stare promised pain and suffering if she ever got her hands on Vanda.

Vanda went on, "I swore you'd pay. Giving you to the German was just a warm-up. When "Santos" here became a last-minute addition to the group, I knew that you'd make an ideal partner for him!"

Leon had a sinking feeling that he knew precisely what Vanda meant, but he wasn't going to ask her to qualify the statement.

Daraja bunched her fists. "If Francisco finds out what you have done, your life will—"

"He knows, you silly fool!" Arms akimbo, Vanda laughed. "Don't kid yourself. Yes, Francisco was distressed at having to give up a beddable *servant*. But I saw it in his eyes. He would not fight me for you, Daraja. You were a distraction for him, and that is all—like so many others!"

Daraja glared, her eyes wide, dry, yet shining in the poor light. "It was nothing personal against you. I had no choice." She raised her left hand, palm open, displaying the truncated little finger. "And you know this to be true."

Vanda taunted, "Do you think I care? I know he's tried many of the more voluptuous comfort women here. But he always returns to *my* bed." She tapped her heaving chest. "Because I have his *heart*!"

Her chain rattling, Daraja offered her back and walked away.

Vanda swiveled on her heel and leveled her gaze on Leon. "I have to talk to my associates. You interest them greatly."

"Nice to be wanted."

"You will be sent for shortly."

"I'll look forward to it. How long will you keep us captive?"

"At dawn, we'll let all of you loose." She turned her back on him and, chuckling, her shoulders shaking with mirth, she left.

The armed guard followed, locking the door after him.

———

As THE HOURS PASSED, Leon got to know something about the others.

As he'd suspected, most if not all of these people were illegal immigrants. Courtesy of the well-intentioned but idiotic Schengen Agreement.

A man dressed in a grubby brown T-shirt, undershorts and sandals stepped forward. By all accounts he was the eldest present and he introduced himself in halting English as Yesal, an Afghan. "I speak no Spanish but I have English," he said.

With the help of Yesal and Daraja, Leon learned their identities and the little they divulged about how they came to be here.

They were a good advert for immigrant diversity and open borders.

Tabish was the only other person from Afghanistan. Sami was a Syrian male. Anamaria was a Romanian woman. Jamal and Meriem were Moroccan husband and wife. And the other two were unrelated Iraqis, Nasim, a male, and Mina, a female.

Considering the mixture of nationalities gathered here, everyone managed to understand the others. The common tongues were English, French and Arabic. Leon was one of those fortunate individuals capable of learning a foreign language with ease. He'd grown up bilingual, speaking English and Spanish, and later learned seven other languages as required in his intelligence work.

Time passed, weighing heavily upon them all.

Leon circulated among them and learned their stories, with the exception of Anamaria, who kept quiet, brooding. He had noticed that while Vanda was in the room, Anamaria had looked daggers at their captor. Not surprising, perhaps, but as both women were Romanian, he guessed that they might have a shared history.

Yesal was wide faced, tanned and weathered, with lines

round eyes and mouth, and a furrowed forehead. He was thirty-six, he said. He had a salt-and-pepper mustache with matching beard and hair. His close-set brown eyes seemed to reflect deep sadness, but he respectfully explained that he didn't want to talk about his past.

It transpired that Yesal had befriended Tabish, who was fleeing the Taliban with a group of Afghans.

The entire family of Tabish had been slaughtered by the fundamentalists. Tabish had studious blue-gray eyes, a hooked nose, a pencil mustache and stubble on his chin. His brown hair hung in short curls. He wore a stained linen shirt of indeterminate color, red-and-white striped undershorts and scuffed leather sandals. He constantly yearned for cigarettes, and he said when he wasn't plagued by nightmares he dreamed of Marlboros.

Sami, a twenty-eight-year-old Syrian spoke rapidly in a mixture of English and French, thick lips a virtual blur. He had narrow facial features, a black beard, mustache and a receding hairline. His sunken eyes were a deep brown. He only wore once-white undershorts and scuffed sneakers, his torso appearing wiry, not muscular. "I flee violence and barbarism so I become less than a slave to men without compassion!"

Speaking in Arabic in a gruff voice, the Iraqi Nasim told Leon that he was a mathematician. He had left his young wife and two-year-old son to find work in Spain, after which he would send for them. He had a swarthy complexion, a heavy brow, a dark brown mustache and chin stubble. "I fear I will not see my family again," he ended, his long face drawn, dark eyes staring, accusing. He also bemoaned the fact that he used to smoke Ghamdan Star cigarettes but hadn't smoked in ages. "I still suffer the withdrawal shakes." Then he laughed mirthlessly. "I could afford to burn money, now look at me!" He wore a tattered gray linen shirt, torn white linen trousers and ancient leather sandals.

He wasn't the only Iraqi. There was another, a female. Mina's face was oval, her nose broad, and she had heavy

hooded dark eyes. She was quiet-voiced, which made it difficult to understand her since she wore a gray hijab, which her
nervous long fingers constantly picked at. A long white
cotton shirt draped to the top of her knees. On her feet were
ornate soft-soled shoes.

She wouldn't communicate with Leon, evading his eyes.
Daraja told him what she had gleaned, her story having been
halting, and brief. By chance, Mina had escaped from the
Islamic State extremists and after a long trek through Turkey
she was one of many smuggled on a lorry from Istanbul, on
and on, traded between gangs. She said little more, save that
for an odd perverse reason all her captors allowed her to
retain the hijab.

"She is a private person who finds her life is in ruins,"
Daraja ended sympathetically.

Every one of them in here was clearly traumatized, but
Mina more than the others seemed to find her situation
almost beyond endurance. And yet she *had* endured. He'd
heard of many who had committed suicide when confronted
with inevitable hardships. Leon could conceive of no words
to alleviate Mina's distress.

The couple from Tangier spoke in a mixture of Arabic
and French, interchangeable at the drop of a verb. Jamal had
abandoned his carpet business because his brother had
attempted to double-cross a criminal fraternity, and Jamal
was rightly afraid of reprisals. He and his wife Meriem ran
away and paid for passage across to Spain. Leon knew it to be
a familiar story, repeated by thousands who risked the
Mediterranean crossing. Their boat began sinking as they
were near the coastline. Fortunately, they could swim and
made for the shore. The pair, sodden and shivering, had been
picked up. On one lorry after another they were transported,
but never separated, though both were molested a number of
times.

Traumatized, fearful, finally they were sold to Señor
Baeza.

"I miss my friends and relatives," Meriem wailed in a

reedy voice. "We should have stayed and fought in the courts, but Jamal has no backbone. He was enticed by the traffickers' promises of good work in Spain!"

Jamal wore only undershorts and moccasins, while she was dressed in a short plain blue cotton T-shirt and jeans cut-off mid-thigh and soft-soled canvas shoes. They were the same height but otherwise contrasted strongly: he was ten years older than her and had a long face, a narrow nose and lips, thick black eyebrows, small yellow teeth, and large ears. Her face was round, her eyebrows dark brown, like her eyes, and she had big teeth. She nervously picked at the hem of her T-shirt whenever she spoke.

Daraja explained that Anamaria was Romanian, like their captor, Vanda. "I don't know, but I got the feeling maybe they know each other." Anamaria had a narrow face, chubby cheeks, plump lips and wide brown eyes with long lashes. Her auburn hair was cropped short. She wore a plain white bra and briefs and yellow plastic sandals. Anamaria hadn't divulged any of her past, however, and was reticent with Leon.

Lastly, Daraja took him to one side of the room and hunkered down with her back to the wall. In a muted whisper, she began, in good English, "My story is similar to the others, save that I wasn't an illegal immigrant."

"Were you snatched off the street in Lagos?" It was known that people peddlers abducted women to order, on the streets of any city, whether in England, Spain or anywhere.

She smiled wanly. "No, not Lagos." She shook her head. "I'm sure it happens there as well. But any women taken would be snatched for the African market, I suspect. Little point in costly transport for them to Europe."

"Fair point, but it might depend on the buyer, I suppose." He whispered sympathetically, "Then tell me, Daraja,"

"I learnt English at school and left college with qualifications in Latin and Italian, and worked hard, became a trained nurse." Her damaged hand kept brushing at a bothersome fly that hovered around her face. "My future looked bright. But before starting on what I knew would be challenging work and long hours in one of the many Lagos hospitals, I wanted to travel through Europe."

Leon's hand darted out, swatted the fly.

She arched an eyebrow. "The beating you took hasn't affected your reflexes."

He said, "Thanks for the medical opinion. Go on."

"So, to begin my adventure, I answered a recruitment advertisement for a live-in nurse for a rich family in Rome." Her mouth down-turned and her eyes gazed into her past. "My family said I could do better. But I argued I didn't want a demanding hospital post just then, I wanted freedom to sightsee." She sighed heavily. "I responded with a CV and a photograph and then I was asked to undergo a Skype interview. I got the job and my flight was paid for." Tears welled in her eyes. She brushed them dry with the back of her hands, and the chain rattled.

"I bid farewell to family and friends at Murtala Muhammed airport and set off, nervous yet excited."

"But?"

Bitterly, she said, "The job was a lie." She stared into the center of the room but he doubted if she saw the other occupants. She was viewing her past which was doubtless etched painfully into her psyche. "I was met at the airport but I wasn't taken to the promised family. I was whisked away to a tenement block."

He said, "You don't have to say more, if you don't want to. The others only sketched in details. I'm sure it was painful for them to do even that."

"Thank you, but I want to tell you." She reached for his hand, held it. "You might survive the forthcoming ordeal. If I am going to die, then maybe you will be able to tell my story. Tell my family."

"Let's have no talk of dying," he said, squeezing her hand.

She nodded and continued to hold onto him.

"As you say, gloss over it. I was sold into prostitution and passed on to different groups."

Anger seethed beneath the surface. He'd dealt with people trafficking scum before, sometimes administering his own kind of rough justice, but there were so many of the bastards. They were like voracious insects, swarming, feasting at the putrid edges of civilization.

"Then," Daraja was saying, "after many months I finally found myself here, working as waitress staff and also as a comfort woman. They say travel broadens the mind. Quite an education, no?"

She put a brave face on her traumatic past. He wondered if she had nightmares.

She said, "I quickly mastered the Spanish language. And then Señor Baeza took a fancy to me."

"I imagine Vanda wouldn't like that."

Daraja snorted. "That was my worry, too. I tried to resist him. But Baeza had an answer for my reluctance."

"Which was?"

"Mateo."

"An unpleasant man."

She sobbed. "Yes, he is. Baeza held me while Mateo bit off my little finger, which he then spat at me." She held up her damaged hand.

"Bastard."

"There are more choice words for his kind, I assure you." She cradled her hand in her lap and rocked against the wall. "I think Baeza was excited by the blood. He... he raped me there... in front of Mateo."

A bolus of bile filled his throat. Leon swallowed it with an effort. He didn't know what to say. No words of comfort would assuage the pain or erase the terrible experience. And she already had lodged in her mind many abominable memories since she was snatched at Rome airport.

She shuddered, licked her lips, and then went on, "After that, I decided I wanted to keep my other fingers and put up

no fight, praying that Vanda never discovered Baeza's infideli-
ty." Black humor was a defense of sorts, he admitted. Created
a veneer, a carapace. He admired her pluck and knew instinctively that no matter what she'd gone through she wouldn't
appreciate his pity.

She said, "Baeza took me to his bed whenever Señorita
Dinescu was away, which was quite frequent. I learned that
Vanda's excuse for her absences was typical of her: "Without
shopping, a girl hasn't lived!" she'd say. Ha!" She spat on the
floor. "You know, to begin with I had the notion that sharing
Baeza's bed might be a way out for me and I might have
some influence on my future; but it wasn't and I had none.
Delusional...that was me. Silly fool that I was! Of course I
soon learned that I wasn't the first nor would I be the last:
Baeza enjoyed cheating on Vanda."

"I wouldn't have thought she was the forgiving type."

Daraja grimaced. "You're right there! She caught us in
bed together. Vanda was furious. She says, 'Again, I am
betrayed!' Baeza didn't know what she was talking about. I
certainly didn't. She slapped him repeatedly and then
slapped me."

Leon ruefully massaged his cheek and his chain rattled.
"I noticed she likes slapping people."

"She does, doesn't she?"

"I'm surprised Baeza took it, though."

"Yes, I truly believed he'd throttle her. After all, he is a
powerful man, big and strong. Yet she laid into him... and he
backed off. And then I was sent to the comfort rooms. I
think she was jealous. Afterwards, I fretted what she had
planned for me. I never saw her for days. Then, on the day
when you arrived, I had just been with Orton—the Englishman, a gentle soul—and after he left Mateo ordered me to
"entertain" a German guest."

"That would be Rudolf. An impetuous nervous type."

She bit her lip, glanced away and absently fingered her
bruised forehead. "Afterwards... Mateo dragged me away and
brought me straight here. On Vanda's orders, Mateo said."

"I'm sorry about that." His words sounded inadequate. Guessing at the ruthlessness of Doina/Vanda, he supposed that even if he hadn't turned up and become captive, Daraja's days of relative freedom would have been numbered.

———

ONCE LEON HAD SPOKEN to them all he explained that he was investigating Baeza's illegal business.

Gradually, as his words were translated among them, there was a buzz of murmuring. They were definitely excited by his disclosure.

He raised a hand to stall further speculation. "I'm sorry. No help's coming now. You heard what the woman Vanda Dinescu said. They destroyed my radio-transmitter."

Sighs and groans followed as the message got across. Briefly full of hope, now they were thoroughly deflated.

He ended by asking if they knew why they were being held in this cell.

A general shaking of heads. Nobody could suggest why. Anamaria moved away and wordlessly hunched in a corner. Perhaps she knew something. And Daraja was quiet, as well.

He debated with himself as to whether he should be honest with them. Subconsciously he bit his lip, but the pain made him quickly regret doing that and he desisted.

Definitely, he knew *why*. He'd paid €50,000 for the privilege of coming here. Like his three fellow passengers, he could afford it.

"The people who have put us in here are hosts to rich trophy hunters. Marksmen," he explained in turn in French and English. He paused while his words were translated further, and then added, "They're going to hunt you—us— and kill us...for amusement."

Like a wave, shock washed over most of them. Yet again he noted that Daraja and Anamaria didn't express surprise. The others appeared devastated.

Several exclaimed, naively:

"They can't!"

"You must be mistaken!"

"That's cold blooded murder!"

Yesal held no illusions, however. "Murder doesn't apply to us. We are illegal immigrants. Worthless..."

Leon raised both chained hands to quell the outbursts, and when they grew silent he went on, "I flew in with three marksmen, a German and two Americans. We've all paid large sums of money for the pleasure of hunting human prey."

"*You* paid to hunt us?"

"You've not been listening!" Daraja berated.

Leon said, "I was undercover, spying, trying to discover if the human hunt was genuine, not fake news. What we'd heard was based on rumor, conjecture. The source—the dark web was not explicit enough. We had no solid proof. That's why I volunteered to come here, to get corroboration. Unfortunately, that woman Vanda Dinescu recognized me from one of my earlier cases and that's why I'm with you rather than calling in the cavalry."

"That jealous bitch!" Daraja exclaimed. "Surely Señor Baeza won't want *me* killed, will he?"

"If Vanda Dinescu pulls Baeza's strings, maybe he won't have much of a say in the matter." Leon hunched his shoulders, undecided. "We'll find out at dawn, I guess."

"When they let us loose?" Anamaria murmured. "The bitch said that."

"Only let loose so we can be prey for their hunt," he amended.

CHAPTER 4

TROPHY BONUS

LEON EMBRACED THE IDEA OF BEING A HUNTER. Even his Spanish name meant just that: Lion Hunter. He could afford expensive private investigations because a few years previously he'd helped a relic hunter. The proceeds from that case provided him with enough wealth to pursue his vendetta against the ungodly. That was quite a long time ago; Angel Ramos had since joined the dust of his cherished artifacts.

His reverie was disturbed when the basement door opened.

Fabio entered, accompanied by two gunmen with their machine-pistols and a dark-haired Spaniard who pushed a trolley that contained a steaming pan, a ladle and two stacks of wooden bowls.

"Food for the condemned men and women!" Fabio called in Spanish. "Line up!"

Whether they understood him or not, the captives all seemed to know what to do. With reluctance, they clambered to their feet and jostled slowly into a ragged line, their chains jangling.

Leon found himself on the end of the queue, immediately behind Daraja.

The man with the trolley poured a slimy yellow

substance into a bowl. "Paella *sin* meat," he said with a smirk. "Yum yum! Step up! You know the routine, one at a time!"

The men and women shuffled forward, taking the bowl of rice and then moved to the walls where they hunkered down to eat with their fingers.

It was Leon's turn. He held out his hand for a bowl.

"Not you," Fabio said. "You're wanted upstairs. The boss wants to see you."

"I'd love to join you," Leon said, rattling his chain, "but I'm tied up at present."

Careful not to block the view of the two gunmen, Fabio moved forward to face Leon and punched him in the gut.

Doubling up, Leon gasped.

Easily riled. A sensitive soul.

He noticed that Fabio's knuckles were slightly raw from their earlier encounter, and that gave him perverse satisfaction.

Fabio shoved Leon towards the door. "Don't do anything foolish," he warned. "We can still hurt you more."

Standing by the doorway, Leon said, "Foolish, me? I don't think so." One gunman went out first.

He knew the layout from his walk here to get his beating, but he still had no idea what was behind any of the doors. Directly opposite his basement cell doorway was another door. Faintly he heard music and, half-turning, he cocked an eyebrow at Fabio.

"That's where our comfort women stay." Fabio shook his head. "But you can forget Mateo's promise. There will be little comfort in the rest of your sad life!" He shoved Leon to move on.

A gunman led, followed by Leon, and then the other gunman and then Fabio brought up the rear.

As they passed the adjacent door on the south side, Leon said, "More comfort women?"

"No." Fabio chortled. "In there we have a new batch of immigrant targets in readiness for next week's rich clients!"

"Quite a production line—or is that extermination line?"

"It's a living." Then Fabio laughed.

This has to stop! Though right now he was in no position to stop anything, except maybe a bullet.

They passed a doorway, the door ajar, and a pungent disinfectant smell wafted out. Probably a communal bathroom, a facility not available to the imprisoned illegal immigrants, the so-called targets. Next to it was another door, this one shut.

Leon observed the regularly sighted emergency lights running along the floor on one side of the passage, similar to those found in the aisles of airliners.

"Noticed them, eh?" Fabio said. "If the generator packs up or runs out of fuel it's pitch-black down here. Those battery-powered lights will guide us out."

"Generators can be so unreliable," Leon answered.

"Yeah."

Reaching a cross-passage, Fabio pointed to a door on the left, at the far end: "That's the armory where your rifle would have come from." He snickered. "The hunter becomes the hunted, how about that?"

Leon made no comment.

Rounding the corner to the right, they came to two doors with the familiar labels for stairs and elevator.

The gunman opened the elevator door and they entered the cubicle.

After the door slid shut, Fabio pressed the button and the elevator rose.

Top floor. Criminal mastermind. Explanations at last!

It felt crowded. Gun snouts were pressed against his sides. He had no intention of disarming any of them. Finally he was about to meet the architect of this project. Only then would he decide what needed to be done.

Nobody spoke as they ascended.

Seconds later, the elevator stopped, made a *ping* sound, and the doors slid open.

Leon was pushed out and then escorted along a short passage.

They turned left and entered a doorway on the right.

They'd entered a large room with a wide window overlooking a balcony. The surrounding land was hazy in twilight, and dark shapes loomed, possibly trees.

The room was a combination lounge-bar and dining room. On one wall were mounted four wild boar heads. There was a huge flat-screen television at one end and at the other end was a dining table with eight place settings.

Seated at the table were Vanda Dinescu and four men. Three of the men puffed on cigars. They all held half-full sherry glasses.

At least one of them was Spanish and Leon guessed possibly a second one was as well. The other two were European, maybe even British.

In the center of the table were tureens emitting the tantalizing aroma of rabbit and garlic. No paella *sin* meat here, then. There were also several plates heaped with eggs, asparagus, olives, shredded carrot, dates, tuna and lettuce. Leon's stomach rumbled. Each place setting had two empty glasses —for water and wine. There were eight uncorked bottles of red and two of white, the latter encased by inflated plastic cool bags.

In one corner was a small galley, manned by a single chef, who busied himself with the oven. In another corner was a well-stocked cocktail bar, crystal glasses glinting. By the bar eight dark red leather armchairs had been arranged in a circle around a couple of coffee tables.

Vanda had changed and now wore a low-cut red evening dress, her neck adorned with a thin gold chain that held a large ruby pendant that snuggled in the deep valley between her breasts. Big gold rings dangled from her ears.

He recognized the man in a black leather shell suit and orange trainers: the goatee beard, shaggy charcoal-gray hair, the square pockmarked face and, dead giveaway, the hole in the throat pointed to the rich lowlife Ramon Calvo. He'd been known to chain-smoke cigars but now, understandably, he was the man without a cigar. Leon nodded to him. "Ah, Señor Calvo, I see you're branching out from providing Eastern European girls for roundabouts."

Calvo's wide-set shark-gray eyes started and he coughed, making an alarming whooping sound. Sadly, he wasn't choking and soon controlled himself and glared.

Leon received a punch from Fabio to his stomach for that quip. Not his solar plexus, fortunately, or he'd be on his knees, wheezing on the floor, if not attempting to cough up bile.

Fabio massaged his fist.

"Fabio," Vanda berated, rising from the table. "Enough of these theatrics."

"You mean I've got the part?" Leon replied.

"No, you failed the audition, Señor Santos."

"That isn't his name," said Calvo, raising a hand-held device to the hole in his throat. His voice was a menacing computerized robotic sound. "After I learned about your failure with the endangered species, Vanda, I checked on this man's identity. Carlos Santos is a phantom. He doesn't exist." He stroked his goatee. "And yet he knows about me."

She said, "I don't care what he knows or what his name is. We're not going to be writing any epitaph."

Chuckles erupted all round.

Such wit.

Leon said, "I get an unmarked grave, is that it?"

"Hardly, old chap," said a man with buzz-cut ginger hair and ginger sideburns. This comment provoked more merriment.

Vanda walked round the table and strode up to Leon. "When I escaped from the complex, I had time to think, Señor Santos. Carlos?"

"You can call me Leon," he said. "If you wish."

"I *wish* I'd never set eyes on you—Leon!"

"Considering my present predicament, it's mutual. I must endorse your statement."

He received another blow to the stomach, and his chains rattled as he held his hands across his midriff as if to ease the pain. He was thankful that he hadn't eaten in quite a while. That rice slop certainly hadn't looked appetizing anyway. He intended to appear weak, in pain, a ruse that might wrong-foot an opponent. And then again, it might not. Wheezing more than was necessary, he said, "Aren't you going to introduce me to your chums, Vanda?" *So I can inscribe their epitaphs*, he thought.

"You have cojones, I'll grant you that!" She gave a brief giggle. "Ramon Calvo you know. I don't want to learn how you know. As for the others." She gestured at the second Spaniard, a man with inky black short hair, his plump lips wrapped around his cigar. "This here's Francisco González Baeza." His sunken coffee brown eyes glared. "He's the brains behind our project."

"And my business partner," Calvo interrupted metallically.

Baeza smiled indulgently, waving a hand with a flourish. His compact body with its prominent belly poorly fitted the gray suit.

"Ah, Señor Baeza," Leon interrupted. "And why did you decide to put the Nigerian woman Daraja in the basement with the rest of us? She seems to have been a last-minute afterthought."

Vanda eyed Baeza who pursed his lips around the cheroot, as if biting back an angry retort. His pallid complexion flushed.

She said hastily, "All in good time, Leon." She waved a hand at the ginger-haired man who spoke earlier. "Simon Maddox. He's an accomplished tracker and marksman."

"Charmed, I'm sure," Maddox said, looking down his nose at Leon. English public school, no doubt. He wore a short-sleeved shirt that exposed tattoos of daggers on both forearms, which, combined with his craggy features, aquiline nose and thick lips belied his cultured voice.

"And finally," Vanda went on, "Orton, who insists on

not being addressed by his Christian name, probably because he is far from Christian in nature."

Orton blew a smoke ring and his thin lips twisted into an indulgent grimace, as if her joke had worn out a long time ago. He had hooded hazel eyes, an oval face, curly blond hair, and a pale complexion. How had Daraja referred to him? Ah, "a gentle soul". Somehow, Leon had his doubts. "I wouldn't like to be in your shoes, mate," Orton said with a nasal twang: estuary Essex.

"Me neither," Leon said. "Take a bit of getting used to, without heels." He flinched involuntarily as Vanda raised a hand, but the gesture was to thwart Fabio delivering yet another punch to his gut.

"Be patient, Fabio."

Leon said, "Thank you, Vanda, for the introductions. It's always helpful to know who one is going to kill."

"He's too flippant for his own good!" said Orton, while the rest of them laughed.

Leon arched an eyebrow. "Do all the occupants of your basement get an interview like this?"

"No," she said. "Only you."

"I'm flattered by the special attention."

"Don't be," she retorted. "I wanted to tell you that after I escaped and I had time to think, I realized you must have carried a tracking device. We had excluded your smartphone already and we were sure our transport could not have been followed. Lazaro was a competent driver, so he would have detected a tail."

He said, "*Was* a competent driver? Isn't he with us anymore?"

"No. Sadly, he suffered an early death. So, it was obvious that the Guardia Civil had been drawn to us by something you carried!"

Leon stamped his foot lightly. "And your pet goons found it."

A third punch to his stomach precipitated waves of nausea, not dissimilar to sea-sickness, though the only occasion he'd actually been seasick, a very long time ago, was when he took a seasick pill. As advertised, it had worked.

Maddox cleared his throat. "While it gives me pleasure to see that dolt use this half-breed filth as a punch-bag, tell me, Vanda, why is this particular prisoner standing here?"

"Indulge me, Simon." She licked her lips and skimmed a warm hand over Leon's chest, brushing at the hair. "This man cost me a great deal of grief. He caused the death of two associates, one of whom was very dear to me. And, much worse, he disrupted a lucrative business."

"We know all this!" Calvo grated in a metallic monotone. "Maddox has a point. Why bring him here? His presence sours what promises to be a most pleasant meal."

She glared at Calvo. "I want this—this Leon—to know what is in store for him." She signed to Baeza.

Baeza stood up and looked at each of them in turn. "Instead of being a hunter, this man will become the hunted," he said and paused a moment to let that sink in. Leon concluded that Fabio's earlier comment wasn't original, after all. Baeza's voice was tobacco roughened. He then added, "My... my comfort-woman Daraja has joined the targets."

Vanda stroked Leon's bruised midriff. "I felt that she was ideally placed to become your partner, Leon."

"Thoughtful of you." Despite the slight pain in his gut, he sensed a sinking in his stomach that had nothing to do with her touch or the current adverse ministrations of Fabio. He guessed where this was going, but spoke anyway. "I usually work alone."

"Oh, it isn't work." She took a step back and folded her arms, which emphasized the bulge of her bosom. "You and Daraja will be chained together. The pair of you will be prey for one of our marksmen. The others in your basement cell will be paired as well. Five couples. Five hunters."

"It doesn't add up," Leon said. "You've got four couples already—you were expecting me to be one of the marksmen, so if Daraja and I are to be targets, too, then that now means you're two hunters deficient."

"That is so." She bowed to Baeza. "Francisco has agreed that Orton and I will join the hunt, gratis." She grinned. "For the sheer joy of it."

Orton said, "I'm really looking forward to the experience."

These people were adaptable, he'd give them that.

Leon glared at Vanda. "*You* are going to hunt Daraja and me?"

She shrugged. "It depends. We will draw lots for selecting our prey."

"Very democratic."

Vanda raised a hand and shouted, "No, Fabio!" before he could receive another blow to his gut. "You and Mateo have had your fun. I want him reasonably fit for his release tomorrow."

"Most considerate." Leon massaged his stomach, chain clacking. "Forgive me, but I'm still curious."

"Aren't you mindful of the cat?" she asked, amusement in her tone.

"I'm going to be killed anyway. You might as well satisfy my curiosity."

"Go on."

"Nobody has yet explained about the trophy that is brought back for the €10,000 rebate."

Maddox laughed. "You won't be claiming it, you fool. The claimant will be the marksman who puts a bullet in you —or one of the others."

"I understand that." Leon persisted, "But—the trophy?"

Vanda almost purred as she said, "Our clients must cut off a hand of their dead prey, bring it back. Whoever is first to return with the trophy will be rewarded with the rebate. A bonus, if you like."

"There are four hands for each couple," Leon persevered.

"You *are* pedantic, aren't you?" She sneered. "Remember, the couples are attached. Be assured, the targets never break free of the chain. A single hand is sufficient proof that the client has dispatched his double prey."

The second kill would not be particularly gratifying to the client, Leon decided. A sitting duck, in fact. "I've got to hand it to you, you've thought of everything."

Orton snorted. "If that was a crass attempt at a joke, mate, it fell flat."

Ignoring his comment, Leon said, "Tell me, what happens to the bodies—afterwards?"

Maddox sniggered. "We feed you to the wild boar. The body bags are dumped far enough from here so we aren't troubled by the putrid stench. The boar in this area have made quite a comeback, their numbers are growing."

"Gratifying to know one is helping in the conservation of wildlife."

Leon was aware that so-called wilding, the uncontrolled breeding of wild boar in the Marina Alta had become a big problem. They appeared in droves on golf courses, in farmers' fields and on country lanes, and were the cause of a number of road accidents. Their diet consisted of foxes, magpies, and farm crops—so they wouldn't be averse to the flesh of human corpses.

"Enough of this!" Baeza scowled and signed to Fabio. "Take him back to the basement."

Fabio said, "*Sí.*"

"I know I haven't paid for the privilege of joining the hunt," Orton asked as Leon was escorted to the door, "but am I eligible for the trophy bonus?"

"No," Baeza said, "but we won't tell the clients. Thinking you are eligible will make them especially keen, no?" He glanced at his gold fob watch. "Now, Fabio, get rid of this scum. Our clients are due for the meal any minute!"

CHAPTER 5

LESS HUMAN

AFTER THE MEAL, BAEZA AND THE OTHERS LEFT THE table and lounged in the dark leather armchairs, most of them smoking cigars and sipping fine Napoleon brandy. Their conversation had lingered briefly on the new captive who, the clients learned, was now called Leon and not Carlos. But Baeza swiftly veered away from the subject, as it didn't seem to greatly please him. He was a hard man to please, though it was evident to Calvo that Vanda had managed it.

Francisco González Baeza was forty-five but looked at least five years older, perhaps because he had neglected himself and indulged in a decadent lifestyle. Before attaining adulthood he'd been a crook, and had persisted in that nefarious career choice, eventually working in a series of casinos, learning the trade and all the angles. As he mingled with moneyed people, he soon learned it was more lucrative to trade in designer drugs. He catered for rich clients in Barcelona but kept clear of the cocaine business. Wisely, he left that to the Galician cartels that had the organizational breadth and depth to deal with the Mexicans and Colombians. It might be a profitable market, he conceded, a kilogram of coke fetching €32,000, but he preferred to retain the use of all his fingers and tongue. He was happy to diversify in other areas and managed to carve out a small empire in the personal escort and land acquisition businesses.

As the years passed, his network of useful clients increased. He diligently kept his ear to the ground, embarking on several recommended shady land deals. His portfolio swelled, too, as did his belly. When he engineered the hostile takeover of a string of casinos, he was exceedingly pleased: at last he'd promoted himself from the small time to the big time.

On his way to the top he had dealt with all manner of lowlife and on a handful of occasions he'd been crossed by illegal immigrant criminals attempting to dislodge him. He and his henchmen dealt summarily with these interlopers. But one particular incident had given him an idea, a beautiful concept.

Teaming up with the equally unscrupulous businessman Ramon Calvo, Francisco had bought forty hectares of land plus this hacienda, which he had converted.

It was a simple scheme, really. They'd cater for rich so-called hunters who hungered for the privilege of hunting human prey. And in the process it got rid of illegal immigrants. Win-win.

"Dear clients," Baeza said expansively in heavily accented English, "I hope you found the meal to your liking?"

Harley said, "The food was excellent, Mr. Baeza. The rabbit fell from the bone."

"I am gratified," Baeza said.

Orton gave a brazen laugh. "And what did you think of your hostess, Harley, eh?"

"I couldn't possibly comment on my female comforter," Harley said.

"Typical politician's response!" Orton's tone was cutting rather than humorous.

Harley glared. "You English really pretend to be well-mannered, but I have found you boorish—especially if you're from the south-east of your little England! The world is bigger than the London bubble and the Home Counties, you know!"

"I'm sorry I asked," Orton replied with a sniff.

"That will be enough, dear friend," Baeza interrupted firmly. "You should not upset our clients."

"Yeah, sorry," Orton said, grudgingly. "Got carried away, didn't I?"

Harley scowled, his eyes mere slits, and his cheeks were flushed. "Hey, no offense taken, fella." His features contradicted his mollifying words.

Baeza said, "That's better." He shifted his attention to Rudolf and Quint. "Now, what about you two—have you anything to say about our hostesses? Were they satisfactory?"

"Yes." Rudolf nodded vigorously. "She was pliable and her exertions they provided me with an appetite."

Quint sipped at his drink, then said, "Whatever rapture you enjoyed today, Rudolf, it will pale into insignificance when you couple with her after you've made your kill."

"Really?" Rudolf leaned forward expectantly.

"Sure. When you've spilled somebody's blood, you'll find your urges will heighten." He smiled lasciviously.

Vanda said, "Sadly, Rudolf, that particular woman won't be available for you on your return."

"Oh." He flushed, his eyes evading hers. "I did not—"

"Don't worry about the way you treated her. She deserved it. No, I simply meant that she's now one of the targets, that's all."

Rudolf let out a sigh of relief. "Ah, I see." He eyed Quint. "I will bear in mind what you say."

"Another comfort woman will be provided for your return," Vanda assured him.

Rudolf bobbed his head repeatedly. "Good, good."

Quint said, "I was pleasurably surprised that this time my woman didn't have on any underwear—just a one-piece that tantalizingly zipped down—"

"Talking about the lingerie, that makes me curious," Harley butted in.

"You're a lingerie fetishist, is that it?" Orton quipped.

"Not as bad as you, I reckon," Harley snapped. "I bet you drooled over your mother's Marshal Ward catalogs!"

"I don't drool."

Amusement in her tone, Vanda said, "I'm pleased to hear it, Orton. So, Harley, what makes you curious?"

Casting an icy glare at Orton, Harley said, "Are all the targets only dressed in their underwear like that Leon guy?"

Baeza said, "You saw him leaving this room, did you?"

"Yeah. Only a glimpse. In chains. Not quite the gladiator look in boxer shorts, is it?"

"Gladiator?" Baeza's faced clouded. "I do not understand the allusion."

"The targets, like slaves, fighting for their lives?" Harley explained as if to a five-year-old.

"The targets won't fight," Baeza said. "They will run."

"And they don't necessarily have to wear underwear," Vanda added. "Minimal clothing is the requirement, however."

Rudolf said, "I would strip them of all their clothes. That will make them feel less human. Like animals. That is what they are destined to be. Animals in a hunt."

"You could be right, sir," Orton said. "I've wondered, myself, about the point."

Harley said, "I doubt if you're being considerate and letting them retain adequate clothing for modesty's sake."

Calvo made a whooping laugh, and then spoke in robotic English: "Modesty—a fanciful term to use with regard to the targets, after what they have doubtless been through, I assure you. No, it is more subtle than that."

"Subtle?" Quint queried. "How is it subtle?"

Calvo wheezed, having difficulty in replying.

Baeza interjected sympathetically. "Allow me, Ramon. If the targets are stripped naked, they will feel, as Rudolf here says, less than human. At the outset, they will feel defeated already, and in that frame of mind they will not try too hard to escape. They will be shriven of any semblance of hope."

"And clothes give them hope?" Quint chortled. "I don't buy that."

"Our targets come from many cultures, many beliefs," Baeza said, "but they all think of themselves as civilized—in their own fashion, I admit. Garments that preserve their so-called modesty confer on them a belief in civilized behavior, despite what they might have undergone before getting here. What do the English say?"

"Manners make the man," supplied Maddox. "And clothes, too, of course. Savile Row and all that."

"Precisely!" Baeza clapped his hands together. "With clothes on, they will sustain hope, forlorn hope though it may be, but hope nevertheless. They will strive harder and try to evade you, the hunters."

"So," Quint said, "letting them keep a little clothing on makes for a better hunt, huh?"

"And footwear lets them run further and for longer," Calvo added mechanically.

Baeza blew through his lips a cloud of smoke. "It is a theory only."

"Well," Harley said, "at dawn tomorrow I reckon we get to put it to the test."

CHAPTER 6

EQUAL OPPORTUNITY

THE FULL MOON WAS VISIBLE THROUGH THE mosquito netting of the window in Baeza's room. Standing and gazing out, Vanda said, "Unzip me, darling." She offered her back to Francisco.

He crossed over to her and roughly pulled the zip down. The red evening dress gaped open to reveal the dimples at the base of her spine and the top of her red lace panties.

"You're not in a good mood," she said. "I can tell." Normally, in this situation his hands would have been caressing her, peeling off her clothing.

As she dropped the bodice of the dress to her hips, he swung her round to face him and gripped her bare upper arms. His deep brown eyes pierced into her. "Why do we have to bother with this charade with that Leon man?"

She slid the dress to the floor, stepped out of it.

Francisco let go of her and she pressed herself against him. "I thought you would be pleased." Her hands cupped both sides of his face.

His voice came in a croak. "It would be easier if we put a bullet in his brain!"

"We discussed that before the meal, dear. It will provide extra sport."

"Will you elect to hunt the hunter then?"

She said, "No. I think we should stick to the agreement and draw straws, don't you?"

"As you wish. I do wonder, is Orton up to the hunt?"

She giggled, twirling a pointed fingernail around his lips. "You're not sure about Orton, but you think I am quite capable?"

His big arms engulfed her, crushed her to him, and his hands clasped her rounded buttocks. "I know you are. Remember Lazaro?"

"Yes. How could I forget him? But he was a poor lover compared to you, darling."

———

Even after she'd made love to Francisco—the session had been delightfully passionate and exhausting, despite his size and girth—Vanda could not fall asleep. He on the other hand had no trouble, and snored loudly, sounding at times like an asthmatic elephant. To avoid the noise, she was tempted to forsake the bed and go to her own room. But the air conditioning wasn't on there. Here, it was quite pleasant, but for his damnable snorting.

The appearance of "Carlos Santos"—Leon—had dredged up uncomfortable memories.

Until then, she hadn't been concerned about snakes one way or the other. She was happy to handle them, especially the constrictors. But seeing Nicholas fall, to succumb to his dreadful fate, invaded her dreams too often, jerking her awake, snatching her from a nightmare, her body lathered in sweat. Now, she dreaded snakes.

She'd hated herself for abandoning Nicholas, but her fear of arrest had overridden her concern and goaded her on to run.

Her heart pounding, she had hurriedly descended the stairs, almost tumbling in her haste twice before she got to the floor, and then she'd rushed into the office. She had made for the wall safe, still carrying in her shoulder-bag the enveloped deposit "Santos" had provided.

Forcing herself to keep calm, she carefully spun the combination dial and opened the small door. Inside was another wad of money and three passports for her different aliases. She also took out the revolver, an Astra 357. If only she'd carried the weapon on her, she could have shot "Santos" and possibly saved Nicholas.

No time for regrets!

While she had no intention of indulging in a gun-battle with the Guardia Civil, the handgun might still prove useful once she'd escaped. She stuffed the passports, the money and the gun in her shoulder-bag.

Hefting the bag, she went through a side door and immediately spotted Lazaro Perez steering the Land Cruiser from the garage. It was as if he'd anticipated her move.

She loped across the intervening ground, frantically waving a hand.

Seeing her, he drove over and braked at her side. He showed his perfect white teeth. "You want a lift?"

"Yes, I do. Good timing, Lazaro."

"You can pay me, I hope?"

"Yes." She opened the door. "We'll discuss that later."

"I heard the choppers, thought it was time to get away."

"Smart move." She slid onto the passenger seat. "Now get us out of here!" She slammed the door shut and rested the shoulder-bag on her lap.

He pumped the pedal and they motored away, leaving a small ephemeral dust cloud.

She craned her neck to peer through the rear window.

There were two Guardia Civil helicopters. Descending, intent on landing between the u-shaped building. Even if they'd seen this car, they wouldn't bother with it—at least, not for now. Their concern would be for the animals and anyone else they could find on the premises. And there were plenty of helpers to round up. She didn't feel in the slightest guilty about deserting them. And the Guardia would probably spend time with Santos, getting the swine to debrief them.

Lazaro Perez said, "I guess I'll have to close up shop now?"

She studied him. His features reflected disappointment. "I regret that it will be sensible for you not to go back there. You should lie low."

"Disappear?"

She said, "For a while, yes."

"We could stay together, yes?"

He might prove useful, until she could determine her future. Then she might have to arrange for him to really disappear. "Yes, of course."

He placed a hand on her knee.

She lifted his hand and put it back on the steering wheel. "Concentrate on driving for now, Lazaro. Later, we will see."

Grinning hugely, he smoothed his mustache with one hand and accelerated.

She settled in her seat and took from the bag her three passports. After spending several minutes studying them, she decided on the Vanda Dinescu identity.

———

RIGHT NOW LEON felt his fifty-five years. He'd lived on the edge so long, it was like a drug. And danger was addictive. Drug addiction got you killed, he reminded himself, looking around the basement cell.

The condemned didn't warrant a last meal. He wouldn't have eaten a thing anyway, and he'd have advised the others to abstain too. Running for your life with a stomach full of food was not recommended.

Fabio and his men had been busy since they arrived about half an hour ago.

Leon was manacled on his left wrist and the attached chain stretched about a meter to Daraja's manacle on her right wrist. The others were similarly chained together in couples.

He'd noted while they'd all been paired up that Mateo lingered over Daraja's shackle, lifting the hand that lacked a small finger to his face, chomping his big teeth like a demented chipmunk, saliva dribbling down his square chin. Taunting. Daraja had cringed. Leon couldn't blame her.

When Mateo had finished, he had pocketed the keys of the shackles' locks. That might prove useful information. Probably not, however, since it was unlikely he'd ever see Mateo again.

The same two armed men he'd seen last evening now escorted them and Fabio as they walked into the passage.

Ceiling lights spanned the length, as usual.

As they passed a cell door on his left, Leon heard hushed voices inside: the following week's human prey.

Next to walk past was a highly disinfected bathroom area. And another room on the left proved to be where a washing machine was thundering away.

Though offering a different perspective, the route in reverse was familiar.

But this time their numbers dictated that they passed through the door labeled "stairs."

Slowly, noisily—their footsteps and clanging chains echoing in the stairwell—their motley group climbed up the stone steps that wound round the elevator shaft. Nobody spoke. Doubtless everyone was deeply immersed in thought —the captives fraught with worry, the captors filled with anticipation.

They passed a half-landing and then came to the ground floor landing, where high-placed windows admitted daylight. Here, Mateo told them to stop. Stairs climbed higher to the roof level, but they were escorted through a door on this floor and entered the broad entrance hall.

Walking through the double doors, they stepped out onto the veranda. Was it only yesterday Vanda had spotted him from her seat here?

Six vacant wicker easy chairs and matching small tables stood on their left.

Dawn streaked across the sky, lending a roseate glow to everything. Even so, it was quite bright and made Leon squint after the poor illumination in the basement.

Leon mused about a hopeful sentiment John Wayne had propounded: "Tomorrow comes to us at midnight very clean. It's perfect when it arrives, and it puts itself in our hands and hopes we've learnt something from yesterday." This new day might be clean at present, and like all new days it certainly held promise. It wasn't going to end clean, though. Not with the promise of death lingering.

And it was already getting very warm.

Nasim and Sami stood next to him and he noticed they were sweating but they wouldn't be sweltering due to the rising temperature, as they'd be used to a hot climate. There was a distinct aroma that exuded from dread. Death had its own smell, too, even more disagreeable.

He fleetingly scanned the cloudless sky. No black specks getting bigger, no helicopters. Clearly, the transmitter wasn't going to bring the cavalry. As he'd feared, Fabio had destroyed it before his position could be confirmed. He was on his own.

Well, he could live with that. Trouble was, though, he wasn't actually on his own. He was chained to Daraja, and he had no way of knowing how she'd react when they had to run for their lives. She seemed to be holding it together so far, although understandably she behaved warily in the close proximity of Mateo, who constantly ogled her.

In fact, not one of the captives had exhibited any sign of panic, not one had struggled against their fate or succumbed to incontinence brought on by fear. Perhaps their varied journeys had taught them the futility of making any protest. A brutal beating with the butt of a machine pistol would instil obedience. On the other hand he noted that Mina visibly trembled. He suspected that her chained companion Sami was seriously handicapped with her as a partner.

Maybe his fellow "targets" were not terror-stricken because they sincerely believed they could outrun a bullet.

Leon and the others were led down the veranda steps onto the hard-packed earth surface, the all too memorable open area in front of the hacienda. He saw the scuffed ground where they'd manhandled him yesterday.

They stood in pairs, silent, waiting.

Ahead, about ten meters away were five wooden posts evenly spaced in roughly a semi-circle, and nailed to each of these was an A4-sized card with a number printed on it. Definitely not an eye-test. Ranging roughly at points on a compass, from 120 degrees to 220, he estimated. Leading from each post was a narrow dirt-track wending its way down into the lush sloping escarpment blanketed in trees and bushes.

"Ah, our targets await us!" Baeza's voice. Behind them.

Leon and the others turned to the accompaniment of jangling of chains.

Baeza descended the veranda steps, smoking a cigar. He now wore desert boots, and a too-tight bush shirt that bulged over the waistband of his matching trousers. Strapped round his midriff was a gun-belt and a holstered revolver. He spoke in English while a couple of men standing by the group translated for those who didn't understand. Well organized, Leon thought. The prey must comprehend in which direction they were intended to flee.

"You will be given a head-start of thirty minutes," Baeza announced.

Leon wondered how much ground they could cover in thirty minutes, particularly if dashing headlong downhill.

"Then," Baeza went on, "the hunt will begin in earnest." He thumbed behind him. "These are the people who will be hunting you."

The five hunters strolled onto the veranda: Rudolf, Quint, Harley, Orton and Vanda. Each carried a Beretta Sniper rifle in the crook of their arm, the webbing sling dangling. Without telescopic sights. Small consolation. They also carried a machete in a sheath at their belts, no doubt required to obtain the "trophy". Only Quint wore any head-covering—a baseball cap. Nobody wore sunglasses.

Baeza chuckled. "So, dear targets, please give them a good run for their money." He rubbed his hands together and his belly wobbled. "We drew lots at breakfast." He pointed to Sami who was chain-linked to the Iraqi woman, Mina. "You're number one." He indicated the numbered post. "You run towards that and beyond." Sami's Adam's apple bobbed as he swallowed. Mina still wore her hijab, and her hooded eyes glinted with tears. "Your hunter is Rudolf."

Rudolf, again wearing his camouflage fatigues from yesterday, pointedly eyed Mina's heaving chest. She lowered her eyelids and her shoulders shuddered. Rudolf leered and licked his lips. He kept tapping a foot, seeming anxious to begin. Raring-to-go Rudolf.

Leon and Daraja were told they were number two. Judging by the position of the post, Leon reckoned they'd been elected to run due south-south-east. He needed to picture in his mind the terrain he'd viewed from the heli-copter. Their hunter was Quint.

Spitting out a ball of chewing gum, Quint said, "I'm going to enjoy this!" He grinned, showing off his perfect teeth, which shone in marked contrast to his black clothing. The dawn sunlight glinted on his spectacles.

Daraja showed concern as her steady gaze roamed over the hunters, lingering first on Rudolf and shuddering, and then she took in Vanda and Baeza. When she looked at Leon, she offered him a faint but brave smile of encouragement. He nodded confidently in response: he needed her to be strong, filled with hope.

The two Afghan men were directed to post number three and allocated to Orton, who wore pale gray and white camouflage clothes, more appropriate to urban warfare than a forest. He fondled his rifle absently, almost endearingly, smiling to himself. When his scrutiny alighted on Harley, his mouth twisted in a superior sneer.

Harley was in a bush jacket, white T-shirt and chinos. He grinned broadly when he was presented with the Moroccan man and wife, designated number four. Harley said, "It's touching, I reckon. You get to die together, maybe in each other's arms, eh?"

The blood had drained from the faces of both Jamal and Meriem. Leon suspected that the pair were so frightened they'd become easy prey to the loathsome small-town politician.

Vanda wore totally inappropriate designer clothing for a hunt: tight-fitting blue denim jeans, a tailored white cotton shirt and sneakers. At least she'd dispensed with ostentatious earrings and settled for gold studs. Her thin lips peeled back in a wide grin when Baeza announced that she was earmarked to hunt couple number five, the Iraqi man Nasim and the Romanian woman, Anamaria.

Vanda pointed to Nasim. "Hey, Mathematician, the odds against you surviving have grown since you're linked up with her!"

Leon wondered about the mooted previous relationship as he waylaid a look of daggers that passed between Vanda and Anamaria. The hate appeared intense and mutual.

Leon caught Vanda's eye. "Hey, I guess you were unlucky in drawing lots, eh? You didn't get me, after all."

She said, "I've seen all our clients' testimonials—even yours, which is bound to be a fake!—and I don't mind in the least. Quint is one of the best in this group, and he's claimed a couple of targets before. I'll look forward to seeing him bring in your hand as a trophy!"

"The best, is he?" Leon answered. "What's to stop all of them from producing fake histories?"

Vanda scowled. "They can lie if they want. It matters not. As long as they have paid!" She giggled. "It amuses me that you too have paid—to become prey!"

"*Touché.*" The irony was not lost on him, either.

She lowered herself into a wicker chair with her weapon resting across her thighs. Three of the hunters stowed their rifles against the veranda wall and sat in the other chairs for their half-hour wait. The exception was Rudolf, who paced the boards of the veranda, chain-smoking his cigarettes.

Baeza addressed Leon and the rest of the so-called targets: "I will signal the end of your thirty minutes with a single shot." He tapped his holster. "That will tell you that our hunters will begin tracking you down." He beamed sincerely. "And when they find you—which they will—they will not hesitate to eliminate you. All of you. Without exemption. This is an equal opportunity hunt!"

He unholstered his revolver—it looked like a Smith & Wesson Model 500—and gestured with the barrel at the numbered posts.

"Get ready!" he bellowed.

He consulted his fob watch and then fired the gun in the air. "*Go!* Run for your miserable lives!"

CHAPTER 7

BAD MEMORIES

WITH THE ECHO OF THAT SINGLE SHOT STILL ringing in his ears, Leon ran with Daraja by his side, their feet kicking dirt in their spurt for post number two. His peripheral vision glimpsed the others heading for their numbered posts as well.

He said, "If you need to stop for any reason, let me know first." He didn't want his arm half-yanked out of its socket by a sudden dead weight if Daraja collapsed.

"I have no intention of stopping. I *can* run. I've been aching to run away for many years."

"Though not chained to a stranger."

"We must take our chances when they are presented."

Still, as they passed the numbered post, she acknowledged it was awkward keeping pace with them shackled together by their wrists.

He agreed. "Let's slow down a bit until we can adopt a workable rhythm."

"It is not easy. Your stride is longer than mine."

"Let's work at it."

Eventually, after perhaps five minutes of jogging, they both adopted a loping pace of equidistance. Left right left right left... And the tugging on the chain eased. Most of the time the chain's length draped loosely between them but didn't get in the way of their legs.

Already, he was lathered in sweat and he could see that her body glistened, too. And yet the sun was barely above the horizon. It was going to be a scorching hot day. But would it be a long day? Or short—and final?

His bruised body protested at the sudden exertion, but he ignored it. In the past he'd been through much worse.

The slope was slightly steeper now, he found, and his knees jarred painfully at each step. And their downhill pace could easily prove treacherous. "Steady!" he called as she jogged out of sequence, seeming to rush a little ahead of him. "We'll build up so much momentum we won't be able to stop!"

She slowed a little. "I said it's not easy!" she said, gasping. "Anyway, what's with all this talk of stopping? I told you already, I do *not* intend to stop!"

"Obstructions!" he barked and leapt a two-foot high boulder, which she skirted, yanking at his arm as she did so. "We might need to stop for obstructions." Spelling it out.

"Point taken," she said, panting.

And then finally they reached relatively level ground and rushed into undergrowth comprising a variety of bushes and tall plants. Leaves brushed against his legs. The ground here was uneven, untrodden, and potentially treacherous.

Daraja shouted a warning and slowed and he adjusted his pace.

An agave loomed in front of them, vicious sharp leaves pointing in all directions.

"Easy, easy!" he urged. "They could give you a nasty septic cut or put out an eye!"

"Noted," she offered, breathless.

As they moved, they disturbed a bird from the undergrowth. Uttering an agitated *poo-poo-poo* it darted into the trees, a flash of brown and orange with broad bands of black and white, with a fan-like crest fancifully reminding him of prehistoric flying reptiles: a hoopoe.

Shortly, he said, "Slow a little, let's get our second wind." His muscles were taut: he didn't want to succumb to cramp. His bruised abdominal muscles ached insistently.

Ignore the pain.

Trotting beside her, he glanced around and over his shoulder.

He couldn't see any of the others, but he could hear undergrowth being brushed aside to their immediate left. That would be Sami, the Syrian and Mina, the Iraqi woman. Neither probably used to racing through this kind of terrain.

SAMI AND MINA RAN AWKWARDLY, in desperation, barging through the verdant undergrowth, not co-ordinating their movements so they found themselves tugging each other at the end of the chain and on occasion almost colliding into each other. Mina's mouth kept sucking at the cloth of her hijab as she gasped for air. Her entire head felt on fire, and her neck and all her back was soaked due to her unaccustomed exertion. Before long, her temple began throbbing and her vision was becoming cloudy.

In the toing-and-froing, as Mina struggled to maintain her pace with Sami, she managed for a second or two to look behind her and realized that they were now out of sight of the dread hacienda. "Please stop for a little," she said in Arabic, their common tongue.

"Stop? Why stop?" He peered across at her, his wide forehead creasing. Sweat dribbled over the ridges and down his face.

"I need to get rid of this." With her free hand she tugged at her hijab. "I can hardly breathe!"

He inhaled a long breath. "All right, but be quick about it!"

They stopped running, but not at the same moment, and stumbled. At any other time, perhaps they might have laughed at their ungainly antics, but this was no laughing matter.

Breathing heavily, Mina said, "I am grateful." Standing still now, her legs trembled.

The irony was that throughout her long trek through Turkey, when she was one of many smuggled on a lorry from Istanbul, and traded between gangs, her captors always allowed her to retain the hijab.

Hurriedly, with her free hand, she tugged off the hijab and flung it to the ground.

At once the sun's rays beat upon her face, her neck, and almost instantly dried the sweat.

"Better?" he asked irritably.

"Yes." True, she was invigorated. Her face was warm, flushed—perhaps from the running, but also from the sunlight percolating through the trees' canopy.

Pulling at the chain to get her attention, Sami said, "Why'd they put you with me instead of with Nasim—he's Iraqi, like you."

Mina raised her hand to her chest and exclaimed, "Huh? Do you think I had a choice in the matter? Why ask me? Idiot!"

"Hey, that's no way to talk to me!"

"Oh, because you're a superior male, is that it?"

"I thought you were the quiet one!"

"The quiet one was me behind the hijab." Tears formed and she blinked them away, shook her head. "We can't argue like this. We must try to be civil."

He bit his lip. "You are right. We should hide, and then when it is clear we can get away!"

His words promised a future. She sobbed, her heart full. "You are very optimistic, Sami."

"We still live. While we live, we have hope, no?"

"All right, Sami, if you say so."

"So. We must run. Now!"

"Yes!"

They ran again, brushing aside the branches of bushes.

Her long white cotton shirt flapped against the top of her knees. A number of times she flinched as her ornate soft-soled shoes pressed on hard sharp stones that protruded from the hard-baked earth.

Despite her abandonment of the hijab, it would be very hard for her to behave civilly to Sami. He smelled like so many men who had forced themselves upon her after she'd been sold as a sex slave. Those who used her had mocked her, letting her keep her hijab while they stripped her of all her other clothing and did unspeakable things, taking great pleasure in defiling her.

Unable to empty her mind of the torrent of bad memories, she bit her lip in anguish, which was a foolish thing to do as she jolted over uneven ground and blood dripped from her lips.

Yet this pain was nothing.

Some recent pains quarried deep into the soul and ate away at it, day by day, no matter how much she prayed to the Prophet.

"Let not hatred of a people incite you not to act equitably; act equitably."

No, the words were false. She hated all men!

"We will survive, Mina, I promise!" Sami huffed and puffed as they ran. "Now that we are chained together, my sole purpose in life is to save *you*!"

He lies. He needs me to keep running so he can save his own miserable life.

She hated all men!

She pushed through the foliage with Sami, and cast a blurry-eyed sidelong glance at him.

His thin torso was covered in sweat. He made promises he could not keep. And he looked terrified.

He wasn't superior, no, not at all.

He was just like her. Frightened of dying.

Yet by his words he deemed himself protective towards her.

She hated all men and yet she was chained to a man who

might be able to save her.

———

THE AFGHAN PAIR, Tabish and Yesal, ran close together, closer than the chain link required. For many months they'd been inseparable. None of their varied captors had bothered to split them up, and their closeness helped them cope, and they worked well as a team. Among the group Yesal had originally fled with had been Tabish and he befriended him, concealing his true motivation, pretending he was fleeing from the Taliban, like all the others.

They knew a smattering of English and Dari, but spoke in Farsi.

"Keep running!" Yesal shouted, his sandaled feet pounding on the hard ground.

As they rushed into the undergrowth, he could see that Tabish's linen shirt and red-and-white undershorts were dark-stained with sweat. His own were clammy and probably were the same in appearance also.

In a matter of minutes, he was exhausted. How much ground could they cover in thirty minutes? Not a lot, not enough. May Allah preserve us!

"We should have stayed in our own country." Tabish gasped, his voice quite harsh. His throat ached for a cigarette. His breath gushed between uneven yellow teeth. "If we hadn't climbed into the back of that lorry!"

Here we go again! Tugging on the chain, Yesal snapped, "Stop moaning what might have been!" Sometimes his friend made him *so* angry! "Think of what we've accomplished, the distance we've covered. So many places we've gone through before we were caught!"

Afghanistan, Iran, Turkey. Asiatic Turkey, the gateway to Europe for them. Once in the Schengen zone of the European Union there were no border checks. Traffickers transported them hidden amongst produce. Until they were robbed and then betrayed, becoming field slaves, their aching backs and muscles powering the EU agricultural dream.

Sold on, repeatedly. Through countless privations, they had stuck together and become ever closer. Very close. Their relationship suited Yesal. *Against all odds, we're in Europe*, he thought. *Soon, if I can get free, I can do honor to the Imam and commit myself to the struggle.*

"So, you speak a little English, but that does not help," Tabish persisted. "These Europeans are always suspicious of us, all of them. Their culture is not ours!"

"We were invited by the Merkel woman. Invitation means friendship. Not so?"

"Yes, but we have not met with friendship. Only this."

Yesal jerked to a halt and clutched Tabish as he jolted on the chain, caught by surprise. He hugged Tabish. "My friend, we must be strong, and if we are, we can overcome anything!"

Can't have Tabish giving up now, not while we're chained together.

"Oh, Yesal, I'm so tired of all this traveling, running!"

"We still have the promise of a new life—if we can escape the accursed British hunter called Orton." Yesal gritted his teeth. He secretly harbored hate for all westerners who he believed had brought only death and destruction to his benighted country. The old men in his village said it had never been the same since the Soviets invaded.

As he held Tabish to his chest, he thought on those months ago when he'd been recruited by a member of an offshoot of Al Qaeda. He'd been instructed to join a group of Afghans fleeing the country for the west. "Lie low and be patient," he was instructed. "We will call upon you when we need you to strike at the heart of the infidel."

When he settled here in Europe, away from these terrible gangsters, he would become a "sleeper." Right now his legs ached with this unfamiliar activity. He would dearly love to sleep. He noticed Tabish's eyelids lower. He disengaged and tugged harshly on the chain. "Come on, friend! We must run. We're not beaten yet!"

"Run." Tabish grunted, his legs moving in time with Yesal's. "Yes, run!"

"We can sleep when we are free!"

———

MERIEM WOULD WELCOME SLEEP, a long undisturbed sleep. Ah, to sleep forever! She didn't want to run any more. But Jamal kept urging her on, pulling on the chain if she dawdled in the slightest. Yet she loved him still, despite the mess he'd created for them.

Families! Who'd have them?

His brother Hakim had been involved in hashish production in the Rif region, which was frowned upon by the family but grudgingly accepted. Then he started working for criminal families dealing in cocaine smuggled into the country from South America.

The various cartels constantly vied for precedence in shifting the drugs into Europe, since there was a great deal of money at stake.

When Jamal found out, he was furious with Hakim. "You bring shame to our family. We could turn a blind eye to hashish." The ancient cultivation of cannabis was only just acceptable. "But this, this cocaine is different. Abhorrent!"

"I cannot spend my days selling carpets, Jamal!"

Hakim's words and attitude hurt Jamal, even though his brother's aversion to the family business was not new. Yes, the carpet emporium had been in the family for many years, but unless he and Meriem were blessed with sons soon, the end of the line would be reached.

"Cocaine is a step too far!" Jamal argued. "You must stop this and get out before your life is ruined!"

Hakim had replied that he was truly scared.

"You must go to the police, Hakim, provide evidence of the illicit trade. It is the only way you can be free of them."

Morosely, Hakim said, "I will think on it." And then he left.

Meriem slept fitfully that night.

Then, five nights after that disagreement, Hakim stumbled onto their doorstep, mortally stabbed. "They—they promised me they will cleanse the earth of all my family."

Devastated, Jamal held his brother in his arms.

Hakim died a minute or two later.

"Oh, Jamal," Meriem had wailed, "why did you interfere? You should have let Hakim ruin his own life—now thanks to you we are all threatened!"

After hours of quarreling, he conceded they had no option but to flee.

They packed portable valuables in a bag and slunk out of their home and shop, saddened that they would never see it again. Both garbed in burnooses to conceal their identity, they had left the town like thieves in the dead of night.

Ironically, they sought passage across the Mediterranean from a people smuggler who worked for the criminal family suspected of killing Hakim. Jamal swallowed his pride and kept silent.

By the shoreline, Jamal paid. "More than I liked to part with," he confided to Meriem. "But one of them recognized me. If I hadn't paid, he would have sent word to his family."

Their little boat was antiquated, constructed of wood and propelled by an ancient outboard motor. It held twelve of them—eight men, two youths and she was one of two women.

The motor lasted about two hours before the fuel was used up.

Adrift in darkness, rising on the swell of waves, the boat lurched left and right, the sea gushing over the gunwales. Whatever loose clothing they could muster was adapted as sponges by the two women and youths to soak up the overspill and wring it into the sea. The men used their hands as paddles and steered by the stars.

She'd been very scared when their boat started leaking

shortly after dawn, frustratingly just as they were in sight of land.

Frantically, they continued to fight the in-rushing sea. Yet, praise to the Prophet, they succeeded moving nearer to the shore.

Then the flimsy vessel ran aground on rocks close to the beach, and seawater spewed up through the damaged hull, soaking them all.

Panicking, everyone clambered over the side.

Meriem found herself in deep water, with no firm ground beneath her feet. She was being pulled under, the sodden weight of her burnoose too heavy to allow her to swim.

Thrashing her arms in panic, fearful of being sucked under, she cried out.

Jamal swam to her side and helped her disrobe. Beneath the voluminous garment she wore a T-shirt and jeans, which proved no hindrance to her swimming. After a few strokes, her feet touched the sloping shelf of shingle beneath the crashing waves.

Hauling herself from the wet sand, she hunched forward and coughed up seawater.

Surf surged at her feet, sweeping in and then receding.

At her side was Jamal. He, too, had divested himself of his burnoose. He leaned close, stroked her wet face. "Oh, Meriem, I am so *so* sorry!"

She shoved him off her, twisted away and was sick. The surf washed her stomach contents away.

Jamal's sorrowful voice was drowned by another, more strident sound.

Sirens blared on the road above the beach.

"Police!" somebody shouted.

Her heart hammering, she snatched hold of Jamal's hand and they splashed through the surf and across wet sand that sucked at their feet, and finally joined the others from the boat, scattering amongst the dunes.

Despite her anxiety, the feeling of the soft dry Spanish

sand sifting under her feet was wonderful. It was as if all their troubles were left behind on the other side of the strait. She didn't care that the sand clung to her wet legs and shoes.

Her throat felt raw due to the vomiting, but she was glad to be alive!

They stumbled past the dunes and patches of marram grass, legs still wobbly after the inactivity on their little boat for so many hours, kicking sand as they went.

Alarmingly, unexpected out of the darkness, a blinding torch beam shone on them.

They were accosted by two burly Guardia Civil officers, who barked in harsh incomprehensible Spanish. The officers were armed, so there was no sense in running.

Meriem's heart sank. Without permission, she and Jamal were entering a foreign country. They were illegal immigrants. It would matter not at all that they were respectable carpet merchants. She'd never broken the law—until now. They could expect little aid, she had heard. There'd been talk of those caught being placed in holding areas where they were "processed" followed by a swift return to Morocco—where all that awaited her and Jamal would be deadly reprisal. She feared their neighbors would ensure that came to pass.

The Guardia Civil officers handcuffed Jamal and her and then forced them to climb into the trunk of the officers' car. This treatment seemed most odd. She'd seen enough television news bulletins to have expected them to be conveyed in some official van with bars on its windows.

The car drove off and she fought against an oppressive fear of the pitch black confines, bounced around against Jamal.

Some time passed and then the car braked.

The trunk was opened and glaring lights almost blinded her.

Beside her, Jamal blinked, bewildered.

The officers manhandled them and pushed them onto

the floor of an empty warehouse. Their mumbled voices echoed.

She and Jamal lay on the cold concrete floor for quite a while, wet, shivering, fearful, while the officers sat smoking in their car.

After what seemed a long time the officers got out and were met by a civilian, a confederate of some kind. She saw money change hands.

And then the warehouse doors were opened and a lorry reversed inside, its exhaust fumes making her choke and cough.

She and Jamal were hastily bundled into the back of this lorry. At least it was slightly more comfortable than the Guardia car's trunk.

Since then, they had both worked—slaved—in fields and illicit factories and, finally, brothels.

As their recent past impinged painfully on her memory, she moaned, her limbs aching.

"What is it now?" Jamal demanded as they ran.

"I've had enough, Jamal. I don't want to live anymore."

"You must—for me, for us!"

"Us? You didn't think of *us* when you brought misfortune crashing down on our heads!"

"Forget the past!" he growled. "This is our chance to get away."

She rattled the chain. "Are you stupid?"

"If we can elude the hunter..."

"Oh, Jamal, your optimism is *so* misplaced!"

———

WHEN NASIM and Anamaria were first chained together, he had attempted to speak to her in Arabic and then French, but she shunned him completely.

His heart sank very low, for he believed that only through teamwork could they hope to evade their hunter. And teamwork necessitated speaking!

She was being selfish, brooding, folding her arms across her chest, and actually shortening the length of chain between them.

He wanted to be sympathetic towards her, but she wasn't helping herself.

Standing anxiously awaiting the gunshot to send them running, he'd found he was studying her. She was attractive, dressed only in a plain white bra and briefs. Her short-cropped auburn hair complemented her big wide brown eyes. So unlike his wife who had much more flesh on her, he had realized guiltily.

Now, as they ran into the undergrowth, he shouted at her in French: "They should have put you with the Iraqi woman!"

Without altering her stride beside him, she replied in that language, her voice surprisingly deep, "Why? I'm Romanian, for God's sake!"

At least she was speaking. Or arguing.

He said, "You will slow me down!"

"God give me strength! I can run as fast as you! We seem about the same age and height."

"You call upon your God a great deal."

"Aren't you religious?"

"No. Allah has forsaken me. If I am to live, it will be for my wife and two-year-old girl."

"So, you remember them, do you?"

"What does that mean?"

She laughed in a jeering way. "I saw you looking at me."

"I can look and admire without tainting my heart."

"If you say so."

"I will be charitable to you, in spite of your tone. I am grateful and glad you are speaking now."

"Our voices may be the last ones we hear."

"Not if I can help it. I don't want to die here!"

"I don't want to die, either!"

He said, "Then we must pull together and try to outwit the Vanda woman."

Anamaria frowned. "How can we hope to best a woman with a rifle?"

"By cunning," he answered. "Trap her!"

"If only we could!" she said with surprisingly intense feeling.

CHAPTER 8

RUN AWAY

THE SINGLE SHOT RANG OUT, SIGNALING THAT THE hunters were now on the move. Fleetingly, Leon's heart went like a trip-hammer. A natural response: fright and flight when danger presented itself. Rationalizing his capabilities, he calmed almost at once. He had no doubt he could evade any of the hunters.

But chained to Daraja, that wasn't going to be possible.

A different strategy was required.

"Oh, God," Daraja moaned. "They're coming!" She made to run, but Leon tugged at the chain, stopped her in her tracks. "Ouch!" she yelped.

"No, wait," he snapped. He held up a hand. "Listen!"

"Listen to what? Didn't *you* listen? Didn't you hear it—the signal?" She pulled on the chain, her lips quivering, and the rims of her eyes moist.

He moved close to her and gently rested a hand on her shoulder. "Tread carefully, this way," he whispered and then led Daraja forward a short distance but was careful to make blatant marks along the track.

"What are you doing?" she demanded.

"Trust me."

WITH HIS RIFLE slung over his shoulder, Rudolf loped along on the trail of the pair which he recalled were named Sami and Mina. And as trails went it was blatant.

So easy to follow.

Getting down on one knee, he noted that the underside of several green leaves of bushes showed lighter in shade than the top of the leaf. It had been pushed aside.

He straightened and hurried on, because he wanted to be in at the first kill.

And if he got this done fast enough, he might reward himself in the killing zone.

He liked the look of Mina. She seemed fragile, even fearful. That wasn't surprising, was it? She had every right to be scared.

He'd always enjoyed it when the women he dealt with were frightened. Especially when there was a threat of a mortgage foreclosure, or a debt was liable to be called in. That hateful #MeToo nonsense put paid to that, though. Started by stupid little starlets who dressed brazenly, asking for it, to further their career, and then crying foul! *Don't go there*, he thought. It is too upsetting. He supposed that when he retired, he'd miss the bank, the power he wielded. People didn't realize how much power bankers possessed. The global crash proved that, right?

Yes, once he'd abandoned the daily grind, he could afford to come on one or two more of these hunts. He felt sure that it would even surpass the powerful fix he enjoyed from time to time in his little office when customers faced ruination and he offered them a way out, with bondage strings attached. He could still indulge himself with the sex and violence, if he was careful.

He stopped and listened, pressing his rifle against his side. No need for it just yet.

Yes!

His heart-beat increased in anticipation.

His prey was not far ahead. He could hear them barging through the undergrowth.

Easy prey.

Fumbling in his camouflage jacket pocket, he pulled free a pack of Entre 23. He tipped a cigarette from the packet, put it in his mouth and, flicking his lighter, lit it. He sucked the soothing smoke into his lungs.

No time to lose!

Puffing on his cigarette, he began to jog, increasing his pace, holding the rifle steady with the flat of his hand.

This was too easy!

And then he halted, his attention drawn by a clump of gray material. He recognized it at once. He'd seen many like this flooding his hometown since Mutti Merkel opened the floodgates. This was the headscarf thing Mina had worn. In her hurried flight she'd discarded it. He picked it up, sniffed at the fabric and breathed in her muskiness and savored the exciting scent of fear.

He wondered what she would look like without this headscarf.

Soon, he would find out—and more.

Getting close.

So close!

———

QUINT SET off at a gentle pace. He was in no hurry. He wasn't interested in a rebate. He was here because he relished the tracking—and in particular the kill.

Scouring the ground, he noted the two sets of footprints. The shoes without heel impressions and the woman's slightly smaller foot size.

At present, the trail was simple enough to follow, as he'd expected. Like the last couple he'd hunted, this pair would run and run, in the hope of outdistancing him. No chance!

When the pair had run over clumps of grass, the blades had been trodden down, pointing in the direction of travel, which was no surprise, either: south-south-east.

He walked alongside the tracks but not on top of them.

Training. Never obliterate the track you're following.

All the while he kept alert for displaced rock chippings broken off by the female quarry. He was impressed to note that the man called Leon avoided such giveaways. But evidently he couldn't control every step of his companion.

That's what made these hunts fun, the pair desperate to live yet liable to put at risk their chained partner.

He stopped and noted a broken cobweb across the path through the bushes, severed at head height, the smallest trace of dew still dripping from it.

Before long he grew disappointed. He had really believed that the Leon guy, hunter-turned-prey, was going to be a challenge, and yet their track was easy to monitor.

———

RUNNING BESIDE NASIM, Anamaria let her thoughts turn yet again to her cousin Doina. She found it difficult to think of her as Vanda. Indeed, since she'd been put in the basement cell, she'd dwelled on little else.

Although it was two years ago, it felt longer since she'd been a waitress in a Bucharest restaurant. The name of the place escaped her. Doina was four years her senior, a qualified zoologist and a successful businesswoman. As Doina had spare rooms in her apartment, she let Anamaria stay rent-free. Doina lived with her boyfriend Basil, but the couple kept to themselves and Anamaria was content to stay in her room and read most of the time. In truth, she'd been shy and didn't socialize.

Basil was eight years older than Anamaria and experienced in the ways of the world. His manner was confident and his Latin looks set her heart on fire whenever they bumped into each other on their way to and from the shared bathroom. He was broody, a man of few words.

And then, while Doina was away for a day and a night at a conference, Basil had seduced Anamaria. She'd been a virgin and enjoyed the earth-shattering encounter so much, not giving a thought to the fact that she and he were betraying her cousin.

After that time, she couldn't get enough of him. Whenever Doina was out, they would make love. Until, inevitably, Doina returned unexpectedly from one absence and discovered them both in bed. She went berserk. Anamaria had never known her cousin to exhibit such a violent temper.

Clutching a bedsheet to cover his nakedness, Basil appeared helpless and fearful. He attempted to explain that he was the innocent party, that Anamaria had seduced him.

His lie shocked Anamaria so much she trembled and wanted to be sick.

Doina slapped his face. "Get out, get out—both of you!"

Tearfully, her heart breaking, Anamaria snatched her clothes, went to her room and, racked with sobs, hastily packed her bag.

Thrown onto the street, she stood, lost, wondering where she could go to. Instead of reading in her bedroom she should have gone out, made friends—friends who could have taken her in.

Moments later, Basil joined her at the curbside carrying a battered old suitcase.

Her nostrils flared and she viewed him coldly, flint in her heart.

He averted his gaze and shifted his feet on the spot. "I'm sorry I lied. It's complicated. I should have told her I love you, not her."

Her heart made an unexpected flip. "You really love me?"

"Yes, of course." He pointed to his suitcase. "That's why I left her."

"Left her?" she scoffed. "She threw you out!"

"No, she regretted her anger. Wanted me to stay. I told her I belonged with you."

He hadn't made up with Doina. "You really left her?"

"I said so, didn't I?"

Impulsively, she hugged him. He'd chosen her over Doina! Minutes earlier her heart had been cold, yet now it overflowed warmly with love for him. "What do we do now? Where do we go?"

He said, "We must stick together. How much money have you got?"

She patted her handbag. "Quite a lot of savings."

"Good." He fished in his pocket, showed her a worn wallet. "And I've enough for us to get by."

"But where do we go?" she repeated.

"We'll leave this country. Only bad memories are here now. We work when we can. You can do waitressing. They always want waitresses, don't they?"

"What will you do?"

"I can put my hand to anything. Just you watch me!"

She watched, all right. He was a great fixer—obtaining fake documentation from a friend, getting her waitress work with ease. All he could turn his hand to was bar jobs, however, which didn't pay well.

Taking advantage of open borders they traveled as man and wife to Hungary, then Croatia where they paid for transport across the Adriatic to Venice, Italy. The city of bridges was like a dream, romantic in so many respects, but it soon transformed into a nightmare for her. Basil worked in a number of bars, but usually got thrown out because he drank the owner's profits. He kept asking her to forgive him, it wouldn't happen again, but it did, often.

Then one day he strolled in, sober, smartly dressed, and announced, "We both have jobs on a cruise ship, my dear!" He promised that he'd changed.

It sounded exciting, a new adventure. And he was sober.

He kept his promise—at least for a while. By the time the ship docked in Valencia, Spain, Basil was dismissed for repeated drunken behavior. As his putative spouse, she had no option but to disembark with him.

They found a cramped apartment in a back street. Here, their deteriorating relationship turned ugly and became abusive. And since she was one of thousands in Spain suffering this kind of fate, she couldn't get much help.

She realized that if she didn't make a break, she would be lost forever. So, one evening, while Basil drank himself into a stupor, she made good her escape, taking all her papers with her. She'd planned ahead, checking advertisements in the newsagent, scanning discarded newspapers. The day before, she'd obtained legitimate employment as an au pair.

She was free of Basil, at last. It had taken her far too long.

Should have made the break ages ago!

Her employer was a smart, decent businesswoman with a ten-year-old daughter.

Yet Anamaria's luck hadn't changed, for her employer's husband had ideas beyond her work remit. One night in the early hours he sneaked into her room, clamped a hand over her mouth and forced himself on her. He threatened to kill her if she told his wife. "It will be our little secret, eh?"

The next night, frantic to get far away from the monster, she squeezed through the bathroom window. She was lost and alone in the city and foolishly in her haste she'd left without any of her papers.

Within an hour or so, while roaming the city and feeling sorry for herself, she was accosted by a man in a car. She told him she was not interested. Seconds later, two men snatched her, bundled her into the vehicle. Abducted, she was sold on.

Finally, many months later, when she arrived at the hacienda in the enforced role as a comfort woman, Anamaria was recognized in a line-up instigated by Doina who now called herself Vanda.

Anamaria would always remember that look of astonishment on her cousin's face.

Vanda had taken her to one side while Mateo watched with amusement.

"Why have you left Basil?" Vanda whispered. "Wasn't he kinky enough for you?" She gestured at the other women in the line-up.

"You had a lucky escape, cousin," Anamaria replied softly. "He beat me terribly. And he was a drunk."

"I do not believe you! He was always loving to me—until

you seduced him. You speak fabrications because of guilt."

"No, no, what I say is true."

"The truth is, my dear cousin, you are wasted here with these comfort women." Vanda's lips twitched with amusement. "Stay with these women for a while, but soon I will have a special place for you." She patted Anamaria's arm. "As an additional chore, you can be a waitress to our clients. You're good at that, I know. But only until I can arrange for you to run away, which is what you seem to do best, no?"

Run away. So, this is what she meant!

She was jerked back to the present, Nasim tugging on the chain. "Watch out, you nearly ran into that tree!" His face was drawn, his eyes red-rimmed, as if he'd been weeping. Dear Lord, compared to her fate, what had he to cry about, eh?

———

ORTON HAD no complaints about how his life had turned out. True, he'd spent most of his adult life as an accountant and administration manager, but he'd always hankered after a more interesting line of work. To obtain that frisson of excitement he'd dabbled in minor fraud over the years. The ill-gotten proceeds had financed a couple of cruises in the Med. His stopovers in Cartagena, Valencia, and Barcelona had strongly influenced him. He found he was attracted to the lifestyle and climate of mainland Spain.

So when he spotted an advertisement in the *Guardian* placed by Mr. Calvo for an administrator of a new business venture, he didn't hesitate and sent off his application.

Mr. Baeza spent two hours interviewing him in a four-star hotel suite in Madrid. In a roundabout way Baeza alluded to the dubious source of the finance and the debatable morality of the project.

Orton didn't balk for an instant. "I'm your man, Mr., er, Señor Baeza."

"I like the way you present yourself, Señor. I think we

can do business together. I can assure you, Señor Orton, you will enjoy your time in my employment."

Orton didn't mind the isolation of the place. He liked to read, mainly erotic novels and thrillers, and the helicopter pilot regularly brought in boxes of paperbacks. It would have been unnecessary if he was allowed a Kindle, but all smartphones and similar devices were banned as far as the hacienda's employees and clients were concerned.

Other compensations included his pick of the comfort women. Before long, he had his favorites, three of them—though never all at the same time!

Yes, he remembered Daraja very well. He'd had her only yesterday. He thought using Daraja as a "target" was an utter waste. But he wasn't about to cross Señor Baeza.

When there weren't any clients at the hacienda, he got the pilot to take him further afield to practice with a rifle, killing the occasional wild boar. The chef delighted in cooking various recipes with the free-range meat he'd bag. Lean, quite dark, the steaks he cooked were rich in flavor and taste, as intense as venison.

And now at last he was on his first manhunt.

Hunting people—unbelievable!

This had to be better than totting up figures on a computer screen any day.

And to think the clients paid thousands for this privilege!

Orton liked the irony. It was all thanks to that interfering Leon geezer.

The only sour note had been that American, Harley, who'd taken a distinct dislike to me, he thought. The small town politician must be a crook if he can afford this hunt. Orton sniggered. It takes one to know one, he allowed.

———

As HE FOLLOWED the trail of broken branches and down-trodden leaves, Harley wondered if he could hang today's trophy on his wall back home. Sure, it was okay to display a lion's head in his office, but maybe not a human hand. Way too gruesome. Of course he could install it in the basement. He giggled. Alongside the head of his wife? No, that would be too gross! Unlikely to garner many votes, either.

The imminent divorce reminded him. He was tracking a married couple.

He recalled watching them, before the starter's gun went off.

They'd looked scared stiff, their faces pale. The woman— Meriem, wasn't it? She'd given the impression she was going to faint on the spot. Couldn't blame her. He had to admit he was a mite anxious as well.

Sure, he'd experienced a high when he'd killed his first animal, a giraffe. And when he shot the old lion, the feeling beat even that.

But this?

His lips were dry. He licked them.

Would he have the balls to go through with it?

Killing people, for Pete's sake! He wasn't a soldier, he was a politician.

Hell, this was an entirely different ball game.

VANDA REVELED IN THE CHASE, and adrenaline coursed through her. She could barely believe her luck. For Anamaria to arrive in that shipment of women had been a shock—and a pleasant surprise.

Anamaria had stolen Basil from her, actually under her very nose! She'd been too hasty, throwing them out. When she had cooled down, she'd realized that, and had vowed that if she ever came across either Basil or her cousin again, they would pay dearly for the betrayal.

Life since then had been a roller coaster. The collapse of her endangered species project had eventually led to Francisco and this venture. Now, life was exceedingly good. She had a lively enough sex life with Francisco, surprisingly even better than it had been with poor Nicholas, or even Lazaro, God rest their souls.

Yes, Francisco strayed from time to time, like most Latin men. She appreciated that some of those comfort women must be a temptation for him. But he always returned to her bed. He seemed to acknowledge she held the whip. She proved he was putty in her hands when she'd exploded on finding him with Daraja.

Already, she believed a certain amount of his authority had been transferred from him to her. Being able to order Mateo to drag Daraja from the German's bed and imprison her in the basement cell had proved she had the power. The hired muscle obeyed her. That fact made her spine tingle.

As for Anamaria's excuses about Basil's behavior, she didn't believe a word of her cousin's protests.

Lies, all lies!

Fleetingly, she wondered how Anamaria ended up here. It mattered not. Whatever had befallen Anamaria was of her own making. Even if Anamaria's story held a grain of truth about Basil, it was of no consequence now. Anamaria was aware of what happened at the hacienda and if released she would, probably out of spite, inform the authorities. Therefore, she had to go. And what better way?

Their situation here was already fraught with Leon Whatever-his-name having bought his way in. Since he'd carried a transmitter, it stood to reason he had been expecting police or Guardia Civil backup. Plainly, they didn't know where the hacienda was yet. How long could it be kept a secret, though?

Perhaps it was time to pack her bags and run? But would Francisco relinquish the hacienda and throw away this huge investment?

On second thought, he didn't need to: he could simply put a stop to hunting illegal immigrants.

Ah, but there was the question of all the bodies. They weren't even buried.

CHAPTER 9

MANIC ROBOT

CALVO AND BAEZA STOOD SIDE BY SIDE, LEANING on the veranda rail. The day was already hot and sweat darkened their shirts. Baeza cupped a glass of red wine and smoked a cigar. Calvo raised his speech tool to the hole in his throat. "You know," he said, "getting rid of that Leon guy will only delay matters."

Today more than usual, his business partner's tinny voice grated on Baeza's nerves. He gulped his wine. "I know." He flicked ash off the end of his cigar.

"If he was onto us, it is only a matter of time before others will soon follow him, investigate..."

"I know, Ramon, I know. In future, we *must* vet applicants on the dark web." Baeza puffed on the cigar and then blew out a gray cloud. "Thoroughly."

Calvo wheezed, and then shook his head. "We're pushing our luck. His being here was a warning."

"But I've invested thousands in this business."

"I've made a considerable contribution as well, you know. It's been a lucrative deal, my friend." Calvo clapped a hand on Baeza's shoulder and chuckled, sounding like a manic robot. "When you came to me with the idea, I grant you I wasn't too keen. *Sí*, I understood your argument. Europe is awash with illegal immigrants that nobody knows about, cares about or will ever miss." He coughed and rasped, "And you were right! We've made a killing all right!"

"In more ways than one, Ramon." Baeza downed the rest of his wine.

"It is no longer a laughing matter, Francisco."

"I *do* understand. You believe we should quit while we are able to? You fear discovery?"

Calvo panted. "I fear nothing. How could I, having come through this damnable operation?"

"But you advise we should quit, no?"

"Yes. I say we should pull the plug before we bring in any more targets."

Lily-livered coward! "Here is a compromise. Shall we quit after next week's clients have had their shoot?" There was still a queue of ten prospective clients anxious to hunt and kill human game. That amounted to a small fortune!

"It is regrettable, I know."

"All that money, Ramon." Baeza suffered a tightening in his chest.

"If we're arrested, we can't enjoy it, can't spend it."

"But we're doing the authorities a favor! We're helping cut the number of illegal immigrants. We lessen the drain they make on the social services."

"Francisco, they're bleeding hearts! They won't see it that way!"

"No, they won't." Baeza took a deep breath and then added, "Very well. One more week. I will arrange for all the other clients to be informed that we are postponing our project."

"Postponing?"

"Most certainly. We will find a new venue where we can continue. It doesn't have to be in Spain, after all. Throughout Europe there are plenty of isolated areas that may prove suitable for our venture. And of course there's no shortage in the supply of illegal immigrants."

"I like the way you're thinking, Francisco!"

"And we can improve on the model. Fit body cams to the

clients, so they can film the hunt *and* the kill. We can make and sell DVDs!"

Calvo's chuckle sounded hoarse and almost obscene. "I can see it now. The Dark Web Oscars!"

———

AFTER A WHILE, Leon and Daraja stopped.

Leon said, "*We're* going to surprise the German, raring-to-go Rudolf."

Daraja's brow wrinkled and she looked askance at him, as if perplexed. "Are you mad?"

"Yes! I'm mad, mad at them using people as prey, treating them as non-persons, calling them "targets", and killing without mercy!"

"Me also. I'm one of the targets, remember? And I have a grudge against the German. But I don't see—"

"From what I've observed of Rudolf, he's an impatient fellow, so I guess he'll outrun the others, including our hunter Quint. Rudolf will definitely want to be first and claim the trophy."

"You *guess*?"

"An educated guess, then?"

"And you—we—are going to surprise Rudolf?"

"Yes. Surprise can be the best defense."

"But he's got a gun!"

Leon offered a smile. "We have something better."

"What's that?" She lifted up her right hand and scoffed, "A chain?"

"As I said, we've got the element of surprise on our side. Though the chain might be useful."

Before she could remonstrate further, he signed for her to be silent.

With the utmost care, he scanned their immediate area and bent twigs and grass stalks in a different direction.

He directed her where to place her feet and, as they went

backwards, in their earlier tracks, he crouched, ignoring the piercing pain signals from his abdomen.

Buying time.

After a while, he directed her to the left, covering these new tracks by gently brushing them with leaves.

When possible, he told Daraja to step on stones to avoid making any imprint.

He wasn't too happy with his efforts, but restrained as he was, it was the best they could manage. It really depended on how alert Quint proved to be. At the very least, he felt confident that they'd hidden their ninety-degree turn to the east.

He knew that, after covering some distance, Quint was bound to realize that their spoor had petered out and he would have to back-track to find evidence of their new direction. Quint's back-tracking would take time. It might be enough for what Leon had planned.

Slowly, silently, crouched low, Leon and Daraja skirted round a eucalyptus tree.

Then he heard them, above the sound of nearby cicadas and birds. It had to be Sami and Mina ahead. They were moving slowly and noisily through the undergrowth. And it sounded as if they were arguing!

He signed for Daraja to stop and they squatted behind a huge ancient fig tree. At least its leaves would hide more than their modesty. They held the chain still and waited.

Soon, not too many minutes later, Rudolf blundered past them, a mere two meters away. It was definitely him, his blue-gray thatched hair and bullet head unmistakable. He didn't see them, too intent on scrutinizing the track left by the Syrian and the Iraqi woman. He left in his wake a mixed miasma of cigarette tobacco smoke and after-shave.

Leon and Daraja held their breath as the German passed.

And then Leon signed for her to go forward with him slowly and carefully. Their hands continued to cover the taut chain links to ensure they didn't clink together and make a noise as they moved.

Maintaining a short distance behind, they followed Rudolf.

Leon had said, "With great care."

Earlier he'd taught her how to sneak up on prey. Let the ball of the foot touch the ground first, then the heel. Lower the weight of the body gradually on the sole of the foot to avoid snapping any twig or kicking any stone. He was impressed. She was a quick study.

They came upon a copse of almond trees choking with mistletoe, and skirted round them.

Not far ahead a shot rang out.

A flock of birds flapped their wings and flew from the trees into the clear blue sky.

Daraja gave a start and gasped.

A woman's scream sounded.

CHAPTER 10

BRUTAL ACT

RUDOLF'S BLOOD RAN FEVERISHLY HOT. HE'D never experienced anything like this rush before. This was so much better than using his fists on women! His mouth was dry, his palms sweaty, and his heart was pumping madly. The Spaniard named Mateo was right.

Sami the Syrian lay dead on a bed of ferns, blood smearing his throat.

A perfect shot!

Well, if he was honest, it wasn't, not really. He'd been aiming for the man's chest. Still, he'd actually killed with a single bullet.

The chattering of birds in the trees had stilled immediately after the report from the rifle. No cicadas made a sound nearby, either.

In the preternatural silence, he could hear Mina the Iraqi panting heavily as she tugged ineffectually at her chain, sobbing, shaking her head in disbelief. Her face glistened with sweat. He noticed her dark hair was cut short and it was unkempt and wet. Her eyes were wide, imploring as she spotted him stepping out from the trees.

Rudolf dropped his cigarette stub to the ground and squashed it under the toe of his combat boot.

She stood, shaking, vulnerable, in her long white

cotton shirt that hung to the top of her knees. Sweat patches darkened the fabric under the armpits, under her breasts and at her belly. A broad sunbeam slanted through the tree-tops, back-lit the woman, made the material almost transparent, so he could glimpse the outline of quite shapely thighs. Her heavy hooded eyes reflected sheer terror.

It was obvious that she expected him to shoot her next.

But he had a more satisfying purpose.

Smiling at the thought, he slung his rifle over his shoulder and boldly walked towards her. She couldn't run, wasn't going anywhere.

The birds in the trees took up their chattering again. Nature reasserting itself.

And his urges were natural, too.

His lips puckered as he withdrew the machete from its sheath. "I want you, little missy," he said in guttural German. "You can be my reward, eh?"

She cowered, shaking her head, as if uncomprehending.

Doesn't anyone here speak German? "If you do as I say," he tried in English, "I'll cut you free, let you go." He gestured with the blade at Sami. "I've got my trophy."

Again Mina shook her head. Whether she meant "no" or still didn't understand, it wasn't clear.

He didn't care if she understood or not. Actions speak louder than words in any language.

His throat dry with expectation, he extended his arm and eased the blade of the machete towards her long shirt. Pressing against the material was a dark triangle between her legs.

Fists clenched, Mina stood as if frozen, though she visibly quivered, the chain taut between her and dead Sami. She lowered her head as he used the point of the weapon to raise her garment at the hem.

Higher he lifted it, revealing knees that trembled, and then thighs that glistened with sweat.

He licked his lips.

Then, abruptly, she raised her head and her eyes widened.

TOO LATE, Rudolf must have realized that Mina wasn't staring at him or his machete, but at something behind him.

Swiftly, in a coordinated attack Leon and Daraja looped their chain around Rudolf's neck.

Leon thrust his knee into the small of the German's back.

"Pull hard!" Leon called.

And the pair of them hauled brutally.

Leon's bruised muscles protested, but he maintained full pressure.

Rudolf gasped hoarsely.

Leon heard Daraja's strained breathing, her shoulders pressed close against his. Then she growled, "This, Rudolf, is the language of pain!"

In response, Rudolf's head darted left and right, but he couldn't see her.

Leon was puzzled by her words and the German's reaction. She'd said something about a grudge, he recalled. He didn't falter in his hold.

The rifle sling dropped off Rudolf's shoulder and the weapon clattered on the ground, and then the machete followed seconds later as they continued to heave on the chain, throttling the banker.

The birds in the trees went silent again, as if cowed by the extreme violence enacted in their domain.

A gurgling sound issued from Rudolf's mouth, saliva drooled from his lips.

Frantically, Rudolf clawed at their hands and the chain pressing into his throat, but in vain. His body jerked as he struggled. Those small feet made a big noise as his combat boots kicked ineffectually at the ground, a deathly rataplan.

Rudolf's hands flopped to his side and his heels rattled

amidst the natural detritus of the forest floor, and then he was still.

Leon caught a familiar unpleasant smell of evacuated bowels. "Let him go," he whispered huskily.

Together, he and Daraja released the chain.

Leon was glad to let go. The strain on his bruised muscles had been intense.

They both took a pace backwards as Rudolf tumbled to the ground, lying on his back.

Dead.

At least this was one banker who finally paid for the global financial meltdown.

Mina stared wide-eyed, her mouth open in shock, not making a sound.

Daraja wiped her mouth with the back of her trembling free hand and looked at him. It was in her eyes: she had never taken a life before. You're never the same after doing that, he knew. An expression of shock and wonder flashed across her features. But he saw no regret, no guilt. Her chest heaved against her black lace camisole with exertion and exultant emotion. He needed to take her mind off their shared brutal act.

He said, "I want to search him."

Breathing in heavily, Daraja nodded and said croakily, "Go ahead."

Then she knelt beside him, looking away, while Leon rifled the dead man's pockets. He found a packet of Entre 23 cigarettes and a lighter, a bundle of Euro notes, and a wallet with credit cards. It was awkward, manhandling Rudolf, but he finally wrenched off the dead man's jacket. He offered it to Daraja. "His trousers are soiled but this will cover you a little."

"No, thanks." She shuddered. "It stinks of death. A death he deserved."

"Okay." He shrugged. The garment would protect his shoulders from the sun, at least. He shoved an arm in one sleeve, flung the other half across his shoulder and used

Rudolf's webbing belt to secure it to his torso. Clumsily, he one-handedly put the lighter, the wallet and euro notes in a side-pocket.

Only then did he look up at Mina. She hadn't moved but stood as if petrified. Staring at Sami's corpse and then at Rudolf.

Leon grabbed the fallen machete. "Let's get up," he told Daraja.

Surprisingly coordinated, they both stood, the linked chain rattling.

Leon leading, they walked over to the dead Syrian.

"Look away," he told Mina in Arabic.

Mina didn't move.

Daraja must have understood his intention, even if she didn't comprehend the language. Solicitously, she moved the short distance to Mina and embraced the shocked woman, shielded her face.

The chain stretched from Mina's wrist to Sami's.

With his shackled left hand, Leon held Sami's arm steady and then swung the blade down, severing Sami's hand at the wrist with one forceful gruesome loud slice. There was little blood, since the heart had already stopped pumping. The shackle fell away from the gory stump.

Leon dropped the arm and stooped, wiped the blade on Sami's undershorts. Straightening up, he sheathed the blade.

He gently disengaged the two women. "You're free now, Mina," he said.

Mina gaped at him. Her features were colorless. The chain and bloody shackle dangling from her wrist clinked, settling at her side, staining her bare leg. She squirmed at the contact, but didn't move otherwise.

"With me, Daraja," he said.

Casting a look of concern at Mina, Daraja went with him to Rudolf's corpse. Leon leaned down and picked up the rifle. With a little difficulty, he checked the small magazine in front of the trigger unit. Four rounds left.

Daraja said, "You're familiar with death and weapons, aren't you?"

"Yes. That familiarity has kept me alive."

"I hope it will work for me, too."

"That's my hope as well. We've got to keep moving. Our hunter Quint won't have been fooled for long by our distraction efforts. I reckon he'll be near."

Anxiety etched her face.

"You've a right to be worried." He pointed the rifle at the dead German. "Quint won't be as impetuous as the late raring-to-go Rudolf."

She waved her free hand at Mina. "What about her?"

He slung the rifle on his shoulder. "We'll take her with us. I'm sure Quint wouldn't hesitate in shooting her. We're her only chance of survival."

Daraja said, "I hoped you'd say that."

They went to Mina's side.

"Come on, my dear." Daraja put her free arm round Mina's shoulder. "We've got to leave this terrible place."

With trusting faith, Mina went with Daraja, holding hands, the chain on the Iraqi woman's wrist chinking, dribbles of red spotting the ground. Leon kept pace on Daraja's right.

Birds again chirruped in the trees and the clamor of cicadas resumed.

Both women hesitantly looked over their shoulders at Sami's corpse.

"We can't help him now," Leon said. "Keep moving!" Inwardly, he fumed. With Mina along there was next to no chance he could conceal all their tracks. From now on, they must rely on speed rather than subterfuge.

At least now he was armed—and dangerous.

———

QUINT KNELT BY A BROKEN TWIG, raised it to his nose and sniffed. The smell of sap could persist for three or four hours. So this was freshly broken. Which was most odd.

He took his time and scrutinized the ground on either side and ahead, but there were no other signs of disturbed vegetation or soil.

What the hell—why not?

At this point, beyond the broken twig, the ground was fresh, unsullied. All traces that he'd tracked earlier were unexpectedly absent from here on.

Damn!

He removed his spectacles and wiped them with a cotton handkerchief from a breast pocket, and then he replaced them.

His prey must have gone to the left or right earlier.

He took off his baseball cap, wiped his forehead with a hand. But which way, and where? And how far back?

How'd I miss it?

So, I hadn't underestimated the guy.

Crafty Leon!

Then he heard a single shot—immediately followed by a woman's scream.

That came from his left.

Damn. Rudolf had got his first kill.

But why wasn't there a second shot?

If one of the couple was killed, the other wasn't going anywhere.

Then again, it depended how accurate Rudolf was. He might only have wounded one of the two targets.

Or maybe Rudolf had made a kill and was going to use his machete on the second target. He recalled Rudolf's attitude and remarks last night, inferring that he preferred to dehumanize his prey.

It didn't matter.

I've got my own prey to hunt.

And I'm in no hurry.

Nothing for it, Quint decided. He'd have to spend time on the lost track drill—back-tracking to the last definite sign.

Nice move, damn you, Leon!

Turning round, Quint put on his cap and slowly, methodically retraced his steps, stopping regularly to listen. At these halts he cocked his head in the direction he was listening and opened his mouth slightly, as this improved the hearing function.

But he heard nothing out of the ordinary, just the strident blare of cicadas and the constant chattering of birdlife, which his experience enabled him to blank out.

His gaze continually swept far and near, right and left, up and down, scanning not only bushes and trees—holm oak, carob and eucalyptus—but also through and beyond them, as he'd been trained.

Now he knew he'd been deceived, he could discern the clever ploys. They'd walked backwards in their tracks, but by doing that they'd shortened their pace and made a deeper impression at the toe. It wasn't that obvious in the grassy patches, but there was the infrequent tell-tale on soil. He should have spotted these clues, but he'd been carried away by the anticipation of an easy kill, so he had underestimated them.

My bad.

From time to time he crouched down, to vary his perspective. He didn't move for a good spell. Since the pair had already exhibited cunning, it was entirely possible that they lay in wait in an ambush and could catch him unawares, attacking with a hefty branch or a small log.

He detected no movement.

Safe to continue.

At last he located the small revealing signs where the pair had successfully concealed their tracks when they veered off to the east.

This new spoor was harder to follow, he noticed. Not surprising. They knew he'd double-back once he realized their fake trail petered out.

He admitted grudging admiration for them.

Still, his senses were on high alert now.

He worked his way through a dense copse of a dozen or

so mistletoe infested almond trees and then stepped into a small clearing.

And he stopped, stunned.

There were two bodies, both men. One was fully clothed and judging by the camouflage fatigues it was Rudolf, while the other was a target whose hand had been severed and then discarded.

His eyes mere slits, Quint studied the surrounding area, but detected no significant movement.

Cautiously, he strode towards the German's corpse.

Rudolf's face was set in frozen agony, eyes starting, his mouth gaping open, the unmistakable rictus of death. Deep impressions round the dead man's throat told all he needed to know.

Strangled.

The cowardly bastards had attacked from behind!

The hairs on the back of Quint's neck bristled. He swung round, wary. Rifle ready.

Still no change in the undergrowth's configuration.

Section by section, he scoured the area and finally he concluded with rising inner alarm that Rudolf's rifle and machete were missing.

The severed hand lay there, mocking, almost giving him the finger.

Quint swore. He had no means to warn the other hunters, or for that matter Baeza, Calvo, and Maddox that one of the targets was now armed.

This wasn't what they'd planned.

No way.

He knelt by a stone that jutted out of a cluster of grass. Specks of fresh blood stained its surface. As there'd only been one shot, the blood was probably from the shackle, not Sami's fatal wound.

His chest swelled and then he released a pent-up breath.

Now his prey had become three.

He grinned. The hunt had just gotten very interesting.

CHAPTER 11

BEAR WITNESS

HARLEY DIVERGED FROM THE TRAIL JAMAL AND
Meriem had left and headed east. It was easy to track Orton,
who was clearly a novice. But then again, why would Orton
conceal his trail? He was the hunter—and the two Afghans
were his prey, ahead of him, not behind. He sure wouldn't
be looking over his shoulder.

Finally, he spotted ahead the pale gray and white camouflage clothing worn by Orton. The Englishman was moving
in a crouching walk, his rifle ready, his movement exagger-
ated, as though he was acting in a Chuck Norris movie.

Slowly, Harley sneaked up behind Orton.

When he got close he smirked.

Now for a little fun.

Purposefully, Harley trod on a dried twig, and it cracked
loudly.

Orton swung round, rifle at hip height. Recognition in
his hooded hazel eyes. "What the hell are you doing here?"
He glowered, waving the rifle barrel in a sideways motion.
"Get your own kill!"

"I have."

"Eh? I didn't hear your shots." Orton let go of the barrel
and thumbed to his right. "The shot I heard came from
there. Quint or Rudolf."

"You're very observant for a novice."

"Don't be so bloody patronizing!"

"Hey, I'm being the honest broker here."

"You may be Mr. Baeza's client, but your Yank brashness cuts no ice with me! Piss off!"

Harley did not move. He was enjoying this. He sighed heavily. "Thing is, I'm here to deprive you of the trophy bonus."

"Eh, what the hell are you talking about?"

"I'd like to eliminate all the others as well." True enough. Harley smiled insincerely, sensing a rush of expectation, a flush of warmth in his cheeks, a tantalizing roiling in his groin. "The thrill of the kill multiplied."

"You're off your rocker!"

"But," Harley went on, "I've settled for reducing my competition by one, at least."

"Eh?"

"You."

"But Mr. Baeza told me I wouldn't get the bonus. Only the clients—you and the other two—are entitled! That's how it works."

"Is that so? As for being entitled, that's what I hate about you Brits. You go around as if you rule the world! Well, that sure ain't the case anymore. Entitled my fanny!"

"Hey, that's no way to talk!" Orton fingered his rifle, as if not sure what to do with it.

"I'll let my finger do the talkin'."

Harley pulled the trigger and killed Orton with a single shot to the chest.

Orton collapsed in an ungainly heap to the ground.

Blood thrummed in Harley's ears. Hell, it was a heady feeling.

My God, I did have the balls to do it. This was the first time I've killed a person. It felt so good!

It was *so good* he wanted to repeat the experience.

This killing caper could get addictive.

He wasn't interested in Orton's targets, the two Afghans.

They could go hang for all he cared. He quickly retraced his steps and soon found the track made by the Moroccan couple. What were they called? Ah, yes, he remembered now: Jamal and Meriem.

With great anticipation he stalked the pair.

If only he could lethally stalk his political opponents as easily.

———

JAMAL AND MERIEM heard the third shot and they both stopped running at the sound. He strained his ears, listening, but couldn't decide the direction of the single report. He gazed at Meriem.

Her eyes were wide, moist, troubled. She let out a heavy sigh of utter despair and embraced him, the chain clinking between them, a constant reminder of their prospective fate.

He caressed her long lank black hair, momentarily recalling happier times, when he'd done this sometimes as a precursor of lovemaking. Now, he did it merely to soothe her. During the most recent terrible months, he'd had to calm her a great deal.

Her T-shirt was soaked with sweat. She trembled in his arms. These days she always seemed to tremble.

She said, "They *will* kill us!"

"That's the general idea, yes."

"Must you always be so matter-of-fact?" she berated.

Most of the time he was at fault, too, he reflected with sadness.

She said, "After all we've suffered we're going to be shot like rabid dogs."

"I tried—tried fighting. You know I did—it seems so long ago. But my defiance came to nothing. Only more abuse, more pain." He let his hands drop to his sides, yet still she clung to him. "It is useless." Until this moment, she'd been the defeatist, the one who feared everything—mostly with good cause. Now, it was becoming all too much for him as well.

"I know, dearest," she whispered against his chest, her tone strangely firm, even strong. "We must forget what they have done to us. Blot it out." Her palms gently tapped him on the chest. "We must take this chance and flee."

"It is hard to run from a bullet." He hated being so rational, so fatalistic.

"We must try, Jamal!" He marveled at where her new resolve had sprung from. When his was crumbling, and he was becoming resigned to an awful fate, she'd transformed.

A tiny glimmer of hope burgeoned in his chest. If Meriem could overcome her despairing pessimism, then he must also. He gently raised his hands to her shoulders, pushed her at arm's-length so as to look upon her beseeching face. "Very well."

He peered ahead and to their right, away from the suspected direction of the shots they'd heard up to now.

His heart lifted, just a little, as he spotted three derelict stone structures only a short distance ahead. Since he'd been in Spain toiling in the fields he'd seen one or two, most of them daubed with colorful ignorant graffiti. Yet these ruined buildings were pristine, blemished only by age. "Meriem, look! We shall hide there—and pray!"

She rested a hand over her heart and her eyes were alight with renewed faith. "Yes!"

Within a couple of minutes they reached a two-story building without a roof and only three walls. External stone steps led to an upstairs floor that had crumbled away, incapable of offering succor. A little beyond were two more similar structures, both in poor state of repair, probably abandoned for decades. Nearby was a solitary tree. A couple of black birds flapped their wings amidst the leaves.

Much further distant was a rounded rock protruding from the earth with sparse lichen and weeds dotted on its surface. A possible place of sanctuary if they could but elude their hunter.

Jamal led Meriem across the fallen debris. "Tread with care," he said. "We don't want to twist an ankle." He gestured at the ground. "We might be able to use a stone as a weapon, if we can catch our hunter unawares." He stooped and snatched a chunk that fitted his hand. The weight of it imparted hope, even strength of purpose.

Meriem reached down on his other side. "Here's one as well." She grabbed the stone and suddenly screamed, backing into him and dropping the stone. "It bit me!"

She'd disturbed a nest of snakes. Three of them! Their angular shaped heads darted away from her and their bodies with a distinctive diamond pattern running along their backs slithered over the ground, quickly hiding amidst other rocks.

His mouth felt dry at the thought that he could easily have picked up that rock instead of Meriem. Tugging on the chain, Jamal pulled her towards him. "Where's the bite? Let me see!"

She offered her shaking free hand with the two bloody puncture marks in the heel of her palm.

Frantically, he bent over her hand and sucked at the bite, his mouth tainted with the iron taste of blood and something bitter. He turned his head from her and spat out her blood and hopefully most of the venom. "I may have caught it in time," he promised, not knowing, dreading that by this act he may have poisoned himself as well.

He feared for her and berated himself for not knowing what kind of snake it was, whether its bite was fatal or not. The sinuous bodies of the three he'd glimpsed didn't resemble the color or markings of either the puff adder or the desert horned viper, though the latter's head was similar. He blanched at recalling an incident outside his local village where a child was bitten by a puff adder. The boy was lucky, saved from death, which could occur within a day, but only by the swift amputation of his bitten leg.

He said, "We can't stay here in the open." Then, pointing to the furthest building, beyond a stretch of tall wild grass, he added, "Let's hide there!"

Together, they moved with extreme caution across the rubble-strewn ground and then more rapidly through the tall grass, all the while Meriem cradling her bitten hand to her chest and sobbing.

Like the others, this ruin was two stories.

Hastily, they climbed the external stone steps, dislodging bits of grit and chunks of stone as they went.

They paused when they reached the landing at the top of the stairs. It commanded a good view in two directions. He couldn't see anybody approaching. He dared to hope.

Ducking through the doorway, they rushed to the far wall and cowered in shadow, grateful for the cool shade.

The floor here was littered with stone shards and pieces of clay bricks. More weapons? But first, he needed to attend to Meriem.

"Here, let me try again." Tenderly, he sucked at the bite.

He spat out a gobbet of red-streaked phlegm.

Agitatedly, Meriem tapped him urgently on his shoulder. "Stop," she said hoarsely.

He lowered her hand as he heard the sound of stones clacking beyond the buildings.

Coming closer.

"This is the end." Meriem wept softly. "Let the poison do its work, my love. I have had enough."

"No, no you were right before. We must live. Must bear witness against these terrible people."

"I feel lethargic already, my love." She kissed him. "The poison—"

"Quiet," he whispered. "He's coming up the stairs."

CHAPTER 12

MEMORABLE DAY

HARLEY WAS STILL FLOATING ON A HIGH AS HE detected the easy trail to follow. His prey had passed two ruins that might have served as a hideout. Now, he saw the footprints in the dust on the first step of the stairs on the side this building.

Got them!

He peered up.

Nothing to see.

They'd be hiding. Hoping.

Fat chance, the fools!

His pulse raced as he climbed one step at a time, the rifle ready, finger on the trigger.

I have the power to give life—or to take it! He beamed, the death of Orton fresh in his thoughts.

Small town politics was nothing compared to this.

When he reached the top step, the landing, he paused, listening intently.

Hell, this was tense. Intense.

His heart hammered away. This was real living.

He licked dry lips and stepped through the doorway, poking the rifle barrel ahead of him, ready to shoot.

Abruptly, someone slammed a big stone on top of the barrel, knocking it down. It clanged and the weapon vibrated and, reflexively, his finger squeezed the trigger, fired, and the bullet hit the stone floor and ricocheted off the walls.

Every movement seemed in slow motion.

A thought flashed: *Stone against bullet. And stone won.*

In the same instant his quarry—both of them—rushed at him, palms of hands pushing his chest harshly, forcing him to stumble backwards. He overbalanced, arms flailing as he was launched off the top step into mid-air. Desperately, his left hand reached out and with clawing fingers grasped the chain slung between the pair of attackers.

He held on tight as he plummeted through the air, and pulled the couple with him.

Pain threshed through his ass and shoulder blades as he thudded to the hard unyielding ground.

Tears squeezed from the corners of his eyes. His whole body felt numb, yet he was aware that he still held onto his rifle. He sat up and excruciating pain lanced into his back.

Through a blur of rising dust and moist eyes he saw the woman kneeling in front of him, her dark eyebrows raised, big brown eyes wide, big white teeth snarling. She raised a stone above her head and then threw it at him. He tried to duck, but too late, and it bashed into his temple.

Hellcat!

It hurt.

In an instinctive defensive move, he swung the rifle round and hit her on the chin with the butt.

She screamed and toppled sideways, reedy voice wailing, "O, my Jamal, *anā āsef!*"

Scrabbling into a sitting position, Harley noticed the other one—Jamal—was writhing in agony, his leg unnaturally twisted under him, the chain stretched between them. Bloody bone protruded from a smashed shin. Through gritted teeth, Jamal called, "Meriem, Meriem!"

Seeming groggy, Meriem shifted on the ground, a hand massaging her bloody chin. "Kill me now," she murmured in English.

Jamal pleaded, "No, Meriem, you don't mean it!" He

turned to Harley and wrung his hands, the chain that linked them rattling. "Please let us go."

"Don't beg!" Meriem snapped. "None of the scum you've begged to showed us mercy! Why should *he* be any different?" Awkwardly, she sat up, defiant, bloody chin thrust out. "Shoot me, coward. A defenseless woman!"

Harley slowly, painfully regained his feet. God, he ached all over! Bastards! He leveled the rifle on the woman.

"No!" Jamal cried.

Harley switched his aim and shot Jamal in the chest. "Surprise!" *God, that was good!* "Put him out of his misery, eh?" he said.

"No!" Tears trailed down Meriem's face as she crawled to her dead husband. She rested her head on his chest and began keening over him, a haunting lamentation that sent a chill through Harley's spine.

Pathetic. Really risible!

Then she slowly raised her head, her cheek smeared with the blood of her spouse, and glared up at Harley with baleful eyes.

Startled at her penetrating, accusing glower, he stepped back a pace.

Then, surprised at how stimulated he felt at having killed yet another human being, he put the rifle aside, resting it against a big stone block, well beyond the woman's reach. He wanted this feeling to last, to savor it.

Never taking his eyes off her, he unsheathed the machete and took two paces towards her.

Pressing against her husband's body, she shrunk from Harley, forehead creased, eyes glaring.

Swiftly, he lunged and grabbed Meriem's free hand.

"No, no, no!" she shrieked.

Her hand felt cold as he tugged at it.

He didn't know if he could do this.

Bracing himself, he then swung the blade viciously, severing the hand from her forearm.

Blood spurted and the sight of it excited him even more. *Yes!*

He stepped back, out of reach, though she didn't pose a threat. She clutched her bloody stump, her whole body shuddering. In shock.

"And you get your wish as well," he said, "but it will be a slow death." He dropped the hand onto the dusty earth. Moving further away, he wiped the blade on Jamal's undershorts and then sheathed it.

Inexplicably, his emotions were mixed as he watched Meriem's life blood seep, darkening her blue T-shirt.

She stared, disbelieving, her lips trembling.

He'd literally fought for his life. As had, bravely, she and her husband.

Slowly, pain lancing into him, he massaged his lower back and winced at the effort. No broken bones. Darned lucky.

Meriem's eyes closed. She looked almost peaceful, serene, slumped on the chest of her dead husband. Pressed heart-to-heart, he supposed. By now both had stopped beating.

Hell, they'd almost beaten him.

Yet he'd triumphed.

And he'd made two more kills.

What a memorable day! For the first time in his life, he was responsible for the deaths of fellow human beings.

Three of them!

Yet, strangely, he wasn't exultant, though he thought he would have been.

To begin with, he'd experienced a kind of singing in his veins, feeling so alive, but now, seeing these two bodies embraced in death, emptiness swamped his gut.

This was nothing like the rush he'd delighted in when he shot Orton. At least Orton had carried a weapon, even if he wasn't capable of using it effectively. This couple only had their bare hands and stones.

It was not a real contest. He'd been caught up in the moment, the blood-lust singing in his veins. His breakfast decided to erupt and he bent over, emptying his stomach on the ground.

Wiping his mouth with the back of his hand, he convinced himself that getting the rebate would offer some compensation for the emptiness he felt.

Gingerly, he picked up his gory dust-covered trophy.

It was time to get back to the hacienda, claim the bonus. And then he thought of Vanda. He liked the look of her, too. Maybe, if he could get Baeza out of the picture somehow, she could be another bonus? He wondered how Vanda's hunting was progressing.

————

NASIM AND ANAMARIA were both out of breath. By mutual consent they stopped temporarily.

His linen shirt clung uncomfortably to his sweating back. He said, "We're losing too much liquid. We're going to dehydrate."

Doubled up, her hands on her knees, she heaved in air, her body glistening in the sun. "Not much we can do about it in this heat. We must keep going." She glanced behind her. "I don't see any sign of Doin—Vanda."

"That's a relief, anyway. I think we should pace ourselves. If one of us collapses with heat exhaustion..."

"I understand. The other will be helpless, too."

He raised his free hand to his brow for shade and peered ahead.

Still some distance away loomed a very large rounded rock, a mound sparsely covered in weeds and small bushes. Sides of the rock were gouged by runnels, doubtless ancient run-off for the region's rare rain.

Nasim said, "If we can reach there, we can hide!" He tugged at the chain and she reluctantly came along.

"You just said we should rest!"

He increased his pace, walking slightly ahead of her. "That was before I saw that rock." He half-turned to face her. "Don't you see? We have a chance. I have a chance to escape, to see my family again!"

"It's all right for you! You have a family to return to. I have nobody."

"You have your life ahead of you! Come!"

After walking a short distance, they came upon a broad cluster of cane which grew about three meters tall. "We can hide in here!" Nasim said excitedly. "Our hunter will lose us in here."

"You hope."

Hope! Yes, hope was alive yet. Nasim pictured his wife Anya and their baby girl Selda, playing in the dilapidated apartment they had occupied near the ruins of what had once been a school. As an unemployed mathematics teacher, he berated himself for being so useless. His savings were diminishing by the day. He did without the main meal every alternate day to conserve money. He had calculated that if he took half the savings as payment for the boat trip across the Med, then that would leave enough for his Anya and Selda to survive on until he could obtain work and then he could send for them. He'd also factored in a three week delay to allow for unfortunate circumstances.

But he hadn't reckoned on those "unfortunate circumstances" meaning that he'd become a labor slave—or a rich man's hunt target.

He was surprised to feel tears on his cheeks. He thought he was devoid of moisture by now. Sapped of strength. No good to anybody. Anamaria or himself—or Anya and Selda.

He saw again Selda's smiling face as Anya waved him off. Her dark eyes glistened with tears, which she nervously brushed away. He'd promised to see them soon.

So he must keep his promise.

CHAPTER 13

MUST END

QUINT TRACKED THE THREE OF THEM WITH relative ease. For a good distance, the frequent specks of blood provided an ideal spoor to follow. But eventually the bloody spots vanished, probably as the source dried in the day's heat. He suspected the blood had come from the shackle rather than any wound sustained by one of the trio.

Having been thwarted earlier, he took his time. He had all day. However he reckoned he would reach them long before the end of the day. The end of their lives, for sure.

He noted that some leaves had been moved, probably by one of the two women. The Leon guy wouldn't be so careless. It was clear that branches had been pushed aside, eased back into place, while other foliage had been thoughtlessly swept through. The women again.

Attempts had been made to conceal the tracks, sure, no doubt by the Leon guy, but they were none too successful because he was covering for three, not merely himself. At least the man had tried.

By now, the sun was quite high, slanting through the openings in the treetops. He was glad of his cap. The heat had long since burned off every last semblance of morning dew. Already, the humidity was almost overpowering.

He wondered how his prey was coping.

———

HEAT AND HUMIDITY pressed oppressively upon Orton's prey, Tabish and Yesal. The two Afghans walked erratically, stumbling, exhausted. Dark patches of sweat stained their clothes, their hair was wet and unkempt, and their faces glistened in the sun.

"I can't believe we've got this far!" Tabish exclaimed breathlessly in Dari, his voice harsh, tobacco-damaged.

"I agree."

"I feared our hunter was close when I heard those shots."

"Our prayers might still be answered," Yesal said, and then, slowing down, he added, "My friend, what is that?" His close-set brown eyes widened as he pointed.

Directly ahead of them was a wide fissure in the ground, stretching to left and right as far as they could see.

"It is some kind of ravine, a gorge." Tabish groaned. "We will have to climb down and then up the other side. We will be sitting targets as we climb out!"

No, this cannot be! Yesal tugged at the chain and approached the gorge, his friend a reluctant enforced follower. Frantically, he looked around, scanning the terrain, and gasped. "No, wait." He pointed. "See!"

Tabish's blue-gray eyes shone. "A bridge!"

"Of sorts," Yesal admitted.

A wooden bridge spanned the gorge on ropes. It was wide enough to accommodate a vehicle, though that must have been some time ago, for now the swaying structure was in an extremely poor state. Several planks had rotted or been broken: there were many ragged holes in the floor of the bridge.

Yesal said, "It could be our way to freedom! Once we're on the other side we can try to bring it down, prevent anyone chasing us!"

"But it doesn't look safe to cross."

"Do not be faint-hearted. Should I go first?" Yesal asked boldly.

"No, my friend, I am younger and slightly lighter. I will lead."

"All right. But tread with care."

Tabish began to cross hesitantly, Yesal following at the end of the chain.

For each step, Tabish tentatively lowered one foot first, taking great pains to test the firmness of the plank. When he seemed to sense no give through his sandals, he lifted his other foot for the next step. With his free hand he held the rope guardrail and cautiously shuffled round rotted planks and gaping holes.

Yesal trod where Tabish went.

Several planks in the bridge floor creaked under their weight.

They had crossed about a quarter of the bridge's span when it began to sway, perhaps its response to unaccustomed load after years of disuse.

"Steady, friend," Yesal whispered, as if speaking too loudly might upset the equilibrium of the flimsy structure. "There is a long way still to go."

"I know. I am sweating with fear."

"No, Tabish, that is the heat. You know this."

"As you say."

Further on they went.

Without warning, Tabish's left sandal slipped on a spot of fungus and as he attempted to right himself his hand missed the rope rail. He slid forward a little and his left leg plunged through a gaping hole. "Yesal!"

As Tabish's thigh crashed downwards, wood splintered and his torso dropped into the hole, and then his head, and finally his chained wrist and hand. Tabish sounded hysterical, shouting incoherently, words bouncing off the gorge walls.

Desperately, Yesal tried to support himself, gripping the rope rail with one hand and taking his friend's weight on the end of the chain.

Creaking, groaning, the bridge swayed perilously.

Warily, Yesal trod forward a pace on the planking and peered through the hole.

Tabish was dangling on the end of the chain above the gorge. Whimpering.

The shackle was digging into Yesal's wrist. Painfully.

"Pull me up, dear friend!" Tabish called.

Yesal slipped on the wooden planks and Tabish dropped further, shrieking.

With his legs splayed apart, Yesal attempted to gain purchase. The weight of his friend threatened to yank his arm out of its socket or pull him through the saw-toothed gap. Sweat poured into his eyes, stinging. His thigh and shoulder muscles ached with the strain.

In truth, he rationalized, Tabish had served his usefulness. Tabish was not on a mission. The fool simply wanted a better life in the west, and was simply an economic migrant.

He's going to pull me to my death, the fool.

Balancing awkwardly, Yesal let go of the rope rail and leaned down, heart hammering as he was fearful of toppling into the hole. With his free hand he grasped a section of loose plank beside his foot, wrapping his fingers round it. He heaved and, with a splintering noise he broke off a length of wood, plucking it clear, though not before he cut two fingers on a big splinter.

"What are you doing?" Tabish shouted.

Yesal put the piece of plank to one side. Tears dribbled over Yesal's cheeks. They'd been close. Friends.

But now it must end.

Steeling himself, and ignoring the pain of the splinter cuts, Yesal heaved on the chain. It was agony, the shackle cutting into his wrist.

Tabish called, "That's it, my friend, you're doing it!"

Looping the chain round his elbow to take the strain, Yesal hauled again until, finally, Tabish's hand appeared through the jagged gap.

"Keep pulling, Yesal!"

Steadying himself, Yesal picked up the piece of broken

plank and slammed its ragged edge against Tabish's wrist, just beyond the shackle.

Blood squirted, spraying onto the floor planks.

Tabish yelled, his harsh voice rebounding from the walls of the gorge.

Yesal caught the anguished glare of his friend and tore his gaze away from those accusing eyes.

All bonds must be broken.

The mission has no room for friendship or love.

Tabish jerked on the chain. "Yesal, stop this! Are you insane? You're hurting me!" He tried reaching up with his free hand, clasping onto the chain that coupled them together, but his hand slid on the blood that had already dribbled there.

Tabish's frantic agitated movement threatened to unbalance Yesal. His back ached, muscles throbbed. His sandals slipped on a blood slick and his heart missed a beat but he steadied himself.

Despite his friend's weight, he stood firm. Feverishly he repeatedly struck with the wood at Tabish's wrist, gouging into flesh, baring bone at the wrist joint, the weakest part of an arm.

Bonds must be broken!

Savagely, he cut into it. His empty stomach squirmed and he gagged on bile that dribbled from his grimacing lips.

Cut, cut, cut!

More blood gushed down Tabish's arm, splashing his face. He shrieked, "No, no! You're my friend! *Why?*"

Yesal couldn't answer, couldn't tell him the truth.

At last, Yesal severed his friend's arm at the wrist and Tabish fell back, truncated limb flailing, body tumbling, his gaping mouth shrieking, the cries bouncing off the walls of the gorge, his body jolting like a puppet or toy against rocks and shrubs, until it finally settled with a dull thud, sprawled on the gorge floor, eyes gazing sightlessly at the sky.

Biting back his revulsion, Yesal sank on his haunches on

the bridge where the planks were firm, and sucked in air. His whole body trembled.

He'd killed before, but this was different. So very different.

Steeling himself to touch the tacky chain, he removed the severed hand from the metal shackle and flung it after his friend's body.

Then his stomach heaved and he vomited bile, hiccupping, wheezing.

Wiping his mouth with his forearm, he sucked in more air and slowly heaved himself to his feet, hastily catching hold of the rope rail.

On unsteady legs, he walked uncertainly across the rest of the bridge, careful to grip the rope, avoiding holes in the planks, testing with a cautious foot at every step.

And at last he attained solid ground on the other side of the gorge.

He was lathered in sweat, but he'd made it!

God is good, he thought.

He didn't have the strength or means to hand to collapse the bridge and stall pursuit. He believed that it was unlikely that anyone would risk stepping on those planks anyway. If the hunter wanted him, then he'd have to find another method to cross the gorge.

He squatted for a moment or two to collect his thoughts and steady the trembling caused by the aftershock of his actions.

Then he straightened and trudged purposefully in a southerly direction based on the sun's position.

Oddly, as he made his way along an overgrown track, he kept glancing to his side, but Tabish wasn't there now. They'd traveled a long way together.

He was as good as free, and yet it had cost him the comradeship and affection of Tabish.

The mission has no room for friendship or love.

If only he could get rid of the shackle and chain! It was possible that if he was found soon by friendly strangers, before he succumbed to dehydration, he could fabricate a story of woe to elicit help. The westerners were soft, they would give him succor.

And when the time was ripe, he would infiltrate their pathetic system and eventually locate like-minded adherents whose sole purpose was to destroy from within all of the infidels and their abhorrent decadent culture.

CHAPTER 14

DEAD WEIGHT

LUSH GREEN FOLIAGE BRUSHED AGAINST THE LEGS of Anamaria and Nasim as they entered the natural concealment of reeds. Anamaria immediately felt safe.

Cicadas made a racket but as the pair pressed deeper into the cane she found that the creatures' noise would stop until they'd passed.

After a while, the ground underfoot started to become soft and spongy.

Water seeped over her sandals.

She noticed that Nasim's feet were partially submerged already, yet he hadn't commented.

"Wait," she cried, "we shouldn't go this way. It's too muddy. We should go around."

Nasim half-turned and grinned. "It's cool on the feet, at least!" He tugged on the chain. "I'm anxious to see my family again, so hurry, this is the most direct route to that rock." He took two more paces forward.

She followed reluctantly, the wet mud now covering her feet.

He said, "Come on!" And then he stopped, jerking on the chain. "Eh?"

Her heart seemed to wobble.

Nasim attempted to take another step but couldn't. His legs began to sink into the ground.

This wasn't muddy ground, it was much worse, like a marsh.

He said, "It's some kind of bog! I'm stuck, can't lift my feet out. Can't move!"

Yet the ground she stood on, though waterlogged, was still firm under her soles.

Firm, so far.

"Try harder, Nasim. Come back!"

Nasim half-turned his torso, his dark eyes filled with alarm. "Help, pull me out!" he yelled.

Her stomach roiled and she succumbed to an overwhelming feebleness for, slowly, inexorably, he was being sucked down, the chain links already taut between them.

In no time at all the surface of the bog reached his waist.

She didn't dare take another step forward.

The pain of the shackle pulling on her wrist was tremendous as Anamaria tried to drag him out.

"Put your back into it!" he hollered.

"I am!" But she was weak. Weak with hunger. Weak with fear.

To make matters worse, their trudging through the marshy surface must have disturbed a nest of mosquitoes. Without warning, a dense cloud of them swarmed around her, buzzing and biting.

With her free hand Anamaria swatted at the biters, splatting some against her flesh, but she couldn't account for all of them.

"Pull me out, please!" Nasim called again, his eyes wide with worry. Then he stared, his mouth gaping in disbelief.

Anamaria peered behind her in the direction of his gaze, and her heart plummeted.

"Oh, dear, oh, dear," said Vanda, striding towards them, her rifle slung over one shoulder.

She wasn't threatening, hadn't unslung or aimed the weapon. "Cousin, help me pull Nasim out!"

Vanda stopped, arms akimbo. "Why should I?"

"Please help Anamaria!" Nasim shouted. "I have a family!"

"I'm here to hunt you both, not save you."

Anamaria said, "But - but if you don't, he will drag me down with him!"

Vanda said, "That's true."

"He'll suffocate—drown, die!"

"He will."

Nasim said, "Don't let me die, not like this!"

"Not like this?" Vanda queried.

Anamaria pleaded, "You must stop that happening to him! It's a terrible way to die!"

"You want me to be merciful, is that it?"

"Yes, please, Doin—Vanda!"

"Very well." Vanda unshouldered the rifle.

"No!" Nasim raised his free hand. "Please, no!"

Vanda aimed.

His dark eyes were beseeching. "Oh, Anya, Selda," he wailed, "I was wrong to leave you both!"

"Your number's up, Mathematician!" Vanda said and fired.

Nasim jerked spasmodically as the shot punched into his chest. He stared at the red stain on his gray shirt. And then he flopped face-first into the quagmire.

"No!" Anamaria screeched. "You—you murdered him!"

Vanda said, "That's the deal, you know. As I just said, I'm the hunter and you two are the prey."

Sobbing, chest heaving, Anamaria attempted to move but her feet were stuck.

Nasim's dead weight was sucking him further down, making an awful *glooping* sound, and the taut chain was dragging Anamaria further forward into the mire. She slipped, righted herself, and slid remorselessly, her legs already covered up to her knees.

Nasim sank entirely from sight. And kept dragging her.

Anamaria prayed. She didn't want Nasim's fate. *Dear Lord, I don't want to die!*

And then it was as if her prayers were answered. Vanda relented. "Here, cousin, grab this!" Holding the rifle by the barrel, she offered the wooden stock.

Anamaria grabbed, her muddy fingers slipping at first but eventually she wrapped her hand firmly around it. "Thank you!"

Gripping the barrel with both hands, Vanda heaved.

Despite her distress over the cold-blooded murder of Nasim, Anamaria dared to admit hope into her breast.

Finally, perhaps Vanda's efforts were being repaid, for there was slight movement, and Anamaria slowly moved out, a little closer to the firm edge of the bog. But she was stretched, her chained arm partly submerged while her free arm was virtually an extension of the rifle. The weight of Nasim was almost too much and caused excruciating pain in her wrist.

Vanda said, "It's no use. I can't pull you both out." She changed her stance and now held her rifle with one hand.

Anamaria bit her lip, heart pounding in her chest. Distasteful though it was, she came to a decision. "Give me the machete!" she screamed in desperation. "I'll—I'll cut his arm free!"

Vanda nodded. "That might do it." Awkwardly, one-handed, she unsheathed her machete.

"Toss it to me!" Anamaria shouted.

"But you'll have to let go of the rifle," Vanda explained in a reasonable tone. "You'll be sucked in before you can use the machete."

"Oh."

"I have the solution!" Vanda yelled triumphantly and leaned forward. Then, alarmingly, she swung the machete down, viciously, the blade cutting off Anamaria's hand at the wrist.

Anamaria shrieked, her face distorted as she saw Vanda

pull the rifle away, the lifeless hand that had been hers still clasping the stock.

QUINT's tight-fitting black T-shirt was soaked with sweat. He removed his cap and wiped his forehead with a forearm and then took off his spectacles and wiped them with his handkerchief. He was annoyed with himself. Tracking Mina, Leon and Daraja shouldn't be this difficult! Three of them, damn it. Should be a pushover.

He'd find their spoor, clues aplenty, soil disturbed, stones upturned, grass bent, twigs on bushes twisted back—and then nothing! As if they'd become ghosts and flown.

Twice he'd had to back-track as the spoor went completely cold.

It all had to be the work of the Leon guy. Damn him!

He peeled back the leather cover on his Rolex. Two hours since he'd set out on their trail. In mitigation, there was the diversion to Rudolf's corpse, which took time.

His one consolation was that his prey never ever escaped.

And this time he'd kill not two but three people. Maybe that fact would silence the social media trolls? Scare them shitless?

A measured approach. Keep calm. The prey would succumb.

Then the niggling thought impinged, like the early warning of a toothache: the Leon guy had Rudolf's rifle—with four slugs loaded.

Quint unslung his rifle, held it ready.

Yeah, a measured cautious approach was best.

Bide your time, Quint.

Anticipation is a major part of the fun.

CHAPTER 15

DECEPTION TECHNIQUES

"MY TROPHY!" VANDA EXCLAIMED. SHE KNEW SHE wouldn't win any money, and doubted if she'd be first back, anyway. But this trophy meant a lot to her. She felt good about shooting Nasim, too. He wasn't the first man she'd shot. Every time it was immensely satisfying. She only wished she could have put a bullet or two into Leon "Carlos Santos". Yes, she envied Quint.

Anamaria stared at her, in shock, the blood having drained from her face. The swamp was already sucking at her hips.

"You didn't think I'd really let you live, did you?" Vanda scoffed. She dropped the bloody hand, slung the rifle over her shoulder, and used a swash of reeds to wipe blood from the machete blade.

"But it was Basil, he's to blame!" Anamaria clutched her bleeding stump to her heaving chest as she continued to sink into the marshy ground, her other arm outstretched, mostly submerged.

"You're still sticking to that hoary old tale? Even as death comes for you?"

"He seduced me." Anamaria looked frantically for something to arrest her sinking movement. But there were no reeds nearby, nothing for her one good hand to grasp. "It was him, not me!"

"Well, as I see it, you're both as bad as each other." Vanda slid the machete into its sheath. "And when I find Basil, I'll be sure to tell him how you met your end. Then he will forfeit his life as well!"

"He told me he loved me!"

"Then he lied."

"He did lie." The tendons stood out in Anamaria's neck. "He's a liar and a drunk!"

"But he was mine, not yours!"

Sobbing, Anamaria let the stump of her free arm drop and it splashed into the marsh that lapped at her waist. "I don't deserve to die because of what I did to you! It was only sex—not—not love."

"Oh, yes you do! Stealing Basil from me hurt more than you could ever know!"

Doina had been pregnant with his baby. Feeling that new life moving within her had greatly affected her and even changed her. Then the grief Anamaria caused sent Doina into a spiral of self-pity and anger. She turned to alcohol and drank to excess and eventually lost the baby. She lost all her friends and her family shunned her. Yet, surprisingly, she survived, hauling herself from the depths of despond, rebuilding herself, finding a steely core she never knew she possessed. One aspect of her transformation was clinging onto the belief that she would find Anamaria and Basil and hurt them just as she'd been hurt by them. And then chance had thrown them together.

Revenge was best served cold, they say, but she was flushed, with the heat pounding from the sun and with the sheer pleasure of getting even.

One day, she promised herself, she would find Basil, and make him pay, too. But for now she was quite content to stand at the edge of the bog and watch Anamaria sink slowly but surely.

Must make sure.

She was determined not to leave until Anamaria had gone from sight for good.

Anamaria's pale face crumpled in anguish, her lips trembling, pleading words growing fainter as she must have realized there was no hope. Her eyes glared. Tears spilled as the mire covered her chin. Then she started coughing, spitting out the muck, choking, and then her nose was covered, and her accusing eyes, until finally her head was completely immersed.

A few bubbles made an eructating sound and then there was nothing but a boggy mass.

Vanda would relish telling the bastard Basil how Anamaria had met her end.

She checked her compass and then picked up Anamaria's hand.

She walked away, not looking back once.

On a whim, she decided not to retrace her steps but cut across land at an angle.

After a short while, she noticed far off and slightly to her right, visible against the stark blue sky, the aerials and TV dish on the roof of the hacienda.

She clutched Anamaria's hand tightly. She'd enjoy showing Francisco her little trophy!

Further on, she noticed a swarm of black birds flying in circles above a collection of derelict buildings. Curious. What had attracted them? She fired the rifle in the general direction of the birds and, raucously, they scattered, flying to the branches of a nearby tree.

Cautiously, she approached the buildings.

And then she stopped, her curiosity satisfied.

She recognized the bodies of Jamal and Meriem, the Moroccan married couple. She could see that Meriem had been deprived of a hand, but the tableau they presented didn't affect her unduly. In her thirty years she'd seen plenty of death and had killed more than once.

Kneeling by the pair, she examined them. One kill had been clean: a single bullet to the heart. The other was messier, however. The Moroccan woman had bled to death. That would have been Anamaria's fate if the swamp hadn't claimed her.

Vanda sensed a frisson run through her frame at the thought. Harley may have derived pleasure from leaving Meriem to die slowly. She remembered Harley's wide white smile, an attractive feature, thankfully not as pearly as Quint's. Though she wasn't too keen on Harley's fluting voice and fostered a strong aversion to politicians of all flavors. Well, it was quite possible this small town American politician was in the running for claiming the rebate. She shrugged. She wasn't able to claim that, but she was pleased to prove herself to Francisco. Prove that she was better, worthier and stronger than the comfort-woman Daraja.

A faint niggling regret hit her: she'd have loved to witness the death of that bitch at the hands of Quint. Both Daraja and Leon.

No use worrying over things you can't change, girl.

Regaining her feet, she studied the bodies one last time. Francisco should consider an alternative method of disposing of them. The evidence was too close to the hacienda. She'd noticed that Ramon was getting jittery, too. Maybe join forces, convince Francisco to curtail further hunts until the evidence could be properly buried? It was a thought, she supposed, and determined to raise the subject on her return. She swiveled on her heel, disturbing a couple of stones as she did so. In that same instant she felt a sudden sharp sting in her ankle. "Ouch!"

She looked down at an angular head and a flicking forked black tongue. Instinctively, she jumped back and stumbled on the uneven surface.

Oh, God! A snake!

Its sinuous diamond-patterned body slithered away.

As she breathed a sigh of relief that the thing had gone, she experienced an overwhelming sinking feeling.

Was this divine retribution?

No, just bad luck!

It mightn't be lethal. But she couldn't be sure.

Dear God, the area round the bite was already swollen. It was on the outside of her ankle, so she couldn't contort herself to attempt sucking out the venom. In fact, she wasn't sure that sucking was a good idea anyway. Wasn't that simply transferring the poison to her mouth?

If the venom was potentially lethal, her choices were limited. As was time. For every second that passed, the stuff was entering more of her bloodstream.

There was no other option.

Biting on her lip, she surveyed the immediate area but couldn't detect any movement. No more snakes, she hoped, and then gingerly she sat on a large stone.

Nervous. Fearful. Scanning the ground as she unsheathed the machete.

She noticed dried blood on the blade near the hilt. Anamaria's blood.

Retribution from the marshy grave? No!

Still, she hesitated a moment. Was this a good idea?

Maybe it wasn't, but there was no alternative. She pursed her lips and, using the point of the blade, she cut a small but deep nick in her skin above and also at the bite area. In response to the self-inflicted pain she cried between gritted teeth, a seething sound, but she was satisfied. Let it bleed profusely. With any luck the blood would drain the poison from her system as it flowed out of her. Would it bleed long enough? In this heat, the cut would probably dry up, the blood coagulate rapidly. Or not. She didn't know.

She was tempted to tear off a strip of her shirt to wrap round the wound, but decided against it. Let the blood flow free while it can.

Cleansing. Maybe.

To take her mind off the pain, she checked the compass again. Oriented herself.

She lost track of time, sitting there. How long? Not too long, surely?

She stood up.

And her head swam a little.

Gritting her teeth, she stumbled in the direction of the hacienda.

Her watch indicated some fifteen minutes or so had passed since she'd been bitten. Even after such a short time passing, her senses started to go awry. Her vision blurred, and she wasn't walking in a straight line.

"Get a grip!" she whispered hoarsely, summoning the will-power that had kept her beyond the clutches of the law. She shook her head and the blurring cleared.

She consulted the compass once more.

Keep on this line of sight, she told herself firmly.

Then she was sure she was hallucinating.

Some shape ahead of her shimmered into view and then disappeared, and then reappeared.

She wiped at her eyes with her fingers, and then waved and laughed on the edge of hysteria as she realized she was waving Anamaria's hand! "Hey, wait up!" she called, though it sounded like a gurgle—not unlike the sound her cousin had made when she sank into the swamp.

The shape stopped moving.

It had a face. A big white smile, but not a dentist's smile.

"Hey, Vanda?"

"Harley?" she mumbled.

He walked up to her. "Hey, are you drunk?" Then he tapped the hand she held. "I see you made your kill." Sternly, he said, holding up a severed hand, "I'm not splitting the bonus, Vanda."

"You can keep it. Baeza said—I and Orton—could—could not claim—claim the bonus—we hadn't paid in the first place." She coughed, hiccupped. "I—I saw—saw your handiwork back there." She giggled. "Handiwork. Get it?"

"What's wrong, Vanda? You seem —"

"I—I've been bit—bitten by—a snake."

"Jesus!"

She dropped her cousin's hand and the world rapidly tilted and went black.

"Here, let me help you," she heard.

She felt Harley take hold of her arm.

Immense relief washed over her. She was saved.

He said, "The hacienda isn't too far now."

———

MINA APPEARED to be in a dream world, happy to be steered by Leon and Daraja. Her eyes were open but vacant. Almost like an automaton, she placed one foot in front of the other, oblivious to the surface she trod. If Daraja didn't hold her, guide her, God knows where she'd end up, Leon thought.

Shortly after the last shot, he had exchanged a look with Daraja.

She nodded. She'd heard. Like him, she'd been counting. "Is that four?" she whispered.

"I think so."

Their concerns didn't seem to affect Mina at all.

Leon whispered to Daraja: "Back there, it seemed personal with Rudolf."

"It was," she replied. "I don't want to talk about it."

Denial. It was one way to cope with the act of murder, whether the deceased deserved it or not.

Birds chattered, now uncaring about the interlopers in their territory. Cicadas persisted, sometimes deafening.

They walked on. Leon attempted to conceal their tracks, but it seemed hopeless as Mina couldn't be left to walk by herself and being chained to Daraja seriously impeded his freedom of movement. But he kept trying, and on some occasions he believed he'd managed to get them both co-ordinated to the point where their spoor was confusing and even a couple of times nigh on invisible. But being cunning with deception techniques slowed them down.

By now it was hot and humid. Their clothing clung, soaked in sweat.

They'd started their run shortly after dawn, which was about six-fifty, so he estimated it was now roughly nine. It was relatively early. A long hot dehydrating day stretched ahead. If they were lucky enough to live through it.

Then he noticed that the sound of birds had ceased abruptly.

The next second they stepped into a large clearing.

An open space meant exposure.

Urgently, he tapped Daraja's upper arm, and then held a finger to his lips. "Stop," he whispered.

He stood still, and Daraja came to a halt. Mina's feet scuffled for a second as Daraja steadied her. The Iraqi stood rigid, staring ahead, as if unaware of her surroundings.

At the far side of the clearing was a derelict two-door red Wrangler Jeep and further beyond that an ancient Elddis caravan. No sign of life. Near the door of the caravan was a pile of black ash, the remains of a campfire. To the right was a considerable pile of empty tin cans, empty whiskey bottles, plastic bottles and milk cartons. A black cloud of flies hovered over it.

Everywhere he looked, it was still.

Not a leaf moved.

No birds chirped.

No recognisable life, save for the constant stridulation of male cicadas, as if the hotter the temperature got, the more manic their courtship cacophony became.

Taking his time, he scanned the foliage that surrounded the clearing.

Nothing untoward.

"It's all clear," he said softly. Gesturing to Daraja, he added, "Maybe we can find something to rid us of these chains."

"Let's hope so."

Daraja guiding Mina, they walked up to the jeep. The Spanish sun had infected the vehicle's red paint with a serious case of alopecia. The two wheels on the driver's side were missing so the jeep stood disconsolately at an acute slant, its deprived axles embedded in the earth.

Mina's head exploded in a spray of blood and brains, instantly succeeded by the heart-stopping gunshot report.

CHAPTER 16

ADRENALINE RUSH

IN THAT MOMENT OF STARTLING DEATH, LEON dived for cover behind the jeep, dragging Daraja with him.

Shit! It must be Quint!

Wincing at the impact of the hard landing on the ground and the strain on his bruised body, Leon gritted his teeth. They were on the vehicle's passenger side, in welcome shadow, and the contrast in temperature was stark, but the coolness didn't lessen the hammering of his heart.

He estimated where the shot had originated: from behind the trees somewhere on the other side—the northern side—of the clearing.

Then he glanced around but spotted nothing that might serve as a weapon. To his left was a jerry-can fixed in its bracket on the jeep. Maybe there were some tools in the rear?

He checked the distance to the caravan—too far to risk running to what amounted to be dubious shelter at best.

Crouching down, he peered past the edge of the jeep to see Mina lying on the hard baked earth.

I didn't spot him!

If it was Quint, he shouldn't have been able to conceal himself so well, dressed all in black. He wasn't a trained sniper. For God's sake, he was a dentist!

Regret and guilt washed over Leon, but he squashed those dangerous unhelpful feelings.

Quint was good, he had to admit.

Never underestimate the enemy.

Quint killed Mina, not me. Why?

An eerie silence followed that single shot and their mad dive for concealment. In the background there'd been the sawing of cicadas, never seeming to tire, but now there was an unnatural hush.

Save for the creaking of the jeep's bodywork protesting against the unremitting attack from the heat of the sun, and the rattling of a chain.

Daraja knelt beside him, shaking violently.

The startling deadly violence had affected her, naturally. He rested a hand on her shoulder. Her flesh was cold, damp with the sweat of mortal fear. "Are you going to be alright?" he whispered.

Tight-lipped, she looked at him, the whites of her eyes glowing in the shade. Tears glinted amidst the sweat on her cheeks. Hesitantly, she nodded.

"We *can* get out of this," he said. "Believe me."

Again she gave a nod.

He hoped his optimism wasn't misplaced.

Carefully, he unslung the rifle and raised it, an awkward action since Daraja's right wrist was attached to his left. Still, there was enough slack. But to accomplish it she'd had to move closer and was virtually squatting in his lap. He felt her body tremble against his.

All of the rifles Baeza had supplied possessed a flash hider on the muzzle. Its main purpose was to reduce the brightness when shooting that might affect night-vision. Its secondary purpose was to make the flash less conspicuous to the enemy. Which was fine, if you were the shooter. But here, he was the target. Naturally, he hadn't been able to see the flash of the weapon, as it had been unexpected. Even so, he'd managed to triangulate distances from where Mina's head had been at the time of impact, and reckoned that Quint was hiding behind one of three trees on the northern side of the clearing.

Assuming none of the shots heard earlier were made by Quint, since he was tracking him and Daraja and presumably not intent on shooting anyone else, then the American had four cartridges left, and so had Leon's rifle.

Every shot had to count. That's why the jeep wasn't being pulverized by a fusillade of bullets.

Quint was being cautious, staying in concealment.

He must have spotted the rifle Leon carried.

His earlier question returned: *Why didn't he kill me first?*

It would have made sense to eliminate any potential armed threat.

Of course he and Daraja were still chained together, and therefore handicapped in a straight firefight. If either he or Daraja had been shot, Mina might have made a run for it. Unlikely in her state of shock, but Quint didn't know that.

Maybe Quint wants to play with us, generate fear. Anticipation of the kill. The adrenaline rush of the killer.

In that case, big mistake, Quint.

While Leon scanned those three trees, the door of the caravan opened. Without deflecting his scrutiny from the trees, Leon's peripheral vision made out a short bearded man who stepped down, walking unsteadily in flip-flops.

"Who's shooting on my property?" the man shouted, his words slurred.

He took three paces and jerked backwards, a fresh red stain on his chest, and crumpled to the ground.

Daraja gasped but Leon only vaguely registered the sound as he spotted the black sleeve of Quint's arm, his hand and rifle barrel, all disturbing the natural symmetry of the tree-trunk.

Leon fired.

Quint swore loudly and slipped behind that tree.

Got you.

Leon calculated they both now had three bullets left.

Leaning his back against the jeep, he arched an eyebrow at Daraja. "Okay?"

Sweat glistened on her face. She licked her lips, whispered hoarsely, "Yes."

He rested a steadying hand on her shoulder and then called out, "Quint, we can stay here all day if we have to! Somebody else will claim the first-kill bonus!"

After a beat, Quint's throaty voice replied, "I ain't going anywhere. I don't need any trophy bonus. I'm here for the killing. My bonuses are these two dead already. The way I see it, I have two more to go."

"You're bleeding. Why not take your bloody trophy from Mina there and let us go?"

"Yeah, and if I break cover you'll treat me like I'm in a turkey shoot!"

"I'll let you go with the trophy. Just leave us be!"

"Are you insane? If you get away, you'll spread the word about this place. That ain't going to happen. No way!"

"You're bleeding," Leon repeated. "We can wait."

"It's only a nick. Flesh wound. A lucky shot." Quint paused, and then added, "Tell me. Is that Rudolf's rifle you've got?"

"He won't need it—or anything else ever again."

"Yeah, I saw what you did. Nice work, fella, attacking the guy from behind. Real brave."

"Luckily, he was too interested in what he was going to do to poor Mina, so he wasn't alert."

"Says you! But your luck can't hold. You ain't creeping up on me, you coward!"

Name-calling wasn't going to elicit any response, and Quint should have realized that.

"Hey, Leon, I remember our chat in the chopper when we flew in. You'd made a kill or two, I recall you said. You weren't talking about wild animals, were you?"

Leon ignored the comment. He noticed that Daraja shifted her position slightly. He yelled, "Look, Quint, we both have enough bullets to finish this. If you're man enough."

"No way. This ain't *High Noon*, fella. I reckon Orton will have heard the shots. He'll be wondering why so many were fired."

That had occurred to Leon, too. "He'll be too busy hunting his own prey," he reasoned. "As far as he's concerned, there's Rudolf and you chasing your targets—that's ten shots between you. No, Orton's not going to think twice, though he might worry that Rudolf or you are about to claim the refund."

"I told you, I ain't interested in the rebate. Let's wait and see, eh?"

Time was on Quint's side. One of the others might come this way, once they'd made their kill. Or if they stayed long enough, Baeza might send the chopper to investigate.

The rising heat and the humidity sapped strength at an exponential rate. Leon continually wiped his palms on the jacket, and tensely gripped the rifle.

Anxiety was etched in Daraja's face.

Must break the stalemate.

He patted her shoulder. "Here, help me get this loose." He softly tapped a knuckle against the jerry-can. It sounded almost empty.

Puzzlement flashed in her eyes. But she adjusted her position so she could assist him.

CHAPTER 17

PURPLE CRYSTALS

THE WOUND IN QUINT'S LEFT FOREARM WAS MORE serious than he'd let on. In this humidity it might not stop bleeding. The pain may be a torment, but he could bite on his lip and withstand it. He sure inflicted worse in his dental chair back home. Despite the throbbing ache, he continued to hold the rifle in readiness. If Orton or even Harley came along, they'd serve as a distraction which would allow him a shot or two to slay the Leon guy and the comfort woman.

From beneath the concealment of a cluster of leaves, he peered at the killing ground.

Suddenly, the black woman stood up.

What the hell?

Salty sweat stung his eyes, blurred his vision. Agitatedly, he wiped it clear with his forearm.

She was holding up something red. Not a white flag, for sure!

Then she flung the thing into the air, in his direction.

Stupid bitch. He laughed. *She'd be throwing stones next.*

He raised the rifle, taking a bead on her.

Before he could fire she ducked out of sight and in the same instant more movement caught his eye. As the red thing sailed through the air, Leon came into sight briefly and fired his rifle.

Quint was ducking into the undergrowth as a tremendous explosion erupted and shards of metal blasted towards him, slicing into the tree trunk he hid behind, scything through the foliage around him.

Birds flapped wings all around, their dark shapes scattering from the nearby trees.

His ears thrummed with the aftershock of what sounded like an airburst.

Of course, she'd thrown a gas can. And Leon had shot at it, exploding the thing!

Fuckin' Hell!

The red fires of Hell: the undergrowth in front of him had been set alight.

Crouching, he walked backwards, keeping under cover.

Disoriented by the percussive noise and smoke, the flames spreading, he stepped sideways, away from the encroaching heat, and his heel hit a half-buried tree root. He lurched to his left to retain his balance and realized too late that he'd stumbled into a shaft of sunlight.

Exposed!

Extreme pain swamped him and the shock of disbelief clouded his mind as the bullet tore at his throat. His hands dropped the rifle and lifted automatically in vain to stem the outpouring of his lifeblood.

He was immediately aware that he couldn't speak or scream.

A gurgling sound filled his ears. Coming from him.

And the world spun in front of him as he slumped into unrelieved darkness.

————

LEON BREATHED A SIGH OF RELIEF. The ploy had worked as he'd hoped. His bullet had penetrated the almost empty jerry can and created a spark as it punctured the metal and ignited the air-gas mix. He'd been lucky. If the can had been full or even half-full, the mix probably wouldn't have been combustible. The explosion and the flames had brought Quint into the open, an easy mark.

That was all he needed. Leon rarely missed his target.

Now, with Daraja in tow, Leon hurriedly skirted the burning vegetation and jogged towards Quint. His rifle was still leveled: he had one bullet left, enough for a coup de grace.

When he reached the American, it was obvious the man was dead. Quint stared sightlessly. Arterial blood had soaked his black T-shirt and trousers and glistened in the betraying shaft of sunshine.

Leon slung his rifle over his shoulder and leaned down, Daraja crouching beside him. He went through Quint's pockets, taking euro banknotes from his wallet. He also transferred the American's Rolex to his own wrist. It would help him monitor the time on their trek to the village. Then he picked up Quint's rifle and swiftly emptied the three remaining cartridges into his left hand and pocketed them. He now had four bullets. Then he stood and swung the rifle against the nearest tree trunk, breaking it.

The chain jerked abruptly as Daraja kicked Quint's chest.

"Serves you right for killing Mina, you bastard!" she shouted at the corpse. Fresh tears shone on her cheeks.

He moved to her side, gave her a hug.

"Can we bury Mina?" she whispered against his ear, as if the dead were prone to eavesdropping.

He held her at arm's length and shook his head. "Sorry, it would take too long. We haven't time. Orton, Harley, or Vanda could come after us. The explosion might bring one or more of them." He pointed to an indistinct track leading south-west, away from the caravan. The jeep probably came along there some years ago, possibly towing the caravan. How it lost its wheels was going to be a mystery for someone else to solve. "We'll follow that trail." He gripped her hands and said gently, encouragement in his voice: "But first, let's see if we can break free of these chains."

"Yeah." She wiped her eyes. "Have we got time for that?"

"We'll make time. But keep alert."

He checked the burning ground. The flames were dying already. There was little risk of the fire spreading. He didn't want to be the cause of hectares of damage. He knew from bitter experience how devastating countryside fires could prove, destroying crops, orchards, homes and livelihoods. He loaded the rifle cartridges. "Let's try the jeep."

On their way over, Leon stopped by the bearded dead man, and Daraja bumped into him. "Sorry," he said. "Just a moment." He knelt on one knee, supporting himself with his rifle, with Daraja having little choice but to kneel beside him.

"He sure was wasting away," she observed.

Leon agreed. The man's hair and beard were straggly, unkempt, and salt-and-pepper in color. He was almost a foot shorter than him or Daraja, slightly built, with no muscle tone, virtually skin and bone, sunken eye-sockets and cheeks. Vibrant life had vacated this person long before Quint's bullet pierced the heart. He noticed that the man's feet were in a bad way, blistered and fungal. A displaced hippy, out of time, literally. He checked the trouser pockets but found that there was no identification, which wasn't surprising. Maybe there were clues in the caravan, he thought, rising.

Leon led them over to the jeep and rested the rifle upright against the door, within easy reach. He rummaged in the rear and behind the seats. He found a pry bar with the jack, a screwdriver, a couple of oily rags, a plastic funnel and another almost empty jerry-can.

He rested their shared chain on the bonnet of the jeep and slid the pry bar into a link midway along. "Hold your end taut," he instructed her.

He had just enough length of chain that allowed him to grip the bar with both hands. He began levering. Sweat dribbled from his face and sizzled on the hot metal.

Gradually, a gap showed in the chain link. After more

effort it widened enough for him to wiggle the other link through the gap and at last they were uncoupled.

"Thanks!" Daraja said, massaging her wrist around the shackle.

"Don't mention it."

Now he could wear Rudolf's jacket properly. He unfastened the belt and slipped his shackled arm with the chain into the dangling sleeve. He felt guilty that Daraja was still skimpily dressed. Maybe he'd find suitable clothing for her in the caravan.

He replaced the belt and then retrieved the rifle.

"Let's see what's inside." He walked with her to the caravan.

They stopped at its doorstep. The door was ajar. "Can you stay here while I see what I can find?"

"What if I hear somebody coming?"

He hoisted the rifle. "Can you use this?"

"I point it and pull the trigger, huh?"

"Yes, but brace the stock," he said, tapping that part, "either against your shoulder or torso. One shot should be enough to alert me, I reckon, and I'll come running. If you must, fire only one shot. We must conserve what little ammo we have."

She nodded. "One-shot Daraja, that's me."

He grinned, pleased she was bearing up. He had no idea what she'd been through in any great detail, though he feared it would have been traumatic. But today she'd been directly involved in the brutal death of one man and had witnessed the sudden death of two other people. "That's the spirit. I won't be long."

Chain jangling at his wrist, he climbed into the caravan, while Daraja stood sentry.

The place was dark. It stank, of stale sweat, putrid food, marijuana, and faeces.

Flies buzzed over abandoned food on the sink unit.

On a small counter-top were two unopened whiskey bottles and about a dozen empty. On a shelf were three cans of baked beans, a half dozen sachets of sugar, four tins of corned beef, three tins of green olives *sin huesos* and two of sardines in tomato sauce. Lying on a small foldable table were three unsmoked spliffs: the guy was probably high when shot and wouldn't have felt a thing.

After a minute or two, his nose hardly noticed the smell.

A hasty examination was enough: no useful tools in here. A hack-saw would have been ideal to sheer off the manacles. But the dead man hadn't seemed capable of wielding anything other than a bottle of liquor.

The limited closet space offered little. The man's shirts and trousers were old and stained and besides were a couple of sizes too small for Leon or, for that matter, Daraja. Still stuck with wearing boxer shorts, damn it.

He checked the drawers and cupboards—one kitchen cupboard was without a door—which between them offered up an assortment of medicines, two antihistamine tubes, and a large jar of potassium permanganate crystals—possibly used for his fungal infection or even for water purification—though on reflection the guy probably hadn't been much of a water drinker. However, Leon did find under the sink a single 1.5 liter bottle of still water: Lanjaron, with its seal unbroken beneath the cap so it was safe to drink. He tried the tap on the caravan's tiny kitchen sink, and brown water gushed for a few seconds and then dripped. The reservoir tank had obviously been empty for a while.

It was apparent that, judging by his lifestyle, if you could call it that, the man hadn't had long to live. Quint had probably done him a favor.

He found a careworn frameless backpack in a drawer under the bunk and emptied the contents of the various pouches and pockets onto the grubby sheets: mainly typed pages of poetry, a handful of faded photographs of school chums, and a passport whose date showed it had expired two years ago: Luke Astley, born in Sunderland in April, 1991. He was twenty-nine and could have passed for someone in his fifties. What a waste!

He snatched a couple of shirts from the closet and tore one of them into strips, which he used to wrap round the jar of purple crystals. He then put it into a side pouch of the pack. Besides being useful for fungal treatment, in diluted form the crystals could disinfect cuts and abrasions. Also they could start a fire with one part sugar and two parts of the chemical: academic for now, since he had Rudolf's lighter, but if that failed, the crystals were a back-up. He then put in the backpack pockets the two other shirts, a couple of polythene shopping bags issued by a Mercadona supermarket, sachets of sugar, a bottle of whiskey, the still water, two cans of beans, the two tins of sardines, and a tin of olives, distributing the weight evenly. Fortunately, the tins all had ring pulls. Quite a dysfunctional Mediterranean diet. He threw in Rudolf's lighter and wallet, a kitchen knife and two spoons, as well as Astley's passport. It was getting the balance right—not too heavy to carry for any distance, but enough to sustain them, since he estimated it could take a couple of days to get to that village he'd spotted when flying in.

Slipping his arms through the straps, he hefted the pack on his back and stepped out of the caravan.

The air was thick with the smell of burnt petrol and wood, but it was preferable to the interior.

Daraja pointed at the backpack. "What have you got there?"

He lowered the pack to the ground. "Not a lot—but it may prove useful later."

She eyed the backpack suspiciously but didn't venture to investigate. She looked around, wringing her hands, the chain clanking. "Are you going to be much longer? I think we should go."

"Just a minute or two more." On his way over to the jeep he picked up two empty whiskey bottles complete with metal screw caps. Then he opened the bonnet and disconnected the battery. Steadying the plastic funnel he poured the battery acid into one bottle.

She stood beside him. "Why are you doing that?"

"It might come in useful."

"You sound like my father. He hoarded stuff that might come in useful. It never did."

He said, "You never know, though." He tore a square off a polythene bag, doubled it up and placed it over the bottle opening, and then tightly screwed the cap on the bottle. That should seal the acid and avoid any reaction with the bottle cap. He wrapped the bottle with a shirt, and then put it carefully upright in the backpack, together with the other empty, which was also cushioned with a shirt for protective padding. Lifting the pack onto his back, he said, "Let's go."

"About time." She sighed and handed him the rifle. "You'd better take this. You know how to use it."

They had only walked a short distance when Leon stopped at a mound of earth heaped with an assortment of stones next to a tree trunk.

A blistered cupboard door rested against the tree, and pinned to it was a faded photograph of a young blonde woman and scrawled on the bottom was: Janine. 1999-2019. R.I.P. XXX. There'd been no female clothing in the caravan. Maybe it was all buried with her.

He said, "I suspect there's a tragic story behind this misper." She was doubtless one of many young girls who went missing, some of them leaving behind distraught family members while others were fleeing abusive relationships.

Daraja said, "He will have joined her now."

"Perhaps." He'd committed Janine's name and date of birth to memory. He adjusted the backpack and then led Daraja along the track he'd indicated earlier.

CHAPTER 18

FIGHT BACK

LEON THOUGHT THEY MADE BETTER TIME NOW
that he didn't attempt to conceal their tracks.

He consulted the Rolex: another hour had passed. By
now, the sun was higher, hotter, and, since there was a
paucity of tree cover here, it beat doggedly on his head.
Should have taken Quint's cap. He glanced sideways at
Daraja. She didn't seem too bothered by the heat.

He stopped to wipe his brow and gather his thoughts: at
some point he would return to the hacienda—either by
himself or with official backup—and shut them down for
good. For now, however, his priority was to get to civilization
with Daraja and then contact Silvano.

"Why have you stopped?" Daraja asked.

"Our assigned hunter is dead and I don't expect any of
the other hunters would consider tracking Quint's prey. If
any of them had been drawn by the explosion, they'd have
confronted us by now."

"If you say so. It makes sense, I suppose."

He assumed that a hue-and-cry would be organized only
when Rudolf and Quint didn't return. At that time, Baeza
was bound to send the chopper—possibly with Maddox—in
a search pattern. He'd mention the threat from the air later.
No need to alarm her yet.

He removed from the pack the bottle of Lanjaron water, cracked the top and removed the paper seal. "Take a sip. We have time."

She was grateful for the drink, even if it was only a sip.

He drank sparingly too, letting the liquid wash around his mouth before swallowing it, and then he replaced the bottle in the pack. The contents would soon be warm, almost unpalatable, but it would still save them.

They continued walking. The heat of the day was unremitting, sapping strength.

After a while they came to a rickety old bridge that spanned the gorge. In the past the structure might have taken the weight of the jeep and even the caravan. Now, Leon wasn't too sure it would even take his weight. There were many holes in the floor-planks. There were rope rails on each side, but too far apart to hold onto both at the same time.

As he slid his arms out of the straps and gently lowered the backpack and rifle to the ground, he noticed a recent sign of scuffed footprints on the ground at this side of the bridge. "Maybe targets have been this way."

She nodded. "Tabish and Yesal were on our right when we started to run. Could be them."

"Well, if they crossed, so can we." He took a step towards the first planks of the bridge.

She said, "No, wait, let me test it."

"You sure?"

"I want to be useful—*but* don't think of putting me in that backpack."

He grinned. "All right. Take it easy, one step at a time."

"Yeah, that's the best way to walk. Why didn't I think of that?" Throwing him a disarming smile, she took hold of the left-hand rope rail as this side of the plank bridge seemed less worn and treacherous.

Tentatively, she began to walk forward very slowly.

The entire bridge creaked and swayed.

Leon's heart was in his mouth as he watched her progress.

Then she hesitated, peered over her shoulder at him. Disquiet etched in her face.

He called, "What is it?"

"The planks," she shouted, "they're tacky—it looks like blood."

Without warning, a number of supports gave way and the boards at her feet splintered apart.

"Leon!" she shrieked.

Wood planks shattered and tumbled into the gorge.

One hand tightly clasping the rope rail, Daraja hung suspended through an enlarged gap, only her upper body visible. Her face reflected the sheer strain she experienced, holding on.

Unhesitatingly, he rushed forward, left hand wrapped around the rope rail, sliding it through his palm as he moved. Dodging holes. Wary of treacherous patches of moss.

Extending his arm.

Grabbed her free right hand, held tightly even though it was slippery with sweat.

"Easy, now." He took her weight. "Get your leg up and through."

Gritting her teeth, she pulled on the rope rail as he supported her other hand. She lifted her right knee through the gap, rested it on the edge of splintered wood, and then raised her other knee and managed to scramble out, placing both feet on relatively solid wood.

He seized hold of her, held her tight against the rope rail. Her heaving chest pressed hard against his.

"Sorry." She gasped. "I guess we won't be crossing here after all."

"No, I suppose not." As he'd held her, he'd looked down. A single body lay sprawled on the floor of the gorge, its amputated hand lying a meter or so nearby. He recognized the colorful red and white striped undershorts.

She'd followed his gaze. "Oh, no..." Her frame shuddered against his. "That's Tabish. Poor man."

"But where's the other one?"

"Yesal." She shrugged and then gestured at the blood on the bridge planking. "Shot?" Her tone had a fearful edge to it. Wide-eyed, she studied both sides of the gorge.

Leon scanned Tabish's corpse. "There are no signs of gunshot wounds on him. Of course, he could have been shot in the back. But then there's his severed hand."

"You think Yesal got away?"

"Looks like it. Maybe Tabish was shot in the back and Yesal was forced to...well, cut off his friend's arm somehow." He pointed beyond the gaping hole in the foot-planks, to bloody footprints leading to the other side. "He definitely went that way, so let's hope he made it to safety."

"Poor Tabish. What terrible luck, to have come so far, only to fail."

"Come on, let's get away from here."

Gingerly, gripping the left-hand rope rail, they walked the short distance back to firm ground, and once there they were both breathless and drenched in sweat. Any elation they might feel seemed misplaced.

He lifted the pack. "After that little scare, maybe a drink of water is called for."

"I was thinking of something stronger, maybe a gulp of whiskey?"

Dehydration was an enemy, for sure, and imbibing whiskey wouldn't help. "I brought that along in case we needed it for an antiseptic."

"Oh."

He lowered the backpack to the ground and pulled out the bottle of Lanjaron. Handing it to her, he added, "Go easy, it's all we've got. We can go without food for a week or maybe more, but without water we'll be hallucinating within a couple of days in these temperatures."

"Couple of days?"

"Yes. It might take us that long to get to the village I saw on the way in."

"Okay." She drank a little, lowered the bottle and passed it to him. She licked her lips.

He took a small gulp and then replaced the cap and put the bottle in the pack.

So far Daraja was holding up well. Not noticeably distressed by these latest deaths: Mina, the hippy, Quint and now Tabish. And her ordeal on the bridge hadn't shaken her, either.

"Right," he said. "We'll follow the gorge, see where it leads." He wished he'd paid more attention to the topography when he'd looked through the helicopter window. But they'd been traveling fast, and it hadn't seemed relevant.

Tabish's body made him rethink his strategy. Now, as they went, he again attempted to conceal their tracks. At least it was easier since he wasn't shackled to Daraja. His efforts were unlikely to fool a trained eye, but he might bamboozle the likes of Harley or Vanda, if either of them, contrary to his logic, was on their trail.

"If anyone comes after us, maybe they'll think we took a tumble down there," she suggested. "Tabish's body could throw them off our scent."

"It's a thought. They might believe we crossed the bridge. We can hope it would fool some of them."

"But?"

"If Maddox comes, he's bound to read the signs correctly and will know the truth almost straight away."

"But nobody's going to be looking for us yet, are they? That's what you said earlier."

"Quite right, I'm just thinking aloud about all the options. We're clear for now."

"For now?"

He didn't answer.

The day's heat intensified and made the hot walk debilitating. The exertion on the fragile bridge had taken its toll.

As they moved along the rim of the gorge side by side, they zigzagged whenever possible in order to seek shade from the small number of trees they came across.

Judging by the height of the sun and the Rolex, he estimated they'd been walking for four hours. Maybe they had an hour or two before Baeza sent the chopper.

Hunger pangs were kicking in, which was to be expected. They could be ignored, he reasoned.

She said, "I could even eat that slop they doled up in the basement cell!" In confirmation, her stomach rumbled audibly. "I can taste those sardines already!"

"We'll eat later."

When they'd covered a fair distance, he spotted a stand of trees that offered shade. "Let's stop and eat."

"About time," she said. "I'm famished!"

"Well, the menu is limited, ma'am. You do have a choice, however. Baked beans or sardines?"

"Beans."

"Then beans it is." They headed for the shade cast by four yew trees.

Gently putting the pack on the ground, he sat with his shoulders against a trunk and opened one of the pockets. He passed her the bottle of water and she took a gulp.

"I could swallow all of it!" she said, reluctantly handing it to him.

"Rationing gets easier the more you adhere to it." He drank and found the water was lukewarm. Not refreshing in the least. He screwed on the top, put the bottle away. He then heated two spoons with the flame of the lighter, and this gave the cutlery a black patina but more importantly any harmful germs should have been eliminated. She held the spoons while he tugged the ring-pull on the can of baked beans.

He said, "We'll share this one."

She licked her lips. "If we're going to make sure it's a fair distribution, shouldn't we count the beans as we eat them?"

"Puts a new meaning on the phrase 'bean counter,' I suppose."

She chuckled fetchingly. "Nah. I'm too hungry to waste time on that!"

They took turns at eating a spoonful.

Baked beans had never tasted so delicious.

They scraped the tin clean with their spoons.

While eating, he had studied the trees. Good. He was pleased, for the Spanish yew was known to have fewer knots in it than the northern European type. Ideal for his purpose.

Daraja licked her spoon clean. "Shouldn't we be getting on?"

"Soon. Rest your stomach for a short while. You've had a big meal."

She raised an eyebrow at him. "Really?"

"I'm going to be a little busy. Rest."

"Okay." She winked. "It's always nice to doze after a full and satisfying meal." She shut her eyes. Soon, her chest started to rise and fall in a steady rhythm.

Leon replaced the cutlery in the backpack and stood up, eyes probing the area.

He quickly found a broken limb of yew that had been lying around some time—it was dried, but still possessed elasticity. He used the machete to cut it to a length of just in excess of a meter, and then cut a notch at each end.

Next, he carefully unpicked a length of nylon thread that stitched one of the backpack pockets, and fitted the makeshift bowstring to each notch, pulling it taut, slightly bending the bow. He pulled back on the bowstring about a half-meter, and felt the draw weight tension: plenty of potential energy to power an arrow, he reckoned. He was satisfied that he'd manufactured a decent short bow.

After that, from other branches he cut eight arrows of equal length, shaved them carefully, making them as smooth as he could.

Deftly, he cut up the hippie's passport cover, preserving the photo page, to create flights for his arrows, which he shoved into thin slits he'd incised at one end.

Daraja shifted, opening her eyes. "You have been busy."

"Nearly done." He took out a tin of sardines from the backpack. "Time to eat again."

"What! You're spoiling me. Are we celebrating something?"

"We are. The start of a new enterprise."

She raised an eyebrow, gazing at the bow and arrows. "And what business is that?"

"*Fight Back*. A catchy name, don't you think? It's in direct competition with *Hit the Target*."

She said, "I pray it will be a success." She sounded dubious, however.

"We can but hope." He opened the tin.

They ate the sardines with the spoons, yet still managed to get their fingers messy.

He couldn't avoid a burp and his mouth was filled with the oily aftertaste. Patiently he cut the sardine tin into strips with the machete. Then, using a stone he pounded and molded the piece of tin into a point on the shaved end of the arrow, and repeated the process seven more times.

"Very Robinson Crusoe," Daraja said. "You know, as I watched you, I got to wondering. You have a rifle, so why bother?"

"I have a limited number of bullets. Besides, if we're still in the wild at night, a bow and arrow can be more effective—and, being silent, won't draw attention."

"Okay, I'm convinced." She paused. "But I'm still a bit worried about the new business. Fight Back."

"When we get to the village, you're free to leave. You haven't signed a contract for the new venture, have you?"

"No." Her eyes shone, amused. "One thing at a time. First, we get to the village, right?"

"That's the plan." He stood and slung the bow over his shoulder and then carefully placed the arrows in the backpack. "Now we can get on."

"Right. I feared we were stuck here forever, playing at Red Indians!"

"I wonder what the cowboys at the hacienda are doing," he replied.

Laughing together, they moved on.

CHAPTER 19

BODY BAGS

SITTING IN THE HACIENDA LOUNGE, CALVO SIPPED at his coffee and looked out of the panoramic window, while Maddox sat at the dining table and cleaned his Webley revolver with an oily cloth.

Baeza paced the floor.

Calvo said robotically, "You seem anxious, my friend."

"It has been too long." Baeza tapped his fob watch. "One of them should have returned with a trophy by now."

Maddox lowered the revolver, turned his gaze on Baeza. "I agree, sir."

"We have never had this kind of delay. This is not normal." Baeza grated his teeth. "I don't like it."

Calvo said, "You worry too much! Perhaps today's prey they are good at running and hiding, no?"

"Perhaps." Baeza didn't sound convinced.

Maddox stood and holstered the revolver. "It's about time the chopper went to collect the corpses, anyway, boss. I'll go along as usual. I might find out what is delaying them."

Baeza stopped pacing. "Thank you, Simon. That would be helpful. Radio if you learn anything—anything out of the ordinary."

"Indubitably, sir."

"Eh?" croaked Calvo. "What do you mean "Out of the ordinary"?" And he received a black look from Baeza.

Maddox said, "I'll be in touch." And he left the room.

———

LEON SAID, "Time to stop and you can rest for a bit."

Daraja didn't reply but seemed grateful for the respite. With her feet she cleared a small area of dry brown pods at the base of a dense dark green carob tree, and then lowered herself to sit with her back to the trunk.

She watched him as he unslung the backpack and put it on the ground. "What are you going to do now?"

"I'm going to make a little preparation—"

"— just in case, hmm?" She started to smile but her eyelids drooped, heat exhaustion clearly making inroads on her stamina.

He had considered warning her, but saw little point in causing alarm, which wasn't helpful. Once Rudolf and Quint failed to return, Baeza was bound to send the chopper to investigate. Even a desultory search was likely to discover the bodies of either Rudolf or Quint eventually and then they'd scour the land in earnest for the "missing targets". This "preparation" might give him the edge if he was confronted by the aircraft.

He rummaged in the backpack and took out the whiskey bottle that contained the car battery acid and then removed the piece of shirt wrapped round it.

First, he needed to perform a little transformation.

He collected a number of stones and used them to build a small oblong crater just smaller than the base of the whiskey bottle. He scavenged dry tinder and put that in the little crater. He unscrewed the whiskey bottle cap, removed the polythene inner covering, and wedged the bottle in the top of the stone crater. Rudolf's lighter ignited the tinder. The bottle glass was tough. He hoped it would be sufficiently heat-resistant: it was all he had to hand.

Keeping clear, he watched and waited. Finally, when dense white fumes spiraled from the bottle neck he doused the fire, taking care not to inhale the fumes.

Now, he needed to let the liquid cool: what remained was concentrated sulphuric acid.

When the glass was cool, he replaced the polythene covering, screwed on the cap and tested it with a gentle shake or two. Thankfully, the concentrated acid didn't penetrate the polythene cover and the bottle cap didn't react, so even in this form it was safe to tote in the backpack.

Reluctantly he poured a small measure of water from the Lanjaron bottle into the empty second whiskey bottle: about a third full, and sealed that.

With great care, he wrapped pieces of shirt around both whiskey bottles and put them into separate side-pockets in the backpack.

Satisfied with his efforts, he went over to Daraja and tenderly shook her shoulder. "Wake up, sleeping beauty."

She opened her eyes, slight confusion in her features but then she oriented herself and squinted at him. "All prepared, are you?"

"Yes. Time to get moving again."

———

THE HELICOPTER TOOK off with only Maddox and the pilot on board. The co-pilot airman was strongly averse to dealing with the corpses of the "targets" so, as usual, he stayed behind.

"Start checking from the south-east," Maddox instructed the pilot. It was the most logical option, passing post number one to begin with.

The aircraft followed the customary track the targets ran along and it was only a matter of minutes before they spotted the two bodies.

"What the hell?" Maddox exclaimed. "Do you see that?"

"Yeah."

One of the bodies was fully clothed in camouflage fatigues.

Maddox unholstered his revolver. "Well, let's land. But be careful, keep an eye out."

The pilot tapped his shoulder-holster. "Sure."

The aircraft hovered briefly and then landed near the bodies, the rotors sending dust and leaves flying in all directions.

The pilot cut the engine.

Scanning the surrounding vegetation, Maddox unbuckled his seatbelt, slid open the door and jumped out.

Ducking beneath the slowly whirling rotors, gun ready, he loped to the corpses.

He was impressed: the Syrian had been killed with a clean shot to the head. But his fellow captive was missing, as was the chain and shackle. The reason for that was obvious: the Syrian's hand was lying nearby.

Maddox scrutinized the German client named Rudolf.

No obvious wounds, but it was clear from the staring eyes, their burst blood capillaries, the dark red of the face, and the massive hemorrhage and scarring round the neck that Rudolf had been strangled. Judging by the damage imprint on the flesh, the ligature used had been the links of a chain.

Gross.

Rudolf's rifle was missing as were his machete and belt. It didn't make sense.

Quite a puzzle.

He recollected that the woman on the other end of the chain was an Iraqi. How could she and the Syrian have strangled Rudolf and then the Syrian man somehow sustained a lethal shot to the head? The gun-wound evinced no powder-burns. The bullet had been fired from a distance, certainly not during a scuffle. Had the woman turned the tables on Rudolf after the German claimed his first kill? Or had the couple outwitted Rudolf, strangled him and then she'd shot her chained partner and cut herself free? The ground here revealed considerable disturbance, possibly as Rudolf died. But the Iraqi woman's footprints appeared a couple of feet away. Damn, he *was* in a quandary.

He hadn't particularly liked the German, but he wouldn't have wished this death on anyone.

The pilot walked up to him. "This looks bad, Mr. Maddox. Real bad." He stood with arms akimbo, shaking his head. He lightly tapped the toe of his boot against Rudolf's side. "What do you want to do about him?"

"We put them both in body bags. That's why we're here."

"Yeah, but this time it's different."

"Indubitably." This poser was doing his head in. "One thing at a time, my friend. Body bags." He double-checked the dead Syrian. No sign of the man's manacle or chain links. He wouldn't need the master key or the hessian bag this time.

Even though they'd done this on what seemed like countless occasions, it took a while and was hot work, lifting each body into a black thick plastic bag, zipping it up, and then carrying it to the aircraft and loading it on the deck between the rear seats.

When they'd finished and both had taken a swig from their bottles of water, the pilot asked, "Do you want to go back to the hacienda?"

Maddox shook his head vehemently. "No, you damned well know we never take the stiffs there!" He screwed the top on his water bottle. "I'll radio the boss; let him tax his brain over this."

———

Sitting in the lounge with Calvo, Baeza gave a start as he heard the insistent buzz of the radio. He lowered his glass of red wine to the table and glanced at Calvo. "That'll be Maddox." He stood and left the lounge, and lumbered into the passage, swung his door wide and entered his own room. On the right was a door to an adjoining office.

Inside the office were a desk, a computer tower, screen, and a keyboard and swivel chair. And in the far corner was another chair, this one in front of a table that held the radio set, which was squawking insistently.

Maddox was calling, and he sounded irritated, even anxious, which was uncommon for him.

"Come in, boss. It's urgent! Come in!"

Baeza sat at the table and clicked the receiver. "I'm here, Simon. Have you found something?"

"Yes, I have, sir, and it isn't good."

While Maddox was providing an explanation of what he'd found, Calvo entered the office. His face paled as he overheard.

"That's unfortunate," said Baeza, gesturing for Calvo to sit in the swivel chair.

Baeza went on, "We have contingency plans for next of kin, I believe. We've never had to put them into effect before but —"

Calvo signed *no, no, no* frantically with his hands.

"Next of kin?" Maddox repeated. "I don't like the sound of that, sir. What about the body?"

"Dispose of it with the others. We can't have the police anywhere near here investigating a death!"

Calvo gave the thumbs up sign.

Maddox said, "That is what I'd intended, sir. Rudolf was careless. He shouldn't have been surprised so easily."

Baeza said, "What do the signs at the scene tell you?"

"One or two targets strangled him from behind, as I told you just now."

"Do you know who did this?"

"No. That's the puzzle. It might have been the Syrian and the Iraqi, or then again it might have been the Leon bloke, but I don't know for sure, as the footprints are all a mess. Trouble is, you see, the chopper's rotors messed with the immediate vicinity."

"That's a pity, Simon."

"I'll check beyond the downdraft perimeter. There may be a trail to follow. Out."

Closing the connection, Baeza turned to Calvo. "This is not good. Not good at all."

Calvo put his device beneath his mandible. "But how?" It came out as a screeching croak. Plaintive, confused.

"Neither the who nor the how is important, Ramon. The important thing is we must arrange something to account for Rudolf's disappearance. Elsewhere."

He moved over to the computer and switched it on. When the screen lit up, he keyed in instructions, and finally found what he wanted. "See." He pointed to the image of a signed document.

"His wife isn't the next of kin," Calvo observed.

"That's right. He has named his secretary, Anna."

"How does that help us?"

"She won't be expecting his return for a couple of days yet. When the time comes, we get in contact with her, tell her Rudolf has wired a lot of money to her bank and she is to wait for him in, say, Rome."

"She won't believe it."

"The money will keep her quiet. She can't make a fuss or she'll have to explain about receiving the money."

"What about the wife?"

Baeza snorted. "She'll learn that he ran off with his secretary. Never to be heard from again!"

Calvo licked his lips in thought. "It might work."

"We can make it work. We have time to plan it. But for now, I'm more worried about what else Simon will find."

———

SIMON MADDOX TOOK his Enfield rifle from the bracket in the helicopter cabin and moved out, treading with care, examining the area as he went.

Fresh sweat soaked the back of his neck. His shirt clung

to him thanks to the exertion of carrying the two corpses to the helicopter.

Whoever had strangled Rudolf might be lying in wait. They had the German's rifle, after all.

Within a couple of minutes he found the approach tracks made by Rudolf's attackers. Now it was beginning to make sense. Two of them, a coordinated assault. Logic told him that the nearest pair would be as he'd guessed: the half-breed Leon and the Nigerian woman.

Grudgingly, he admitted that they'd done well. Not only did they creep up on Rudolf but they killed the poor unsuspecting bastard.

Next, further along, he found the tracks of the Iraqi woman which joined those of the other two.

Soon, he detected where the three left the area—heading almost directly due south. Dried blood spots showed on a couple of stones, he noted.

Then, on the right, he was surprised to spot additional tracks. These were combat boot imprints and indicated that the Yank called Quint was on their tail.

Studying the tracks, he relaxed, knowing the three fugitive targets wouldn't linger to pose a threat but would have moved away, doubtless concerned about the pair's own nominated hunter, Quint.

He pursed his lips in thought. He had a choice: go after them now or collect and bag more bodies.

By rights, Leon and the woman were Quint's prey.

Maddox decided on the spot: he'd leave them to the Yank. Pick up their corpses later.

He returned to the aircraft and stowed the rifle.

The pilot discarded a half-smoked cigarette. "What now?"

"We continue as planned. One extra body isn't going to matter. There's plenty of room. So let's go and bag more corpses!"

Chapter 20

Rogue prey

With Ramon Calvo standing beside him, Baeza bit his lower lip as he stood leaning on the rail, looking out from the veranda. Their gin and tonic glasses were half full on a small table. He'd needed a stronger drink than wine: the death of Rudolf was troubling. Worse, though, he was worried by the absence of anyone returning with a trophy hand.

On all previous hunts there'd been no problem. The clients had slain their targets by mid-afternoon at the latest. He glanced at his fob watch and then peered down the slope, beyond the numbered posts.

Despite their heated arguments, he cared a great deal for Vanda. In every way she was his match, a strong wilful woman. True, he wandered, but none of the other women ever satisfied him like her, though that Nigerian had come close. He was a fool to cheat on her, he supposed, but it was in his nature, in his blood. His father had been the same.

Then he was jolted, yanked from his thoughts.

Movement at the edge of the greenery caught his eye, alerted him.

Finally, the bearer of a trophy!

The bushes were pushed aside and not one but two people emerged from the foliage.

His breath caught in his throat. *Madre de Dios.* Seconds earlier he'd been thinking of her—and now...

He pointed. "Look! Isn't that Vanda?" His mouth went dry.

Someone was beside her. The way they were moving. Something was wrong.

Calvo raised his electrolarynx device to his throat. "Who's that with her?"

Baeza squinted. "The American, I think... Harley!"

"Yes, I can see now. At last—a hunter with a trophy!"

This didn't feel like a time to celebrate, Baeza thought.

Harley was supporting Vanda. The pair slowly stumbled up the slope.

"Trophy be damned!" Baeza snapped. "They're in trouble!"

Seconds later, the pair had reached the numbered posts.

Must go to her! Heart pounding, Baeza lumbered along the veranda and hurried with an ungainly gait, descending the steps. By the time he reached the ground, he was puffing, but he didn't ease his pace.

He heard Calvo trailing behind him, panting, coughing and spluttering.

Baeza hurried across the open space and reached the pair. Immediately he went to Vanda's other side and helped support her. She didn't recognize him, her eyes seemed glazed. "Vanda, my dear, it's Francisco," he whispered, the words catching in his throat. Her complexion was pallid, and now her eyelids drooped, unresponsive.

Between them, they walked Vanda towards the hacienda steps.

On reaching them, Calvo fumbled with his throat device, and wheezed, "Harley, you're the first back. Congratulations."

"Gee, thanks."

Calvo pointed to Harley's head. "What happened to you?"

Harley groaned. "Oh, that. My targets fought back."

Calvo exchanged an anxious look with Baeza.

"That's never happened before," Baeza said.

Harley brandished a hand that was covered in dried blood and threw it to the ground. "Make no nevermind. I beat them!"

Vanda murmured something unintelligible; it sounded like "cousin."

By now Baeza was alarmed: she appeared seriously unwell, her face beaded in sweat.

Baeza demanded, "Harley, do you know what happened to her?"

"She was bit by a snake," Harley said. "Before our paths crossed."

Vanda moaned, clutching at her belly, writhing in their grip.

"She's been sick twice," Harley added. "I reckon she's in a bad way."

"I can see that!" Baeza swore. "You shouldn't have let her walk!"

"Hey, I couldn't carry her all the way here!"

Baeza shook his head and trailed a hand across his face. "No, you are right. I am very worried, though. Quickly, we must take her to her room."

Manhandling her, Baeza gleaned pleasure from the looks of surprise on the faces of both Calvo and Harley as he lifted Vanda in his arms. He knew from their many previous frolics that she wasn't too heavy, and he was strong, but even so it was strenuous work and he broke into a sweat. Yet he managed, carrying her the remaining distance towards the veranda and up the steps.

They followed as he crossed the veranda and elbowed open the double doors and entered the hall foyer.

"This way." Baeza indicated the door on the left. "Quickly, Ramon!"

Calvo stepped in front of him and swung it open.

A double bed was set against the far wall, the sheets in disarray. Baeza gently lowered her onto it. Then he knelt at the bedside and brushed a trembling hand over her perspiring brow. He peered behind him at Calvo. "Ramon, there's antivenin in the kitchen fridge. Go, please and get it!"

"Yes, yes, of course." Calvo rushed out.

He shouldn't be too long, Baeza thought. The elevator to the basement, then a dash to the kitchen, and back again.

Harley said, "You're prepared for snakebites?"

"Yes," Baeza replied. "A year or so ago one of our clients disturbed a snake. His description of it suggested it was a horned viper—the Lateste's viper. He reacted badly and died as he was being airlifted to the hospital. I didn't want a repeat of that. So we shipped in antivenin for the species. The death of a client is bad for business."

"Hell, yeah, it sure is. Talking of clients," Harley added, glancing at the door, "what's happened to the others?"

Calvo rushed in, breathless, with a hypodermic and an ampoule.

"Well done, my friend." Baeza snatched them from him.

"As you will have gathered, Harley," Baeza went on as he prepared the hypodermic, "you're the first to return. I must admit we had expected one of you long before now." Expertly, he injected the anti-venin into Vanda's arm. She whimpered weakly. "Maddox has taken the helicopter to collect the bodies and he will also locate your two fellow hunters."

"You bring the bodies of the targets here?"

"No, that would not be sensible. We deposit them in a gorge some kilometers to the south. Fresh food for the wild boar."

Harley puckered his brow and then, shiftily, he eyed Baeza. "You said *two* hunters? Shouldn't that be three—Rudolf, Quint and... your guy, Orton?"

Rising to his feet, Baeza put the empty hypodermic on the night table. "Unfortunately, Rudolf was slain. We assume he was killed by that police spy, Leon."

"What!" Harley roared. "Hey, I don't like the sound of

that, Señor. When I paid for this little caper, I didn't expect to be hunted by rogue prey!"

HARLEY WAS MOLLIFIED when Baeza clapped him on the shoulder and said, "I've heard Simon say that he always enjoys the company of a woman after a kill. You would, too, no?"

"Yes." Harley had to admit that he felt horny. Truth was, if Vanda had been fit, he'd have enjoyed her warm company, rather than excitable "number six" or one of Baeza's other comfort women. Sure, Vanda was Baeza's woman, but hell, right now he'd be happy to kill for her! Killing could become addictive, he realized. Still, Vanda wasn't in any shape to fight over. For the present he settled on the offer. "I guess I might like that, Señor Baeza."

"Good. I will arrange for two women to entertain you in your room."

"Two?" Harley tendered a politician's grin, oozing sincerity. "I sure as hell like this arrangement. I'd prefer to shower first, though."

Baeza chortled. "Let the women shower with you."

"Yeah! Why not?"

A while later, as arranged, Harley entered the lounge/dining room, feeling clean, debauched, smug and flushed. He puffed on a cigar.

Baeza was already there and gave him a glass of thirty-year-old Sanchez Romate brandy. "You have had a good shower?"

"Thanks. I did. Real good. Especially appreciated the help from the ladies."

Baeza smirked briefly and then his features grew serious as he raised his glass. "I want to thank you for bringing Vanda back. It is very probable that you have saved her life."

"Glad to." Harley puffed on his cigar. "How is she?"

"On the road to recovery. The antivenin is doing its good work. She is sleeping now."

"That's sure a relief." Harley sipped the dark mahogany colored liquor. A rich plummy flavor. "Nice—as good as any French cognac, Señor Baeza."

"Thank you." Baeza inclined his head. "I thought the occasion warranted celebrating with our best."

Mateo entered the lounge carrying his laptop. "You wanted to see me, Señor Baeza."

"Yes." Baeza waved a hand at Harley. "Credit this client with the agreed rebate."

"Sí, Señor." Mateo placed the laptop on the dining table, opened it and tapped on the keypad. Then he turned to Harley. "Please to sign in your password. Then the funds can be released to you."

"Sure." Harley put down his glass and sauntered over to the table. With his cigar hand, he keyed in his code.

Mateo completed the transaction. "It is done, Señor Baeza."

"Good. Now, leave us, Mateo."

"Sí, Señor." Mateo exited.

Harley turned. "Thanks for that, Señor Baeza."

"It is your right, as I stipulated at the beginning. You were the first to return with your trophy. I am a man of my word."

Harley raised his glass and beamed. "I appreciate that."

"And, even if you had not been first, I would have authorized an additional rebate for you since you brought Vanda back to me. I will be forever grateful to you, good sir."

Chapter 21

Cold blood

Leon reckoned they'd been on the run for about six hours and in that time they must have covered at least twenty kilometers, allowing for stoppages. By now the sun was directly overhead and hotter than ever.

They came to a slight depression which slanted to the edge of the gorge. From here he spotted a narrow steep track, possibly a goat trail worn into the side that descended into the gorge. At the start of the track there was a cluster of old hoof-prints which, he reckoned, belonged to a donkey. The greenery in the gorge would offer protection from the sun and, more to the point hide them from any probing helicopter.

Gingerly, they made their way down. A short way along, he noticed a series of mesh nets strung across the gorge and festooned with foliage. Typical camouflage. Puzzling.

The sudden temperature drop was an abrupt relief and most welcome as they stepped into the shadow cast by the walls of the gorge.

He licked dry lips. And his stomach rumbled, which wasn't surprising, since all he ate yesterday was a light breakfast at the airport, and today's half-tin of sardines and beans was not exactly fulfilling.

His nose twitched and his stomach roiled at the rank

stink of human habitation that wafted on a light breeze that funneled through the gorge.

Stopping, he pulled out the water bottle and offered it to Daraja. "I'm baffled by that netting," he whispered. "So let's take a good swig in case we need to start running."

She held the bottle to her lips but didn't raise it. He was impressed that she caught on so fast when she answered in a subdued voice, "You don't expect trouble, do you?"

"No, but if we're going to ask our bodies to move fast, we need a little refreshment now." He shrugged. "I'm just being cautious."

"Okay. So far your cautiousness has kept us free—and alive."

Her forthright attitude appealed. He was eternally grateful he'd been paired with her.

She drank, her throat moving with the water intake. He peeled his eyes away from her and surveyed the area beneath the camouflage netting.

The deep cleft in the earth was wide. About fifty meters ahead he glimpsed what resembled shanty dwellings on the floor of the gorge, a short distance before a bend.

Children's voices carried, bouncing off the rock walls. Originating some distance further along.

She said, "That doesn't sound too threatening." She passed him the bottle.

He took a gulp of lukewarm water, rinsed his mouth and swallowed. His stomach rumbled again. Screwing on the top, he replaced the bottle and then removed the rifle's magazine and pocketed it.

"Why'd you do that?"

"Don't want a loaded gun near children, do we?"

"No, I suppose not."

Cagily, he cast about and then saw a cluster of bushes in the gorge wall on their right, growing out of a small dark cleft. He unslung the backpack and thrust it in there with the bow.

She said, "What are you doing now?"

"I've carried that for quite a few hours." He pointed at the shacks, adding, "I'm not making a gift of the contents to anybody."

The corner of her mouth curved. "I understand. It pays to be distrustful."

"It does."

"And besides," she said, straight-faced, "later on that stuff might be useful."

He offered her a grin in reply.

————

MADDOX THOUGHT that all the targets should have reached this far south by now. He directed the pilot to veer right, to make a beeline west. The helicopter hovered at sufficient height that he could study the ground without the downdraft disturbing the vegetation and soil cover.

He identified what he surmised was Quint's trail, heading south. After all, Quint had no reason to disguise his tracks. Good. That confirmed his theory: the American dentist was after that pair, the half-breed and the Nigerian, plus the Iraqi woman in tow. He told the pilot to change tack slightly, to the south-west, and he began searching for the number three targets.

It didn't take long to locate a body.

Damn! Yet another hunter!

This one was in pale gray and white camouflage clothing, which he recognized.

What the hell's going on?

He told the pilot to land sufficient distance away to preserve the scene and any spoor that might prove significant.

As soon as the engine shut down, he unbuckled. This time he didn't bother worrying about an ambush. He left the rifle in the cabin, quite content with his holstered Webley. Careful not to spoil any existing tracks, he sprinted towards the body. He knelt and heaved it over, already knowing that it was Orton.

Surprise—or shock—was etched in his fellow Englishman's face.

He examined the solitary wound. A heart shot.

Unsheathing his hunting knife, he slid the blade into the wound and dug deep. Eventually he extracted the bullet: a 7.62 x 51mm slug. He wiped the blade, the bullet and his hands on Orton's jacket.

A quick check of the fallen rifle revealed the magazine contained its original five rounds. Orton's surprise must have been total. The machete was still sheathed on Orton's belt.

Evidently, Orton was killed in cold blood. But by whom? Orton's prey? Unlikely. And there was no way that fellow Leon could have done this; his tracks were too far away and led further south.

He glanced over his shoulder at the surrounding undergrowth, an unwelcome prickly sensation on the back of his neck. He rubbed his neck with a hand. Don't be so paranoid, he told himself.

Carefully, he scrutinized the ground, and confirmed that tracks made by the two targets were clear enough, heading south—in the direction of the gorge some miles away. Judging by the temperature of the body, the age of the targets' tracks and the fact that they were underneath the corpse, Orton was slain *after* the fleeing pair had left the scene.

More tracks indicated other boot impressions, and their approach was from the west. The tread size told him it was male. So Orton's killer had to be Harley, not Vanda.

He returned to the helicopter and with the pilot's help Orton was placed inside a body bag, which they carried between them to the aircraft.

Maddox then got onto the radio to update Baeza.

After he'd explained, he ended, "I can't be certain, but the indications are that Harley killed Orton. In cold blood."

Baeza's room door was ajar and Harley had been about to knock and enter when he heard the crackling of the radio. A politician down to his follicles, he let curiosity get the better of him and silently slipped inside. He scanned Baeza's bedroom quickly. Despite the lingering flush of after-love-making with those two women, he was struck by a pang of jealousy, to think Vanda cavorted with Baeza on this king-size bed. Shaking his head to clear it of salacious thoughts, he checked the rest of the room: a Picasso print of *Guernica* on the wall above the headboard, a sideboard, nightstand, a Van Gogh print of *Sunflowers* on the far wall, a door leading to a bathroom, and, on the far side, a second door, which was open. The sound of the radio came from in there.

Standing just inside the room he could see Baeza sitting at the radio station, gripping the receiver so tightly his knuckles were white.

Harley's stomach lurched as he clearly heard Maddox's voice: "I can't be certain, but the indications are that Harley killed Orton. In cold blood."

Oh, fuck!

After a lengthy beat, Baeza said through gritted teeth, "That isn't how the game is played. We have gone to great pains and considerable expense to obtain suitable targets. We do not want our clients killing our staff!"

Maddox's laugh sounded tinny on the radio. "Not the ideal TripAdvisor customer feedback you want, is it?"

"Do not be flippant, Simon. This is serious."

"Yes, of course it is, boss. Any sign of Harley or Vanda?"

"*Sí.* Harley got here almost carrying Vanda."

Guardedly: "Harley's with you now?"

"Not in the room, but yes, he is here at the hacienda."

"What are you going to do with him?"

"We can confront him when you return with your accusation. Until then, he can remain in ignorance, no?"

"If you say so, you're the boss. Excuse me, but did you say he was "carrying" Vanda?"

"I did. She has been bitten by a snake."

"Oh, that's bad luck. You've administered the antivenin?"

"Yes, of course!"

"Keep your shirt on, boss."

"I am concerned for her wellbeing. That is all."

"I realize that."

"You will continue to retrieve the corpses and dump them?"

"Yes. By my reckoning, I have six targets to pick up yet. Couples numbered three, four and five."

"What about the female half of number one?"

"All indications are that she went off with the Leon guy and the Nigerian woman."

"Ah, I see. Are you going to track them down?"

"I think Quint's on their trail. Let's be honest, Quint's done this before, knows the terrain. I expect he'll catch them and dispatch all three."

"You will make sure, though?"

"Yes, of course. I'll check after we've dumped whatever bodies I can find. Then we'll do a broad sweep and see if we can spot the others before they get away."

"They will not get far in this heat," Baeza said, wiping his brow. "The nearest civilization is over forty kilometers away."

Harley had heard enough. It sounded like he wouldn't face any repercussions concerning Orton's death until the helicopter returned. Couldn't bluff it out, or call it an accident; he had no excuse to be on Orton's trail.

But what could they do, even if they could prove it? They couldn't call the police, that's for sure.

Still, it might be prudent to pack a bag.

Before he vamoosed, however, he wanted to see Vanda and check on her.

Chapter 22

Cave house

As Leon and Daraja reached the floor of the gorge, the additional shade from the overhead camouflage netting proved even more welcome, though the trapped hot air meant it felt more humid.

Further along were silhouettes that resembled people amidst a strange other-worldly forest of odd shapes.

"Be careful," Leon whispered, "we don't know how they feel about strangers."

"I can't blame them if they want to stay here," she said. "At least it's cooler."

They moved closer, warily, and now the weird creations loomed, constructed from a hodgepodge of metal parts: Leon recognized bits of a fridge, sections of bicycle frames and poles from scaffolding or maybe children's swings, all forming sinister deformed winged creatures, misshapen humans, and lanky aliens.

Strung between two vaguely humanoid formations was a washing line where a variety of clothes hung to dry, flapping in the breeze. And beyond them a donkey was tethered, grazing on sparse bunches of weeds. Nearby, but out of reach of the donkey, was a sizable vegetable patch and behind that a collection of nine small off-white wooden crosses planted in the earth. A pet cemetery? Crosses signified that whoever lived here must be religious after a fashion, at least.

To one side of the cemetery was a circle of stones and suspended above them was a wooden trestle with a rope dangling into the center of the stones.

Leon moved closer, said, "It's an illegal well."

Daraja said, "Makes me even thirstier just seeing it."

"It's estimated there about a million of them throughout Spain. Some less obvious than this one, simply boreholes in the ground, maybe twenty or more meters deep, tapping into the water table. As they're unregulated, they seriously deplete the water reserves. And, they can be dangerous. It's not unknown for children to stumble into them and perish."

At mention of children, he was surprised to see seven youngsters of assorted ages and physique step out from behind the metal sculptures. Beneath pronounced brows the children's eyes peered with blatant curiosity. Their clothes appeared to be made from flowery brown and gray curtain material, whether blouses, skirts, shirts or trousers: making him mindful of deprived escapees from *The Sound of Music*.

Daraja said, "At last, civilization."

"I don't think this is civilization as we know it."

The children stared directly. A couple of the older girls shuffled to one side, both of them with a crooked gait, their eyes never leaving Daraja.

Almost at once Leon detected the similarities in their facial characteristics. More than one had squinting or misaligned eyes. Among them was a young pregnant girl. She seemed too slight and short to even be a teenager yet. A blind infant clung to her skirt. Two babies were being nursed by young girls.

A short distance behind them stood shacks constructed from sheets of corrugated metal, mold-covered hardboard, and paint-spattered tarpaulin drapes.

They'd stumbled upon an isolated small shanty town.

Higgledy-piggledy, mildewed old fridges and rust-pocked

ovens littered an area beneath the right-hand wall of the gorge, doubtless the raw material for more bizarre sculptures.

Cut into the left side of the gorge was a door flap in the form of a gray-brown blanket. At that moment it was swept aside and a stocky bearded man in his forties or fifties emerged.

"Welcome to my home," the man said, his Spanish delivered gruffly. He was short, muscular with broad shoulders, and possessed a broken nose and long greasy unkempt curly black hair streaked with gray and tied in a short ponytail. He swept an arm in the direction of the children, his forearm covered in thick black hair. "I am the patriarch of this family." He moved to face Leon and held out a hand in greeting. "Manuel. Manuel Esquiva Ramirez."

"I'm Leon and this is Daraja." He shook hands. The grip was firm, strong, and no-nonsense. "We've got ourselves lost."

Manuel's thin lips peeled back in a roguish grin, revealing sharp yellowed teeth. "Looks to me like you lost more than your direction." He chuckled, the sound rumbling from the barrel of a chest. His deep-set brown eyes glinted, candidly appraising Daraja. Then he ran a hand over his torn unbuttoned cotton shirt that revealed a hair-covered chest. "I mean, you lost most of your clothes as well." He sniggered at the jest, slapping hands against his careworn corduroy trousers.

Leon smiled briefly. "It's a long story, Manuel. Can we trouble you for a drink of water? We're parched."

A willowy woman in a multi-colored skirt and suede jacket ducked past the blanket to stand alongside Manuel. Her long black hair, also streaked with gray, was tied in a much longer ponytail down her back. Leon guessed she might be in her late thirties. She had high cheekbones. Her thin lips didn't offer a welcome.

"This is Trinidad," Manuel said, wrapping a possessive hirsute arm around her. He shook her playfully and eyed her knowingly for a second or two.

Trinidad nodded barely perceptibly. Narrow dark eyes weighing up both of them, she considered the chains dangling from their wrists. "I don't know where he has left his manners." Her voice was hoarse and deep, that of a heavy smoker. Still no welcoming smile. Holding aside the blanket "door," she beckoned to the mouth of the cave. "You are welcome. Come in, have a drink."

Leon didn't think she meant the "welcome" to be heartfelt and offered it under duress. No matter, both he and Daraja were definitely dehydrated. Go with the flow.

Manuel said, "You'll have to leave your weapons outside. House rules." He made a beckoning gesture and a broad-shouldered man in his twenties came forward. He had small dark brown eyes and an askew nose. "My eldest son Antonio will look after them for you."

"No problem." Leon gave Antonio the rifle and then unbuckled the sheathed machete and handed him that, too.

Manuel studied Daraja for a short time and then nodded, as if satisfied.

Considering their minimalist clothing, it should be obvious they carried no other weaponry.

Awkwardly, as if familiar with the weapon, Antonio checked the rifle magazine. "It isn't loaded."

"I used my shells while hunting," Leon lied.

"It isn't loaded," Antonio repeated.

Leon said, "I know. Anyway, that seems the safest thing, with children about, don't you think?"

"Children, yes..." Antonio seemed agitated, even confused, and stood clumsily holding the rifle. "Children..."

"Go in, go on," urged Manuel agitatedly.

Leon stepped inside with Daraja by his side. Out of the corner of his mouth he whispered, "Stay alert."

Her brow wrinkled. "All right."

A clinging smell, perhaps of boiled chicken, assailed his nostrils.

Manuel entered after them. And the children followed, their eyes continually staring, as if these strangers were from another planet—which might not be too far from the truth, Leon mused.

The interior was lit by a couple of low wattage filament light-bulbs strung on the cave ceiling. The floor was flagged with mismatched ceramic tiles.

It was indistinct, but he heard the sound of a generator, somewhere in the back of the cave.

The place was furnished with an ancient flea-bitten two-seater sofa, a couple of armchairs exuding stuffing from their sides, a grumbling refrigerator, a chest freezer, a kitchen sink, and a wooden dresser stacked with crockery.

In the center there was a long wooden table, covered by a cloth with a hand-embroidered flowery-pattern. The table was flanked by two long benches with an upright carver chair at each end. Neither the kitchen cupboards nor the dresser harmonized, all jarred with different colors, design and handles. A cooking stove was linked by a rubber hose to a silvery butane gas cylinder. Bubbling on the hob was a large saucepan, very likely the source of the fatty smell that clung to the air.

Standing hip-shot next to the sink was a woman perhaps in her twenties. She wore a flowery green blouse and skirt—different curtain remnants, perhaps—and black pumps. She, too, had an askew nose and high cheekbones. Her narrow dark eyes studied Leon as if in confusion or dread. She brushed a hand through her long black curly hair and queried in a high-pitched voice, "Papá?"

"Josefa, these are our guests," Manuel said calmly.

"Oh." Her plump lips curved to reveal sharp teeth. "Welcome." She sounded only marginally more welcoming than Trinidad. Her gaze briefly lingered on Leon's partially uncovered torso and then flicked away, almost guiltily.

In this part of the cave at least they had no TV and no radio. That didn't bode well for communicating with the outside world.

Cut into the rock on either side were openings with ill-fitting wooden frames and doors, doubtless leading to living quarters for this rather large family. He counted five doors. That's a lot of digging out, he thought.

Most cave houses he'd been in only had an entrance that also served as the exit. Despite the gas stove and cylinder, fire risk was minimal. Even so, he felt uncomfortable. Instinct and training taught him to always consider an escape route.

He and Daraja stood by the dresser while the young children sidled past them, glowering.

Trinidad thrust a couple of tin mugs at them and then took a plastic bottle of water from the fridge, which grumbled and vibrated as she closed its door. She poured the water into the mugs.

Fleetingly, Leon wondered if he should have brought the bottle of potassium permanganate to purify the water. Too late now. He sipped it—refreshingly cool and he could detect no visible impurities. It was slightly bitter to the taste, but welcome. "Thanks."

Daraja drank hers and then lowered the mug. "Thank you. We really needed this."

As they drank, their chains had jangled.

"I see you've got a problem there, the pair of you," said Manuel. "I think I can sort it out for you."

Leon said, "As I mentioned, it's a long story."

"We won't pry, Señor. We are not prudes, either. We know people play strange sex games."

Daraja said, "It's nothing like that."

Manuel's chuckle rumbled. "As you say."

Antonio and another lad winked and leered.

Trinidad said, "Paco, Antonio, that's enough. Stop it!"

Paco was shorter than his brother, with narrow shoulders and a wiry frame similar to Trinidad's. He had misaligned eyes and a withered left hand.

"Leave them be, Trini," Manuel said. "They're just boys being boys." He went to the dresser and rummaged in a drawer. Finally, he held up a metal ring with a number of keys hanging from it.

Leon thought they resembled skeleton keys.

Manuel inserted several keys that seemed to fit but didn't work, fiddling repeatedly until at last he found a good match and unlocked Leon's shackle.

After Daraja's was unlocked, Leon said, "Thanks."

They both massaged their wrists.

Daraja said, "We're really grateful."

"Glad to help."

"How'd you get those?" Leon asked, indicating the keys.

Thrusting out his chest, Manuel gave a satisfied smile. "Made them all. Various sizes, quite useful. I have a small tool turning shack in the cave next door."

"He's good with his hands," Trinidad murmured gruffly, running her palms over her hips suggestively.

Antonio and Paco sniggered and she gave them a black look, which instantly made them desist.

Manuel said, "She means I trained in metalwork. A long time ago, mind you. In Barcelona."

Leon said, "We noticed your sculptures outside. Unusual." He disliked most so-called modern art, whether painting or sculpture, believing there was a strong hint of the emperor's new clothes about a lot of it. No harm in being polite to hosts, though.

"I scavenge most of the stuff from the communal bins."

Trinidad added boastfully, "He sells some of his sculptures to the village."

"My Trinidad's no slouch, either," Manuel barked, smacking her behind. "She's an excellent seamstress. She embroidered that tablecloth and makes all the children's clothes!"

"So we see," Daraja observed with a fleeting smile.

With a swagger of her wide hips, her ponytail flicking left and right, Trinidad moved to the stove. She stirred the pot, and said over her shoulder, "We don't have much but you're welcome to share our meal."

Knowing looks passed between the family members. It was as though they all held their breath in anticipation of an answer.

"We rarely have guests," Manuel added. "It would be an honor."

Leon swallowed the rest of the water. "Thanks. We appreciate the offer." Yet in truth his stomach squirmed at the smell of whatever sickly sweet concoction Trinidad was cooking on the hob. But they'd be foolish—and disrespectful —to refuse the hospitality. They still had a long way to go to that village he'd seen and needed to keep their strength up. "That's generous of you."

"You can stay the night if you wish." Manuel indicated a door on the left. "It's our guest room."

Guest room? I thought they didn't get many guests.

"Thanks for the thought." Leon bowed slightly. "I know it sounds ungrateful, but we should be getting on as soon as we've eaten."

A fleeting look passed between Manuel and Trinidad.

"That's a pity," Manuel said.

"People will be wondering where we are," Leon explained. Then an idea struck him. "Do any of you have a mobile phone?"

"No." Manuel held his sides and laughed. "We like to keep ourselves under the wire."

Continuing to stir, Trinidad giggled. "That's us. Off the grid."

And Antonio repeated, "Off the grid..."

CHAPTER 23

GUEST ROOM

HARLEY TENTATIVELY KNOCKED ON VANDA'S DOOR and opened it when her faint voice called, "Come in!" She lay fully clothed on the bed, head and shoulders raised on two pillows. Despite her condition, he couldn't deny he was attracted to her physically. Her complexion was still wan. But her toasted brown eyes lit up and her thin lips curved with pleasure on seeing him. He was encouraged: she seemed genuinely glad he was there.

He said, "Hey. Okay to talk, is it?"

She nodded.

After shutting the door he walked to her bedside. "How're you feelin'?"

"I'm a bit woozy." Her brow wrinkled slightly. "Why are you here? You are our client. I don't know if Francisco would approve."

Harley dismissed Francisco's non-approval with a shrug. "I was concerned and wanted to see how you were."

"That is most considerate of you. I think I will survive." Her trembling hand clasped his, warm, gentle. Her eyes were welcoming, the lashes long. "Thanks to you."

"Gee, that was nothing." He liked the idea that she hadn't let go of his hand. "Glad we stumbled on each other."

"Me, too. Stumbled is right!" She raised an eyebrow. "You seem troubled, Harley."

"Has Baeza been to visit you yet?" He could feel a pulse in the heel of her hand, and it sent his own racing.

"Not that I am aware of. But he might have been here while I slept, of course."

"Yeah, sure."

"I am grateful for your concern, Harley." She squeezed his hand. "Now, tell me, what is it about Francisco?"

"I'm a mite worried…"

"Worried? In what way?"

"I reckon he thinks I killed Orton."

She let out a gasp and finally released his hand, raised two fists to her heaving chest. "Orton's dead?"

"Yes, that's what I overheard Maddox say on the radio."

"That is terrible. He seemed healthy. Do we know what caused his death?"

Lying came easy. He'd been a politician long enough, it was second nature. "He was shot, so says Maddox."

"That is worrying. I assume he was shot by one of us, the hunters?"

That seemed logical, naturally, since none of the targets carried guns. She may be "woozy," he reckoned, but she was still firing on all cylinders. He admired that in her, too. "I don't know," he replied. "Maddox isn't back yet. Maybe he'll tell us more when he flies in."

"But why does Francisco think you killed Orton?"

He lifted his shoulders and instantly remembered his wife had told him more than once that this action belied his sincerity. But Vanda wasn't his wife—and hadn't shared his bed yet. "Maddox found Orton's body. Put two and two together and made five." Dramatically, he slid a hand over his face. He couldn't summon tears at will like some consummate politicians, but his voice did manage a convincing croak. "And I sure don't want a fake murder charge lodged against me!"

Her hand gripped his tightly, giving his a reassuring

squeeze. "He can't very well go to the authorities." She paused, her eyes burning into him. "Did you—did you kill Orton?"

His free hand on heart, he lied: "No way, of course not!"

Her hand fell away from his. "Then you have nothing to worry about. Simon was probably a bit jealous of Orton. They are both English, but so different, you know?"

"Yeah, the English are a strange breed."

Her long eyelashes fluttered. "Orton is—was likable. He was amusing, joked about his accountant occupation. Simon isn't likable at all, he is full of himself. He is a predator. He enjoys killing for its own sake."

"Ah, killing..." He grinned at her, sensing his pulse race at the memory of shooting Orton. "Well, I sure see how blood lust can dominate!" *Isn't that the truth?*

She said, "You can, can you?"

He licked his lips, and finally answered, surprised at how sincere he was at this moment: "Until today, I suppressed my anger. Maybe I needed a shrink. Wife and mother-in-law were grinding me down. The divorce business has been taking its toll. You know, they both want to take me to the cleaners."

"Until today, you said?"

"Yeah. Making those kills. It changes a man—or woman, I guess, eh?"

"Yes." She giggled, her gaze fading into an indeterminate distance as if remembering her own kills. "It does, doesn't it?"

"Of course, I forgot. You got to stand in for that Leon fella, didn't you?"

"Yes. And it was *most* satisfying. As you say." She gave a start. "Do you know what happened to Leon? Has Quint returned with his trophy?"

She must really have hated the Leon guy.

He said, "Nobody but us has come back yet. And Francisco has already paid me the trophy rebate."

"Oh." She sounded disappointed. "I am pleased for you," she added in what seemed an afterthought.

Her lids flickered, and then lowered.

"Hey, you need to rest." Impulsively, he leaned towards her and planted a kiss on her forehead, which was dry and warm, not feverish. "I'll leave you for now. Drop by later, honey, okay?"

"Mmm, I would like that. Mmm..."

———

LEON AND DARAJA were led into the "guest room" by Josefa and then she stopped at the door, said, "We will knock for you when the food is ready." She left, shutting the door behind her.

This room was furnished with a double bed covered with clean sheets and a metal headboard and footboard, a single ladder-backed chair against the wall, a sideboard, and on the bedside table an empty brass wash basin and brass jug of water. The walls and ceiling were bare rock. A large cockroach scuttled into a crevice, hiding. The floor was untiled, bare earth compacted by constant use—by guests?

Not having eaten much, Leon felt weak, but he knew it would pass.

"Is it safe to stay here?" Daraja asked. "Won't Baeza track us?"

"It depends on what, if anything, they've learned so far. The threat of discovery is real. But there's no getting away from the fact that we need food to sustain us—more than a can of beans and a tin of sardines can provide—if we're to keep up our strength."

"Well, the smell of food in there got me salivating."

He grimaced. "It doesn't smell too appetizing to me, but we should be grateful, I suppose."

"They are poor. It is good of them to offer us their food."

"Yeah, you're right."

"And then," she said, "after the meal we leave, right?"

"Yes."

"Right, that suits me."

"You don't sound too happy about staying here."

"I'm not," she said. "I'll be glad to get to that village you're aiming for."

"Well, I guess it's a good twenty kilometers off—that's three or four hours' walk in this heat."

She said, "That long? I'm not looking forward to it, I must admit. And I'm not used to this much exercise... I—"

Raised voices outside the room interrupted her.

Maybe they were speaking in anger, though Leon knew only too well that his countrymen might sound like they're arguing when they're simply chatting vociferously and loudly. And they were as bad on their mobile phones. It sounded like the high-pitched voice of Josefa and the gruff tones of her father, Manuel.

Daraja gestured at the door. "Did you see how all of the children stared at us?"

"I did. They're just curious. As Manuel said, they don't get many strangers here in the gorge."

"That might be true." She quivered. "But they give me the creeps."

"I know what you mean." He lowered his voice. "I suspect there's been some inbreeding among them, too."

CHAPTER 24

FOGGY MIASMA

PEERING THROUGH THE HELICOPTER CABIN windshield, Maddox saw about twenty black crows flocking to the entrance of a ruined building, one of three derelict properties.

The birds were ideal detectors: usually, a murder of crows signified the proximity of a body—in this case, he mused, a very appropriate collective term.

He tapped the pilot's shoulder. "Let's investigate."

The helicopter hovered near the ruins, the rotors disturbing the crows, which took wing, finally roosting in a nearby solitary tree.

Once they'd landed and the engine was switched off, Maddox opened the door and clambered to the ground, gripping his Enfield rifle. "Keep alert!" he told the pilot.

"Yeah." The pilot patted his holstered revolver, rolled his eyes, and then pulled out a cigarette and lit it.

Warily, Maddox approached the buildings. It was simple enough to detect the three sets of footprints—all leading to the ruins.

A cursory check of the first and second buildings was all he needed because the tracks led beyond them to the third one.

He heard the flies first.

Rounding a corner, he saw the two bodies at once and immediately recollected they were the married couple from Morocco, targets allocated to the client called Harley. Still chained together. The woman was slumped on top of the man. Her hand had been cut off and wasn't lying anywhere near. Considering the amount of blood that had seeped into their clothing and the ground, she must have bled to death. He batted flies away and shoved the woman to one side. A quick examination of the man revealed he had sustained a compound fracture to the leg but had died from a bullet in the chest. Crows had already harvested their choice morsels and pecked out the eyes. The gruesome display didn't bother him, it was all too familiar.

Squinting against the sun, shading his eyes with a hand, Maddox watched the carrion birds. He was inclined to leave the bodies for the damned crows, but then he dismissed that idea as being too macabre. Besides, it would be careless. Somebody might spot the corpses here, yet once encased in body bags, they'd be lost from view in the gorge.

Turning on his heel, he made his way to the chopper.

The pilot said, "Everything all right this time?"

"Indubitably. What we've come to expect. By now I imagine Harley has turned up at the hacienda with his trophy. Just the two body bags this time. And the sack."

"Normality. That's a relief!"

Swatting at the flies, Maddox used his master key to release the shackles on the two deathly cold wrists and then put them in the hessian sack. Having done his bit for equipment recycling, he attended to Meriem first, the pair of them placing her in a black body bag. She was light, no problem. When the bag was zipped up, he slung her over his shoulder and hefted her to the aircraft while the pilot got busy bagging Jamal.

When Maddox returned to the death zone, Jamal was bagged and zipped. The pair of them lifted Jamal between them and carried him and soon dumped the bag on top of the others.

By the time they were through they were lathered, their shirts darkened by sweat.

Maddox said, "In future, we should bring a trolley, make life easier, eh?"

The pilot shrugged. "Most of the ground is too rough. It would be hard work pushing a trolley."

"You're probably right." Maddox studied the birds. It was as if they knew that they'd been deprived of their feast. Almost as one, they broke cover from the tree and flew high, swarming to the south-south-west.

Maybe they're heading for the other bodies?

Worth a try.

"Follow them," he told the pilot. "They may be after another feast."

———

A VARIEGATED ASSORTMENT of bowls was laid on the long table, each accompanied by a large spoon. Trinidad ladled into Leon and Daraja's bowls a watery broth that consisted of meat, potatoes, and green peppers. A little girl helped Trinidad with the serving of the broth and Leon noticed the child had seriously crooked legs so was forced to walk with an awkward gait. Accompanying the broth was fresh fluffy white bread which they learned had been baked by Josefa that morning.

Broth was not the best choice for a hot day, he thought, yet within the cave the temperature was much cooler. If he recalled correctly, cave houses retained a constant temperature of roughly eighteen degrees Celsius.

Trinidad, Antonio and Josefa sat opposite him and Daraja, while Manuel occupied the far end, at the head of the table. The other children filled the rest of the benches on both sides and, as the meal progressed, Manuel introduced them with evident pride.

Paco of the distinctive misaligned eyes and withered left hand was the youngest son aged eighteen and had long brown matted hair, a straight nose and jutting chin.

Eugenia was twelve, thin and gaunt, with long unkempt brown hair. She had a similar nose and chin to Paco and had buck teeth. When she spoke, she stuttered.

Remedios was thirteen and pregnant, which might account for the slump of her narrow shoulders. Despite her gravid state, she had a wiry frame. None of her features really set her apart, whether the untidy long black hair, the straight nose or the receding chin. She seemed to have difficulty hearing and her voice was loud and whining.

Maria Rosa was twelve, with broad shoulders and a surprisingly well developed physique for her age. Her hooked nose and high cheekbones were distinctive attributes. Her hooded black eyes squinted continually as if she had problems with her sight. She handled her knife awkwardly, Leon noticed, then realized why: her left hand only had two fingers and no thumb.

Lula was only eight, of slight frame and squinting eyes: "a wonderful helper."

They never learned the names of the three infants and two babies who were asleep in metal-worked cots.

As though ravenous, the children slurped the broth, breaking the bread, spreading crumbs everywhere. They constantly snapped at each other, the girls giggling, the boys snorting good humoredly. Trinidad paused in her eating a number of times, her face a radiant glow as she watched the children.

Leon chewed the stringy meat, which was salty and fatty, and forced himself to swallow it as it was essential sustenance. He was glad of the liquid part of the broth to wash it down. Out of the corner of his eye he saw that Daraja seemed happy enough with the food. Compared with the fare in the hacienda's basement cell, he supposed this was probably a gastronomic delight.

The uncomfortable feeling they'd remarked upon earlier

persisted. During the meal, many of the family kept eyeing him, as if he were a specimen in a jar. Then as he waylaid their interest, they'd look away, almost guiltily.

Leon made small talk while attempting to obtain useful information as to their whereabouts. "Are you not lonely here—wherever we are?"

Manuel gulped noisily from his spoon, and then wiped the hairy back of his hand against his gray-streaked mustache. "How could we be lonely? We have the family!"

Opposite, Leon apprehended a slight curl of distaste in Josefa's plump lips.

Trinidad said, "We live for our family."

"We prefer it this way." Manuel glared purposefully at his family. "Don't we?"

A chorus of "yes, Papá" rose up. But Leon noted that the lips of Eugenia and Maria Rosa remained sealed, not joining in the refrain. *Curious. Not quite happy families, then?*

Stroking his beard in thought, Manuel went on, "We have been living in this place for quite a few years. Nobody troubles us. It is ideal. We are almost self-sufficient."

Daraja said, "I saw the vegetable garden."

"That is all Paco's work. He has green fingers, which compensates for his left hand."

Paco said, "Thank you, Papá."

Leon offered with caution, "You appear to have an idyllic lifestyle." He tried not to stare at the pronounced jutting chin and buck teeth of Eugenia and Paco, or the misaligned eyes of Paco and Remedios.

Leon returned his attention to what Manuel was saying: "When we need things we cannot provide here, I will drive to the village with one of the children. It varies but we go about once a month. I will trade with the townspeople, buy neces- saries." He smiled benignly. "The girls fight for their turn to go with me, don't you?"

Mutedly, Josefa and Eugenia said in unison, "Yes, Papá."

Again, Leon noted a sour glare in Josefa's narrow dark eyes.

What didn't Josefa like? She was probably sulking, an overspill from her earlier argument with her father. Leon didn't much care. The prospect of getting a lift to the village from Manuel beckoned.

Leon said, "Really? The village? How far away is it?"

Manuel licked his lips. "Too far for you to walk today. Easily twenty kilometers."

Guessed right, then.

"How do you get your vehicle to the road from here?"

Shaking his head, Manuel said, "I don't. At the end of the gorge, about a half-kilometer away, I walk up a gentle slope. It's no hardship. No exertion in this heat, eh?"

Antonio interrupted, "Except when we have to carry your sculptures, Papá!"

"Aye, there is that. And when I bring material to work on." He gestured with his spoon, which dribbled broth onto the tablecloth. "The car is parked at the top."

"Is it safe to leave the car there?" Leon asked.

"Not a car. It is a pick-up." Manuel scooped the remains of the broth with a hunk of bread, and ate it. "Yes," he mumbled, spitting a few crumbs. "It is safe. I have made a sort of carport from brush and branches so it cannot be seen." He grinned broadly, tapping the side of his hooked nose. "The truck cannot be taken away, either—I take the rotor arm and distributor cap!"

"Very sensible," Leon conceded, forcing himself to spoon the final mouthful of sludge from his bowl and swallow it.

"Cannot be too careful." Manuel sniggered and winked at Antonio. "Many thieves about, you know."

Antonio said, "Thieves."

"Sad but true," Leon agreed.

Expelling a burp, Manuel shoved his empty bowl away. "After the meal, we always indulge in a libation, no?" He cast his gaze around the table and all of the family inclined their heads in accord.

The older children sniggered behind their hands.

Trinidad smacked Antonio's hand and glared at the others. "Stop that at once! Manners! We have guests!"

Leon raised an eyebrow. "Libation?"

"Yes." Manuel lifted a finger. "You must try a glass of our home-made liquor."

The studied look from all of them implied that to refuse would be considered a terrible insult. Despite his misgivings about their lifestyle, Leon appreciated that they had been hospitable. "Yes, it would be my honor to taste your liquor."

Rubbing his hands together, Manuel licked his lips in apparent anticipation. "Trini, my dear, the drinks, please."

Without saying a word, Trinidad rose from the table and sashayed to the kitchen sink, her pony-tail swishing. She rooted around in the dresser cupboard and brought out four mismatched glasses and a decanter of golden liquid and placed them on the kitchen counter by the sink. Her back to them, she poured and then turned, all smiles, and carried two brimming glasses for Leon and Daraja, which she stood on the table in front of them. She returned to the sink and poured two more, brought them for Manuel and herself. She sat and fondled her glass, a thin smile on her lips.

"What about us?" Antonio asked, smirking.

"Yeah, we're old enough!" That comment generated much amusement.

Trinidad scowled. "Later! We have guests. Be nice."

Antonio and Paco rolled their eyes. Eugenia giggled.

Manuel raised his glass. "Welcome, dear friends!" And he gulped the entire contents and then licked his lips and mustache.

"The same!" Leon drank half his glass. It was tart and yet sweet, but not unpleasant, and surprisingly smooth. It concealed the greasy aftertaste of the broth, too. "And thank you for the generous hospitality."

Trinidad said, "Think nothing of it."

Daraja sipped at her drink and then stood abruptly. "Is it okay if I put some water in mine?" Without waiting for an answer, she got up from the bench seat.

Trinidad was about to rise, but Daraja waved at her to stay seated. "Don't trouble yourself, I'll get it." She moved to the fridge and swung open the door.

Instead of lifting out a bottle of water, she took a step back and simply stared open-mouthed.

Trinidad exhaled heavily and got to her feet. "You shouldn't have done that." She hurried to Daraja's side.

Leon wondered why Daraja's face had taken on a shade of gray, as if it was drained of blood. The concern etched on her face was troubling, too.

He stood, anxious to investigate, but he found his legs were unexpectedly weak. He reached for the table top to steady himself and missed it, unavoidably sinking to one knee on the tiled floor.

A foggy miasma occluded his vision.

"Leon?" Dimly, the voice of Manuel penetrated: "Are you all right?"

Leon formulated a response, mumbling something, but couldn't hear or even decipher his own words.

Hazily, he sensed his body being helped to walk by Antonio and Manuel, their faces switching from shimmering blurs to recognizable identities.

"I—I... am not... well," he murmured.

"Sunstroke, perhaps?" Manuel's voice. Soothing. Or was it a mocking tone?

Manuel said, "If your wife wishes to throw you off a roof, make sure it's a low one."

Antonio said, "Too late for that advice, Papá!"

Leon was sort of walking between them. Helpful of them, his hosts.

Daraja, where was she?

Vaguely, he noticed the bed he'd seen earlier. When had he seen it? An age ago.

Hey!

Too rough to be friendly, they threw him onto the bed, and it creaked noisily in sympathetic protest.

Indistinctly, the voice of Daraja sounded in his ears, irate, voicing dissent.

And then—blank.

CHAPTER 25

LIVE SPECIMEN

As THE HELICOPTER HOVERED OVER THE WIDE crack in the earth, Maddox spotted a flock of black crows clustered round the floor of the gorge, just beyond the rickety old bridge he'd seen countless times. This lot might be the same birds they'd seen earlier. Or maybe not. It didn't matter. In this area, the killing zone, experience told him the birds were an unmistakable sign of more corpses.

Getting closer, the aircraft hovered above the bridge and the birds dispersed, flying to conceal themselves in foliage.

And then he saw the feast they'd abandoned: a body sprawled on the floor of the gorge—either Tabish or Yesal— and without a chain attached. Freedom at a price. But where was the other target?

There was no way the aircraft could descend into the gorge here. And he sure as hell wasn't going to climb down to retrieve that body. "Leave that one as carrion for the crows!" he told the pilot, pointing out the windshield.

"Good decision, sir!"

"Right. Let's go and dump these bloody body bags!"

"Right away, sir!"

The chopper lifted higher and followed the gorge, heading roughly westwards.

Maddox pondered upon the Afghan target's severed

wrist. Trapped animals had been known to bite off a limb in order to escape. This was no different, he supposed, though the biter must've had big teeth! Baeza wouldn't like it, though: it meant that one of the targets was running free.

His priority was to dump the corpses. He could then decide what to do next. Maybe get the pilot to search further south, from the other side of the gorge, in the hope of locating the runaway Afghan.

He sensed a fluttering in his stomach. It was a while since he'd done any hunting from a chopper. Always an exhilarating experience.

———

LEON'S HEAD THROBBED, but as he raised a hand to massage his aching temple, he realized he couldn't move either hand. His eyes opened and he noticed that his wrists were tethered with rope to the metal headboard, as if he was involved in a kinky sex game. But he knew this was no game. It was getting ridiculous, though, being captured twice in as many days! And the Rolex was missing—his second watch pilfered. His body seemed to have seized up, probably with lying here inactive for—how long?

He turned his head, which did nothing to improve the ache, and saw Daraja lying alongside him, her eyes closed, her chest rising and falling steadily. She too was secured to the bed. Their feet were tied to the metal footboard. She was still wearing her camisole, briefs and shoes, and he was in his boxer shorts and shoes. The jacket he'd taken from Rudolf was draped on the back of a chair against the far wall. There was no sign of the belt and machete.

Daraja shifted a little and opened her eyes. "How's the head?"

He looked askance at her. "It aches, just like a hangover. You?"

"I'm not so bad. I didn't drink much liquor. I went to get some water, remember?"

"Yes. I remember you opening the fridge. You appeared distressed."

"I was."

"What did you see in there?"

"Three severed human arms. Defrosting."

He nodded. "That explains the taste—"

Her eyes went wide. "How can you be so accepting? We ate the flesh of somebody!"

"I've been around, Daraja. Sadly, little shocks me these days."

"I was almost sick when I realized."

"Understandable. So, besides being incestuous, the Ramirez family are also cannibals."

"Where do they get the... meat?"

"Targets like us, I guess."

She shuddered. "Dear God, the thought of that makes me sick. Since I was taken, I've seen terrible things, but this..."

"I know. They seem to have shut themselves off from the modern world. I've heard about similar cases. There was a community not far outside Sydney, Australia, a few years back. About forty of them, all related, obsessed with sex." He studied her, concern in his tone. "They haven't molested you?"

"No. But I think it is only a matter of time."

Aware of aspects of her history, he understood how she could be so sanguine about her immediate future.

She jutted her chin at the ceiling. "They all scarpered and left us when a helicopter flew over a short while ago. But I don't doubt they'll be back soon."

"That explains why the chopper needs fuelling from the hacienda. I wonder if they were searching for us—or donating more bodies for the delectation of our hosts."

"Ugh!"

At that moment the bedroom door opened and Manuel entered alone. "Ah!" He shut the door and folded his arms. Leon noted that he was wearing the Rolex watch.

Manuel beamed. "You are conscious again!"

"Why have you done this to us?" Leon said. "We mean you no harm."

Chuckling, Manuel sat on the edge of the bed on Leon's side, near his hip. "You're being tracked down by the hunters from the big hacienda." He pointed vaguely in presumably a northerly direction.

Leon said, "Are you going to send us back to them? Is that your plan?"

"No, no, nothing could be further removed from my intentions." Manuel slapped a hand on Leon's bare shoulder.

Despite himself, Leon flinched. Was that slap to test the muscle tone, making an assessment for future taste, or plain exuberance?

Manuel said, "It is rare for us to meet a live specimen."

"You've seen plenty of the dead ones, though, haven't you?"

"Yes. I abhor waste." Manuel's gaze shifted, lingering on Daraja, and he licked his lips and mustache. "As you must realize by now, those bodies supplement our diet. Unfortunately, our freezer only has a limited capacity. As much as I hate it, a lot of it does go to waste—or to feed the wildlife."

"You haven't answered my question," Leon persisted. "Why drug us, why tie us like this?" Let's hope they weren't going to strip the fresh meat from us while we were alive. He'd heard of primitive cannibal communities doing that to their enemies.

"It did not go unnoticed that you studied my children with great interest, and doubtless noted that some of them have, what shall I call it, physical issues..."

"I noticed. But I'm no moral arbiter. That's your business—your family's business, not ours."

"So it is." Manuel rested a hand on Leon's chest, brushed his palm through the hair. A predatory touch, just like Vanda's. Manuel heaved a sigh. "It is unfortunate that to sate themselves they are inclined to mate with each other frequently."

Daraja said, "But they're your children. Why do you and your wife let them do that?"

"My wife?" Manuel chuckled. "You are mistaken, young woman. Trinidad is my sister. We, too, have urges. Always have." He stroked his beard and his deep-set eyes sparkled. "We satisfy them." He leered at Daraja. "My eldest children have expressed an interest in both of you. So you should feel honored." He rubbed his hands together. "It seems fortuitous that you have dropped in on us."

Leon said, "Why fortuitous?"

"My eldest daughter Josefa will mate with you, Señor. We will keep you here so you can copulate with all our females and so improve our gene pool enormously."

Leon gritted his teeth, then asked, "And my companion?"

"She can satisfy Antonio. To begin with. Then, afterwards, Paco, and perhaps even myself." He rocked back on his heels. "We are not racist, we would be happy to welcome a dark-skinned child into our family community."

This was insane. "You'll keep us here for nine months?"

Manuel said, "Or longer, possibly."

"But we'll get bed sores, our muscles will waste away in that time!"

"You will be allowed up to perform necessary functions and stretch the legs. One at a time. Be aware that the other will die should one of you attempt to escape." Manuel turned away, rose from the bed and clapped his hands. "Antonio, Josefa!"

The door swung open and the two of them entered.

Josefa's eyes evaded her father and Leon. She gazed on Daraja lingeringly. "I am ready, Papá," she said feebly.

"I am as well, Papá." Antonio slid his tongue over thin lips and leered at Daraja. He wore Rudolf's belt and the sheathed machete.

Manuel waved a hand at Leon and Daraja. "My children, they're all yours." He leaned a shoulder against the wall, clearly settling in to enjoy the show.

"Papá," Josefa said plaintively, "I don't want you to watch."

"Why not? I've done so before."

"That was different, Papá." She walked to him, at Leon's side of the bed. "It was with my brothers. Family! This is a stranger. And a captive."

Brushing two fingers on his mustache, Manuel chortled. "Enticing, no?"

"Papá, please!" She stamped her foot.

Easing himself off the wall, Manuel raised an eyebrow. "You understand what I want?"

Josefa lowered her eyes. "Yes, Papá," she said, but her tone was far from enthusiastic or even willing.

A little roughly, he held her chin, raised her head.

She glared at him. "I birthed Remedios, Papá—your daughter!"

"She is deficient, you know this!" He swirled a finger at his head. "She has silly moods just like Antonio!"

"Hey, my moods are not that bad!" Antonio objected. "Not bad, my moods…"

"Shut it, boy. This is between me and your sister!"

"Paco thought she was good enough to get pregnant, Papá!"

"He's a gardener," Manuel snapped, and let out a barking laugh. "He enjoys planting seeds!"

"As you know!"

"Aye, and look at the result. He gave you Lula!"

"Don't talk like that, Papá. Lula's a kindly soul."

Antonio said, "Papá, we've had these arguments before."

"I said be quiet, boy! You haven't done so well, have you? Eugenia, for God's sake!"

Josefa sobbed, "I was too young, Papá. You shouldn't have forced Antonio and me."

"Forced? Antonio didn't need forcing!"

Antonio said, "Hey, Papá, I love Josefa!"

"Ha, love? You lust after all your sisters!"

Josefa cried, "Papá!"

Ignoring her outburst, Manuel jabbed a finger at Josefa. "You know Eugenia doesn't have your looks or your good sense. She can barely speak properly! In fact you have not given us any *good* babies for years."

"I have tried. I've miscarried *eight* times."

"I know, and four of them were since the blind infant was born. You must understand, my girl, we need new blood. This is your *last* chance to show you are still fit to add to this family of ours."

"And if I disobey? Will you eat me, too?"

"Don't be absurd!"

"Well?"

"You will lose your status. A servant to all the family, a drudge. Eat meat? Hah! You will feed off our scraps!"

Her cheeks flushed. She lowered her gaze. "All right, you win, Papá. As usual. I will obey."

"Good." Manuel snorted. "I trust you don't object to Antonio having fun with this one while you obey me?"

She shook her head. "No, Papá. He is my brother and the father of our daughter."

"Am I not your father—and the father of our Remedios?"

Tears welled on the rims of Josefa's eyes. "Please, Papá, we've been through all that." She growled, "Go now!"

"Very well." Manuel shrugged. "I will leave you to it." He ambled to the door, abruptly swiveled round and raised a fist. "But the next time you use this man," he growled, gesturing at Leon, "I promise you, I *will* watch!"

Antonio giggled. "Go, Papá, go. Leave us to have a little fun!"

"That's my boy!" Turning on his heel, Manuel opened the door and left, slamming it shut behind him. Bits of rock crumbled at the jamb.

Leon watched, helpless. Pointless to struggle. He was more concerned for Daraja.

Antonio unsheathed the machete and approached Daraja. He slid the blade under her camisole.

She squirmed, her eyes hard, blazing.

The blade lifted sharply and cut the flimsy fabric, which fell to either side, baring her breasts. "Nice," Antonio whispered throatily, his small dark brown eyes glinting. "Nice." He moved two paces back to stand beside her midriff.

She was breathing heavily, stomach and chest rising and falling.

"Nice." His tongue poking between lips, Antonio tapped the blade against Daraja's black lace briefs.

———

MADDOX ENJOYED THIS PART IMMENSELY. While the pilot hovered over the gorge, Maddox slid open the door and peered down.

Strewn across a small area were black shapes that glinted in the sun. Body bags, many of which had been cut open. Moving among them were wild boar and rats and black crows, all feasting on the human remains. While the birds dispersed at the sound of the chopper, the boar and rats were unconcerned.

Maddox hauled the first bag to the lip of the deck and tumbled it out. It fell, head over heels, though he had no idea which was which, and landed amidst the older dead denizens.

The boar and rats flinched, moved a little, but continued their foraging.

One by one, he tipped the corpses out.

By the time he'd come to the last body bag, his thoughts turned to Quint and his prey. There'd been no sign of any of them. Assuming Quint had finally dealt with Leon Whoever, his female chained partner and the Iraqi target of Rudolf, then there was just the runaway Afghan to consider. Need Baeza know about that? It didn't matter one way or the other. It isn't my responsibility, after all, he told himself.

But there were still the two corpses—Quint's targets—to account for, so it might be worth a final sweep.

Sliding shut the door, he moved to sit next to the pilot. "How's the fuel?"

"We're good. What did you have in mind?"

"Let's do a final sweep. We've got three corpses unaccounted for."

"Three? I reckon on four."

"Just fly. I'll do the counting. Okay?"

"Certainly, Mr. Maddox. At once, Mr. Maddox."

Cheeky bastard!

CHAPTER 26

TAINTED FRUIT

SUDDEN MOVEMENT FROM JOSEFA DISTRACTED Leon.

In a swift unexpected action, Josefa picked up the brass water jug from the bedside stand and leaned over Leon and Daraja, swinging it hard at the side of Antonio's head.

Water splashed out of the jug as it made contact with Antonio's temple, soaking the faces of both Leon and Daraja.

The machete still in his hand, Josefa's brother slumped to the floor. He must have been unconscious because he made no sound or any further move.

Daraja swore. The blade had missed cutting into her flesh by inches.

"What the—?" Leon began but stopped.

Josefa put a finger to her lips.

"Hey, Antonio, sounds like you're having a good time, eh?" That was Paco's voice.

"He's riding her!" Josefa called, gripping the dented jug till her knuckles turned white.

"Well, tell him to hurry up, I'm ready right now!"

Girls giggled.

"Enough, Paco!" bellowed Manuel. "Be patient and leave them be!"

Pressing a hand against her chest, Josefa whispered to Leon, "I no longer want to be part of this family." She replaced the jug. She leaned close to Leon, narrow dark eyes intense, her voice hushed. "Will you help me escape?"

A no-brainer. "Yes, I'll help."

Josefa let out a huge breath. "Good." She walked round the bed to her unconscious brother and snatched the fallen machete. Swiftly, she cut the ropes tethering Daraja's wrists, and then her ankles. Returning to Leon's side of the bed, she cut his ropes as well.

Leon's muscles seemed to creak as he sat up. He needed to massage his entire body, he reckoned, but settled for his wrists.

"You will keep your promise?" Josefa said, still gripping the machete.

"Yes." He slid off the bed. "Where's my rifle?"

"It is against the wall by our cave entrance. Antonio said it is no use, it is without bullets."

"Your brother's not too bright, is he?" Leon lifted the jacket from the chair, shook it. The four bullets jangled. He slid his arms into the sleeves, put it on.

Daraja stood, in vain attempting to cover her breasts with the two sides of the slit camisole.

As quietly as he could manage, Leon lifted Antonio onto the bed and gestured at him. "Daraja, I think his shirt and trousers might fit you."

"They'll do." She began stripping Antonio. He wore purple Y-fronts; she left them.

Leon strapped on the webbing belt. Josefa handed him the machete, which he used to cut fresh lengths of rope to tie Antonio to the bed. A strip cut from a sheet served as a gag, in case he regained consciousness and wanted to raise the alarm.

"Not a good fit," Daraja said, pulling Antonio's trousers over her hips, "but they'll serve." The shirt's buttons fastened most of the way, but not higher than her cleavage.

While Josefa helped tie Antonio's feet, Leon asked, "What made you want to leave now?"

"This is the only chance I have had. When I was twelve, I had Remedios, sired by my father." Then she scowled at her unconscious brother. "When I was thirteen, I gave birth to Eugenia, the tainted fruit of my union with Antonio. Paco gave me Lula when I was seventeen. And one of the infants is mine, too, from yet another seed planted by Paco. I never named her and he has no time for her." She finished with the ropes and stepped back, arms akimbo. "I think I should be sterilized, I have no luck with children. Eugenia has a speech impediment, Remedios has much difficulty with her ears, Lula's legs are crooked and the infant is blind."

"Those deficiencies may be caused by the incest—inbreeding," Leon offered. "With the right man you could give birth to a baby with no problems."

"I hope you are not offering," Josefa said.

"No. Just suggesting you should not give up on bringing life into the world. You're still young and healthy." Alas, her multiple miscarriages might be due to her incest-donated genes, but he kept that thought to himself.

"That may be so. But I do not want any more children gifted by these people."

Daraja tentatively hugged her. He could see why Daraja had chosen the caring profession.

Leon moved to the door. "When we leave this room, it might get unpleasant, even rough," he warned. "Josefa, I'm liable to hurt members of your family."

Josefa's lips curled and she spat on the dirt floor. "Family?" she seethed. "You heard Papá," she whispered hoarsely. "I have no feelings for any of them! I curse the day I was born! I—"

Banging on the door interrupted her. "Hey, Antonio!" Paco shouted, "you don't usually take this long!"

His comment caused gales of laughter from the young females.

"Come on," Paco insisted, "it's my turn with her now!"

Leon inclined his head, hearing an unmistakable noise.

Manuel barked, "Wait, what's that? Sounds like the helicopter has landed close by. Paco! Go and check it out, see where it is!"

"Aw, Papá!"

"Go, Paco! Do as you are bid! We don't want any more visitors!"

———

THE HELICOPTER LANDED near the lip of the gorge, but far enough from the down-sloping track so that the rotor draft didn't destroy any spoor traces. By lucky chance from the air Maddox had spotted the imprints at the top of the track and ordered the pilot to land. He knew that the signs could have been left by other people, not the hacienda targets, but he doubted it. Who the hell else would be out here? Perhaps the missing Afghan hadn't crossed the bridge after all. Yet there were *two* sets of footprints.

Maddox opened the door and jumped to the ground as the engine cut off.

He soon identified the footprints of Leon and the Nigerian woman. He grinned, quite pleased with himself. This final sweep was likely going to pay off, after all. The pair of them had done well, to get this far—especially by outwitting Quint. What happened to Quint if these two had eluded him? And there was someone else supposed to be with them—an Iraqi woman. All of that was a puzzle for later.

He returned to the aircraft. "I'm going to investigate. Wait for me here!" He took his Enfield rifle from its retaining bracket.

The pilot said, "I'll wait. That's what I do. Fly and wait. Oh, and hump body bags."

Ignoring him, Maddox loped towards the head of the sloping trail.

Watchfully he descended the track.

———

AT THE ENTRANCE Paco swept the blanket door-flap aside and warily walked out.

He started in surprise. Maria Rosa and Lula, who was carrying the baby, appeared from behind an old fridge. "It landed there," Maria Rosa said and pointed to the top of the sloping trail cut into the side of the gorge.

Paco raked his fingers through his hair. "Oh."

Maria Rosa said, "You want me to come with you?" Was that a come-hither tone?

"No, you stay here and watch Lula and... the baby." Never did give the baby a name, did we? He couldn't even remember whose baby it was. It wasn't his; that he did know.

"You would say that, wouldn't you?" Maria Rosa snapped. "Why don't you watch Lula yourself? She's yours, for God's sake!"

Maria Rosa was six years younger than him, yet she behaved grown up most of the time. She was jealous of Remedios since she was carrying his third child.

"Yes, and I'm a proud father." Lula had been touch-and-go, born under-weight and premature. Yet the little scrap survived. She was a fighter. "I told you. Stay here. I'll go and see what they want."

"Suit yourself." Maria Rosa's hooded black eyes glared. "The men in this family always do."

Shrugging off her words, though they stung, he began to climb the slope.

———

SPOOR TOLD Maddox the pair had stopped halfway down this slope. He searched and quickly found an old backpack hidden behind a bush. He was puzzled by its contents, especially the oddly colored whiskey. He was tempted to pocket the money but decided to leave it all for now. *Concentrate on the prey*, he told himself. The rewards, the loot and the whiskey, all of it could be attended to later.

Warily, he edged down, noting the camouflage netting that spanned the gorge here.

Odd. What was all that about?

Then he saw the semblance of dwellings, which might explain the netting. He'd had no idea about this place. Baeza was going to be unpleasantly surprised to learn people lived here.

Not good. They were potential witnesses.

Odder still, he caught sight of strange metal constructions, sculptures of weird shapes, some of them rather sinister.

What the hell?

———

"JOSEFA," Leon whispered, "where does your father keep the rotor arm and distributor cap for his truck?"

"It will be in his bedside drawer."

"We need that transport."

She nodded.

He unsheathed the machete, wielded it. "Maybe I can get past everyone with this. When we leave this room, show me your parents' bedroom."

"Be careful," she whispered, "they can get nasty."

So can I, he thought.

He turned the door-handle. "Stay close."

Opening the door, he strode into the living area, with Josefa and Daraja behind him. He lifted the machete threateningly.

About two meters away, Manuel and Trinidad stood in front of the kitchen counter and stove.

Remedios and Eugenia were on the other side of the kitchen table, each holding a small pile of dishes, Remedios balancing hers against her pregnant bump.

All of them stared, their faces showing surprise. Every eye was leveled on the weapon.

None of them made a move.

Puzzlement creased Trinidad's brow as she stared at Josefa. She was doubtless confused to see that her daughter appeared free and not a hostage.

Leon spotted the rifle resting against the wall on the left of the cave entrance doorway.

Manuel's face hardened and then grew red. "Josefa, what is the meaning of this?"

"I've had enough, Papá. I'm leaving—with these people!"

"Ingrate!" her father snapped.

"What have you done to Antonio?" Trinidad pleaded. She jabbed a finger at Daraja. "She's wearing his clothes!"

"He's unconscious on the bed," Daraja replied.

"He is not hurt?"

"He will have a headache."

Leon barked, "We haven't time for this. Josefa, get your father's bunch of keys!"

While they'd been speaking, Leon had sidled slowly towards the entrance door. Nobody attempted to stop him. He reached the doorway and the rifle. From here, he could slink out. No, he wasn't going without Daraja, or, for that matter, Josefa. He'd made a promise.

He quickly snatched the rifle and fumbled for a cartridge in his pocket and loaded the rifle in the blink of an eye.

Then he slid the machete into its sheath and aimed the rifle at the family.

He noted the stern looks on their faces as Josefa lifted the bunch of keys from the dresser drawer on the other side of the big room.

"Might come in useful," Daraja said.

Josefa pointed past her parents to a door that stood ajar. "The bedroom, that's where you'll find the rotor arm."

"You bitch!" Manuel snarled.

"Mamá," wailed Remedios, "why are you doing this?"

Taking a bold step forward, Eugenia held her sister's hand. "She's never been a good mother to us, Remi!"

———

MADDOX'S HEART JUMPED. He raised the rifle as a young man with a withered left hand walked up the trail.

The youth froze at sight of the rifle.

"Don't move an inch!" Maddox warned in whispered Spanish.

Docilely, the youth nodded and lifted his hands in surrender.

Cautiously, Maddox descended and approached the youth.

"What's your name, lad?"

"Pac—Paco."

Maddox jacked a bullet into the rifle's chamber, aimed the barrel at Paco.

Then his eye was drawn by other movement.

Two girls stepped out from behind a looming bird of prey effigy. One of them was broad shouldered, well developed. She raised a hand to shield her hooded black eyes, studying him, and he noticed the hand only had two fingers. The other girl was younger, slight of frame. Both her legs appeared crooked. She supported a baby on her jutting hip. She squinted at him, perplexity on her face.

If people were living here, then Leon and the woman might be with them. If he could convince these people to turn over to him the so-called fugitives, then he wouldn't have to slaughter them all. He'd killed African poachers before, and relished it, but never any children. That idea didn't sit too well.

Without warning, the girl with the baby wailed in alarm.

Pivoting on his heel, Maddox aimed at the two girls but immediately eased off and relaxed.

Neither one was armed, so they were not a threat. And he had no great urge to kill any kid.

Silly little tyke! She shut up, anyway.

Still, can't be too careful. He gestured at the girls with the weapon and they backed off, moving to hide amidst the remnants of an old fridge and a cooking stove.

He turned to the young man. "Go ahead of me, Paco. When we get to the bottom you can tell me all about your two visitors."

CHAPTER 27

LOST CAUSE

EVERYONE IN THE CAVE HOUSE SEEMED TO FREEZE as a wailing sound reached them from outside.

"What was that?" Eugenia asked fearfully.

"What?" bawled Remedios, with hands to her ears. She appeared to be in distress.

Trinidad crossed herself. "That was my poor Maria Rosa!"

Remembering that Paco had been sent outside, Leon moved away from the doorway, still covering them all with the rifle. Only one bullet loaded, but he was sure none of them would risk rushing him. He was acutely aware that not long ago a helicopter had landed and time was pressing.

Keep calm.

Stay alert.

Manuel half-turned, eyeing the kitchen counter top. There were five knives of various sizes sheathed in a block of wood.

Leon said, "Don't try it, Manuel."

Scowling, Manuel hunched his shoulders and glared at Josefa. She stood by the dresser, holding the bunch of keys.

It was a stalemate. If either Daraja or Josefa attempted to go into the bedroom, they'd have to walk past Manuel and the others. He wouldn't be surprised if Manuel used either woman as a shield. The rotor arm was a lost cause, then, as was the vehicle.

Then everything changed. Fast.

Paco stumbled in through the doorway, eyes wide, mouth open, gasping.

He was immediately followed by Maddox with his raised rifle.

Leon identified the weapon: an Enfield L85A1 with a magazine capable of holding thirty rounds.

Potential carnage.

Maddox's gaze darted to Leon. He said in English, "There you are, you bastard!" Pointing the rifle barrel at Leon and Daraja, he snarled, "Both of you, come quietly. We don't want any witnesses. We'll fly you out alive."

Leon didn't hesitate. He pivoted and fired from the hip.

It was a rushed shot, yet surprisingly accurate. The bullet hit the breech of Maddox's rifle with a sharp metallic sound, was deflected and traveled under Maddox's jaw and exited through the roof of his skull. He fell to the tiled floor, blood spreading in a pool by his head.

Children screamed.

Paco leaped forward, grabbing Leon's rifle barrel, forcing it down. The lad was brave, since he didn't know there was only the one cartridge loaded, which had been spent. He'd be aware that there was no threat from the sheathed machete anyway. He was young and wiry with deceptive strength, and held onto the rifle tenaciously despite his withered hand.

Leon kneed Paco in the groin and swiveled round, braced his shoulders and threw the lad sideways. Paco instinctively let go of the rifle in an attempt at breaking his fall, and rolled into the solid table leg, his head hitting it with a thudding sound. The lad slumped at an angle, features blank, mouth gaping open.

"Paco!" Eugenia cried.

Before Leon could reload the weapon, Remedios jumped

on his back, one fist pummeled his head, the other arm around his neck, constricting his breathing. She bit into his left earlobe, drawing copious blood.

Christ, she's eating me alive!

She was a child, though. A pregnant child, at that.

They *were* cannibals, he reminded himself.

Less of the tender treatment!

Holding the rifle with his right hand, he bunched his left into a fist and executed a sharp back-hand strike that slammed into the side of her head.

With a dull grunt, the grip of her teeth relaxed and Remedios slid to the floor, unconscious, his blood smearing her mouth.

"Remi!" Trinidad shrieked.

Leon lifted a hand on his ravaged ear, unable to stem the bleeding.

Trinidad had picked up a skillet from the stove and was moving warily on him, thin lips peeled back to reveal sharp teeth. A mother defending her brood. "You've hurt our children!"

And behind her, Manuel had taken advantage of the distractions to snatch a big carving knife from the kitchen counter and he too strode forward, his face dark, a mask of anger and hate. "You repay our hospitality like this!"

Deranged, clearly.

Standing by Maddox's body, Leon dabbed at his ear with his jacket collar. He quickly checked the Englishman's rifle. The magazine was damaged so he couldn't use the weapon, and the cartridges were 5.56 x 45mm so no use for his rifle.

The bleeding from his ear had stopped.

Hastily, he unholstered Maddox's revolver and pocketed the Webley.

Everything had happened so fast, Daraja hadn't moved, but now she grabbed a chair from the head of the table, lifted it with an effort and stepped in front of Trinidad. She aimed its legs at Trinidad, the cross-pieces pinioning her chest, halting the willowy woman's advance, and slowly she forced Trinidad back.

As the matriarch lashed ineffectually with the skillet, she stumbled backwards and lost her footing and fell directly into Manuel's path. Before he could react, his outthrust knife blade sank between Trinidad's shoulders.

"No!" Manuel howled.

Paco was regaining his senses, even managing to get to his knees.

Daraja swung round and hit Paco over the head with a leg of the chair.

While loading the remaining three cartridges from his jacket pocket, Leon surveyed the scene.

Eugenia stood with her hands covering her ears, staring, her body trembling. Paco and Remedios lay unconscious on the dirt floor. Josefa hadn't moved from the dresser and still clutched the bunch of keys tightly to her chest. She stared, aghast. Manuel was on his knees, cradling in his lap Trinidad, his beloved sister, his incestuous partner.

Leon said, "Josefa, forget the rotor arm." He toed Maddox's body. "He came by helicopter."

Josefa inclined her head in understanding, but her face was blank, bloodless. She must be in shock. Trinidad was her mother, after all.

"Daraja, she can't stay here, so bring her with us. We're flying out *now*."

Moving past the distraught Eugenia, Daraja went to Josefa and took her hand, led her towards the entrance.

Seconds later, they emerged into daylight, blinking. Though muted by the shade cast by the gorge walls, it was still a striking contrast to the cave's poor illumination.

"You are going now?" Maria Rosa asked, wide eyes staring fearfully at him.

The younger girl clung to the baby.

Leon said, "Yes. We mean you no harm."

Maria Rosa said, "The other man who went inside threatened us. Where is he?"

"He won't be threatening anybody again. He's staying."
Leon couldn't resist adding, "He's probably your dinner."

Daraja shuddered.

"Come on," he urged Daraja, "let's go!"

"*Adios*!" Maria Rosa called.

Slowly, glancing over their shoulders, the three of them
negotiated the warren of metal sculptures and domestic
appliances.

Walking at a steady pace, they passed the docile donkey
and the illegal well, and then climbed up the sloping track.

Leon looked behind.

Nobody had rushed from the cave's entrance. The children had gone and were probably inside.

Faintly, he heard weeping and wailing. A family in shock.
Perhaps they were mourning.

Halting at the halfway point, he located the backpack. It
had been moved, but the contents were all present and
untouched.

He took the bow and arrows as well, put them in the
pack and slung it on his shoulders. "Josefa, give me the keys
now."

She handed them to him and he pocketed them. "Stay
behind me," he said and then led them to just below the lip
of the gorge, where he stopped and signed for them to
hunker down.

"Stay quiet," he whispered.

First, he checked behind them, the base of the track
they'd climbed, but there was no activity from that quarter.

Then he peered over the lip.

The Agusta-Westland helicopter was parked sideways to
the edge of the gorge. The pilot sat with the cabin door
open, smoking. Looking into space, uncaring. Very likely
bored.

Leon jacked a bullet into the chamber and then signed to
the others to follow him.

He stood, crossed the lip of the gorge and headed
towards the aircraft, the rifle primed and ready.

Movement attracts the eye, even if it's caught peripherally. The pilot saw them and at once his face filled with alarm, which wasn't surprising. Maddox had left him but now coming back instead were two women and an armed man. He flung away his cigarette.

The pilot's hand darted to his shoulder holster.

CHAPTER 28

DUBIOUS PURPOSE

LEON STOPPED WALKING. BREATHING STEADILY, HE raised the rifle.

The pilot's automatic slid from its holster.

Aimed.

The pilot's automatic moved in an arc, centring on Leon and his group.

Fired.

Simultaneously the pilot jerked and let off a wild shot. Then he slumped in his seat with his head pressed against the cockpit windshield.

"Why'd you do that?" Daraja slapped his upper arm with the flat of her hand. "He could have flown us out of here!"

Leon said, "He callously dumps corpses of innocent victims into the gorge, and you ask that?"

"I suppose you have a point. But—"

"Besides, I can fly that." He ran towards the aircraft.

"Oh, that's all right, then," she said to his departing back. She shoved Josefa. "Come on." The two women scampered after him.

When he reached the cockpit, Leon leaned in and placed a finger on the pilot's neck: there was no pulse. He removed the pilot's watch and put it on his own wrist. Maybe he'd be able to keep this one! He estimated there was at least two hours to sunset. Half-raising the man, he unclasped the dead fingers from the Sig P-232 automatic. It was the 7.65mm caliber model, so it held eight rounds. He shoved the gun in another pocket. Getting quite a collection now. He searched the pilot's pockets and found a spare magazine clip. He wasn't interested in the wallet, but he pocketed the folding money.

"What now?" Daraja asked, standing next to him. She sounded remarkably calm. Doubtless accustomed to sudden death in his presence.

"We radio for help." He reached for the radio console and stopped. "Shit. That stray shot he fired, it busted the radio!"

"But you can still fly it, can't you?"

"All being well." He checked the instrumentation. A note pad fixed to the console was blood-spattered, but all the dials and the facia were intact. "Yes, the bullet didn't do any other damage." He hauled the pilot from his seat and flung him out of the aircraft. He felt nothing for the dead man, someone who'd clearly accepted his role as carrier of innocent corpses, dumping them as instructed. Just obeying orders—for a salary.

Josefa, standing close by, visibly cringed as the body hit the ground. Perhaps she'd never seen a whole dead body, only parts served up in her mother's stews. At least it seemed as if she was surfacing from her state of shock.

He said, "Come on, both of you, get in!"

Docilely, with Daraja's help, Josefa clambered in and he guided her to the seat in the rear that he'd occupied yesterday.

Daraja was soon beside him. "I'll sit in the back with her."

"Good idea. Strap her in and keep an eye on her. She might never have flown. I don't want any hysterics. I need all my concentration on flying this thing."

"That gives me a lot of confidence."

"No worries. Cazador Airways are happy to have you on this flight!"

"Cazador?"

"My real surname."

"Oh."

He returned to the cockpit and slid the door shut, and then strapped himself in the pilot's seat. Scanning the console, he familiarized himself with the readouts and indicators, the compass, the ceiling buttons and knobs. It was a while since he'd last flown a chopper. He wiped his damp palms on the chest of his jacket. He needed two dry hands and both feet to fly.

Switching on the batteries, he opened the fuel valve and the engine started.

An escalating whine as the engine droned.

The choppy sound of rotor blades whirling through the air.

The procedure flooded back.

Just like riding a bike!

With the collective lever in his left hand he slowly twisted the grip, opening the throttle to full, and the rev counter reflected the increase.

While vital seconds passed until the engine reached its operating speed, he watched through the cockpit windshield, but none of the Ramirez family appeared at the lip of the gorge.

If he'd been too hasty attempting lift, the main rotor blades would have dashed against the fuselage. Now, as the rpm hit the mark, he raised the lever and the aircraft lifted a little. He constantly adjusted the collective pitch, not too much or the revs will decay.

Simultaneously, he depressed the left foot pedal to counteract the torque caused by the main rotor.

Within a minute or so after ignition the aircraft began to leave the ground.

He heard Daraja let out a pent-up breath.

At this point his right hand felt the cyclic lever become

sensitive and he pushed it forward slightly. This moment of transition from vertical to forward motion made the craft shudder and the nose pulled up, which he expected. Familiar tilt and sway.

He pushed the cyclic forward a little more and they moved ahead smoothly.

Within seconds, they were over the gorge. Below, he saw Antonio and Manuel running out of the cave entrance, their fists raised. Thankfully, neither held a gun.

Leon's right foot pressed the pedal to adjust the tail rotor, and they turned, veering to the south, flying in the direction of the village.

For some distance he steered the aircraft to follow the gorge. After a short while he noticed on the left a group of crows flocking. He guessed that was where the pilot dumped the body bags. He glanced at Daraja. She hadn't noticed. Just as well, she probably knew a number of the dead, since she'd "worked" at the hacienda before becoming one of their latest "targets."

Smoothly he edged the aircraft away from the gorge and found a road which he followed at a height of twenty feet.

Presently, they neared the outskirts of the village.

A farmer drove a tractor in a field and in his wake white egrets flocked. His back was to the road; he didn't hear or notice the helicopter.

A road-sign warned of a roundabout ahead.

On their left they passed a field that was partially flooded. The irrigation lock was open, and water bubbled through.

Leon eased on the collective lever, descending gradually, adjusting the airspeed.

He checked the airspeed dial: slowing to twenty knots.

The roundabout was directly ahead: it was quite big, a rounded mound of decorative pink and gray gravel with no foliage. Two roads branched to left and right, bordering cultivated fields of mostly alfalfa and artichokes. A third road led towards the village. Irrigation ditches ran alongside the roads and on the side of one a heron perched, unconcerned.

He brought the nose of the chopper up to decrease airspeed. Momentarily he lost sight of the roundabout mound, and reduced the collective. This was the tricky bit, he recalled. He eased the cyclic back to reduce momentum and then forward a fraction to level the altitude. He kept the rate of descent low, adjusting the collective slightly, sensing the old dropping sensation in his stomach. A dust cloud surrounded them and then the landing skids contacted the ground and the cabin juddered slightly and his seat belt straps jolted against his shoulders.

He remembered the parking brake and armed it and reduced all power.

Dust settled. The rotors drooped.

Daraja said, "Well done!" She unbuckled, moved forward and slid the door open.

"I know this place," Josefa said, anxiety in her tone as she freed herself from the seatbelt.

"You've been here before?" Daraja helped her out, and then jumped down to stand beside her.

Josefa spoke in a monotone, pointing to a dust-covered green plastic chair on the verge of the nearest road junction. "Papá sometimes would leave me here sitting in that chair, to lure men. He also brought Eugenia instead of me." Leon knew there were plenty of similar chairs placed a round-abouts dotted around the countryside, all serving the same dubious purpose. Josefa screwed tight her eyes, as if attempting to blot out images, memories, and her brow creased. "They always wore protection so I couldn't fulfill his wishes and conceive from strange men."

"My God," Daraja exclaimed, hugging her, "your own father!"

Josefa sobbed and nodded, yet her eyes were dry.

Leon delved in the backpack and then got out.

Josefa fidgeted with her hair. "That was not as bad as other times..."

Leon said, "What happened then?"

"Papá would hide in that ditch and attack and rob the men who stopped for me."

He said, "Well, Josefa, you're free of him now." He passed her the wad of money he'd taken from Rudolf. "This should help you get away."

She accepted it, but stood hesitant.

He pointed along the road. "You can go to that village."

It was tempting to give her a message to pass on to the Guardia Civil or the local police but he decided against it. It would prove awkward for her.

And, besides, this was personal now.

Josefa's face paled. "I've never been in the village alone— always with Papá. Some days he robbed houses with those keys you took."

He turned to Daraja. "Do you want to go with Josefa?"

"What are you going to do?"

"I'm returning to the hacienda. I have a score to settle." He jangled the bunch of keys. "And I'd like to free the other captives."

Daraja thrust out her chest and set her jaw. "Then I will go with you. I have scores to settle as well."

The determination in her features convinced him he couldn't dissuade her. In truth, he was used to having her by his side.

He rested a hand on Josefa's shoulder. She flinched so he let go. "Will you be alright?"

She briefly clasped his hand. "I will. Thank you." She stepped off the roundabout and stood on the far curbside, clutching the money to her chest. "Take care. Both of you."

Leon and Daraja clambered into the helicopter cabin. She slid the door shut, and then sat beside him.

He started the lift-off sequence.

They waved to Josefa. Her dress was wafted about by the draft from the rotors. She covered her face with a hand to ward off the dust.

Moments later the aircraft was airborne.

His left foot pressed on the pedal and they turned, heading north.

He caught a glimpse of Josefa walking along the dusty road, heading for the village.

After a minute or two, once he'd settled into routine, he said, "I'm a bit hazy about the layout of the hacienda." He told her he only knew about the helipad, the generator and the basement, stairs and elevator. "Can you fill me in on the rest?"

"Yes. I got to know it." She detached a pad from the console, tearing and discarding a handful of blood-stained pages, and unclipped a pen. She began drawing a plan, a page for each story: basement, ground floor, and top floor.

When she'd finished, she showed him the first sheet.

He studied it while gripping the collective and cyclic levers. He didn't need to use his feet at present. The altitude and attitude were level. Just fine.

The top floor comprised Baeza's private room at the front on the south-western corner, opening onto a balcony that stretched the width of the building.

"I know it well," she said sourly. "The radio equipment's in there also, inside an adjoining small office." There was a corridor that ran the length of the building from the stairs and elevator, and this gave access to six so-called client rooms. "One of them would have been reserved for you, of course."

"Of course. With all the mod cons, I suppose?"

She said, "En suite. And a comfort woman."

"I could do with a shower, but I'd forego the comfort woman."

"You and me both—for the shower. No Wi-Fi for clients, however."

He said, "Keeping the clients cut off from the outside world. Makes sense."

There was also a lounge-bar with galley, dining table and television.

He nodded. "They took me there to have a chat with Baeza and the others. What about the ground floor?"

She presented him with another sheet. "Vanda Dinescu's room is to the left of the entrance hall—though she spends most of the time in Baeza's room."

"When she's not away on shopping trips?"

"That's right. Calvo's room is next to hers. A corridor runs from the hall and along here are other rooms—Mateo's, Fabio's, Orton's, Maddox's on the south side, a kitchen, canteen and accommodation for the aircrew and the armed guards on the north side."

"Outside, at the back you'll find a chicken coop, a vegetable garden and a lemon and orange orchard. And on the west side is the generator, which you know about."

"We passed a second basement room with captives in it—on the south side. What else is down there?"

She showed him a third sheet. "Next to that room you saw is the communal bathroom, and next to that the laundry. On the west side are two rooms—the armory and a store-room. The comfort women are held at the far end on the north side."

"Yes, I remember. I was told about that."

She was silent for a moment or two. Probably remembering her role there, before Baeza had taken a fancy to her. Then she said, "We must free them as well. None of those women volunteered to be there. And next to them is accommodation for the maintenance men and kitchen staff and female cleaners."

"Will the staff be loyal to Baeza?"

She said, "Difficult to say. Maybe the kitchen staff will be."

"Do the staff know about the captives?"

"They're bound to know. They change the sheets for the comfort women weekly, and meals have to be brought for everyone, including the "targets"—as you saw."

"Well, if they get out of this, they're going to be looking for a new job."

She hunched her shoulders. "Do I care?"

They lapsed into silence for a while.

Much of the terrain they flew above was familiar.

Eventually, Daraja broke the silence. "This is preferable to walking, no?"

"Definitely." He checked the airman's watch. Plenty of time before nightfall. "Daraja, get the backpack, will you? I need to show you something which is really going to be quite useful."

"Ah, useful at last? Good!"

After Daraja had retrieved the backpack, he delved inside and gave her detailed instructions.

She confirmed she knew what to do and they settled into a tense silence for the remainder of the journey.

The landscape that had taken them hours to walk sped beneath them in minutes.

Finally, he pointed ahead.

Looming on the horizon was the hacienda building perched on top of the plateau, with roof aerials and dishes jutting against the deep blue sky.

He said, "There's *our* target."

CHAPTER 29

TROUBLESOME PEOPLE

VANDA WOKE WITH A START, FLEETINGLY wondering where she was, and desperately waved her arms left and right to ward off the attack of hundreds of hissing snakes. She jerkily sat up and instantly realized she was in her bed in her room.

Alone.

No snakes.

And remembered the snakebite.

Breathing rapidly, she pressed a hand against her hammering chest and then checked her foot. It was bandaged, but it didn't feel swollen or too sore, more like a dull ache.

The image of the American's face swam into focus. Harley had saved her.

What of Francisco? Was he concerned for her? Or moping after the comfort woman Daraja? That was academic, she reasoned. The Yank, Quint, would have shot her by now.

The ghost of a smile played on her lips as she saw again Anamaria sinking into the quagmire, eyes pleading. That revenge was *so* sweet.

Parts of her memory were hazy, but she recalled having a conversation with Harley in here, while she lay recovering.

Something he'd said... Francisco thought Harley had killed Orton, was that right?

Harley genuinely seemed anxious for her wellbeing. She was touched by that.

In stark contrast, she couldn't remember seeing Francisco while she lay in bed. Of course he could have visited while she was lost to the world.

She raised a hand to her forehead, vaguely remembering a touch of lips. "Drop by later, honey, okay?" Harley's words.

He was protective towards her. Sometimes, she brought out that in men. Lazaro had shown that trait after they escaped from the endangered species complex. He believed he was an unrivaled Latin lover, all smiles and smarm. But she was genuinely grateful to him for providing transport for her getaway. She was not averse to showing gratitude. When they found themselves in Madrid in a one bedroom apartment, she rewarded him.

Unfortunately, she soon discovered that Lazaro had a serious weakness.

He gambled.

She wasn't going to let him fritter away her ill-gotten gains. She knew that he resented her not giving him any of her money and was jealous of her bulging closet of garments from Punt Roma, Zara and Balenciaga. One morning it came to a head when he jumped from the bed and opened the closet, rifled her clothing.

She said, alarmed, "What are you doing?"

"You have money for all these!" he had snapped. "Why won't you give *me* money? We're good together, aren't we?"

"I don't have to pay for a gigolo, you know, Lazaro!"

"I know, I know. I didn't mean it like that. It's just—I'm a bit short."

She purred, "Come to bed and we can correct that."

"I'm being serious."

"So am I." Invariably, their disagreements ended with lovemaking.

But her patience was wearing thin.

Then, one evening, while they both played at the roulette wheel of the Casino Catalina, she noticed that Lazaro was being discreetly shepherded towards the elevators. He looked uncomfortable, even flustered, his brow beaded in sweat. She doubted if his concern centered on the appropriateness of his quite threadbare tuxedo.

Clasping her clutch-bag, she abandoned the roulette and, her long green silk gown swishing, sashayed up to the two heavies on either side of Lazaro.

She said, "Where are you taking him?"

Small unintelligent eyes scanned her and their owner's lips curled at sight of her apparent charms. "None of your business, lady."

"He is my business. He goes, I go."

Leering, the talkative one said, "Suit yourself. There's room for one more."

Lazaro stared at her, whispered, "You shouldn't be here."

"No talking, please," said the silent one.

The other added, "You can sing all you want when we get to the office."

Lazaro's face abruptly matched the white of his dress shirt.

When they exited the elevator they were met by the sounds of television screens blaring from several offices, their doors ajar. Horse racing and boxing, mostly. Bets and the odds were being shouted across the rooms.

As they entered a large plush office, she realized it must be sound-proofed, for as the door shut behind them she couldn't hear any of the noise from the corridor.

They were escorted to a broad mahogany desk and sitting behind it was a corpulent man with sunken coffee brown eyes, a seamed round face, and a pallid complexion.

"Why the woman?" the man said, his voice rough-edged, possibly on account of the six half-smoked cigars in the ashtray. He shifted his compact body in his leather chair.

"She's with Perez, Señor Baeza."

Baeza scrutinized her, from head to toe, and his smile told her he liked what he saw.

He had a broad nose, plump lips, designer stubble on his chin, and short, inky black hair. He wasn't handsome, but he exuded power. She believed power was an aphrodisiac, and she wanted to bathe in it.

Baeza said, "What's your name?"

"Vanda Dinescu. Don't you have a first name, Señor Baeza?"

His eyes sparked. "Francisco." He raised an eyebrow at her and thumbed at Lazaro. "So tell me, Vanda, what is he to you?"

She held her clutch-bag in front of her, outwardly quite relaxed, while her insides churned. "More to the point, Francisco, what is Lazaro to you?"

"Normally, I ask the questions."

"Normally?" she prompted boldly.

"I like the look of you."

She said, "And it is mutual."

"So I see. Then I will indulge you. The answer to your question is quite simple. He owes me money. A great deal of money."

She studied Lazaro. He was visibly trembling, still held between the two heavies.

"You're not going to get what he owes if he's wearing concrete boots in the Manzanares."

"That is true. But he pleads poverty." Baeza smiled enticingly. "Though his choice of female friend is far from poor."

"Tell me what he owes."

Baeza told her.

She said, "I can pay that."

Baeza stood up, leaned across the desk. "Then we have a deal."

"Thank—thank you, Vanda," Lazaro croaked.

Baeza sneered at Lazaro. "What should we do with him?"

In one swift movement Vanda opened her bag, pulled

out the Astra revolver and pressed it firmly against Lazaro's chest. "This." She pulled the trigger once.

Lazaro gaped in surprise.

The sound was loud.

Followed by silence.

The two heavies took a pace back, hands reaching for their shoulder holsters as the body dropped between them. There was very little blood.

Vanda put the gun in her bag, snapped it shut. "We still have a deal, don't we?"

Francisco Baeza's grin was broad and approving. "We do." Gesturing at the two heavies, he said, "Clear up the mess. And be discreet about it!"

Slowly, deliberately, she took a fresh cigar from the humidor on the desk and put it in her mouth, moistened its end with the tip of her tongue and then placed it between Francisco's plump lips. Using the desk lighter, she lit it.

Holding the cheroot between his teeth, Francisco Baeza grinned.

She decided that her new protector would prove useful.

Later, she was surprised at his athleticism in bed, despite his girth and weight.

Now, though, she hankered after a younger, fitter man. Perhaps a politician was a better kind of crook.

She sat upright and swung her legs off the bed.

I need a shower.

Standing, she swayed and almost lost her balance. She flattened a hand on the nightstand and steadied herself.

Weak.

Shivering.

Aftershock, probably.

Still need a shower.

Tentatively, she began to walk to the bathroom, awkwardly stripping as she went. Her confidence in her ability to walk increased as she divested herself of the clothes. Clothing that reminded her of her mortality, of her own brush with death.

———

Baeza sat hunched in front of the radio, his head in his hands. He hadn't realized until now what being cut off from the helicopter could mean. They were seriously isolated here. No other means of transport. Out of the corner of his eye he noticed movement. Calvo had entered the small office and now stood by his side.

Calvo said gratingly, "Still no word from the pilot?"

"That's right. Or Maddox."

"Could the Englishman have deserted us?"

"Why would he do that?" Baeza snapped.

"Maybe the intervention of that police informer—Leon—it might have worried him, no? Given him the jitters."

Baeza smirked. He hadn't considered that, but the idea was ridiculous. "He hasn't been paid. Maddox is fond of money."

"Then why doesn't he answer you on the radio?"

I wish I knew! Baeza shrugged. "Must be some kind of mechanical breakdown." *Madre de Dios, no, not a crash!* "I mean, a problem with the radio."

Calvo glanced behind him at the open door and whispered, "What about Harley? Maddox said he probably killed Orton."

That mechanical "voice" could be very irritating at times! "I'm troubled by that, I admit. Still, I am reluctant to do anything yet. Harley saved Vanda, remember that."

"I am pleased for you. It would be a shame if Vanda had died."

"A shame?" Baeza ran a hand over his scalp. "I didn't realize how much I want—need—her until she was almost taken from me."

"Harley saving Vanda does not take away the concern I have about Maddox's accusation. Harley might have killed Orton to make sure he won the trophy rebate, no?"

Men have killed for much less. I've disposed of troublesome people for much less. Baeza said, "That is possible, yes."

"Or Harley might be in league with the Leon guy, no?"

"It is all supposition."

"Harley could be a plant put in by one of the cartels who doesn't like you, no?"

"That, too, is possible. Unlikely, but any of those suggestions is conceivable."

Calvo said, "But?"

"But we will wait for Maddox to return and I will speak to him first before I confront Harley."

Then he heard it and released a pent-up sigh.

The sound of the helicopter grew louder as it approached.

Baeza stood up. "Ah, it won't be long now," he said with assurance. "Then we can have a reckoning, all right?"

LEON STEERED the helicopter directly in the direction of the generator on the western side of the hacienda, and then hovered above it. "Now, Daraja!"

She slid open the cabin door and picked up the two bottles she'd already placed on her seat. Hugging the bottles to her chest, she unscrewed the caps, which she dropped to the deck.

Steadying herself against the cabin bulkhead, she carefully removed the polythene cover from the neck of the concentrated sulphuric acid and poured an agreed quantity into the whiskey bottle that was already one-third filled with water. As soon as the reaction began, she leaned out a little, bracing herself against the downdraft from the rotors, and dropped the home-made bomb unerringly on top of the generator. Then she tossed the bottle containing the remainder of acid after it.

The heat created by the reaction should be sufficient, Leon hoped.

Yes! The glass bottle exploded on impact and the contents immediately ignited the inevitable smears of fuel and grease.

Seconds later, there was a tremendous explosion and flames erupted, flaring upwards.

Daraja slid the door shut and grasped the back of her seat to steady herself as Leon swerved the aircraft away, towards the rooftop.

Taking great care and holding his breath, he managed a perfect landing on the painted "H" of the helipad.

No sooner had the skids touched the roof than he switched off the engine.

In the following silence he heard Daraja release a breath that signified relief. At about the same time he, too, decided to breathe again.

They unclipped their seatbelts.

"Stay with the chopper." He gave Daraja the pilot's automatic and pointed to the doors that led to the stairwell and the elevator. "Watch those doors. If anybody attempts to come through, shoot at the door. That should keep them away."

She hefted the gun. "With pleasure."

From the backpack he took out the short-bow and arrows and then put the pack on his back. Slinging the rifle strap over his shoulder, he slid open the cabin door, jumped down and sprinted to the western edge of the roof where a column of black smoke now rose from the blitzed generator.

IN THE COOL cave house Manuel Ramirez knelt with Trini lying in his lap. With a trembling hand he wiped the tears from his eyes.

He gazed upon her face, her high cheekbones catching the overhead light. Her narrow dark eyes would glint no more with humor or love. Her thin lips would never again curve with the promise of lust to be sated. She lay in his arms, her long black hair, streaked with gray, still tied in a ponytail. His constant companion for almost forever.

And the years they'd savored together flew before his mind's eye, gloriously exciting, thrillingly secretive, and joyously passionate. And it got even better when they had fled home and began a family—no, a dynasty—of their own. No rules, no constraints, just love.

Dimly, he was aware of the children weeping and wailing. Even Antonio, who had been freed by Paco, cried: it was unusual for the lad to show this kind of emotion.

No words were spoken. They were all speechless, trembling before a grief that nobody could console.

Her last words had been, "Look after all the children, my love." And then the light had faded from her eyes.

His heart pounded and he was surprised at that, since it felt broken into pieces. His love, his only love, was dead. The sexual congress they had enjoyed with their children was a different kind of love.

A heavy weight crushed his chest. His one true love had been stabbed by the knife he'd held in his own hand.

Yet he suffered no guilt. Only anger.

Those strangers had caused this. Nobody else.

They had been instrumental in Trini's death, and to compound that they had abducted their daughter, dear Josefa!

Racked with sobs, Manuel struggled to stand, lifting Trini in his arms. Though his heart was shattered, still must he walk through the valley of shadow, and keep going.

"Papá," Paco pleaded, "what are you going to do?"

"I am taking her away from this place."

"But we bury our babies here, Papá," said Eugenia, her hands massaging her bulge.

"Their deaths were natural. Our mother's death was not. It was murder."

A heavy silence followed his words.

Grating his teeth, he snarled, "They forced her into my blade. I am not to blame! It was them!"

Eugenia and Remedios said in unison, "Yes, Papá, that is the truth of it."

He laid Trini on the table, on top of the embroidered flowery cloth. Reverently, he wrapped her in it, like a shroud, and covered her face.

CHAPTER 30

SILENT RAPTURE

"*MADRE DE DIOS*! WHAT THE HELL WAS THAT?" Baeza exclaimed, as his heart pounded and his stomach sank. He and Calvo stared at each other while a loud explosion shook the walls of the little office.

A tremor, an earthquake? Over the years he'd been close to a number of earth tremors. The most surprising had been when he was in an apartment where the windows of the balcony's sliding doors had bowed in and out with the shockwave, a disconcerting rippling effect that coincided with a short, sharp thunderclap. And yet the epicenter had been kilometers away.

"It came from the west side," Calvo offered in a metallic croak.

They both rushed out, through the bedroom and into the passage.

Baeza saw Harley running for the stairs with a bulging leather bag.

"Hey!" Baeza shouted.

Harley stopped and said, "Did you hear that?"

Baeza said, "We did. It was probably just an earth tremor."

"Tremor? It sounded like a bomb to me."

"I doubt that, sir." Baeza pointed at the bag Harley carried. "Where are you going?"

"If that's a tremor, then it could be followed by a full-blown earthquake," Harley replied. "I reckon I should get Vanda away from here before it hits."

"I appreciate your concern for her safety, sir." *Why the concern?* He'd been with Vanda when they returned, hadn't he? What had they been doing together? Don't be absurd, he berated himself. She'd been bitten by a snake! He stamped on his feelings of jealousy. The American was being chivalrous: a rare trait for so many of his countrymen.

Harley said, "Hell, I'd do it for anybody. But she's still recovering. Needs assistance, right?"

"You are right, of course. Most considerate." *Why wasn't my first thought to feel concern for Vanda's safety?*

Harley waved and walked on and quickly entered the stairwell door, slamming it behind him.

Baeza started to go after him but Calvo yanked his arm and said, "You must see to the building, my friend. That is your priority."

With reluctance Baeza answered, "You are right." He went with Calvo to the elevator door and stabbed a finger at the button, but there were no indicator lights, and no sound: the elevator wasn't functioning.

"The explosion could be the generator," Calvo suggested.

"I'll check!" Baeza rushed down the passage, through the door and out onto the top floor balcony. Moving to the right-hand end, he leaned on the rail and peered round to the side of the building.

He swore.

Calvo was right again. The generator was on fire, smoke billowing!

No alarms. Because there are no electrics.

Was it some kind of failure, an accident? His stomach lurched. Or sabotage? And if sabotage, committed by whom?

He watched below as two guards ran round the corner, one of them carrying a machine-pistol, the other a foam extinguisher.

Then Calvo joined him at the rail. "*Madre de Dios!*"

Baeza was filled with an abrupt lightness. "At least the fire can be fought and hopefully put out."

Calvo rasped in a deflating tone, "Restoring electricity might be a problem, though."

———

PEERING FROM THE ROOF, Leon looked at the generator. Flames darted and licked the remaining twisted metal structure, reflecting red and orange against the building's walls. He heard voices below and to his left. He risked looking.

Baeza and Calvo were leaning on the side rail of the top floor balcony. The angle was hopeless. He couldn't get a good shot at either of them from here.

At that moment, two men rounded the corner, running from the front of the building. One carried a Steyr machine-pistol, the other held an extinguisher.

Leon recognized them as the armed guards who watched his "softening up" and shepherded the captives.

He was tempted to unsling the rifle, but he wanted to conserve his bullets and also maintain an element of surprise. There were still captives to release.

Strike silently.

Taking aim with the bow, he loosed an arrow.

The guard with the machine-pistol fell dead, a shaft protruding from his throat. The man holding the extinguisher hesitated, staring at the arrow, and then he turned, and looked up.

Leon shot an arrow directly into the gaping mouth and the extinguisher dropped to the ground.

The fire continued to rage.

He had no qualms—they'd been complicit in using the captives as prey for the rich hunters.

Before either Calvo or Baeza could see him Leon backed away from the edge. Then he beckoned to Daraja to join him.

She pocketed the pilot's revolver and hurried over. "What now?" she asked.

———

As the two guards crumpled to the ground with arrows protruding from them, Calvo's robotic voice echoed, "Francisco, they're both dead. We're under attack!"

"Sometimes you state the obvious, Ramon," Baeza growled, glancing at the lip of the roof. No sign of anybody there, though. "Those arrows came from the rooftop. Now we know there was a very good reason for the helicopter's radio silence." He bit his lip, weighing the possibilities. The conclusion was inevitable. "I fear the pilot's dead as well."

"Oh, no! I knew we should have quit. I told you!"

"Will you keep calm? We can still get away."

"We can?"

"Stay with me, my friend." Baeza hurriedly returned to his room, Calvo close on his heels.

Baeza swung wide the Van Gogh print on its hinges and quickly spun the combination dial and opened the wall-safe. He removed a Smith & Wesson Model 500 revolver and then filled a leather briefcase with money from the safe's two shelves.

He turned to Calvo. "Let's get the navigator."

———

Clutching his bulging leather bag, Harley burst into Vanda's room on the ground floor. He shut the door behind him.

She still lay on top of the bed, but she'd changed clothes since he last saw her. Now she was wearing a short black lacy nightdress, showing a lot of leg. Her ankle sported a fresh bandage. She had raised herself on an elbow and was staring in concern at the wall where jagged cracks had appeared in the plaster. Judging by her complexion, she was in shock.

She swung round to face him. "Harley? What're you doing here—what's happening?"

He lowered the bag to the floor and knelt by the bed, held her hand, which was warm. His nostrils flared as he caught a strong tantalizing hit of perfume. "Baeza says it might have been a bomb," he lied. She'd lived in Spain long enough to be untroubled by earth tremors, so he concocted the more threatening scenario.

"Bomb?"

"God knows, honey. And where from, eh?"

"It can't be ETA, can it?"

"Honey, I sure don't know. I'm not great at Spanish politics."

She said, "The big bang—explosion. He thinks a bomb could have caused that?"

"Who knows? I reckon it was the generator." He reached past her, breathed in more exotic fragrances, and clicked the switch of the bedside lamp. But, as he expected, it didn't work. "See? Maybe the generator malfunctioned, overloaded, blew up." He put an arm round her shoulders, helped her sit up. "Come on, we must get you out now."

She swung those long shapely legs off the bed. "But if it's only a breakdown, why must we leave?"

Nothing wrong with her logic. He waved a hand at the new cracks in the wall. "The building may not be safe anymore."

"Oh." Her hand glided provocatively over her nightdress. "I can't go anywhere like this!"

He liked her just as she was, but common sense intervened and he nodded. "Stay there—I'll get your things."

Rushing across to the closet, he slid open the door. There was a long rail crammed with a medley of colors and fabrics. He snatched a pair of jeans and a red silk blouse from their hangers, and a pair of slip-on shoes from the floor.

Hurriedly returning to her, he handed her the clothes. "Put these on." He dropped the shoes at her feet. "And hurry!"

Unabashed, she pulled the nightgown over her head and flung it onto the bed. He gazed in silent rapture at her upturned breasts, the dark inviting nipples and areolas, the flat stomach and lush dark brush between her legs. Then she slipped into the blouse and buttoned it up. He watched, mesmerized, as, standing shakily, she slid her legs into the jeans, zipped up and then shoved her feet into the shoes.

He grabbed his bag and shoved it under an arm. "Ready?"

"I think so."

"Here, let me help." With his free hand he held her arm, steadied her, and felt her warmth. He was pleased to sense her reliance on him.

Slowly, they moved to the door, Vanda limping only slightly.

He said, "Does the bite hurt?"

She shook her head. "The foot, the ankle, it is stiff, that is all. I can manage."

"Good girl."

They got to the door and stopped while he reached for the handle.

She said, "No, wait!"

"What now?" He was annoyed at letting his exasperation show. "Is there a problem?" he asked in a sweeter tone.

"My papers—passport, money." She jutted her chin at the dressing table next to the closet. "In the drawer."

There was only the one drawer. "Okay. I'll get them. Stay there."

"I'm not going anywhere without you."

He liked the sound of that.

She rested her shoulder against the wall by the door while he crossed the room and rummaged in the drawer. Then he half-turned. "Three passports? And a gun?"

"Yes." She grimaced. He construed the facial tic as pain,

but it might have been her annoyance or frustration. He guessed it was due to her pain. "Yes," she repeated. "Bring the passports, the gun, and the money."

Hesitantly, he removed the passports, a wad of euros, a sheaf of official-looking documents, and a revolver. Not much left. A little jewelry. He took that, too. Stuffed them all in his leather bag, and then closed it.

Seconds later, he was by her side again.

She said, "What about my clothes?"

She'd obviously had time to think of that while he was filling his bag with her identities and gun and such.

"I'll buy you whatever new clothes you desire."

"You will?"

"I promise."

She cast a parting glance around the room. "All right. Let's go."

He opened the door and they passed through into the wide entrance hall.

Fabio was running from his room at the far end and stopped in the hall as he spotted them. "Señor, what's happening?" he asked in English.

Harley said, "Señor Baeza is coming down." He gestured along the passage to the stairwell door. "Wait for him. He'll tell you everything."

"Sí. Right. But do you want help with Señorita Dinescu?"

"Thanks, but no, I can manage. Señor Baeza asked me to take her away now." From the corner of his eye he caught a look of puzzlement on Vanda's face. He'd explain later. "Fabio, go see to your boss, okay?"

"Okay."

And then Harley held Vanda against him and guided her across the hall, through the double doors onto the veranda and down the entrance steps. It felt good, to have her so close.

As they reached solid ground, he breathed a great sigh of relief.

But where to go?

He saw the numbered posts. Back the way they'd come? There was no decent road for miles, that's why Baeza used the helicopter.

"Where do we go now?" Vanda asked. She wasn't too out of it; in fact, he reckoned she was incredible.

"Away from here." Sure, stating the obvious. He pointed at the smoke billowing round the side of the building. "That fire might spread." It might, but he doubted it.

"Yes. You are right." She offered him a weak smile. "I am glad you came for me."

"I sure am as well," he said with feeling. This could be the start of a swell relationship.

———

LEAVING HIS ROOM, Baeza and Calvo hurried along the passage to the door that gave access to the stairwell.

Baeza opened the door.

Here, on the top floor landing, he was surprised to find Fabio.

"Señor, I came up when I heard the explosion."

"Good man!" Baeza clamped a hand on Fabio's shoulder. "We're under attack! Stay here and guard the stairs. We're going to get the airman. When we get back, all of us can get to the roof and fly out."

"*Sí*, Señor. That is a good plan." Fabio beamed, doubtless pleased to be flying out.

"Good man!" Baeza repeated.

At each landing and half-landing, high-placed windows were sited in two walls of the stairwell shaft, admitting daylight. Only the basement had no windows, only emergency lighting.

He left Fabio behind and led Calvo down the stairs, their footfalls echoing.

———

LEON HAD no way of calculating how many people were in the building. He knew about Baeza, Calvo, Mateo and Fabio. The latter two he dearly wanted to meet again, but this time on his terms. The helicopter had also been manned by a navigator, who was armed, he recalled. And, as Daraja said, the place must be run by several staff—cooking food, providing maintenance, and doing the laundry—all of whom might be strenuously loyal to Baeza and the others.

He said, "We have to go down."

She said, "Your logic astounds me. We certainly can't go up!"

Which way, though?

They could go via the fire escape staircase, which he'd used on arrival, but then they'd be exposed.

He waved the bow at the block building in the northwest corner. "This way."

They jogged to the two doors, each with a simple emblem.

There was an elevator door and to its left a normal door with a stairs logo.

By rights the elevator should be out of action after the destruction of the generator. Even if there was a standby power source, the cubicle could easily become a trap.

The stairs door opened onto a landing and stone steps descended, effectively going round the elevator shaft.

"Stay close," he whispered.

She said, "Like a limpet."

Cautiously, he led the way down, trying not to make any noise, which proved difficult as the slightest sound was magnified.

They passed a half-landing and then arrived on the landing of the top floor, ready for the final flight to the basement.

The access door from this floor opened and Fabio stepped through.

CHAPTER 31

SKELETON KEYS

BAEZA AND CALVO REACHED THE GROUND FLOOR
landing, where they stopped.

Below, the stairs ran on to a half-landing and then to the
basement access door.

Baeza opened the door and strode into the entrance hall.
On their right was Calvo's room and next to that, Vanda's.
His throat constricted with concern. He wanted to check
that Vanda had gone, that Harley had spirited her away to
safety.

He turned to the right, intent on finding out, but Calvo
grasped his arm, steadied him.

"Francisco, where are the aircrew's quarters?"

Releasing a heavy sigh, Baeza said, "The pilot and navigator are bunked this way. Along here." He pointed at the
passage on their left, and then led Calvo past a slightly open
door. He peeked inside and saw a two-tier bunk, a wash-
basin, a small table and two chairs, and a single window
looking out onto the vegetable garden and chicken coop.
Nobody there, which was to be expected, since the armed
guards normally stayed here but now lay outside with arrows
poking from their corpses.

The next door was shut.

Baeza didn't bother to knock. He opened the door and was met with the fug of an unventilated room.

The navigator was asleep on the top of a set of two-tier bunk beds. His clothes were draped on the back of a chair, a belt and holstered Smith and Wesson Sigma automatic on a hook on the wall, his scuffed slip-on shoes lying on the floor by the bottom bunk.

Turning to Calvo, Baeza said, "He slept through that explosion?"

"I pray he is sober!"

"One way to find out." Baeza reached up and shook the airman by the shoulder. "Come on, man, wake up!"

Groggily, the airman opened his eyes, blinked, and then screwed them up. "Hey, what the hell you doing here?"

"I own the place—and you!" Baeza snapped. "Now get up!"

"All right, all right!" Rubbing sleep from his eyes, the airman sat up, swung his legs over the edge and dropped to the floor, bare feet landing firmly. He wore a white vest and white boxer shorts.

Baeza said, "Get dressed."

"Why the rush all of a sudden?" He slipped his arms into his shirt. "I'm off duty, you know."

Baeza sucked on his teeth and then hastily explained, ending, "We need to get to the roof and fly out—now!"

The airman eyed the bottom bunk. "What about—?"

"I fear he's dead."

The airman swallowed, crossed himself and stepped into his trousers, fastened the belt and holster. Hastily, he slipped on his shoes and began buttoning his shirt.

Baeza grabbed his arm. "No time for that! Come on, man—we need you!" Baeza propelled him towards the stair-well door, Calvo trotting at their heels.

———

FABIO'S small mouth made an O-shape beneath the black mustache and his pebble eyes widened. He then came to his senses and reached inside his jacket for the gun in its shoulder-holster.

Leon reacted swiftly, delivering a side-kick that sank into Fabio's midriff.

Fabio expelled a whooshing sound and dropped the automatic, which clattered on the stone steps, and finally lay halfway down.

Leon followed through with a punch aimed at the side of Fabio's head, but the man raised a forearm, deflecting the blow.

He may be flab, but he's tough, Leon thought, fishing in his jacket pocket. He clasped the bunch of skeleton keys and threw them to Daraja who stood at the far side of the landing. "Catch!"

She caught them.

"Go on down," he shouted. "Free the others!"

Next instant, Fabio jumped at Leon, hands extended as balled fists. His stance indicated he was a brawler, not a fighter. Probably more comfortable when holding a weapon —or backed up by a fellow gunman with a machine-pistol.

Daraja clasped the keys to her chest, hesitant.

As Fabio charged bullishly, Leon kicked at his kneecap, but it didn't crack. The man buckled slightly, and Leon slammed a knee into Fabio's ribs, this time sure that he heard a cracking sound, and simultaneously thrust an elbow in the man's face.

Leon barked, "Go, Daraja!"

Fabio's nose leaked blood. Wheezing in pain, he flung two wild punches, but Leon neatly repelled them with his forearms.

He glimpsed Daraja descending towards the basement.

Fabio's pebble black eyes seemed feral. He wiped his bleeding nose with a sleeve and snarled incoherently.

Leon remembered the beating he'd undergone under Fabio's fists while Mateo watched. All day the bruises and the aches had been a constant reminder. Even so, he wasn't filled with red rage, only cold dark purpose. He kicked the same kneecap again, this time unbalancing Fabio. But, as the man fell sideways, he frantically snatched at Leon's jacket and clamped on tight, hauling Leon down the stairs with him.

Together, they tumbled, bashing into the concrete walls and hitting the stone steps. Hurting and jarring Leon's hip, thigh and pelvis until, finally, he came to rest bundled against the wall of the next half-landing. The backpack had protected him most of the time, though he wondered about the state of its contents. Thank God the sulphuric acid had been thrown out and had done its job.

Fabio was sitting about a meter away, looking as bruised and dazed as Leon felt.

Leon's rifle had dropped from his shoulder in the tumbling fall and lay halfway up the stairs, its stock and trigger housing busted.

Both of them regained their feet at about the same time.

Fabio's face contorted as he rushed forward, hate filling his eyes.

Leon's powerful defensive punches should have incapacitated Fabio if they'd connected to the head, but Fabio swerved and avoided them, and then blindly embraced Leon in a bear-hug.

Up close, Fabio stank of body odor, and his breath was rank.

With his arms pinned to his side, Leon could only move his legs, but not enough to knee the bastard in the groin.

Like some ill-matched dance couple, they pivoted and pirouetted on the half-landing, until Fabio's feet came to the stone edge and trod on air, and he lost his balance and, together, they staggered and then fell down more stairs.

The force of landing on the basement floor pushed the air from both of them and broke Fabio's grip.

Here, the stairwell was only illuminated by emergency lighting.

Fabio regained his feet first, swaying slightly, panting, his face twisted with pain—with any luck, probably from the cracked or broken rib.

Leon lay on the floor, his back aching. He thought cutlery or a tin can had dug into him. He moved to get to his feet and pain lanced into his pelvis. He withdrew the machete in defense.

Fabio wiped his jacket forearm against his bleeding nose. "You'll need more than that to beat me!" he snarled. "I'm going to break every bone in your body!" He spat out blood and a tooth and charged with surprising swiftness, instantly kicking Leon's hand. It was a lucky kick: the machete went flying.

WITH THE NAVIGATOR and Calvo behind him, Baeza opened the door and stepped onto the stairwell's ground floor landing. Hearing grunts and other noises, he peered into the gloomily lit bottom of the shaft.

He gasped in surprise, and then swore.

Fabio was fighting the Leon guy.

He ground his teeth.

So, that damned swine was responsible for the attack on the generator. Surely he couldn't have done it by himself? Did he have any other help?

I'm not staying to find out, he thought.

Fabio can deal with him.

He turned to the navigator and Calvo. "Come with me. Quickly, to the roof!" He took out the Smith & Wesson revolver, in case there was anybody left behind with the helicopter. Then he ascended the stairs in a rush and they followed, their footsteps echoing.

IN THE EERILY LIT BASEMENT, Daraja loped along the main passage, her breath unsteady. She clutched the skeleton keys to her chest and felt her heart pounding. The pilot's automatic in her pocket banged against her thigh. Antonio's clothes were not a good fit. Earlier that hadn't bothered her much, but now, as she ran, they chafed at her crotch and under the arms. Ignore it. Do what needs to be done!

She was all too familiar with the basement, from her time first in the comfort room, and then in the targets' cell. Uppermost in her mind was the sheer dread of discovery and being taken captive again. She reached for the gun, but there was nobody about. No one exited the doors on the left, so presumably the kitchen and maintenance staff had gone up to the ground floor when the generator blew and the emergency lights went on. She left the gun in her pocket and passed the laundry and bathroom doors on her right. No one there either.

All good, all clear.

Reaching the cell next to the one she and Leon had occupied, she stopped. She was surprised that she was short of breath. She could hear talking inside.

Fumbling with the keys, she tried three before she finally managed to find one that not only fitted but also unlocked the door.

Taking a big breath, she flung it open and was assaulted by the overpowering smell of the place.

There was no emergency lighting in the cell, but light from the passage filtered through the doorway, creating looming shadows on the bare walls, revealing ten partially clothed men and women, anxiety etched on their spectral faces.

The cell resembled the one she'd been held in. All eyes were on her, unease changing to puzzlement. Each of them had their wrists chained together. She dared not linger trying to use the keys on their shackles.

"Get out—you're free!" she yelled in English, waving a hand at the open door.

Variations on her words in other languages were passed among the huddled captives, dismay and disbelief on many of their faces.

Some of them gasped, others grinned, and a couple of women and a man broke into tears.

"Come on!" she urged. "Hurry!"

Finally, they started moving to the door and began streaming out, their wrist chains jangling as they ran along the passage towards the elevator and stairs, their shadows darting on the walls. Two or three of them mumbled "Thank you!" as they passed her.

———

IN THE SAME instant as the machete clattered on the floor, Fabio kicked at Leon's head.

Leon blocked the foot with a forearm savagely hitting the ankle and instantly locked his hands round the shin, twisting it with all the power he could muster, standing as he did so.

Fabio tumbled off balance and fell, hitting his shoulder on the stone floor. He rolled onto his back, winded, groaning, and Leon jerked hard, breaking Fabio's ankle.

Screaming in agony, Fabio attempted to rise.

But Leon dived headlong on top of him and forcefully slammed his forearm into Fabio's throat, pushing the man's head against the stone floor, crushing the trachea.

Air gushed from Fabio's mouth and his eyes started wide in shock as his lungs were deprived of any more air and oxygenated blood ceased to flow to his brain.

Nobody was home behind Fabio's staring eyes.

Gingerly rising to his feet, Leon picked up the machete and sheathed it.

He left the body and limped to the access door. Agonizing pain lanced from his hip.

Warily, he opened the door and peered out.

A lot of murmuring sounded further along the passage ahead on the left. Must be Daraja freeing the captives.

He turned right and hobbled along the adjacent passage, past the junction on his left that led to the basement cells and the comfort women's rooms. He saw chained men and women hurrying along the passage, heading in his direction. He grinned. Yes, she'd freed them!

Well done, Daraja!

Directly ahead, on the right was a store room. He tried the door, and it was unlocked. He opened it.

Inside on the left were metal shelves crammed with a variety of cardboard boxes and assorted bottles of cleaning agents, bleach, glycerol, packets of baking soda and soap flakes, rolls of toilet paper and packs of paper towels. And on the right were plastic buckets, dust pans and brushes and three shelves stacked with bedding.

Leaving the door open, he went to the adjoining door which was labeled "Armory." Not surprisingly, this was locked. Fortunately, it was a basic pin and tumbler lock.

He could wait for Daraja to eventually come along with the skeleton keys. But he couldn't risk the delay. By now Baeza and others were bound to be armed and decidedly wary. If his hip didn't give him so much gyp he could have kicked the door in, he supposed. Instead, he unslung his backpack and discarded the broken bow and four snapped arrows. He kept the remaining two intact arrows, as they might prove useful.

Then he used the machete to cut off two metal buckles from the backpack. Applying the blade as a lever, he bent one buckle into an L-shape, which would serve as a tension wrench, and the second he straightened out then quickly hammered three ridges in one end to form a lock pick rake. After that it was simply a matter of inserting the tension wrench to jiggle the tumblers and use the rake to unlock each pin sequentially. It only took a few seconds for his improvised lock-pick to unlock the door.

He opened the armory door and went in.

Stacked on a couple of metal shelves were cardboard boxes of cartridges of various calibers. Other shelves were home for leather and webbing holsters and automatic pistols. On one side was a rack for ten Beretta Sniper rifles, with five empty slots.

WHEN THE LAST of them had exited, Daraja extracted the key from the door lock and shifted her attention to the comfort room door, almost directly opposite.

At that instant that door opened, Mateo filled the doorway and walked out, his laptop in one hand. His free hand was fumbling in his pocket, presumably for the key.

On seeing her, his eyes widened in surprise, as if he'd seen a ghost. But he recovered quickly and said, "You came back from the dead!"

Then he made that appalling chomping motion with his teeth.

The stump of her little finger tingled uncomfortably and her heart sank. Her suddenly clammy hands dropped the bunch of keys.

CHAPTER 32

SMALL MERCY

LEON RETURNED TO THE STORE ROOM AND selected a glass bottle containing glycerol, a roll of toilet paper, a couple of cotton sheets and put them in a plastic bucket.

Back in the armory, he emptied the bucket and then ransacked the shelves, opening the cartridge boxes. He dumped the bullets into the plastic bucket. Using the machete he broke open a number of bullets on a shelf, and spread the powder on top of the shells in the bucket.

Quickly but calmly he opened the backpack and took out the wrapped jar of potassium permanganate. It wasn't broken, yet even so the contents would still have been usable if the jar had shattered during the fight with Fabio. He poured the crystals into a section of torn sheet, tying it with a knot.

Satisfied, he rested this bundle on top of the bullets.

Nearly done.

———

BEFORE DARAJA COULD TURN to run, Mateo's free hand grabbed her upper arm, swung her round and pushed her forcefully against the wall. She hit it hard with her chest and forehead.

Dazed and winded, she slumped to her knees.

As the pain hit, her mutilated hand twitched.

Mateo's teeth. She shuddered at the thought.

No, I couldn't bear it, not again!

He placed a foot on her left calf, pressed hard.

Tears of anguish—and frustration—trailed her cheeks. She hurt in her chest, her head and her leg, and her damaged hand seemed to throb in sympathy.

Then she remembered the automatic in her pocket.

Blinking away tears, she stared over her shoulder at him, while surreptitiously sliding her right hand down her side and wriggling her fingers into the pocket.

A tight fit.

Relief surged through her as her fingers touched the firm metal hand-grip.

She might have helped strangle Rudolf, but she'd never shot anybody before.

But this bastard deserved it!

She tugged out the Sig P-232.

Mateo moved his foot from her calf and the relief was sudden but short-lived because he then stood hard on her right hand before she could raise the weapon.

And she dropped the gun.

He lifted his foot off her hand. "Well, you have been busy, eh? Letting out our captives and you've even found yourself a gun!" He pressed the cold metal of a gun barrel against her temple. "I've got a gun as well. A Glock's better than a Sig any time. And I know how to use it!"

Her hand hurt fearfully, but she was sure the bones weren't broken.

Small mercy.

She blinked and shut her eyes.

He was going to shoot her in the head.

This was how it ended then? All the striving to stay alive.

Wasted. Might as well blow out my brains. I wasn't using them. Should have gone with Josefa when I had the chance!

Daraja prayed.

Mateo said, "I reckon the boss will be pleased to get you back!"

Her eyes sprung open and her heart pounded with renewed hope.

A reprieve!

He swiftly lunged, retrieved the Sig automatic, and flung it into the empty cell. Then he jabbed his gun-barrel into her neck. "Get up!" he ordered. "You will come with me!"

Docilely, thankfully, she stood and turned to his leering face.

"Now, move, or I'll bite off another finger!"

At least he wasn't threatening to blow me away.

Feeling crushed, defeated, she limped alongside him. The hurt to her chest and forehead seemed insignificant while pain shot through her from both calf and hand.

He kept the gun on her all the way as they followed the released captives. She glanced behind her, past him and saw the comfort women escaping too. She allowed herself a little smile. Distracted by her, he'd forgotten to lock the door on them. A small victory.

Soon, she found herself behind the bunched tail end of the captives she'd released a minute or so earlier.

There was a bottleneck as they struggled to get through the doorway.

A woman exclaimed, "Oh, dear God, he's dead!"

Daraja had no idea what she was talking about. As Mateo forced her past some of them, nobody objected or voiced concern about Mateo's presence. They merely wanted to get out.

———

LEON BROKE open five boxes of bullets, stacked them around the bucket.

Now, he laid a thick wad of toilet paper on top of the knotted bundle containing the crystals.

Finally, he wedged the open bottle of glycerol between the bucket handle and tipped it at a slight angle on its side so that the liquid dripped onto the toilet paper slowly and steadily.

That's the delay mechanism set up, then.

Time to go.

He got up and left, closing the door behind him. Just as well he hadn't kicked down the door. A contained blast would be more effective.

———

MATEO SHOVED a woman aside and pushed Daraja towards the open doorway that led to the stairs.

Despair engulfed her as she looked left and right, seeking succor in vain.

Her heart gave a slight flip as she glimpsed Leon coming out of the armory.

And then her new-born hope died as Mateo forced her inside.

"*Pronto, puta*! We have a chopper to catch!" Then he stopped abruptly and gasped. She faltered, too, as she almost stubbed her toe on a corpse. She recognized him immediately.

"Fabio?" Mateo said.

The press of bodies behind them was insistent.

"Move," Mateo told her gruffly. "We go up—up to the top!"

She trod round Fabio's body and started to climb the stairs.

CHAPTER 33

DISSOLVED PARTNERSHIP

As Leon exited the armory he spotted Daraja at the same instant as she saw him. He wouldn't have been concerned, but he'd also seen Mateo, directly behind her, brandishing his Glock automatic.

And then they were gone.

And other freed captives surged around the doorway.

Though his body rebelled with insistent aches, he broke into a halting, quite painful run. He was only too aware that his extemporized delayed ignition could kick in at any moment, since it wasn't particularly precise.

He hurried in limping fashion along the short passage and soon reached the last of the captives at the door to the stairs. Over his shoulder he saw the comfort women hurrying towards them. Through the open doorway he peered up the stairwell at the half-landing and spotted Mateo, his automatic in one hand, a laptop in his other, and then he'd vanished behind the elevator shaft.

Aware of critical time passing, he followed, barging past released captives as he went. Not anxious about the impending explosion, but concerned about Daraja's fate. She'd been through too much to die now.

At the next landing, the door was wedged open as the captives burst out onto the ground floor.

He noticed that only Mateo—and Daraja in front of him —continued climbing the stairs.

Obviously they were heading for the roof.

Damn. The helicopter!

It made sense. Logically, the remaining aircrew man must already be there, all set to take off.

He cursed, thinking he only had the machete and two arrows, no other weapon. Then he remembered Maddox's Webley revolver in his pocket, and took it out, quickly checked the cylinder: six shells. Enough.

———

Baeza clambered through the helicopter cabin doorway. "Get this thing in the air!" he commanded the airman. "*Pronto!*"

"Yes, sir, at once!"

Moments later, the engine engaged, revved.

Calvo stumbled at the door, coughing and spluttering for breath. Standing by the doorway, Baeza reluctantly gave him a hand up. "Sit in the back," he ordered. "And wheeze quietly!" The man was really becoming a pain.

Then he noticed movement at the doorway at the head of the stairs. "Who the hell?"

It was Mateo and ahead of him he was shoving Daraja.

Baeza was filled with a warm glow of satisfaction. He was not too surprised that Daraja had survived being hunted by Quint—especially since he'd moments earlier seen Leon fighting Fabio. No, he was pleased to have her almost within his grasp because she'd pay dearly for her part in this shameful mess!

"Wait for us!" Mateo called and ran with her towards the aircraft, the laptop clutched under his arm.

"Ah, Daraja!" Baeza exclaimed. "Perfect!" He gestured frantically for them to hurry.

Finally, they got in, both breathless.

Baeza said, "Good work, Mateo!"

"*Gracias*, sir!"

Mateo holstered his automatic and pushed Daraja towards the rear, to sit next to Calvo. Mateo sat on the other side of her.

Baeza leered at Daraja. "Harley may have taken Vanda with him, but I've still got you, eh?"

She didn't look too pleased. Too bad. She'd please him, soon enough.

He then slid shut the cabin door and returned to his seat.

"Belt up!" the airman ordered.

Obediently, they snapped on the seatbelts and Mateo slid the laptop under his seat.

The rotors started whirring, picking up speed.

Mateo swore loudly. "Sir! Sir, look! That cop spy!" He pointed out the window. "Another one back from the dead!"

Baeza winced and spat out a number of expletives as he saw Leon at the doorway to the stairs. Damn Fabio, he'd failed. Then he relaxed slightly, since Leon didn't pose a threat since he wasn't carrying a gun.

"I'll stop him, sir!" Mateo unbuckled, crossed the floor of the cabin and slid open the starboard door. An air-blast surged in from the rotors.

"Stay in your seat!" the airman shouted. "I want a stable take-off!"

Ignoring him, Mateo crouched by the doorway and withdrew his Glock. With one hand holding the door-frame, he aimed and fired the automatic.

———

TWO OR THREE bullets whined against concrete on Leon's right.

Bracing himself against the downdraft, Leon ran towards the aircraft, crouching low despite stabs of pain from his bruised torso and agonizing hip. The machete sheath slapped against his thigh. He was mindful of the Webley in his jacket pocket, but he was reluctant to use it, as he had no wish to shoot Daraja by mistake.

He ducked more bullets, trying to count them. The weapon had a capacity of fifteen cartridges. He'd gambled that while the helicopter airman attempted to attain a stable attitude on take-off, adjusting for the movement of a passenger on the deck, Mateo's aim would be adversely affected. Downside: there was always the chance that a stray bullet could prove lucky for Mateo and fatal for Leon Cazador, P.I.

Finally, the revs must have been adequate, for the helicopter's skids lifted from the rooftop.

In such close proximity to the blur of the rotors, Leon found the sound of them and the engine was deafening. The pressure wave from the downdraft was considerable, blowing his hair and the jacket back.

Mateo kept shooting, but fortunately he was a lousy shot.

He'd dearly love to shoot back with the Webley but still couldn't risk it!

Then the noise of the aircraft and Mateo's shots became swamped by a massive explosion that erupted from the south-west corner of the roof.

There went the armory.

Everything seemed to happen in slow motion, his senses were so highly tuned.

Mateo sank inside the cabin, out of sight.

The air-blast hit Leon as he launched himself into the air.

A flying metal shard whizzed past his head and parts from the aerial equipment flew everywhere. Nuts and bolts punctured the fuselage and he felt a dull thud against his back. A piece must have hit the pack.

Yes! Both hands gripped tightly onto the starboard landing skid.

He hung on.

When the glycerol made contact with the potassium permanganate crystals, the ignition would have been almost instantaneous. It would have burned fiercely and intensely, initiating a chain reaction with the spilt gunpowder, the flammable sheet and the surrounding cartridges.

He hadn't anticipated how severe the explosion would prove, though. He'd intended it as a distraction while also destroying their weapons and ammunition.

As he'd sailed through the air, he'd seen a whole section of the roof crumble. Maybe the earlier explosion when the generator blew had weakened that side of the building.

The aerials and dish toppled, and the dish rolled over the edge of the roof.

He screwed-up his eyes into slits against the blast of air from the main rotors.

His unexpected excess weight on one side made the aircraft lurch.

For a heart-stopping instant the tips of the rotor blades came near to hitting the rooftop, but the airman reacted swiftly, expertly adjusting the craft's attitude. Leon doubted if he'd have been able to respond so well in the pilot's place. Yet each movement Leon made as he attempted to swing his legs up and around the skid affected the aerodynamics. The aircraft wobbled and shook as it climbed higher into the air, heading south.

I'm a sitting duck here!

Where was Mateo? How many bullets did he have left?

He spotted the chained captives together with a number of staff members and half-clad women exiting the building and running down the slope, past the numbered posts. It felt like an age since he and Daraja had run for their lives there.

Shouting came to him through the open door.

"We're going to crash," Calvo stated in a metallic voice oddly without emotion.

Even above the noise, Leon heard Baeza: "I'm sick of hearing that bloody robotic voice!"

Then there was the loud report of a handgun.

Seconds later, Calvo was tipped out of the open door,

and Leon saw a bloodstain in the man's chest and the next instant the corpse tumbled towards the ground.

"Hey, you want to crash us?" the airman shouted.

"We're lighter now, eh?" Baeza laughed. "I've just dissolved my partnership!"

The aircraft continued in a southerly direction, with Leon dangling in the air, clinging on for dear life.

———

As they flew past the numbered posts and the lush foliage, the aircraft continued to swing in an ungainly fashion while the pilot attempted to counteract the weight and movement of their unwelcome stowaway.

Mateo was shaking his head, as if he had a hearing problem. His forehead was bleeding from a deep cut and his chest was peppered with small bloody holes caused by the explosion's flying debris.

"Stop that and come to your senses, man!" Baeza shouted at Mateo. "Where is he?"

"I—I'll take a look, boss!" Mateo moved ponderously to the open doorway, and clung onto the doorframe, his gun arm wavering as he tried to get a bead on the elusive Leon. He seemed reluctant to lean out too far as the land raced beneath them.

"Get back in your seats, both of you!" the airman pleaded, in vain.

Baeza stood with one hand on his seat to steady himself, hesitant, watching Mateo. "Well?" he shouted above the noise of the aircraft. "Do you see him?"

Mateo bawled, "No! Maybe he fell!"

Daraja whimpered.

Baeza glared at her.

She clenched her fists in her lap and stared at him, insolently.

"Get back in your seat!" the airman repeated loudly. "And shut that damned door!"

On his way to his seat, Baeza called, "Mateo—the door!"

Mateo scowled. Legs braced for balance on the tilting deck, he leaned across to grab the door-handle with his left hand, intent on sliding it shut. He blanched as he detected the glint of metal moving up through the doorway.

———

LEON SAW Mateo attempt to bring his automatic around, but it was clear that his balance was precarious, his footing unstable, and he was suffering from numerous small wounds.

Holding on with one hand, Leon appeared at the lip of the doorway and instantly thrust the machete up between Mateo's legs.

Mateo gave a high-pitched cry, more like the squeal of a pig. He lost his grip on the doorframe and the Glock fell past Leon's head.

Ignoring the blood running down the blade and covering his hand, Leon tugged fiercely and tipped Mateo through the doorway and over his shoulder.

Leon ducked the flailing feet which missed his head by a fraction. The blade slid free as Mateo tumbled out.

Mateo shrieked as he plummeted towards the ground.

A pity, I'd so wanted to repay Mateo with a lot more pain.

Leon sheathed the bloody blade and in the next second he swung his legs up and scrambled onto the shifting deck of the cabin. The lip here was slippery with spilt blood.

Clutching the doorframe, Leon got to his feet.

The airman shouted, "We should have stabilized by now, but I can't fly straight! Debris from that explosion may have damaged the tail rudder!"

Baeza peered behind him, as if checking the tail of the aircraft. Spotting Leon, he swore and unbuckled his seatbelt and stood unsteadily.

"No," the airman cried, "I'm having difficulty enough without you wandering about!"

Baeza ignored the man and holding onto the back of his seat with one hand, he withdrew his revolver and aimed it at Leon.

Daraja launched herself from her seat, wielding Mateo's laptop. The edge of it hit Baeza in the side of his face and he fired blindly, stumbling against his seat. He kicked at her, his toe connecting with the laptop. The computer flew from her grasp, skittered over the deck past Leon and fell out the open doorway to the vegetation-choked land below.

Daraja backed off as Baeza wiped blood from his cheek and aimed his revolver at her.

Instinctively, she ducked, but not to avoid a bullet.

For an instant Baeza hesitated, his brow creasing in puzzlement.

In spite of the engine noise the unusual cries of *krrrkrrr* were deafening as a black mass of carrion crows loomed in front of the cabin windshield, rising up, directly in their path, eclipsing visibility.

The airman swore.

The cabin darkened.

Baeza turned to look and swore.

Daraja screamed.

"*Krrrkrrr!*"

The aircraft lurched sideways.

Baeza lost his footing and fired wildly.

Leon held grimly onto the doorframe and bent his legs to steady himself.

The engine made worrying unpleasant noises.

Red and black splattered the windshield, further obscuring the view.

"We're going down!" the airman called. "Brace, brace, brace!"

CHAPTER 34

ROASTED FLESH

LEON BRACED HIMSELF AGAINST THE BULKHEAD OF the aircraft as the deck canted at forty-five degrees. Out the side window he watched the lip of the gorge approaching at a sloping angle. And directly ahead was a black mass glinting in the dying light of day. Rocks?

Hitting them, we won't stand a chance.

No, they were not rocks.

For God's sake, they were body bags, a score or more of them!

He tried to maintain his footing and reached for Daraja's outstretched hand, but then the aircraft struck with a deafening tearing crashing of tortured metal, the port side making contact first, ploughing into many body bags, the rotor blades scything through flesh and bone.

Then the engine stalled and the cabin came to a juddering halt.

Onboard alarms blared.

The sudden jerk threw Leon out the open doorway amidst a scattering of black feathers.

Old training kicked in and he somersaulted clear.

Made a relatively soft landing on bagged corpses.

And was immediately assaulted by a stomach churning smell of putrefaction.

He raised himself on an elbow.

Several black rats scurried away from him in all directions.

The rodents were not alone. Snorting and squealing, four wild boar scattered a short distance before coming to a halt and staring, there small eyes red, glaring.

Getting to his feet, he saw the helicopter. Fire had erupted on the rotor cowling and mast, probably caused by leaked fuel ignited by a random spark. The aircraft was pitched slantwise. One rotor blade was buckled, and another was wedged in a pile of black body bags, and one landing skid was sticking in the air. Flesh, gore and feathers splattered the windshield and, together with scythed body parts, covered much of the area surrounding the stricken aircraft.

"Daraja!" Despite his painful hip, he tried to run, but it was awkward on the uneven spongy surface. He kept stumbling, righting himself, while crossing the squelching terrain of bagged corpses. Almost at each footfall a noisome miasma erupted. He kept gagging at the rank stink, a mixture of the charnel house and the smell of boar and rat.

"Leon!" Daraja's voice. She was still inside.

He jumped and grabbed the projecting landing skid and heaved himself up and finally reached the lip of the open doorway. "Daraja!" He leaned in and, surprisingly, the left side of his face felt hot.

Heat from the flames that snaked from the cowling above and to his left intensified as paintwork burned and blistered.

If the fire found the fuel tank, it would blow.

A single glance told him the airman was dead, his chest crushed against the cockpit controls.

Ominously, there was no sign of Baeza.

Groggily, Daraja was crawling up the sloping deck. "Leon, help me!"

He reached in with his outstretched hand.

Sheer relief showed in her face as his fingers closed on hers.

He said, "Come on, let's get you out!"

"Now, why didn't I think of that?"

He hauled her towards him, and embraced her.

"Hold on tight," he told her.

She said, "I'm not letting go, be sure of that!"

He jumped with her by his side.

The landing was soft, on a couple of body bags, one of which burst, releasing putrid matter and a noxious smell. The uneven surface meant they both lost their balance as they landed and tumbled head over heels.

They finally came to rest against a rigid corpse bag.

Gingerly he pressed a hand against the viscous surface of a bag to raise himself.

He said, "Are you all right?"

Lying partially obscured by a body bag, she nodded, and then winced, raising a hand to her bleeding temple. "Leon!" she cried.

As he saw the alarm in her face he instinctively ducked his head and experienced an intense pain in his shoulder.

Baeza had kicked him—doubtless aiming for his head.

The pain from the powerful blow was acute. Breathing through clenched teeth, Leon rolled away, sinking into a cleft between two body bags.

Baeza stood unsteadily, blood streaming from a deep cut in his cheek that laid bare bone.

Then the helicopter exploded.

A piece of metal slammed into the bag next to Leon's head. Gray matter oozed out. Luckily, he'd been shielded from most of the blast by the bags he lay between. He heaved himself out of the cleft.

Daraja was lucky, too. She seemed unscathed as she unsteadily got to her feet.

The carcass of the aircraft still burned. The stench of roasted flesh added to the assault on his nostrils.

Screaming unintelligibly, Baeza jumped on Leon's back.

The unexpected force and weight of the man drove Leon to his knees before he could react.

Baeza's left forearm was pressed against Leon's throat, cutting off his air supply. Baeza's right fist pounded against the side of Leon's head. This was no pregnant girl but an overweight adult. Baeza's legs were wrapped around him so he couldn't get at the sheathed machete or the Webley in his jacket pocket.

Clumsily, Daraja ran on the irregular surface and finally stood in front of them, pummeled Baeza's face with her fists.

Until Baeza swiftly hit her with a powerful backhand.

Daraja stumbled backwards and tripped.

Tensing his muscles, Leon rolled sideways. As soon as he landed on top of Baeza, he wrenched the man's arm free and yanked hard, breaking the wrist.

Squealing loudly, Baeza shuffled backwards, feet scrabbling frenziedly, cradling his limp wrist.

Saliva drooling from his mouth, Baeza's right hand seized a piece of ejected metal from the exploded aircraft and charged.

Out of the corner of his eye, Leon spotted other movement.

Oh, hell!

Manuel Ramirez was clambering on top of the body bags, lugging a large blue cool-box. And he was with his son Antonio. The lad was carrying a petrol-powered chainsaw.

Must be harvesting fresh morsels for their fridge, Leon reckoned as he rolled away.

Leon side-stepped Baeza's charge and then, as he withdrew the Webley revolver, he slipped on slick blood.

Baeza slashed viciously with the piece of metal. Clanging. A hard jarring blow, knocking the handgun from Leon's hand. Then he followed through with a second attack.

Baeza's metal shard sank into a body bag near Leon's shoulder as he rolled sideways, nursing his bruised hand.

He glimpsed Manuel and Antonio facing Daraja.

Manuel laughed hysterically. "You!" he yelled, lowering the cool-box.

Where's the gun?

"What have you done with Josefa?" Manuel demanded.

Daraja said, "She's safe, safe from you and your family!"

"Because of you," Manuel snarled at Daraja, "my Trini is dead! I've brought her here."

She said, mockingly, "What, didn't you have the heart to eat her?"

Her words angered Baeza. He pulled out the chunk of metal, which made a sucking sound, and attacked again.

Leon dodged, rolling over the squelching bags.

"I heard the 'copter," Manuel was saying, "I couldn't believe my luck! We'll feast on *you* tonight!"

Antonio started the saw. It made a rasping, hungry sound.

Leon withdrew the machete.

Baeza leaned forward, swinging the chunk of sharp metal.

Leon brought the machete up to deflect the downward motion of the metal shard, and there was a metal-on-metal clang on contact, and his arm juddered so much with the force of Baeza's blow that he dropped the weapon.

Grinning broadly, Baeza lifted the metal shard again, threateningly.

Chapter 35

Black crows

Leon's left hand sank into a bag and instinctively clasped a thick bony limb. It came away with a squishing sound as he tugged, slamming it full into Baeza's grinning face. The thigh bone smashed into the man's mouth, and tore his lips and broke some teeth.

Grunting, shrieking, Baeza stumbled backwards and then sank to his knees, one useless limb resting on his blood-stained thighs, blood dribbling from his smashed mouth. He looked to the left and to the right. A boar was approaching him from each side. The color of the flames from the burning aircraft reflected on their vicious tusks.

Baeza was no longer a threat. In fact the boar would ensure he wasn't going anywhere—except straight to Hell.

Leon swung round to face Manuel and Antonio, who were closing in on Daraja.

On Leon's right, Daraja was backing away from Antonio and his rasping chainsaw.

Antonio stood on a bag that partly covered the remains of a corpse that had been scavenged by the animals.

Next to Antonio stood Manuel, his cold eyes watching Daraja; his lips peeled back in a hateful grin.

Swiftly, Daraja knelt and grabbed the length of torn body bag Antonio was standing on. Straightening up, she tugged sharply and Antonio lost his footing, tumbling backwards. Unable to control his fall or the saw, he inadvertently steered the saw-teeth to cut into his thigh above the knee. Yelling in extreme agony, he flung the saw away, and its grating noise stopped immediately. Blood gushed. An artery had been severed: he was bleeding to death.

Two minutes of life left, probably.

"No, no!" Manuel lumbered towards his son.

Daraja said, "Watch out for those boar!"

Perhaps scenting fresh blood, two wild boar clambered on top of the bags, heads down, aiming for Antonio.

Seeing them approach, Manuel waved his hands to scare them off. He seemed confident. Maybe he'd done it before while scavenging.

If he had, this time they ignored him. Their blood-lust was up. They'd scented fresh meat, not a corpse that was hours' old baking in the sun. Fresh blood. Warm steaming flesh.

One wild boar charged Manuel and its tusk gored his thigh and ripped into his groin, its weight toppling him onto his back. Arms threshing, he screamed, "Keep them away!"

Leon unslung his backpack and delved into it. He had two arrows, and they had survived intact from the fall from the chopper.

Daraja said, "Careful, Leon!"

Snuffling and snorting, a second boar went for Antonio's bleeding leg. Antonio was beyond caring, motionless, probably dead.

Manuel sat up with his shoulders against a pile of bags, his face twisted in agony. The animal that had attacked him stepped back, feet stamping on the bagged corpses, and then it charged.

Boldly, Leon lunged forward, stabbing the boar in the eye with an arrow point.

Squealing, the animal lurched to the side, the arrow protruding from its eye cavity.

Watchful, Leon held the single arrow in readiness.

The wounded boar continued to squeal plaintively, walking unsteadily in circles, while two others trod on the bagged carcasses, perhaps curious, perhaps incensed by the smell of blood, getting closer.

Then Leon spotted the Webley, lying close by. He lunged for it, picked it up and shot the boar he'd wounded, putting the poor creature out of its misery. The other two backed off at the loud sound of the loud report.

Manuel said, "Please, take me and my son to hospital!" Tears squeezed from the corners of his eyes and trailed down his cheeks. "I'm in agony!"

Daraja said, "Don't trust him, Leon!"

Holding the revolver in readiness, Leon was fleetingly tempted to shoot Manuel Ramirez.

Manuel sobbed. "Honest, we need medical help now! The truck, take us in the truck!" He threw a small bunch of keys.

Leon caught the keys in his left hand. He glanced at Antonio. The second boar was eating ravenously and noisily, its snout blood-stained.

Several other wild boar encroached unflinchingly, not shy in the least, clearly wanting their share.

Leon said, "Your son's dead." He pocketed the keys.

"*Madre de Dios!*" Manuel crossed himself, winced in pain, and then placed his hands on his gashed crotch. Big black flies buzzed. "*Me*—take me!"

Leon shook his head. "You've feasted on human flesh. Now you can find out what it's like to be the main course."

He held onto the revolver in case he or Daraja was attacked by a boar. With his left hand he clutched Daraja's arm. "Let's go."

"No!" pleaded Manuel. "No, you can't leave me!"

They turned their backs on Manuel Ramirez and ignored his screams as two wild boar fell upon him.

Black crows hovered. A flock swooped down for fresh pickings, spoilt for choice. Their cawing soon became deafening.

Careful to avoid foraging boar and scurrying rats, Leon and Daraja scrambled hand-in-hand over the tail-end of dumped body bags and finally attained firm ground. Once here, he shoved the revolver in his jacket pocket.

The trail was clear, hard-baked earth ascending the southern side of the gorge in a narrow gentle slope.

By the time they'd reached the lip, the sun had dried the putrescence, dirt and blood on their clothes, making the material slightly stiff.

Poking his head above the natural parapet of the gorge, Leon spotted Manuel's truck. He pulled out the Webley, hoping young Paco hadn't come on the journey with them and stayed with the truck. He had little interest in any more killing.

He breathed easy. There was nobody else inside or near the truck.

"Come on, Daraja!" He gripped her hand and they walked quickly to the vehicle.

It was a Ford 1980s pick-up and, not surprisingly, its paintwork was flaking, the wheel-rims were black with grime and oil, and the seats were badly worn in places, padding showing through. Rust probably held the chassis together. Four square tiny ITV stickers made a column on the windscreen, implying the vehicle had passed its road-worthiness inspection for the last four years, which gave him hope. On the floor of the flatbed was the flowery tablecloth from the cave house, now blood-stained.

Impulsively, Leon bowed to Daraja. "Transport awaits, ma'am."

"Thank you." She gave him a quizzical look, adding, "Sir."

"Hey, don't stand on ceremony. Leon, remember?"

"I was playing along—the moment, you know?"

He said, "Playing. Seems an age since that concept entered my head."

"Well, too much work and no play makes for a dull life, no?"

He grinned. After all they'd been through it was refreshing to lighten up. "Something like that." He opened the door, which creaked, and she slid onto the bench seat, knocking her head on a rosary that dangled from the rearview mirror.

He threw his backpack on the floor by her feet and then got in behind the steering wheel.

The interior smell evoked unpleasant memories of the cave house.

Slammed shut the door.

Opened the window to access fresh air.

Dusty dashboard littered with sun-bleached papers and receipts.

Checked the fuel gauge. Half-full. More than enough to get to the village.

Moment of truth. He inserted the ignition key and gunned the engine. It ticked over all right, though there was a clunking noise under the bonnet and the whole truck seemed to vibrate as the engine idled. Needed serious maintenance, more than simple tuning, but it would serve even if it did sound as if it was on its last legs.

He put it in gear and, handbrake off, he gently pressed the pedal and the vehicle jerked into motion, beginning a jarring ride over the uneven surface. Still, it moved along at a steady if labored pace, leaving a trail of dust in its wake.

She rested a hand on his. "Thank you for saving my life."

He looked at her. Sincerity shone in her dusky brown eyes. "You heft a pretty powerful laptop yourself," he replied with a smile, returning his attention to the track. "You stopped Baeza shooting me."

"I was scared, to be honest, did it without thinking."

"Sometimes, it doesn't pay to think—just act."

"The laptop was the only weapon to hand."

"It did the job. Maybe the police will find it," he mused. "It might provide more links for them to track down."

She sobbed and he glanced at her. Tears flowed, cutting through the grime, but they wouldn't wash away today's memories. "The body bags. I knew some of those poor people!"

"I thought you would. I'm only sorry we couldn't prevent the carnage." He was aware that three so-called targets had perished. "Sami, Mina and Tabish were killed that we know of. Maybe some of the others from our group escaped the hunters."

She wiped the tears with the heel of a hand. "I fear two couples didn't—including Anamaria."

"Oh?"

"Baeza said that Vanda got away with the American, Harley."

"Ah, I see."

"Yes. Will you track down Vanda and Harley?"

Leon said, "Perhaps. But I doubt if she'll stick with him." He laughed without mirth. "I can't see her becoming a political activist, promoting him as the next candidate for President!"

"As you say, she'll probably use him and then drop him."

"That sounds about right. She seems adept at evading the law."

He changed gear and gently pressed on the accelerator. A little faster, but not too fast. He didn't want to push the engine too hard. Steady as she goes. Better than walking.

The truck bumped and juddered over the rough ground. The backs of his sweaty thighs stuck to the seat.

They left the gorge of death behind, heading along the track in the direction of the village.

There were moments of uncomfortable silence when he was sure she'd be reliving a number of terrible experiences from her past, but there was little he could do for her.

To break one of the silences, he said, glancing at her, "In English, my surname means "hunter". I wondered, does Daraja mean something?"

"It does, actually." She offered him a faint smile, as if glad to be talking about anything other than what had recently transpired. "My mother insisted on naming me. Don't laugh, but it means someone who is valuable and important to everyone."

"I'm not laughing. That's a lovely definition—and true. Sadly, the people who've mistreated you did not appreciate your value."

"Value?" Playful or cutting tone? He wasn't sure.

He said, "Your worth, I meant. Valuable as a person, as a friend."

"Oh. What about the "important" bit?"

"You're important to me, Daraja. We've endured a lot." Without taking his eyes from the track, he gestured at his clothes and hers. She was covered in dark unsightly stains and smelled dreadfully and he knew he was just as bad. "Wouldn't you agree?"

"Yes, I agree—we've been through a lot!" She added, "After this, we need a hotel and a long shower—and a change of clothes."

He pointed to the backpack. "There's still enough money to pay for new clothes. Though I must admit not many villages have clothing shops. In fact, not many have hotels. We can but hope there's a room available."

"You said *a* room?" she queried coquettishly.

"A slip of the tongue."

She said, "I don't mind sharing."

"How old are you?"

"Twenty-six. Why?"

"I'm old enough to be your father. We keep it platonic, right?"

"Whatever you say, Pops."

He took his attention from the track for a second or two, appraised her and pulled a mock-disgust face. "I must admit you do need someone to scrub your back."

She smiled, her eyes shining. "I'll scrub yours if you'll do mine."

"Deal." He returned his concentration to driving. "After we've cleaned up, I'll contact the local police. The authorities need to know about Baeza's hacienda and everything else."

She glanced through the rear window of the cab. "They've probably already seen the smoke."

"True. But if they want to investigate, they'll have to arrange for a helicopter to fly there."

"I suppose so. He liked his privacy, didn't he?"

"His nasty little enterprise relied upon it."

He turned off the track and motored onto a metalled road.

The smooth surface was a huge contrast and a great relief.

The truck picked up speed, which meant more air rushing in the open windows, clearing a little of the stifling heat.

He said, "I need to tell the authorities about what's left of the Ramirez family. The children will be taken into care, I imagine."

"Manuel was a dreadful man," she said, "but he didn't deserve that fate."

Leon said nothing. Although he'd instinctively attempted to save the man, in the final analysis he believed that Manuel's fate was most appropriate.

Darkness hovered as the sun sped towards the mountain peaks on the horizon.

He switched on the headlights, hoping the battery would take the extra load.

He drove past a familiar sign, a small metal square comprising a black triangle and a white triangle, indicating *coto privado*—hunting ground. Legally, the season was from October through December on weekends, the usual prey being boar, rabbit and fox. Until today when illegally it was also humans.

The airman's watch told him it was 9:30. The sky on their right was a glorious sunset, flamed various shades of red.

He concentrated on the road. He thought he'd seen enough red for one day.

AFTERWORD

Leon Cazador informed Captain Silvano Lopez of the Guardia Civil of the situation and almost immediately a full-scale operation was set in motion by the authorities. That evening a fleet of helicopters equipped with searchlights and heat-detecting apparatus was dispatched and they combed the area surrounding the still burning hacienda building. In all, they located eight illegal immigrants each with their wrists still chained together, nine so-called comfort women and twelve distraught hacienda staff.

Next morning, one body of a chained captive was discovered lying in the rubbish on the northern escarpment behind the building. Post mortem determined the man had died of a heart attack. The second body to be retrieved was that of Tabish lying in the gorge.

Two of the freed captives were granted political asylum, while the remainder were processed for ultimate repatriation. Considering their experiences, it seemed that they were glad to return to their homeland.

Mateo's Toughbook CF-30 laptop was eventually located and retrieved, and it had lived up to its name. The shock-mounted hard drive survived the drop from the helicopter and provided links to previous *Hit the Target* clients and their bank accounts, together with their withheld surnames.

Initially, the authorities were reluctant to make public the nature of the *Hit the Target* organization. Full disclosure would occur once a wide-ranging investigation had been completed.

The wife of banker Rudolf Kraus was informed of his death, though few details were supplied. Rudolf's mistress Anna read about her lover's demise in the daily newspaper *Bild*.

Harley Coleman was identified as a passenger on an Iberian flight to Rome. On the same flight was a certain Vanda Dinescu. But thereafter their trail went cold. Enquiries were made at Harley's home town, but he never came back and a new incumbent had to be voted in. His wife continued with her suit for divorce, changing the grounds to desertion.

Leon suspected that while Vanda had gone to ground, she would surface again one day using a different alias and with another illegal money-making scheme.

The passport details of murdered hippy Luke Astley bore fruit. In 2015 he'd been a schoolteacher in Sunderland when he ran away with an underage schoolgirl, Janine Bentley. An autopsy of her remains determined that she died of a drug overdose, aged eighteen. When informed, her parents were devastated and had to accept the death of hope and the heart-breaking consolation of "closure".

The Ramirez children, with the exception of Paco, were taken into care. Two months later, Remedios gave birth to a healthy boy but never revealed that the father was her brother Paco. Being eighteen, Paco was free to go but could not return to the illegal family cave. He was not questioned regarding his complex family relationships.

The lengthy process of retrieving the bodies—and in the majority of cases, body parts—began in earnest. One aspect of that activity included taking DNA samples. But little expectations were fostered that the identities of the dead would be discovered. Blood traces on the ruined bridge were also sampled.

Josefa was taken in by a local convent and became a novice nun.

Leon provided funds for Daraja to purchase new clothes. He also arranged for her to obtain a replacement passport and other documentation. She bought a plane ticket to Lagos, where she was briefly reunited with her parents. Strangely, she found that her heart was now in Spain and she returned to take up a nursing post in Barcelona's Hospital de San Pau.

Some six months after the events at the hacienda an explosive device was detonated on a heritage streetcar, the Tramvia Blau outside the Avenida Tibidabo metro station. Eight innocent passengers were killed and twenty-five passengers or passers-by were injured, some of whom were seriously maimed. Al Qaeda claimed responsibility. As a result of cross-checking with the blood samples from the bridge over the gorge, it was established that Yesal was the suicide bomber. Daraja was a bystander at the scene and thanks to her swift medical action saved two lives. She then helped tend the wounded.

UAR, the counter terrorism branch of the Guardia Civil, traced two members of Yesal's terrorist cell to an apartment in the city's El Raval barrio. The Rapid Reaction Group was called in and a firefight ensued. The two terrorists were shot dead and, fortunately, there were no other casualties.

Leon Cazador continued with his crusade to hold back the encroaching night of unreason and fight injustice in all its forms and where necessary mete out his own rough justice.

It's what he does.

A Look at Book Two:
No Prisoners

Some perpetrators of crime deserve only one fate—no prisoners.

When Leon Cazador discovers the body of a fellow investigator who was working with the British National Crime Agency to infiltrate a pedophile group that uses the pursuit of golf as a cover for their organized abuses, he refuses to chalk it up to coincidence.

Seeking justice for his fallen friend, Leon is presented with another missing person's case. But this one is decidedly different. Diving deeper, Leon finds himself one step closer to uncovering the deadly pedophile ring that took down his comrade.

Finding missing persons is all in a day's work for Leon. But can he fight his ultimate nightmare in a race against time to save a group of innocent children and exact revenge on their abusers?

AVAILABLE AUGUST 2022

ABOUT THE AUTHOR

Nik Morton has sold over 100 short stories, edited periodicals and contributed to magazine articles, chaired writers' circles, run writing workshops, and judged competitions. He has edited many books and was sub-editor of the monthly magazine *Portsmouth Post* (2003-2007) and Editor in Chief of a U.S. Publisher (2011-2013). He has had 32 books published—including 3 books in the psychic spy *Tana Standish* series and 8 westerns—and co-written 4 books in the *Floreskand* fantasy series. His *Write a Western in 30 Days – with plenty of bullet points!* is a best-seller. With his wife Jennifer, Nik lived in Spain for several years (2003-2019). They have since returned to England, residing in Northumberland—near their daughter Hannah, son-in-law Harry and grandchildren Darius and Suri.